W9-CDD-355

NANCY
DREW®
COLLECTION

Nancy Drew
Mystery Stories

COLLECTION

The Bike Tour Mystery • The Riding Club Crime
Werewolf in a Winter Wonderland

CAROLYN KEENE

Aladdin Paperbacks
New York London Toronto Sydney

This book is a work of fiction. Any references to historical events, real people, or real locales are used fictitiously. Other names, characters, places, and incidents are the product of the author's imagination, and any resemblance to actual events or locales or persons, living or dead, is entirely coincidental.

ALADDIN PAPERBACKS
An imprint of Simon & Schuster Children's Publishing Division
1230 Avenue of the Americas, New York, NY 10020

These titles were previously published individually by Aladdin Paperbacks.

This edition specially printed for Sweetwater Press
by Simon & Schuster, Inc.

The text of this book was set in New Caledonia.
Manufactured in the United States of America
First Aladdin Paperbacks edition October 2004

Library of Congress Control Numbers: (Bike Tour) 2002100862, (Riding Club) 2002115458, (Winter Wonderland) 2003109058

ISBN 1-4169-0079-9

NANCY
DREW®
COLLECTION

The Bike Tour Mystery

Contents

1

Welcome to Ireland

"And how long do you intend to stay in Ireland, Miss, uh . . ." The passport clerk glanced briefly over the U.S. passport in front of him. "Miss Drew?"

"About two weeks," Nancy Drew replied. "I'm going on a cross-country cycling tour."

The clerk's green eyes flicked up to glance at the tall, willowy American teenager with red-blond hair. He smiled. "Well, I'm hoping your legs are strong, then. Ireland's got a powerful lot of hills, especially here in the West."

Nancy smiled back. "Oh, I think I'm up to it. I've been training for a few weeks, with my friend George." She pointed to the athletic-looking dark-haired girl standing in line behind her.

"Well, best of luck to you." He flipped her passport

to a blank page, punched it with his stamping machine, and handed it back. "Next!"

Nancy walked past the desk and joined her other friend, Bess Marvin, who had already passed through the immigration interview. "Isn't it exciting, Nancy?" Bess said. "Everyone here is so friendly and warm."

Nancy suppressed a smile. She was used to Bess's quick assumptions, but they still amused her. "You can't judge a whole population by one official," she said. "But yes, the Irish people are known for being very friendly."

"I can't wait to get on that bike and start whizzing through the countryside," Bess went on, twirling a lock of her blond hair. "Those pictures in the tour company's brochure made everything look so picturesque. Thatched-roof cottages, woolly white sheep, crumbling stone walls . . ."

"Just don't expect leprechauns, shamrocks, and pots of gold at the end of every rainbow," warned Nancy with a giggle.

George Fayne strode toward them, hitching her carry-on bag onto her shoulder. "Well, that's over. Now on to the baggage claim. We'd better grab a cart—Bess brought a mountain of luggage."

Bess stuck out her tongue at George, who was not only her close friend, but also her cousin. "I didn't bring that much!" she protested. "After all, we'll be here two weeks. And we need at least two outfits per day. You can't expect me to go to dinner wearing the same clothes I've been bicycling in all day."

"Why not? That's what I plan to do," George said.

"Then remind me not to sit near you at the dinner table. Whew!" Bess waved a hand in front of her nose.

The three girls trooped through a pair of glass doors to the swarming baggage claim area. Most of the bags from their flight had already circled into sight on the luggage carousel. Nancy quickly spotted her black suitcase, thanks to the neon green ribbon she had knotted onto its handle. George's big purple duffel bag was next to it. The two girls lifted their bags off the conveyor belt.

Bess frowned as she began to search through the mounds of bags already removed from the carousel. "Two tan suitcases, just like my carry-on. Oh, there's one!" She sprang over to the edge of the carousel and checked the ID tags on the suitcase. "No, sorry. That belongs to someone else. It's just like mine, though."

"Bess, you'll never learn," George groaned. "You buy this year's trendiest luggage style, and everyone on the flight has the same bags you do."

"I always find them eventually," Bess shot back. "It isn't my fault you're in such a hurry."

"The rest of our tour group *is* waiting for us," Nancy reminded Bess. She exchanged wry glances with George. The three girls traveled together often. The scenario was familiar by now.

As Bess scurried off to inspect another tan suitcase, Nancy was jostled from behind. Ever alert, she shifted around to see who it was.

A broad-shouldered man in a black wool overcoat was shoving through the crowd milling around the neighboring carousel. Something about his heavy-browed, tight-mouthed face made Nancy uneasy. Eyes trained on someone ahead in the foot traffic, he seemed in a great hurry.

As he hoisted a duffel to his shoulder, Nancy idly noted that the little finger was missing from his left hand. With the instincts of a trained detective, she glanced at the electronic sign above the adjacent carousel, noting that its flight was from Sydney, Australia.

"Found them!" Nancy heard Bess announce. She turned to see Bess stacking her carry-on atop two larger suitcases. "And we don't need a cart, George—my new suitcases have wheels on them."

"So you do learn from experience." George grinned. "After I've toted your heavy bags down so many long terminals!"

"We still have to pass through customs inspection," Nancy reminded her friends, nodding toward a final set of doors.

"Ooh—will they open our cases?" Bess asked, looking concerned as she maneuvered her tower of luggage toward the doors.

"Probably not—but they do perform random checks of passengers' bags," Nancy said. "I think they zero in on people who look suspicious."

As they passed through the swinging doors, Nancy noticed one passenger who'd been called over to the customs official's table—the man in the black overcoat from the Australian flight. And from the expression on his face, Nancy guessed he wasn't happy about being inspected.

Nancy's curiosity was piqued. Her father, prominent River Heights attorney Carson Drew, often told her she was a natural detective. Back home, she'd worked on several important cases. Even though she was on vacation, she couldn't help being intrigued by shady activity.

Bess and George were hurrying ahead toward the exit doors. The Irish customs officials were apparently not interested in checking the three American girls' bags. And Nancy eagerly followed them, looking forward to meeting the rest of their cycling tour group.

Emerging from the customs area, the girls looked around for their tour leader. They spotted him easily—a twentysomething man with curly brown hair, holding up a cardboard sign reading, MCELHENEY TOURS. They walked over to him. "Mr. Prendergast?" George asked.

The young man smiled. "Call me Bob," he said in

an American accent. "Are you the girls from River Heights?"

"Yes—I'm George Fayne. And here's Nancy Drew and Bess Marvin." George gestured toward her friends.

Bob shook hands all around. "Glad to meet you. Did you have a good flight?" The girls nodded their heads. "Good. Some of the other folks are here—let me introduce you."

He led the girls over to a small waiting area with vinyl couches. Three other newly arrived passengers were slumped on the seats, surrounded by suitcases and looking weary from their flights.

"We've got the whole American contingent now," Bob said cheerfully, parking Bess's stacked bags for her. "Everyone, here's George Fayne, Nancy Drew, and Bess Marvin, from River Heights. Girls, this is Carl Thompson—he's from Boston. College professor, right, Carl?"

A large man with a bushy brown beard and twinkling dark eyes stood up. "Assistant professor in chemistry—but thanks for the promotion, Bob."

"Anytime," Bob replied brightly. "And here are Jim and Natalie de Fusco, from California."

"North or south?" Nancy asked as she shook hands with the young, suntanned, blond couple.

"Near San Diego," Jim de Fusco said. "I work construction, and Natalie manages a surf shop."

"And you're missing surf season?" asked George.

"Truth is," Natalie admitted, "when you live near sunny beaches year-round, you get tired of them. Believe it or not, we hope for chilly, rainy weather every day."

"Great," Bob declared. "Because this is Ireland, and I can promise it will rain. Now, if you'll excuse me—I've got two other tour members coming out of customs any minute." He darted away.

"Does it really rain so often here?" Bess wondered, looking out the airport window at a clear blue sky.

Carl gave a philosophical shrug. "Sure. But look on the bright side—that's why western Ireland's one of the greenest places on earth."

"I think rain's refreshing on a bicycle ride," George said. "Who wants hot weather when you're pedaling up and down hills?"

"I'm with you on that," chuckled Carl.

"I'm surprised that we have an American tour guide," Nancy remarked to the group.

"Bob told me his specialty is cycling, not Ireland," Jim said. "But he's led several groups around here the past couple of years. He says it's a great country for cycling—not too many mountains, and lots of sight-seeing."

"Oh, I can't wait," Bess said.

A moment later, Bob returned with a striking pair

of girls, one redhead and one brunette, both nearly six feet tall. "Here we are," Bob said. "I'd like you to meet Rhonda and Rachel Selkirk." He repeated everyone's names for the newcomers.

"G'day, all," brunette Rhonda said in a broad Australian accent. "Glad to be here at last. That flight from Sydney seemed to take forever—I'm really knackered."

"Sorry, but I have to ask," Bess said. "You two look so much alike. Are you twins or sisters?"

Red-haired Rachel laughed. "Just sisters. But don't worry—we get asked that all the time."

"Now, everybody, collect your things and we can load them into the van," Bob said. "Terry, our driver, has got it parked right out at the curb."

As the tour group began to gather their gear, a porter came up behind the Selkirks, pushing a cart. On it were a few handsome leather suitcases and two large, narrow packing crates that were curved at both ends.

"Whoa—you brought your own bikes?" George exclaimed. "Wasn't that expensive?"

Rachel looked vague. "I guess so," she said. "But we prefer to ride our bikes rather than what the tour company provides. Not to knock your bikes," she added apologetically to Bob.

"These bikes were custom-made for us," Rhonda added, tossing her shoulder-length brown hair.

"Seemed a shame not to use them, eh?"

"Those girls either are pro cyclists or they're awfully rich," Bess whispered to Nancy as they followed the others out the terminal's exit doors.

"Probably the latter," Nancy replied softly, "judging from that expensive luggage. And pro cyclists aren't likely to join a tour like this."

"If they've had bikes custom-made, they must really be into cycling," George muttered, joining her friends. "And they look like they're in top shape. I'll bet they're super cyclists."

Nancy laughed. "And you're already determined to outride them," she teased her friend. "George, this isn't a race. We're just here to get some exercise and see Ireland at a leisurely pace."

George nodded, but she kept studying the tall, athletic-looking Selkirks.

The group headed for a cherry red van parked at the curb, with MCELHENEY TOURS painted on the sides. A rumpled Irishman with a gloomy expression stood by the open side doors. "This is Terry O'Leary," Bob announced. "He'll drive your luggage from one night's hotel to the next while you cycle along. He's also the guy who can repair your bikes—so be nice to him."

Terry flashed a gap-toothed smile, but Nancy wasn't convinced it was genuine.

The tour members piled their luggage beside the

McElheney van, then followed Bob to a sleek black minibus parked just behind it.

Waiting to board the passenger van, Nancy sensed a commotion on the sidewalk behind her. Out of the corner of her eye she recognized a black overcoat. It was the man with the missing finger from the Sydney flight!

Then a connection clicked in her brain.

Nancy peered inside the van. The Australian girls were sitting inside. Rhonda was rooting in her purse for something.

Then Rachel looked out through the window—and spotted the man in the black overcoat.

And Nancy could swear Rachel froze in fear.

2

The Gang's All Here

"Rhonda, wasn't that—?" Rachel began, poking her sister in the arm.

But Rhonda, barely looking up, cut her off. "Don't be silly, Rache," she said, tossing her thick brown hair. "We've only been in Ireland an hour. How could you possibly recognize anyone?"

Nancy watched Rachel's expression as she sank back in her seat. She didn't look at all convinced, Nancy thought.

Climbing onto the bus, Nancy told herself to put the incident out of her mind. *You've been working on too many mysteries lately,* she scolded herself. *You imagine crimes wherever you look. Just relax and enjoy your vacation.*

With everyone aboard, the minibus pulled away.

After navigating the tangle of roads around Shannon Airport, they were soon rolling across open countryside. Nancy's first impression was an overwhelming sensation of green.

"So that's why green is always used to symbolize Ireland," George said, gazing out the window. "I've never seen such an intense color."

"Look at that old stone cottage," Bess exclaimed, pointing. "Isn't it charming?"

"There sure is a lot of farmland around here," said Natalie de Fusco, across the aisle.

"Yeah, but what tiny farms," George said. "There's the next farmhouse already. And I don't see any big red barns like back home."

"What I love are the crooked stone walls between the fields," Jim said. "Do you know, they don't even use mortar to make those walls? They just pick up stones from the fields and fit them in place. But they're remarkably strong—some of those walls are well over a hundred years old."

Natalie rolled her eyes. "Trust you, Jim, to know all the construction details."

The bus curved around winding roads until, less than an hour later, they pulled up to a large rambling house, a quirky pile of eaves and gables in warm yellow stone. "Wow, what is this—someone's country manor?" Bess asked, impressed.

George scanned the tour itinerary Bob had passed

out to the group. "It says this is our hotel for the first night—Ballyrae House. We're in a town called Lahinch, on the western coast."

"Terry has already arrived, I see," Bob said, standing up and spotting the red van in a side lot. "Your luggage will be taken up to your rooms. In the meantime, let's gather for a quick meeting."

Bob led the way through a marble entry hall and into a wood-paneled parlor, where a young couple sat in a pair of leather armchairs. "Ah, I see our final two cyclists are here," Bob said. "Folks, meet Derek Thorogood and Camilla Collins, just off the ferry from England."

As Derek and Camilla shook hands and learned the names of their tour companions, Nancy noticed Bess's dazzled expression. Even Nancy had to admit that Derek was handsome, with his shaggy dark hair, lazy gray eyes, and clean-cut features.

"Here goes Bess with another crush," George whispered in Nancy's ear. "I bet she hasn't even noticed that Derek brought a girlfriend with him."

"I heard that," Bess muttered, whirling around. "And just because they travel together doesn't mean they're boyfriend and girlfriend."

"No, but I'd say it's a pretty good clue," George shot back. "That and the fact that Camilla's draped herself all over his shoulder."

"Relax, girls," Nancy broke in. "Time will tell

whether or not Derek is 'available.' And even if he isn't, who cares? This seems like a great bunch of people. I'm looking forward to riding with them—all of them."

As a waiter passed around cold drinks, Bob asked the members of the tour group to sit down. "This is probably a good time to go over the protocols for our tour," he announced. "You all have copies of the itinerary I passed out."

Several members of the group waved their itineraries in the air.

"Hang on to these," Bob advised. "They'll be your bibles for the next ten days. There's a page for each day, which we'll supplement each morning with a detailed road map of that day's route. The itinerary tells where our lunch stop will be—usually a historic site. I've typed up a brief paragraph describing each lunch sight, but you can use your own guidebooks for more details."

"Got mine," Carl said, holding up a thick paperback book. From the dog-eared pages, Nancy guessed Carl had done plenty of pre-trip research.

"We also describe other sights you'll pass along the way," Bob continued. "Some of you may want to stop and explore. Others may be more interested in keeping up a good cycling pace. You're free to go as you please."

Natalie de Fusco frowned. "But aren't we going to ride as a group?"

Bob shook his head. "After a few years of running these cycling tours, I've learned that that doesn't work. You're all at different levels of cycling ability. Some people may want to ride forty or fifty miles in a day. Others may get tired after fifteen or twenty."

"That'll be me," Camilla Collins admitted. Noting the English girl's fair skin, manicured nails, and carefully styled brown hair, Nancy guessed she wasn't the outdoors type.

"Well, we've designed the tour to work for all levels," Bob reassured them. "As often as possible, I've plotted out a longer route and a shorter route for each day's ride. And if you want to quit after the morning ride, Terry can drive you from the lunch stop to that evening's hotel."

"What if you want to sleep late in the morning?" Jim de Fusco asked, winking at Natalie.

"Well, then Terry can drive you to catch up with the tour at the lunch stop," Bob said, with a sideways grin. "But seriously, I wouldn't advise that—it's always better to ride in the morning, when the air is cooler and clearer."

Nancy raised her hand. "It sounds like we're going to be all over the place," she remarked. "How will you keep track of everybody—for safety's sake?"

"Glad you asked, Nancy," Bob said. "Each morning when I hand out the day's maps, I'll also give a cell phone to each couple of riders. Both Terry and I are programmed into the speed dial, so you can call us anytime. If you get lost or need a repair, we'll find you. Terry can get there faster, of course, since he's got the van."

"You won't be in the van?" Rhonda asked.

"No, I'll be on my bike, riding along with you all," Bob explained. "I'll try to catch up with every group at some time throughout the day. And, of course, we'll all meet at lunch."

"You said 'each couple of riders'—are we assigned to ride in pairs?" Derek asked, his gaze flickering for an instant toward Camilla. Recalling Camilla's comment, Nancy guessed he was a more serious cyclist than his girlfriend.

Bob shook his head. "I hope you'll ride with different people each day," he said. "That's the great thing about riding with a group—getting to know one another. Of course, the really fast riders may not care to stay too long with the slower riders. So we'll be flexible. The only rule is, always ride with at least one other person, and always have a phone with each group. Beyond that, you can sort it out for yourselves."

A satisfied murmur arose from the crowd. "Sounds like they've thought out all the problems," George remarked to Nancy and Bess.

"Well, I'm glad I won't have to keep up with you two all the time," Bess said, sighing in relief.

Nancy chuckled. "You should have followed George's training plan for the past month, Bess. You'd be in a lot better cycling shape now."

"I know, I know," Bess admitted. "But it seemed so boring at the time."

"Well, don't complain to me if every muscle in your body is sore tomorrow night," George teased her cousin.

Bob Prendergast lifted his voice above the crowd. "Everybody, listen up! We've got several bikes parked outside." He gestured toward a pair of French doors leading to a side terrace. "I know Rhonda and Rachel brought their own, but the rest of you have to choose a bike to ride throughout the tour. So can we step outside?"

Everyone eagerly jumped to their feet and went outdoors. Terry O'Leary stood beside a row of gleaming ten-speed bikes. Their slim aluminum tube frames were painted a bright variety of colors.

"Dibs on the powder blue one," Bess called.

"Better try it out first," warned Terry O'Leary. "Forget the color—you want one that'll suit your height and arm reach."

Bess, blushing with embarrassment, obediently swung her leg over the bike so that Terry could measure how her feet hit the pedals. "Seat's a bit high yet," he muttered. He whipped a hexagonal wrench out of the pocket of his grubby corduroy pants and lowered the seat post. Next he adjusted the angle of the handlebars. "Now it'll do, miss," he said gruffly. Bess pushed off, tottering, on the blue bicycle.

The rest of the group crowded around the various bikes to make their choices. Nancy selected a dark green bicycle, while George settled on a bronze-colored one. "These are good bikes—not as good as mine at home, but still very rideable," George said approvingly.

Rhonda Selkirk spoke up from the terrace wall where she sat with her sister. "Funny how heavy those aluminum frames look, now that I'm used to titanium," she said casually.

George shot Rhonda a glance that wasn't all that friendly. "The weight difference can't be more than a pound or two," she said.

"True," Rhonda replied agreeably. "Still, every ounce matters when you're climbing a hill."

"Remember, these are touring bikes, not dirt bikes," Bob spoke above the hubbub. "Those narrow tires don't have thick treads, so they puncture easily—you may get flats. I'll give you all tire repair kits so you can put on a temporary patch, pump up the mended tire, and ride on. Then Terry can put a new inner tube and tire on that night."

"Better still, don't ride over any nails or broken glass," Rhonda joked.

Bob grinned. "That, too," he said. "And one more thing: You Americans, don't forget to ride on the left-hand side of the road!"

One by one the tour members claimed bikes and then drifted off to their rooms. Nancy, Bess, and George found the large room they were sharing on the second floor. "Too bad," Bess said, gazing out the window at rolling countryside. "I peeked in Rhonda and Rachel's room across the hall, and they have an ocean view."

"Wouldn't you know it," grumbled George.

"Now, give the Selkirks a break," Bess said. "They can't help being rich. And Rhonda may be a bit spoiled, but Rachel's okay."

"You know," Nancy said, "I didn't tell you guys about this before, but in the airport I noticed this one shifty-looking guy on the Sydney flight. I swear Rachel recognized him as we drove off—and she looked pretty upset."

"Did Rhonda see him?" asked Bess.

"That was odd, too," Nancy said. "Rhonda shook her head at Rachel without even looking to see if she knew the guy. It was like she knew he was there, but didn't want to admit it."

George touched Nancy's forehead as if testing for fever. "You need some time off, Nan," she said with a grin. "You're getting a little paranoid. Anyway, it happened back at Shannon—I bet we never run into that character again."

An hour later, the girls went down to meet the group for dinner. "Now we'll get the view," Nancy said as they entered the dining room. A huge picture window on the west wall showed a brilliant sunset sparkling over the Atlantic.

Rachel Selkirk joined the River Heights girls at the window. "What a ripper of a view!" she said. "I'm so glad we chose to do this cycling trip. You can really get in touch with the landscape when you ride through it instead of just staring out the window of a car."

Nancy was just about to reply when she heard a slither and a soft thud behind her. She whirled around to check out what had happened.

There lay Rhonda Selkirk, collapsed in a heap on the dining room floor.

3

A Wee Bit of Trouble

Derek Thorogood jumped up from where he had been sitting, next to Rhonda. "I was talking to her, and she just got all woozy. She started swaying about in her chair, then she tipped over."

Everyone in the dining room broke out in worried murmurs. Almost as one, they rose from their seats and gathered around the spot where Rhonda lay sprawled on the carpet.

Bob Prendergast pushed through the onlookers. "Rhonda?" He knelt quickly at her side and laid a hand against her cheek.

"Her breathing seems to be okay," Bess pointed out. She'd worked at Nancy's side often enough to have a pretty good idea of what to look for in an emergency. "Does her skin feel cold and clammy, or hot and feverish?"

"Neither," Bob said shortly. "Still, I think we'd better call a doctor. I'll go ask the innkeeper to phone a local physician." He searched the ring of faces around him for Rhonda's sister. "Rachel—everything will be okay."

Rachel, looking numb with shock, gave a tense little nod. Bob jumped up and jogged out of the dining room in search of the inn's owners.

Some instinct made Nancy take a careful look around at the circled tour group. To her surprise, she saw that Derek Thorogood was quietly lifting a camera up to his face. Could he really be planning to take a picture of Rhonda lying unconscious? Why would anyone be so intrusive?

But before she could do anything, Natalie de Fusco's voice broke in. "You were sitting with her, Derek—what happened?" she asked.

All eyes turned on him. Derek swiftly slid the camera under his blazer. He pointed to the glass of orange soda sitting on the table at Rhonda's suddenly empty place. "She had just taken a few sips of that Orange Squash," he said, and his dark eyebrows knit in concern.

Nancy heard a little gasp from behind her. She wheeled around to see Rachel, her face completely pale beneath its sprinkling of freckles. "But . . . but that was *my* soda!" she cried out.

Nancy gripped the back of the chair next to her. She didn't want to jump to conclusions, but *if* the orange soda was responsible for Rhonda's blackout—then had it been intended for Rhonda to drink, or for Rachel?

As the group rallied around Rachel, Nancy sank back on a nearby table, her mind racing. Glancing at her watch, she did a swift calculation. Rhonda couldn't have been in the room longer than five minutes before Nancy arrived. Most poisons and drugs take at least twenty minutes to take effect. Of the ones that work immediately, most cause vomiting, convulsions, or gastric pain. But Nancy could see Rhonda lying there on the red-patterned rug—not writhing, not thrashing around, not even breathing very hard.

Nancy rose to her feet and began to move toward the suspect glass of soda, careful not to let anyone notice her.

But Carl Thompson got there first. He picked up the half-full glass, raised it to his nose, and sniffed. "No unusual odor," the professor remarked. "If the drink had been laced with cyanide, it would smell like almonds."

Nancy exchanged a quick glance with Bess. Maybe she wouldn't have to reveal her identity as a detective after all.

"Do you really think anyone would put cyanide in her drink?" Natalie asked.

Carl shrugged. "I'm not a detective—just a chemist," he said. "But if something in the glass caused her to pass out, it was either a poison like cyanide or some drug—a barbiturate powder, maybe. A drug wouldn't have a distinguishing scent, however."

Trying to act like an ordinary bystander so as not to make anyone feel uncomfortable, Nancy asked Carl, "How would you find out? Could you run a chemical test of the remaining soda?"

Carl smiled. "Well, I'm no traveling lab. But I could probably improvise. With a few household chemicals, I could run some preliminary tests."

"We don't need testing yet," Bob Prendergast broke in, rejoining the group. "There's a physician driving over from the next town to look at Rhonda. Let's wait for his diagnosis. This could be a simple medical situation—a reaction to some medication, or something like that. Meanwhile, could someone fetch a blanket? If Rhonda's blood pressure's dropped, she needs to stay warm."

As though relieved to have something definite to do, the members of the tour bustled around. Nancy took advantage of the stir to draw Bob aside. "Did you contact the police?" she asked.

Bob's eyes darted nervously sideways. "Well, uh, no, not yet. I don't see any need to make a fuss. Rhonda wouldn't want the police involved."

"How can you know that?" Nancy asked.

Bob flinched. "It would be a violation of the Selkirks' privacy," he explained. "And I promised them—" He choked off what he was going to say, casting his eyes downward.

"If I were in their situation, I'd want the police called," Nancy said gently.

Bob's eyes flew up to meet hers. "What do you know about their situation?" he challenged her.

Suddenly, Nancy heard a shattering sound from behind. She whirled around.

The glass of orange soda had been knocked off the table where Carl had so carefully set it aside. A puddle of sticky orange liquid was soaking into the red-patterned carpet, oozing around a few big shards of glass.

Terry O'Leary was already on his knees, mopping up the spill with a pile of paper napkins. "Sorry—clumsy me," he muttered. He plucked glass shards up with his fingers and dropped them into the nearest waste bin, then scrunched up a handful of soggy orange napkins and threw them away.

Nancy clenched her fists at her sides. Now they'd never be able to have that liquid tested!

Nancy caught George's eye and jerked her head upward, indicating the need to talk privately. George nodded and glanced at Bess. Bess looked back at Nancy and fluttered her eyelids in reply.

Nancy backed quietly out of the dining room, hoping no one would notice her going. She trotted up the staircase to the girls' room. A moment later, George came in, followed soon after by Bess.

Nancy was tense with anger and disappointment. "Terry O'Leary spilled Rhonda's glass of soda," she fumed. "Now we'll never learn what may have been in it. If I could even get my hands on one piece of glass, there might have been enough soda on it to test."

"It's a tough break—no pun intended—but accidents do happen," Bess said.

Nancy's blue eyes flashed. "I'm not so sure it was an accident. What if Terry *meant* to spill that soda? He heard Carl say he was going to test it."

"Why would Terry want to prevent Carl from testing the soda?" George asked.

"I'm not sure," Nancy admitted, "but I got the distinct impression that Bob wasn't eager to call in the police. And Terry does work for Bob."

"You think Terry and Bob have something to do with Rhonda's passing out?" Bess looked amazed.

Nancy sighed and shrugged. "It's possible. One thing's for sure: Something fishy is going on here. I get the sense there's something about Rhonda and Rachel that we don't know. And this mix-up with the soda bothers me."

"Maybe we should find out more about Derek,"

George said. "He was right next to Rhonda at the table. He had a perfect opportunity to slip something in her drink, didn't he?"

Bess flushed. "How dare you accuse Derek of doing anything wrong!"

George blew out an impatient little breath. "Come on, Bess! Just because you think the guy is gorgeous doesn't mean he's innocent."

Bess glared at her cousin. "It's not just because he's gorgeous. If he had poisoned Rhonda, why would he point out to everybody that she'd just drunk the soda? He would've tried to hide it if he'd been messing with her drink."

"You've got a point, Bess," Nancy said. "All the same, we can't rule him out. I think he was just about to snap a photo of Rhonda while she was lying there. How rude is that? I'd like to know a little more about Derek Thorogood myself."

"You bet," George chimed in. "I mean, he came with Camilla, but he's been hovering around Rhonda and Rachel ever since we arrived. What gives?"

Bess rolled her eyes. "Maybe he's just being friendly. There's no crime in that."

"I'm not saying he's a criminal—I'd just like to know more about him," Nancy said. "And that goes for everybody on this tour. All three of us must keep our eyes and ears open. Now, let's go back downstairs before anyone misses us. Maybe the doctor's here."

She pushed open the door to their room and stepped out in the passageway, casually tucking her hair behind her ears. A movement down the hall caught her eye.

A few yards away, Derek Thorogood crouched in a narrow cranny, hunched over something in his right hand. He was talking quickly and softly to himself. Sensing Nancy's presence, he froze against the wall.

Nancy's sharp eyes picked up the gleam of a tiny electronic device in Derek's hand. It looked like a tape recorder!

Derek thrust the device hastily into his pocket and jumped up. A glib smile spread over his handsome features. "Oh, Nancy, I came up to find you. Thought you might like to know—all's well after all. Rhonda came to, just after you left. Seems none the worse for her scare, thank goodness."

"Well, that's a relief," Nancy said in a guarded tone of voice.

"The doctor never came, but Rhonda swears it was nothing. No medical condition, she's not on any medicines, nothing of that sort. So it was probably an allergic reaction to something in the soda." He blithely waved his hand. "Or maybe jet lag. Anyway, they're about to serve dinner. Where are your two friends?" He looked over Nancy's shoulder.

"They came up to . . . use the bathroom," Nancy said.

"You mean the 'loo.'" Derek smiled and began to guide Nancy toward the stairs. "I'm making it my mission to teach you Americans the local lingo, you know."

"I appreciate it," Nancy said, flashing him a smile. She had to agree with Bess: Derek Thorogood *was* good-looking, and charming, too. But she still didn't trust him.

The low-beamed dining room rang with chatter as Nancy and Derek entered. Nancy glimpsed Rhonda and Rachel at a table with the de Fuscos, looking as if nothing had happened. Derek led Nancy to a table near the picture window. "Well, that was enough excitement for one evening, I can tell you," Camilla said, smiling up at Nancy.

"Yes, indeed," Nancy replied. She took a seat next to Carl Thompson.

Derek rubbed his hands together and began to back away from the table. "Well, I'll just leave those other seats open for Beth and Jo, shall I?"

"Bess and George," Nancy corrected him. "But they can find other seats. Like Bob said, we should all mingle and get to know one another." She patted the chair beside her for Derek to sit down.

"Yes, yes—well, all the more reason why I should sit somewhere else. Right, Camilla?" And before she could reply, Derek had gone to join Bob and Terry at a table by the door.

I can still keep an eye on him from here, Nancy thought, shifting her chair slightly. She lifted her menu and began to decide what to order.

But the next time she remembered to look up, as the soup plates were being taken away, she saw that Derek's chair at the table near the door was empty.

4

A Need for Speed

"So what if Derek *did* leave the dining room?" Bess said as the girls talked in their room later.

"Bess, you've got to admit he's acting suspicious," George argued. "First, Nancy saw him try to snap a photo of Rhonda while she was knocked out. Then he was whispering into a tape recorder. Then he steered Nancy to a table away from Rhonda and Rachel so she couldn't ask them any questions."

"And after I sat down, he sat somewhere else so I couldn't ask *him* any questions," Nancy added, tugging a brush through her hair.

"Then he snuck out of the dining room for almost fifteen minutes," George said.

"Maybe he had to finish recording his tape," Bess suggested.

"Yes, but why was he making a tape recording in the first place?" George demanded, pointing her toothbrush accusingly at Bess.

"None of it makes sense yet," Nancy said. "But like I said, we should be alert for the next few days. I can't help thinking Rhonda and Rachel are the key to everything."

"We should ride with them tomorrow," George said, "to keep an eye on them."

Bess raised her eyebrows. "You two can ride with the Selkirks," she said, rolling over on the bed. "Not me. Those girls are as tall and strong as Amazons, plus they have those fancy titanium bikes. There's no way I'd keep up with them."

Nancy fought a yawn. "Well, there's no way I'll keep up with them, either, if I don't get to bed. I didn't sleep much on the plane last night—too excited. On River Heights time, it's only four P.M., but it's ten here and I'm totally zonked. Let's turn in."

"I'll take Rhonda, you take Rachel," George murmured to Nancy the next morning. They glanced over to where the Selkirk sisters stood beside the hotel steps in their high-tech riding gear—snug black knit shorts and zip-up spandex jerseys.

George self-consciously adjusted the legs of her form-fitting blue shorts, bought new for this trip. Her banana yellow jersey was emblazoned with the name of an Italian racing team. Nancy and Bess had opted for ordinary clothes: khaki cotton hiking shorts, roomy T-shirts, and windbreakers.

"You ride with them, and I'll ride with Derek Thorogood," Bess offered. George gave her a sarcastic look. "Well, you said we should watch him, too," Bess said, a twinkle in her eye.

It was a bright, clear morning with a balmy breeze. As the tour group gathered outside the hotel, Bob Prendergast handed out the day's maps, along with plastic water bottles. "Lunch today is a picnic overlooking the Cliffs of Moher," Bob reminded everybody. "Be there by twelve-thirty."

"Or, as we say over here, half-twelve," Derek added, waggling his eyebrows.

Nancy walked her bicycle over to the Selkirks. "Love your matching magenta bikes," she said. "But how do you tell them apart?"

Rachel smiled. "Easy—I've put silver tape on my handlebars, and Rhonda's got black." She pointed to her down-curved handlebars.

Bob Prendergast joined them. "Who's riding with whom today?"

Nancy turned to Rachel. "Could we ride together?" she asked quickly.

Rachel shrugged as she lifted her silver helmet to strap it on. "Sure, why not?"

"Okay, Rachel and Nancy, here's a cell phone for

the day." Bob handed Nancy a bulky, slightly outdated model of cell phone. "Push speed dial one to reach me, speed dial two for Terry."

"I could ride with you, Rhonda," George piped up, standing behind Bob.

"Great, Rhonda and George are a team," Bob said, handing a cell phone to Rhonda. "I'm glad you're mixing partners. Have a good ride!" He bustled off to finish equipping other riders.

Rhonda shot an annoyed look at George. "Hope you don't mind riding fast," she snapped, slinging her black helmet on top of her glossy dark hair. Rhonda swung onto her bike and pushed off, with George scrambling in her wake.

Rachel smiled at Nancy. "I have to confess—I have a serious need for speed myself," she said. "That's why Rhonda and I hoped we could ride together. But I'm willing to give you a go."

"Thanks," Nancy said, fitting on her own helmet. "Don't worry. I like to ride fast, too."

Nancy and Rachel swung out of the hotel parking lot, turning right onto the road that led north. They cycled downhill into Lahinch, its main street lined with shops and restaurants.

"This looks like a popular resort," Nancy shouted to Rachel, who was riding ahead. "I even saw a dive shop back there. Funny, I wouldn't have thought of scuba diving off the coast of Ireland."

Rachel nodded but said nothing.

A moment later, Nancy tried again. "That looks like a good golf course up ahead. Camilla was saying last night that County Clare's a big golf area—lots of famous courses." She paused, fishing for a response. "Do you play golf?"

Rachel shifted in her seat so she could shout to Nancy. "Sorry—don't mean to be unfriendly—but I don't like yabbering and yakking while I'm riding. It interrupts the flow, don't you think?"

Nancy cheerfully replied, "Okay." But she felt crestfallen. She'd hoped to learn some details about Rachel by talking to her. But even more important, she'd hoped to gain Rachel's confidence. Now she was afraid Rachel would write her off as a chatty air-head.

And a chatty airhead who couldn't cycle seriously, Nancy added to herself a few miles farther on. Everything was all right so long as they rode down-hill. But just past Lahinch, the road narrowed and began to climb. George's training regimen had im-proved Nancy's wind, stamina, and leg strength, but she still didn't know how to shift gears on hills like Rachel did.

Nancy stood up on her pedals to gain extra power as she pushed her bike up the challenging slope. Looking ahead, she saw that Rachel was still seated, pedaling rapidly but smoothly.

Nancy fumbled with her gear lever, shifting down so that she could pedal with less resistance. But it was too late—she'd already lost momentum. The distance between her and Rachel lengthened by the second. Nancy gritted her teeth, determined not to ask Rachel to slow down.

Even without turning, Rachel must have sensed that Nancy had fallen way behind. She halted and got off her bike at the top of the hill. Nancy toiled up the last few steep yards, trying hard not to show the exertion.

"Now this is what I call a view," Rachel said as Nancy finally reached her side.

Nancy nodded gamely and pivoted toward the northwest. What she saw made her completely forget her cycling efforts. Stretching ahead before them, for about five miles, was a stretch of spectacular coastal cliffs, their sheer sides ribboned with five layers of different-colored rockface. On the stony ledges nestled huge flocks of puffins and other seabirds. To the left the Atlantic Ocean gleamed and danced.

"Takes your breath away, eh?" Rachel asked.

It took a second for Nancy to realize that Rachel was kidding her. "Oh—so *that's* why I can't breathe," she said, playing along. "And I thought it was from riding up the hill."

Rachel laughed along with her, but Nancy felt

embarrassed. "A new bike always takes getting used to," Rachel said tactfully. "Best get a drink and stretch your calves before we go on."

Nancy nodded and dismounted, hardly daring to admit what a relief it was. Leaning her bike against a signpost, she took her water bottle from a bracket on her bike and took a long swig.

"Looks like we still have some uphill riding to do," Rachel said. Crouching down, she ran her fingers through the gravel on the road's edge by Nancy's bike. "What's that out there?" She pointed north, where a few dark islands dotted the sea.

Nancy peered at her map for a moment. "Looks like those are the Aran Islands," she finally decided.

Rachel stood up suddenly. "Well, we should get going." She grabbed her bike and swung up onto the seat. "Ready?"

"As ready as I'll ever be." Nancy stuffed the map in her pocket and jumped on her bike. Rachel was off with a spurt of gravel before Nancy could fit her shoes into the toe clips on her pedals.

The two bikes sped smoothly down the brief slope that followed the hilltop, but soon the road angled upward again. This time, Nancy paid more attention to gear shifting, clicking down to a lower gear each time the pedals began to strain. *Now I've got the hang of it,* she told herself. She kept her eyes trained on the red reflector below Rachel's seat and fought to match Rachel's pace.

Then suddenly everything went wrong. Nancy's front wheel jerked and wobbled. She heard a grating sound on the pavement. The bike began to lean sideways. Nancy squeezed her handbrakes hard.

The red reflector on Rachel's bike whizzed uphill and away.

Nancy hopped off and examined her front wheel. As she feared, the tire was totally flat. Even worse, it looked like the steel rim of the wheel had cut through the rubber treads.

"Rachel!" Nancy called out. The Australian girl was already at the top of the hill, but she circled and coasted back down to Nancy.

"Looks like you've come a cropper," Rachel said as she saw Nancy's flat. "You won't be able to mend it with the patch kit. Better call that Terry bloke and have him pick you up."

With a sigh, Nancy phoned Terry and told him where to find her. As she hung up, Rachel began waving. "Look! Jim, Natalie, and Carl are just down the hill," she said. "You don't mind if I ride with them, do you? I'll leave you the cell."

"That's fine. Terry will be here soon," Nancy said, swallowing her regret.

After the others had ridden away, Nancy rechecked her tire. She frowned. The tread and the inner tube had a long, straight cut in them—not a simple puncture or a jagged rip.

A worrisome thought struck Nancy: Had Rachel done something to the tire at the top of the hill?

Nancy replayed the scene in her mind—Rachel crouched by Nancy's bike, making Nancy gaze out at the ocean and then pore over her map. She'd had time to slash Nancy's tire. But had she done it?

And if she had, why?

"Nancy, stop brooding about that flat," Bess shouted above the music. "You covered the day's route all right after Terry fixed it, didn't you?"

Nancy shook her head. "Yes, I know. Sorry. But it isn't just getting a flat—anybody could get a flat tire. It just seemed so odd—"

Nancy was cut off by the night's entertainment. The musicians finished with a flourish, and wild applause filled the Currach Pub right up to its low, oak-beamed ceiling. The tour was spending the night in Doolin, a fishing village famous for the music pubs along its short main street. Across the room, Nancy glimpsed Rhonda and Rachel, both safe and sound, sitting at a table with Derek and Camilla. *There's no reason to suspect Rachel caused my flat tire,* Nancy scolded herself. *Just because she didn't want to chat while we were riding—and just because she was eager to ride away with other people. She's focused on her cycling, that's all.*

Nancy told herself to stop fretting. After all, when would she hear such delightful music again? Getting into the spirit, she started to stamp her feet with the chorus. Her thigh muscles twinged painfully.

George noticed and giggled. "Don't worry, Nan—I'm sore, too," she whispered. "So much for keeping up with the Selkirks."

Nancy grinned and glanced back over at the Australians' table. Derek was leaning over and whispering in Rhonda's ear, while Camilla, looking oblivious, swayed to the music.

But where had Rachel gone?

Nancy stiffened and looked around. Though the room was crowded, it was small. Despite the noise and the haze of smoke from a peat fire, every cheery corner was visible. And Rachel was nowhere.

Nancy rose uneasily and started to move toward the door as the sea chanty ended. The applause was dying down when she heard an awful clatter outside, followed by a moan of pain.

Dashing outside, Nancy nearly tripped over Rachel, sprawled on the cobbled street with the pub's heavy wooden sign lying beside her.

5

No Thanks

Bob Prendergast came hurrying out the door right behind Nancy. "Go ask the pub owner for some ice, and have him call a doctor," he said, kneeling beside Rachel. His fingers gently probed the side of her forehead, where Nancy could see a small, bloody gash. "And send Terry out."

"Here already, Bob," came Terry's voice from the shadows beside the pub door. Nancy turned to look at him, standing with his hands thrust in the pockets of his baggy corduroys. How had he arrived so fast and so silently? Nancy wondered. Had he come from inside—or was he outside the whole time?

"Fetch the first-aid kit from the van, Terry," Bob said, not looking up.

Nancy hated to leave the scene of the accident,

but she knew it was crucial to get medical help as soon as possible. Luckily, the pub owner had heard the commotion and was already at the doorway. He promised to bring out some ice as soon as he had phoned a physician. "There's no one directly in town," he warned Nancy. "Doolin's not so big as all that. But Dr. Finney lives only a couple miles off—I'll ring him up."

Bess and George joined Nancy as she headed back outside. "Rachel's been knocked out—it looks like the pub sign fell and hit her in the head," she said anxiously.

"Derek was inside the whole time—I know, I was watching him," Bess said, reading Nancy's mind. "Just in case you were wondering."

As they emerged again into the clear, crisp night air, Nancy was relieved to see Rachel beginning to moan and stir. "My head," Rachel murmured. "Wicked pain . . ." Her eyes fluttered open and then squeezed shut again, as if even the dim light from the pub door was too bright.

A curious crowd had begun to spill out of the doorway. Rhonda pushed her way through, glaring. "Can't you all clear off?" she snapped.

"Yes, that's enough now, you lot," the pub owner said. Handing a bag of ice to Nancy, he shooed the gawkers back inside. Bess and George reluctantly followed them.

Rhonda bent over Rachel. "What were you thinking of?" she scolded her sister. "Why did you go outside? You know you shouldn't slip off on your own."

Rachel winced. "Leave off, Rhon," she replied groggily. "Gotta . . . have a life . . ."

"Where does it hurt, Rachel?" Bob asked.

Rachel lifted a hand weakly and touched the top of her skull, on the right side. "Something heavy—out of nowhere—"

Rhonda glimpsed the blood on her sister's forehead and sucked in her breath. "The sign—it really hit you! Give us that ice, Nancy." She started to lift Rachel's head, but Bob stopped her.

"Best not to move her, in case she's had a concussion," he suggested. "Lay the ice against her head from the side and wait for the doctor."

"No doctor!" Rachel burst out with surprising vehemence. "I'm all right." She pushed herself up onto her elbows with a sudden, forceful effort.

"Now, Rachel, it's best to get checked out," Bob said. "With head injuries, you never know."

"Then send the doctor to the hotel," Rachel declared. "I'm not lying here in the gutter anymore. Help me up, Rhon."

Rhonda took her sister's elbow and helped her to her feet. "We'll be all right, Bob," she said. She cast a worried look up and down the shadowy street. "I'll see she stays in bed. Send the doctor along."

Nancy noted Bob's anxious expression. "I could have Terry drive you in the van," he offered. "He should be back any sec." He glanced around, just realizing that Terry hadn't returned.

"No!" Rhonda insisted. She quickly added, "I'll walk her back. It's not far. Fresh air might do her good—better than being jolted in a van."

"I'll be fine," Rachel announced, lifting her chin as she took a wobbly first step. "Not to worry."

Bob stepped back, hands hanging helplessly at his sides. Nancy stood with him, watching, as the sisters moved tentatively down the sloping street toward the inn where the group was staying. An only child herself, Nancy didn't always understand sibling relationships. But she knew enough to see that this one was complicated indeed.

Jim de Fusco popped out of the front door. "Is Rachel okay?" he asked. "We heard she was hurt, but we didn't want to hover."

"I'll go reassure everyone," Bob said. "Nancy, tell Terry I'm inside. And don't stay out too long—the night air's cold, so close to the sea." He ducked back inside the pub.

"What happened?" Jim asked Nancy.

She pointed to the wood sign on the pavement. "Apparently that fell and clonked Rachel on the side of the head."

Jim knelt to inspect the thick slab of wood, carved

in the shape of a wicker-framed one-man boat. "So that's what the pub's named after—a currach fishing boat," he said. He ran his hands over the wood. "Nice carving. Real craftsmanship."

"This makes two accidents in a row," Nancy remarked. "Rhonda passed out last night, and now this with Rachel. If it *was* an accident."

With a professional eye, Jim studied the end of one of the chains from which the sign had hung. "Hard to tell how it happened. This chain link is twisted, like it had torn loose. Maybe the other side was rusted . . ." He picked up its mate, then gave a low whistle. "No, this one's been cut, clean through, like someone hacked it with a saw."

"Let me see." Nancy bent down to examine the two chains. "So once this chain was severed—"

"The other one would eventually break," Jim replied. "It couldn't hold the weight on its own. These chains are pretty thin to carry such a heavy sign. If I'd hung it, I'd have used a thicker chain."

Nancy looked solemnly at Jim. "So possibly someone meant for Rachel to get hurt."

Jim screwed his mouth to the side. "Maybe. I'd sure like to know why the one chain was cut."

"So would I," Nancy said grimly. She swiveled and began to hunt around the pavement. If she could find a discarded hacksaw, or even a pile of iron shavings . . .

Her eyes fell on a patch of white on the ground,

right where Rachel had fallen. She stooped to pick it up. On a crumpled piece of paper was scrawled, "R—Meet me outside—D."

Nancy chewed her lip. Who had written this note? Someone whose name started with "D." Derek Thorogood? He had been sitting at the table with Rachel, Nancy remembered. Why had he needed to see her privately?

She turned to face Jim. "We should let Bob know what we found," she said. "I'll go to the inn to talk to Rhonda and Rachel."

Jim nodded and went back inside. Drawing a steadying breath, Nancy headed down the street toward their inn. She fingered the corner of the note in her pocket. *Think logically*, she reminded herself, like her father had always told her. *Don't make quick assumptions.* For instance, why assume the note was for Rachel? R could just as easily stand for Rhonda. Either girl might have dropped it when she came outside tonight.

The note might have nothing to do with the accident, Nancy mused. But still, it was worth checking out. It was no more puzzling than the other facts in this case so far.

The lilt of music-making coursed through the evening air, only the tune changing as Nancy passed each of the village's pubs in turn. But she was thinking too hard to notice.

Reaching the inn, Nancy marched past the front desk and straight upstairs. With its whitewashed walls and polished plank floors, the inn was more rustic than last night's lodgings, but it was cozy and quiet. The Selkirks' room was at the end of the third-floor hallway. Nancy rapped on their door. "Who is it?" Rhonda called.

"Nancy Drew. I have to talk to you."

After a brief silence, Rhonda called back, "Another time, Nancy. Rachel needs to sleep."

"If she's had a concussion, she should stay awake," Nancy warned. "Are her pupils dilated?"

"Go away!" Rhonda replied.

Then Nancy heard Rachel's low murmur. A moment later, the door opened. Rachel faced her. "Come on in, Nancy," she said. "I am feeling groggy, I must admit, but we can talk."

Nancy glanced at Rachel's pupils, which she was glad to see were normal sized. "How many fingers?" she asked, holding up three fingers.

"I already did all those tests," Rhonda said, leafing through a magazine on the bed. "And it's not like you're a doctor, Nancy."

"No, I'm no doctor," Nancy admitted. She paused, making certain of her own decision. "But I *am* a detective," she revealed.

Rachel's eyes widened. Rhonda slapped shut her magazine. "For real?" Rachel asked.

Nancy nodded. "I'm just an amateur, but I've solved lots of cases. No one on the trip knows, except Bess and George. But I think you need someone to look out for you. Knowing my background, will you let me help?"

Rachel fidgeted. "Thanks, but no thanks, Nancy. It's sweet of you to offer, but we don't need protection. Those were two random accidents."

Nancy raised her eyebrows. "That falling sign may not have been an accident," she said. She told them what she and Jim had discovered.

Rhonda snorted. "That's ridiculous," she said. "Even if the chain was cut, it was probably done as a prank by some kid from town. They must hate us tourists for overrunning their village."

Nancy looked skeptical. "But tourists also provide jobs for their parents. I don't think they mind us that much."

"Look, I don't know why the sign fell," Rachel said earnestly. "But I'm sure it's nothing."

Nancy bit her lip. In her experience, people acted scared when they were told someone was out to hurt them. Why didn't Rachel care?

Nancy flashed the note she'd found. "I found this lying on the ground where you fell, Rachel."

Rachel glanced at the scrap of paper. Her face hardened. "Never saw it," she claimed. Yet Nancy thought she saw Rachel's pale skin flush beneath her freckles.

"Me neither," Rhonda spoke up, though Nancy hadn't asked her.

Just then, another knock came on the door. "Hello, it's Dr. Finney. Miss Selkirk?"

"You'd better go now, Nancy," Rhonda said firmly. "See you tomorrow." And Nancy had no choice but to walk out.

"I never eat this much for breakfast," Bess exclaimed, rising from the table. "Eggs, bacon, toast, *and* those yummy fried tomatoes."

"You were hungry, and no wonder; you spent all day yesterday exercising," George said. "Today will be more of the same. That's why I had two bowls of oatmeal—so I can keep up with Rhonda."

Nancy wrinkled her nose. "I'm not sure Rhonda will agree to ride with you today—or Rachel with me," she said. "Not after I spilled the beans to them last night. What was I thinking?"

"You were thinking they'd be glad to know you're a detective," Bess consoled her. "And anyone else would be. I think their reaction is highly suspicious."

Nancy smiled, grateful for her friend's loyal support. "Well, we should ride together today, and enjoy ourselves. I'll go find Bob and get our map and cell phone."

"Meet you by the bikes," Bess agreed.

Stepping outside, Nancy marveled at another

sunny day. "So much for all the Irish rain," she said to herself.

The tour group's bikes were lined up along a low stone wall, their chrome fittings glinting in the morning sun. None of the other cyclists were out yet. Nancy strolled to the corner of the hotel to check if Bob was anywhere nearby.

Rounding the corner of the white stucco inn, Nancy glanced down a narrow alley where a few cars were parked. Two people huddled together about fifty yards down the alley, in close conversation.

Nancy froze. It was Rhonda—whispering earnestly with the stranger in the black overcoat.

6

Look Both Ways

With long, determined strides, Nancy headed toward Rhonda and the mysterious man. Something's up with those two, she told herself, and I'm going to find out what it is.

But as soon as she began to approach, the man saw her from the corner of his eye and immediately started to back away from Rhonda. He raised his voice, and Nancy clearly heard him say, "Thank you, miss, I'll find it on me own."

I'll bet that was for my benefit, Nancy thought.

Moving with surprising agility for such a large person, the man whisked around a corner before Nancy reached Rhonda. The Australian girl turned to face Nancy, looking startled.

"Why, Nancy," she said, adjusting the zipper on

her neon green spandex jersey. "G'day. Ready for today's ride?"

Nancy refused to be distracted. "Who was that man you were just talking to? Everything okay?" she asked.

Rhonda pursed her lips. "What man?"

"The man in the black coat," Nancy said, her fists on her hips.

"How should I know?" Rhonda replied with an airy shrug. "He was just a tourist asking for directions. He took me for a local. Fancy that! I told him I was probably just as lost as he was."

"Lost?" Nancy narrowed her eyes. "This is a small village. How could anyone be lost here?"

"Well, he got mixed up—didn't know which pub was which, I reckon," Rhonda explained, waving her hand.

She turned on her heel and started to hurry away. Unfortunately for Rhonda, the cleats on her cycling shoes clattered and slid on the cobblestoned street. Nancy, wearing her low-tech cross-trainers, easily caught up as Rhonda headed for the main street.

"The funny thing is, I've seen that man before," she persisted, closely observing Rhonda's expression. "The day we landed at Shannon Airport. I remember noticing him because he's missing one finger."

"Is that so?" Rhonda's face was like a mask of total

unconcern. "I didn't get that close a look. You've got a knack for identifying people. Must be your "detective eyes."

"Yes," Nancy said, ignoring the dig. "But don't you think it's strange he would show up here? That can't be another coincidence."

"Why not?" Rhonda said calmly, walking on up the street. "Ireland's an awfully small country, and this is one of its most popular tourist stops. I reckon half the people who came through Shannon the other day will be driving up and down this coast. It's no surprise you'd run into someone twice. I wouldn't worry about it. Now, excuse me, I've got to buy some film for my camera." She popped into a small shop that was open early, leaving Nancy alone on the cobbled pavement.

Frustrated, Nancy went back to where the bikes were parked beside the inn entrance. Bess and George were packing supplies for the day's ride in their canvas panniers—bags fitted onto a bracket mounted over the rear wheels.

"Bob gave us our map and cell phone," Bess told Nancy. "We can get going whenever you're ready. Maybe if we get a head start on the others, we won't have to ride so fast."

Nancy chewed her lip for a second. Her natural desire to help people was winning out over her stung sense of pride. "Slight change in plans," she announced. "I think we should do everything we can to follow the Selkirks again today."

Bess groaned and sagged against the stone wall. "Why?"

"You'll never guess who I just saw," Nancy explained quietly, hoping none of the other gathering tour members would overhear. "Remember that suspicious guy I noticed at the airport?"

Bess raised her eyebrows. "The one with the missing finger?"

"Yes," Nancy said. "And guess who was talking to him? Rhonda."

George whistled softly.

"She said he was just asking directions," Nancy added, "but the way they were talking sure looked like they knew each other well."

George glanced around to look for the Selkirks. "Once again, Rhonda pretends not to know something she obviously does know," she muttered.

Nancy nodded. "And it does seem significant that this guy's in town, doesn't it? Considering what happened to Rachel last night."

"But after that note you found, I thought it was Derek who lured Rachel outside," Bess said.

"Ooh, do I detect a change of heart?" George needled Bess. "You're not defending Derek anymore. Could it be because he spent all last night flirting with both Rhonda and Rachel?"

Bess blushed slightly, but she held her ground. "Working with Nancy, I've learned one thing: Don't ignore the evidence."

Nancy pushed up the sleeves of her yellow windbreaker. "I wish we knew whether the note was for Rhonda or for Rachel."

"I had a thought in the middle of the night," George said. "Suppose Derek passed the note to Rhonda, and Rachel saw it. Maybe she went outside to stop Derek from having a private date with her sister."

"Or Rhonda went outside to stop Rachel from meeting Derek," Bess said. "The possibilities in this love triangle are endless."

At that moment, Derek and Camilla strolled out of the inn. As Camilla pulled on a pair of stretchy leather cycling gloves, Derek walked behind, his hands resting on her shoulders. Camilla halted for a moment and leaned back against his chest, smiling warmly up at him.

"They look lovey-dovey this morning," Nancy observed. "Isn't it weird that Camilla doesn't seem to mind Derek flirting with the Selkirks?" She fit her helmet over her hair. "This isn't just a love triangle, it's a love quadrangle. Something's definitely weird."

Now Rachel appeared at the inn doorway, pausing for a moment on the flagstone step to draw in a lungful of breezy sea air. She had a strip of gauze around her head, half covering her copper-colored hair, but she was decked out in full cycling gear, black and fluorescent orange. Nancy had to admire the Australian girl's spirit, even though she did question her judgment.

"Hey, Rachel, how's the head?" Natalie de Fusco called over in a friendly voice.

Rachel smiled shyly and touched her bandage. "I'm feeling super, really I am," she replied. "Takes more than a little knock on the head to put me out of action. The bandage is just so my helmet won't irritate the cut. But the doctor says I'm perfectly fit to ride."

Bob Prendergast turned around from where he was discussing the day's route with Carl Thompson. "I know the doctor gave you a clean bill of health, Rachel," he said, "but could you promise to take it easy today? Just so I don't have a heart attack?"

Rachel chuckled. "Anything for you, Bob."

"Then take the inland route instead of the coastal one," Bob advised, pointing to two different roads on the photocopied map. "It's five miles shorter and a lot less hilly. You're riding on a rocky plateau instead of up and down seaside bluffs. Besides, it's more interesting scenery."

"Whatever you say," Rachel agreed.

As Rachel strolled toward her bike, Nancy stepped forward. "Morning, Rachel," she said.

Rachel shot her a wary glance. "Morning, Nancy. Hi, George and Bess."

Inwardly, Nancy groaned. Telling the Selkirks that she was a detective hadn't helped her get close to them, as she had hoped. In fact, it had driven them away.

Luckily, George was thinking fast. "Looks like Rhonda's not here yet," she said brightly. "Want to ride together this morning, Rachel? That way, I can compare your speed with your sister's."

Evidently, George had pushed the right button. A competitive gleam lit up Rachel's face. "I did promise Bob I'd go easy," she said with a mischievous smile, "but a challenge is a challenge. Let's go!"

Nancy flashed a look of gratitude at her friend. With a wink, George took her ten-speed by the handlebars and walked it over to where Rachel was getting her magenta bike ready.

"What about Rhonda?" Bess asked Nancy, craning her neck to look around. "She still hasn't shown up. Are you going to try to ride with her?"

Nancy shook her head. "I don't think she'd let me, judging from how she talked to me this morning." She sighed. She suspected she would like Rachel and Rhonda if she ever got to know them better. Now, that didn't look likely.

"No," Nancy decided. "If we want to keep an eye on Rhonda, we'll just have to ride close behind her."

Bess made a face. "And here I was looking forward to a leisurely day of cycling. I guess this means we won't be able to take the shorter inland route."

"Sorry, pal," Nancy said, playfully bumping her friend's arm with her fist. "If Rhonda takes the coast road—and I bet she will—we've got to follow."

Across the paved area, Nancy saw Rachel swing her left leg over the crossbar of her bike. George thrust her feet in the toe clips on her pedals. "See you at lunch!" George called out with a wave to Nancy and Bess.

Bumping over the cobblestones, Rachel darted onto the main road, inserting herself into traffic right behind a small green car. George stood on her pedals, pumping to catch up.

George turned onto the road, eyes trained on Rachel, who was already picking up speed.

Suddenly, the tour's cherry red van roared out of the side alley. Terry O'Leary was at the wheel. He gunned the van, lurching onto the road—aiming for George!

7

A Vicious Cycle

Scared by the engine's roar behind her, George clutched her brakes and wrenched the bike aside.

Nancy dropped her bike and ran toward George. For a moment, Nancy lost sight of her friend as the van screeched between them.

Suddenly, Nancy heard a sickening thud.

The van jerked to a stop. Terry O'Leary threw open his door. "Eh, what is it now?" he grumbled.

Nancy ran around the corner of the van, Bess at her heels. George sat on the pavement, looking dazed.

"Now I know why cyclists wear helmets," George said, looking up at her friends. "I flew over the handlebars and landed on my head, but I'm actually fine."

Terry stood behind Nancy, awkwardly opening and closing his fists. "You want to watch where you're riding," he said to George. "You can't just go barging into oncoming traffic."

Bob came bustling around the van, looking agitated. "Terry, you idiot!" he lashed out at his driver. "How many times do I have to tell you?"

"Coming out of that alley, I couldn't see her," Terry protested, his pale gray eyes shifting nervously.

"Then that's when you should drive slowly," Bob said, sounding exasperated.

"But I had to accelerate to get up the incline. There were cars coming," Terry defended himself.

"Yeah, right—the dreaded rush hour traffic in Doolin," Bob muttered sarcastically. "Are you okay, George?"

"A little shaken, that's all," she said, standing up and brushing off her blue cycling shorts. "A scrape on my leg, maybe."

"She scratched the paint!" Terry complained, pointing to the side of the red van. "And after we just got a new paint job."

Bob groaned. "Terry, forget the paint! One of our guests got hurt—and it could have been a lot worse. Now shut up and get me the first-aid kit."

Terry flashed a dark look at Bob and hurried to the passenger door. He handed Nancy a flat metal box with a Red Cross on its lid. Inside, Nancy found some alcohol and a cotton pad. She began to swab George's scraped knee clean.

"Where's Rachel?" George asked.

"She went on riding—she didn't even see your collision," Bess reported. "Rhonda showed up and went to catch up with Rachel."

"So much for riding with them," George said with a sigh.

"It doesn't matter," Nancy said, repacking the first-aid kit. She glanced over at Terry and Bob standing a short distance away. Bob was talking angrily; Terry hung his head and listened with a smoldering look on his face.

"I wouldn't be in Terry's shoes now for anything," Bess said sympathetically.

Nancy crooked an eyebrow. "Maybe. But it looks like Bob has read him the riot act plenty of times before. There's some bad history between them. Wish I knew what it was."

Bess followed Nancy's gaze. "You don't think Terry's up to something, do you?"

Nancy considered. "Well, it was Terry who spilled that suspicious soda two nights ago—and last night he was close by when the sign fell on Rachel."

George shivered. "You don't think Terry was *trying* to hit me just now, do you?"

"It happened so fast, I'm not sure what I saw," Nancy admitted. "But something about this guy doesn't add up."

Knowing that George wasn't really hurt, the rest

of the group soon mounted their bikes and set off. Nancy, Bess, and George followed. The three girls soon passed the de Fuscos, then Derek and Camilla, who were dawdling along.

Before long, they reached a fork. "We got a late start—might as well take the shortcut," Nancy said, turning onto the road heading inland.

"Yes!" Bess pumped her arm.

"Rhonda and Rachel probably followed the coast road," George guessed.

"Don't bet on it," Nancy said, peering along the road ahead. "I see two tiny figures way ahead. They're far away, but one of them is bright green and the other one orange. And if I remember correctly—"

"Rachel was definitely wearing orange this morning," Bess said. "And Rhonda was in green."

Nancy grinned. "Ready to kick it up a notch?"

Bess groaned, but Nancy and George began to pedal hard, and she had no choice but to keep up.

"They're leading a stiff pace," Nancy called out. "So much for Rachel taking it easy."

"It's a good thing they didn't notice we're behind them," George shouted.

"Yeah—I'd hate to see how hard they'd ride if they were *trying* to go fast," panted Bess.

"Hey, they just pulled over to the side of the road," George said. "Now we can catch up."

"Why did they stop?" Nancy wondered aloud.

"Looks like they're checking out that herd of sheep," George guessed.

"*Flock* of sheep," Bess corrected her cousin, leaning over her handlebars. "Cows go in herds, sheep are in flocks. Aren't they fluffy and adorable? I can't wait to see them up close."

"Uh-oh." Nancy began to reach for her hand brakes. "We may be more up close than we want."

The gray asphalt ahead was slowly covered by white as the immense flock of sheep began to wander onto the road. A chorus of *baa*s rose on the air, echoing off the grassy hollows.

"Slow down—they're blocking the road!" George called out.

As Nancy pressed her hand brakes, she gazed past the sheep. Rhonda and Rachel had hopped back onto their bikes and were pedaling away. Rachel waved jauntily over her head at Nancy and her friends, stranded amidst the woolly flood.

"Do you think they did that on purpose?" Nancy asked as she stopped, helpless, surrounded by sheep.

The animals' fat sides heaved under thick, ivory-colored fleeces. Tiny black hooves clicked aimlessly on the pavement. "I didn't realize how many there were," Bess said, glancing skittishly from side to side. "This is creepy. How long do you think it'll take them to cross the road?"

"They aren't exactly crossing," George said, frowning. "There's no dog or shepherd guiding them. They're just crashing around like bumper cars."

"I bet Rhonda and Rachel opened that gate," Nancy said, pointing to a swinging wicket at the edge of the nearby pasture. "They lured them onto the road to stop us!"

Looking back up the road, Nancy saw a pair of cyclists approach. It was Derek and Camilla. Nancy grimaced, embarrassed.

As the English pair coasted up, Bess waved to them. "Looks like Rhonda and Rachel let these sheep out," she called out, "and now we're stuck."

"Trust a pair of Australians to know about sheep," Derek said with an amused smirk. "But don't worry, we'll help you herd them back."

It took some doing, but fifteen minutes later they had steered the sheep back into the pasture. Derek fastened the gate shut. "The Selkirks got you this time," he teased.

Nancy gave a rueful shrug. "Let's just head on to lunch."

At the crest of the next steep hill, they looked down the hillside, expecting to see the vivid green expanses they had become used to. George braked to a stop. "Wow! What happened?"

The others braked, too. Below them stretched a vast panorama of creased, craggy gray rock. Bess shivered. "I feel like we just took a wrong turn and ended up on the moon."

"Amazing," Nancy exclaimed. "I've never seen a landscape quite like this."

"This must be what they call the Burren," Derek read from the map.

George pointed downhill. "Look, there's Carl. Let's catch up to him."

"You go on—I want to snap some photos," Derek said, pulling his camera out of its case.

As Nancy and her friends waved good-bye and pedaled on, something struck Nancy. *Odd,* she thought. *A panoramic lens would be the thing to catch this wide landscape. So why does Derek have that huge telephoto lens on his camera? That's like what cops use on a stakeout.*

Carl Thompson had parked his bike by the side of the road and was kneeling on the gray rock. "We didn't see you pass us earlier," Bess remarked as they reached the professor.

Carl looked up and grinned. "I didn't. I left early, while you all were still at breakfast. I wanted to give myself plenty of time to explore the Burren—it's the main thing I came here to see. As a geologist, I find it fascinating."

"Geologist? I thought you were a chemist," Bess said.

Carl smiled modestly. "Double specialty."

"Well, I find it fascinating, too, and I'm neither a geologist nor a chemist," said Nancy.

"What kind of rock is it?" George asked.

"Limestone, mostly," Carl said. "This kind of region is called 'karst.' You see how it has heaved around over the centuries? That's what caused all these cracks and fissures in the surface—or, as the locals call it, the 'pavements.' Now, look inside the fissures. You'll find a whole secret world."

The girls dismounted, and bess poked a finger into one crevice. "You'd almost expect tiny people to be living there."

George punched her cousin's shoulder. "No leprechaun sightings, Bess, please!"

"It's a beautiful place," Nancy said, sitting on her heels and gazing around in awe. "So primitive-looking."

Carl nodded. "The Selkirks said it reminded them of the Outback. Except, of course, that the rock there is red sandstone, not gray limestone."

Nancy raised her eyebrows. "The Selkirks? When did they come by?"

"About ten minutes ago," Carl said. "They stopped to look at it with me, too."

Nancy got up, peering along the road ahead.

There was no sign of the sisters, but they could be hidden in a road dip. "Well, thanks so much for the info," she said. "We'd better get moving."

"See you at lunch. We're stopping at the Cave of Ailwee," Carl said. "Carved by an underground river out of limestone. Fascinating!"

Bess and George remounted their bikes, too, saying good-bye to the professor. They hadn't gone far before George said, "There they are!"

Two tiny figures—one in neon green, the other in fluorescent orange—were outlined against the horizon, scooting briskly along. Sunlight glinted off their magenta bikes.

Bess moaned. "They're so far ahead, how can we possibly catch up?"

"They probably think we're still back with the sheep," Nancy reasoned. "That'll buy us some time." She stood up on her pedals and began to pump hard.

From the top of the plateau, Nancy saw the scene unfold like an old silent movie. As the Selkirks coasted down a long hill, a blue car turned onto the road. As soon as the sisters passed it, it began to pick up speed.

Nancy tensed up, clutching her handlebars. How ever fast the Selkirks might be riding, the blue car was going faster.

The Australians shifted toward the left, giving the

car room to pass. But instead of swerving around them, the car kept bearing down toward them. Rachel glanced over her shoulder, balancing on the rim of the asphalt.

Bess let out an anguished cry. "The car's going to run them off the road!"

8

The Chase Is On

The blue car surged toward the Selkirk girls. The screech of its tires ominously carried across the high, still air to Nancy, Bess, and George.

As if in slow motion, Nancy saw the car ram the rear wheel of Rachel's bike. Nancy squinted to try to see a bit better. Rachel, looking like a mere flicker of orange, flipped off the road and into a ditch.

Twisting around in her seat, Rhonda let out a scream, tiny and futile-sounding at this distance. She bailed out, leaping off her bike just before the car reached her. She tumbled into the same ditch where Rachel had landed.

The blue car, without a pause, revved up and sped away.

"Come on—we've got to go help!" Nancy cried.

The three River Heights girls began to race their bikes down the long, winding road. "Did you get a good look at the car?" George asked Nancy as they rode abreast.

Nancy shook her head. "Too far off—no way I could get a license number. I couldn't even identify the make. I don't know European models as well as I do American ones."

Dropping into a dip in the road, the girls briefly lost sight of the Selkirks, but when they came out again they saw Rhonda and Rachel climbing out of the ditch, brushing themselves off. "They don't look badly hurt," Bess shouted, relieved.

Just then, Nancy heard another car engine roar behind them. She swerved sharply behind George to let it pass, almost crashing into Bess.

Looking over her shoulder, Nancy saw it was the red McElheney Tours van. Terry O'Leary was bent over the steering wheel, jaw jutting forward, glaring at the highway. He beeped the horn and raced by, evidently headed for Rachel and Rhonda.

"That was convenient, wasn't it?" George said, slackening her pace.

"Too convenient," Nancy replied. "How did he know they'd had an accident? Let's hurry."

"Why?" Bess pleaded. "Now that help has arrived—"

"How do we know Terry will help?" Nancy answered. "He almost hit George this morning, remember? I don't want to leave him alone with Rhonda and Rachel."

Nancy whizzed down the hill, soon pulling up to the accident site. Rhonda and Rachel sat slumped by the roadside, near where Terry had parked the van. Terry was hiking up out of the steep ditch, holding aloft a magenta bike. "This one's got a bent wheel," he announced. "I'll have to go into Galway to get it replaced. You can ride along in the van—but you'll have to skip the cave." He blinked, his eyes sliding from one of the sisters to the other. "Which one of you belongs to this bike?"

Rhonda and Rachel traded glances. "It's mine," Rhonda said, climbing to her feet. She winced as she tried to rotate her shoulder. "I don't mind missing the cave. I feel a little banged up, anyway—must have landed funny."

Rachel looked past Terry. "Hello, Nancy," she greeted her. "Glad to see you. Thanks for phoning Terry to come help us."

"I didn't phone Terry," Nancy said, feeling guilty that the idea hadn't occurred to her.

They heard a whirr of wheels behind them. "It wasn't her—it was me," Carl Thompson announced, pulling up. "Derek and Camilla and I saw you from up the hill."

Nancy twisted around and looked up the hill.

Derek and Camilla sat on their bikes at the summit—and Derek was peering through his telephoto lens. Nancy winced, remembering Derek pointing his camera at Rhonda after she passed out that first night. Did the guy have no sense of shame?

"Well, thanks a million, Carl," Rachel said.

Terry carried the bike with the bent wheel to the van. As the sun shone on its handlebars, Nancy noticed they were covered in silver tape. *Funny*, she mused. *I thought it was Rachel who put silver tape on her handlebars, not Rhonda.*

"Should one of us go along with you?" Nancy offered. The idea of leaving Rhonda alone with Terry worried her.

Nancy thought she saw Rhonda stiffen. But before she could say anything, Terry whirled around, glaring at her. "No!" he barked. "No room. I've got the whole lot of luggage back there, and all the lunch as well. I barely have room for one bike and a passenger."

Rachel stood up, flexing a bruised leg. "I'm happy to ride on to the cave—it's not too much farther. I hear it's a beaut, with an underground waterfall and all."

"I'll get a doctor to look at your sister," Terry grumbled. He slammed the van's back door and stomped to the driver's side.

"Enjoy the cave, Rache," Rhonda said to her sister

with a wink as she climbed into the van.

"Feel better," Rachel replied.

Nancy anxiously watched the van pull away, hoping that Rhonda would be safe.

The van left, and the five cyclists—Nancy, Bess, George, Rachel, and Carl—got back onto their bikes.

"I owe you girls an apology," Rachel said as they reached cruising speed. "That was a sneaky trick Rhonda and I played on you with the sheep."

"What trick?" Carl asked.

Bess rolled her eyes. "We got stuck in the middle of a flock of sheep crossing the road."

Carl chuckled. "That must have been an experience."

"It was," Nancy agreed. "Well, I appreciate the apology, Rachel."

"Rhonda and I saw them milling around by the gate and couldn't resist," Rachel confessed. "Especially since you three seemed so keen to catch up with us. It was just a prank."

"Unfortunately, that incident with the car wasn't just a prank," Nancy said, still concerned about Rhonda's departure. "We saw it all from a distance. Did you recognize the car?"

"Recognize it?" Rachel looked puzzled. "No way. I don't know anybody in Ireland. Anyway, I never got a good look at the car. It was behind me the whole time."

"You know, it looked like the car hit your bike,"

Nancy said. "Rhonda only jumped off hers. Yet her wheel was bent, not yours. Isn't that strange?"

Rachel bit her lip. "Well, actually, it was my bike that got hurt. Rhonda said it was hers because she knew I wanted to go see the cave."

Nancy nodded. That explained the silver handlebar tape. But she wondered grimly if Rhonda had bought more trouble than she knew.

One thing Nancy had to say: The car accident had changed Rachel's attitude. She no longer seemed intent on ditching Nancy. They hung out together for the next couple of hours, enjoying their picnic lunch and then exploring the Cave of Ailwee. Though the underground cavern was illuminated, there were plenty of shadowy corners and eerie echoes. At one point, a simple drip of water off a stalactite made Rachel jump, and her foot slipped on the clammy cavern floor. Nancy grabbed her elbow just in time. Rachel flashed her a smile of gratitude.

Maybe Rachel has realized it's good to be with a detective, Nancy thought to herself. *Especially when so many dangerous things have happened—coincidence, or not.*

When they emerged from the cavern, blinking in the afternoon sunlight, Terry was waiting in the parking lot with the red van. He had already collected the bikes and had returned to drive the cyclists to Galway City. "There's not enough seats for everybody to ride at once. We'll have to make two trips," Bob explained.

"I'll go on the second shift," Derek volunteered. "Rachel, why don't you wait with me?"

Nancy noticed Camilla, standing behind Derek, give him a little jab in the ribs. *Good for you*, Nancy thought.

Rachel hesitated. "Actually, Derek, I'd like to get to Galway and make sure Rhonda's okay."

"I saw her at the hotel; everything's fine," Bob assured Rachel. "She had a soak in a hot bath and she's feeling one hundred percent."

Nancy blew a tiny sigh of relief.

"I could use a hot bath," Natalie de Fusco put in. "I call first shift."

Nancy, Bess, and George agreed to ride with Derek and Camilla on the second trip. After the first group had driven away, Derek and Camilla strolled around the grounds. "Look—Camilla's giving Derek a piece of her mind," George noted dryly, nodding to where the English pair were having a heated conversation.

"It's about time," Bess said. "Even I'm tired of the way he throws himself at the Selkirks."

"Jealous?" George asked.

"Not anymore," Bess said. "He may be totally hot-looking, but who'd want a boyfriend who flirts with other girls?"

"Do you still think he's behind all these accidents?" George asked Nancy.

Nancy cupped her chin in her hand. "I don't know. He couldn't have been driving that blue car. He was riding right behind us."

"It wasn't Terry O'Leary, either—he showed up in the van soon after," Bess pointed out.

Nancy nodded. "But Terry could be working with the driver of the blue car," she suggested. "We know he was somewhere nearby, since he arrived so fast. And he sure was eager to take Rhonda away in the van. Thank goodness she got back okay."

"One thing occurs to me," George said. "What if all these incidents are aimed at McElheney Tours itself? It could be sabotage from a rival company. That falling sign and the poisoned soda might have been aimed at anybody. And it was me who got hit by the van this morning."

"Yes, but you were right behind Rachel," Bess pointed out. "It could have hit you by mistake."

"Well, it is a theory," Nancy said. "But three out of four incidents so far have involved the Selkirk sisters. I'm afraid we'll have to see what happens next, if anything."

Terry and Bob soon returned, and the five remaining tour members piled into the red van. The drive around the bay didn't take long. Soon they were sweeping down into Galway City. The girls sat up eagerly, looking out the van windows.

Bob slid forward on his seat to deliver his usual travelogue. "Lots of people think Galway City is Ireland's prettiest city," he said. "The downtown area is remarkably well-preserved and quaint, but there's a university here and lots of arts and culture. In its heyday as a port, Galway had a thriving trade with Spain—it's said that Christopher Columbus made his last stop here on his way to America. In the sixteenth century . . ."

Nancy leaned back and let Bob's words wash over her. It would be nice to be in a city again for a night, she decided. She enjoyed riding from village to village, but her legs weren't used to so much exercise—especially not at the speeds she had to ride to keep up with the Selkirks.

Nancy must have dropped off, because the next thing she knew, George was shaking her awake. "Nancy, we're here. Bess is going up to the room. I want to check out this cool pottery store I noticed as we were riding into town."

Nancy shook herself. "Pottery? I'm up for that." She climbed out of the van and followed George down the sidewalk from the hotel.

The girls plunged into the narrow medieval streets of downtown Galway City. Like a maze, the streets twisted and wound between overhanging old buildings. "This is so cool!" Nancy exclaimed.

"Here's the shop," George announced. She marched into a quaint-looking shop front with tiny windows. Inside, however, was a well-lit, modern store, its open display shelves lined with beautiful hand-thrown pieces of glazed ceramics by local artists.

Browsing among the shelves, Nancy reached out to touch one bowl. It would make a perfect gift for Hannah Gruen, the housekeeper who had cared for Nancy ever since Nancy's mother died. Nancy lifted the bowl gently, admiring its smooth, greenish glaze and sinuous curves.

A man's hand was reaching into the case from the other side to grasp a mug. His coat sleeve was heavy black wool—and the little finger was missing from his left hand!

9

Slipping Away

Holding her breath, Nancy sidled around the floor-to-ceiling display case. Was it the same man she'd seen at Shannon? The same man who'd been talking to Rhonda in the alley that morning?

Peeking around the corner of the display case, Nancy got her first really good look at the mystery man. His broad shoulders, massive forehead, and terse expression were what had drawn her attention before. Now she took in his short, greasy brown hair and small, dark eyes. He looked like he was in his mid-thirties. Beneath the formal-looking overcoat, he wore faded jeans and sneakers.

As the man looked over his shoulder, Nancy ducked so he wouldn't see her. "Miss?" she heard his harsh, nasal voice call out to the shopkeeper.

"Yes?" The shopkeeper strolled over to him.

"The sign says this pattern is called Clostermeade Manor," the man said. His accent certainly sounded Australian, Nancy thought.

"Yes, that's what the potter named it."

"I had an aunt who was parlor maid at Clostermeade Manor before she came out to Australia," the man said. "She always showed me pictures of the place. Tell me, would Clostermeade be near here?"

Leaning forward to listen, Nancy brushed accidentally against a display shelf. The ceramic pieces on the shelf wobbled and clinked.

She could hear the man hastily plunk down the mug and brush past the sales clerk. Nancy whirled around and pretended to browse on another shelf. *Please don't recognize me*, she wished silently.

Then she heard a heavy tread and the shop door swishing open. Nancy sprang to where she could see the doorway. A broad-shouldered back, clad in black wool, was shoving hurriedly out to the street.

"George, come on!" Nancy called her friend.

George, well-used to Nancy's sudden moves, set down the casserole dish she'd been admiring. "I'll be back," she promised the shopkeeper as she bounded across the store, following Nancy out to the street.

Nancy hesitated a moment on the sidewalk. "The way his body tilted, I'd guess he went to the right," she decided, and sprinted down the sloping street in that direction.

George was right behind her. "Who was it, Nan?"

"The Australian guy with the missing pinkie!"

Nancy felt pretty sure she'd seen a black shape turn left by the red-painted shop front across the way. Dodging and weaving through the afternoon shopping crowd, she raced around the corner after him.

Her quick eyes picked him out up ahead, this time popping into an alley to his right. Nimbly, Nancy leaped over a woman's shopping bag set down on the cobbles, and ducked under a display of finely woven shawls. She couldn't lose the trail this time!

Running into the mouth of the alley, Nancy spied the black coat up ahead. The man was running hard now—obviously he knew Nancy was after him. She urged her legs to go faster, willing herself to ignore the sore muscles of two days' bicycling.

The man swung left into a larger street. I'm closing in on him now, Nancy thought triumphantly. But as she turned left at the corner, she skidded to a halt. He was nowhere to be seen.

Nancy pivoted to the right, wondering if he'd faked her out with a false turn. She couldn't see him there, either.

Maybe he went into a store, she mused. But which? She peered into the large front window of a jewelry shop, but he wasn't there. She slipped into a bookstore across the street, searching between its rows of bookcases. No luck.

Nancy's throat tightened. The trail was swiftly growing cold. In the heart of a city, there were so many places where a man could hide.

Discouraged, she retraced her route through the winding narrow streets. She spotted George leaning against a brick wall. "Nancy, I lost you. Where'd you go?"

"He got away." Nancy sighed.

"Well, cheer up," George said. "When I couldn't find you, I circled around this block, and guess what?"

Nancy said eagerly, "You saw him?'

"No, but I saw his car." George's eyes gleamed. "Or rather, I saw the blue car. But all the evidence suggests it's his, doesn't it?"

Nancy drew a careful breath. "We can't assume anything. But let's go have a look."

George led Nancy around a couple of corners and emerged in front of a beautiful little gray stone church, crammed between two larger buildings. There was an empty space at the curb by the wrought-iron church gate.

George's face crumpled in disappointment. "It was right there! A blue four-door sedan—same size, same color, same style as the one that chased Rhonda and Rachel today."

Nancy swallowed her hope. "Don't fret, George. We have no proof it belongs to our Mr. Black, anyway."

"But if we could have seen who got into it . . ." George slammed her fist into her palm in frustration.

"He may have run back to get the car as soon as he shook me off his trail," Nancy said. "If so, we have no hope of catching him on foot."

"Well, at least I wrote down the license plate number," George said.

Nancy clapped her friend on the shoulder. "Good work, George!"

"Hey, I haven't tagged along on all your cases for nothing," George remarked. She bent over and fished a folded scrap of paper out of her shoe. "One bad thing about these cycling shorts: no pockets," she noted with a rueful grin.

Nancy studied the paper, a torn-off bit of newspaper. "G500A7," she read.

"Are you going to ask the police to check it out?"

Nancy scrunched up her nose. "Frankly, George, I don't think they'd cooperate. This isn't River Heights, where the police might check a license number for me because they know me and my dad. The Irish police—or the Garda, as they're called—have no reason to take my word I'm a detective. And there's no actual crime to investigate. Rhonda and Rachel haven't reported anything to the authorities, remember."

"What if we got Bob to report the incidents?"

George suggested. "His company does a lot of business in Ireland. Considering how important tourism is around here, I'd think the police would be anxious to protect innocent travelers."

Nancy cocked her head. "It's worth a try. My sense is that Bob is getting worried about all these accidents. And if he isn't, he should be."

Nancy looked discouraged when she joined Bess and George in their hotel room a couple of hours later. "What did Bob say?" George asked.

Nancy plopped down on the bed with its sprigged muslin counterpane. Tonight's lodging was a charming bed-and-breakfast, full of antiques. "Bob says he can't go to the police without Rhonda's and Rachel's permission," Nancy reported. "He was adamant about it."

"Why are they so reluctant to take any help?" Bess wondered, turning from the mirror where she'd been admiring her pale blue sweater.

Nancy shrugged. "I don't know, but Bob's so afraid of crossing them, he can hardly think straight. He kept saying this is just a string of ordinary mishaps—but from the tone of his voice, I don't think he believes that himself."

Wearily she opened her suitcase, pulling out the navy knit dress she planned to wear to dinner. The tour group was eating tonight at a seafood restaurant on Quay Street, near the Galway harbor.

"I suspect Rhonda and Rachel aren't just any customers," George said. "They certainly seem rich, for one thing."

"I agree," Nancy said. "All the more reason why someone might really be after them."

"Like our Mr. Black?" Bess asked.

"Or Terry O'Leary, or Derek—or whoever was driving that blue car," Nancy said, pondering as she unbuttoned her shirt. "We've got an open field of suspects. One thing I do know: Mr. Black knows I'm on his trail, and he sure acts like he's got something to hide."

"So this is officially a case, Nancy?" George asked.

Nancy blew out a sigh. "If it is, it's a weird sort of case. I don't really have a client—Rhonda and Rachel never hired me."

"In fact, they keep avoiding you," George said.

"That's not true. Rachel's friendly again," Bess remarked.

"Yes, but that was today, when Rachel was on her own. With Rhonda back on the scene, I bet things will be different," Nancy warned.

"Gathering evidence will be tough," George said. "We're constantly on the move; not only the suspects, but the victims as well."

"And we ourselves have to keep moving," Nancy added. "We can't go back and forth investigating the scenes of these crimes."

"Especially not when we're only on bikes," Bess said.

"All the same, I've got to do something. I can't just sit around." And Nancy pressed her lips together in a determined expression her friends knew very well.

Nancy made a point of lingering the next morning over her breakfast of soda bread and grilled fish. She watched as the other members of the tour went off to start their rides: first Rachel and Rhonda; then the de Fuscos and Carl Thompson; and finally, Derek and Camilla with Bob. Bess and George were the last to get on their bikes. "Bob thinks I'm riding with you guys," Nancy reminded them as they stood in front of the hotel. "So don't ride too fast, and I'll catch up as soon as I'm done."

"Keep an eye out for Terry," George reminded her. "The van's still in the parking lot, waiting for him to load the luggage."

"I'll be careful," Nancy promised. She waved to her friends as they wheeled into the quiet street outside the bed-and-breakfast.

As soon as the coast seemed clear, Nancy walked back into the bed-and-breakfast. Looking as nonchalant as possible, she went up the mahogany staircase to the second floor. She sauntered down the wide, sunny hallway to room number four, the room where Rachel and Rhonda had slept last night.

A red-haired teenager was bustling down the hall with an armload of dirty sheets. "Oh, miss?" Nancy said. "I just checked out of room four, and I'm missing something. Could you open the door so I can check if I left it in my room?"

The maid shrugged. "No bother, ma'am." She dropped the linens in a heap and pulled a master key from her apron pocket. In a minute, Nancy was in Rhonda and Rachel's room.

She was taken aback to see how messy the girls had left the room. *They must be used to having servants pick up for them*, she thought. Sheets were half pulled off the bed, and wet towels lay in puddles on the carpet. Balled-up candy wrappers were strewn over the desk. A half-empty bottle of nail polish stood on the TV set, brush balanced precariously on top. Empty soda cans were lined up on the antique dresser, leaving white rings on its dark polished top.

Keeping an eye on the half-open door, Nancy began to methodically inspect the room. She started with the wastebasket, but it was empty. Beside it, however, lay a crumpled copy of a tabloid newspaper. She scooped its pages into order and stuffed it in her small daypack to read later. Who knew—it might contain a clue.

Just then, the door was thrust open. Nancy straightened up with a jerk and whirled around.

There stood Derek Thorogood, looking as shocked to see her as she was to see him.

"Derek—what are you doing here?" Nancy gasped.

Derek glared. "First you'd better tell me what *you're* doing here, Nancy."

10

Who's After Whom?

Nancy knew she had to act cool. "I'm doing Rhonda a favor. She asked me to come back and grab her guidebook." She dug her hand into her daypack and pulled out her own travel guide to Ireland. "See? Here it is."

Derek tilted his head in a way that told Nancy he wasn't convinced. "Well, I came back to get a cable for my laptop. Silly me—I left it in the outlet."

"In Rhonda and Rachel's room?" Nancy cast him a suspicious look. What was Derek up to?

Derek raised his eyebrows, looking innocent. "This is their room?"

"Unless you wear nail polish, it is," Nancy said, pointing to the bottle on the TV set.

"Oh, I never wear nail polish;—at least not in the daytime," Derek joked. He flashed Nancy a charming smile—one he used to get out of jams, Nancy suspected. "But you're right—now I realize this wasn't my room. I get so confused, staying in a new hotel every night."

It struck Nancy that Derek might have come back here for the same reason she had: to search Rhonda and Rachel's room. But why? What could he be hunting for?

"You'd better go look for your own room," Nancy said. "Good luck finding your cable."

"Now that you've fetched Rhonda's book," Derek said, nodding toward the guidebook in her hand, "you can accompany me."

Nancy stifled a groan. She'd never be able to search the room with Derek hovering around, and he seemed to know it.

Their eyes locked, each one determined not to leave the other in the room. The standoff ended only when the maid peeked around the door. "Did you find what you left, miss?"

Nancy gave a sigh of surrender. "Yes, thank you." She trudged out of the room, Derek following her. The maid pulled the door shut behind them. Nancy heard the lock click.

"So which room was yours?" Nancy said, trying to pin Derek down.

"Other end of the hall, I think," Derek said. He strolled to an open door with a brass numeral 8 on it. "This was it. I remember now."

He stuck his head briefly inside the room. "Not here. Perhaps I unplugged the cable after all, and packed it in the side pocket of my case. I'll check tonight. Not to worry—if I've lost it, it's easily replaced. Well, Nancy"—he gestured toward the staircase—"shall we go?"

Nancy strode down the hallway and downstairs, fighting to hide her irritation. *Only a temporary setback*, she told herself. *Tonight I'll find a way to search Rhonda and Rachel's bedroom, wherever we're staying. That'll be better, anyway, while their stuff's actually in the room.*

Walking outside, Nancy saw Derek's ten-speed propped against the garden fence beside hers. "At least now we can ride together," Nancy said.

"Super. I've got one of the mobiles," Derek said, showing her the cell phone, "and a copy of today's map."

Just then, the red tour van came rumbling out of the parking lot. Terry O'Leary braked when he saw them and rolled down his window. "No lagging about," he said crossly. "You'll be missing the ferry. There's not another for hours."

"We'll hurry," Nancy promised.

Luckily, their ride was all downhill from the B&B

to the harbor. A steam ferryboat was waiting at the docks, its engine rumbling. As soon as Nancy and Derek rode up the gangplank, the crew raised it and the boat set off. "Whew, that was tight," Derek said lightly. "Shall we find the others?"

George and Bess looked relieved when Nancy arrived on deck. "Glad you made it," George said. "Find anything?"

"Just Derek," Nancy murmured. Bess and George raised their eyebrows. But Derek was moving toward them, and she couldn't say more.

The ocean air was salty and brisk, and Nancy tugged her baseball cap tighter over her red-blond hair. Derek leaned suavely on the railing next to Bess and launched into a stream of chatter, but Nancy tuned it out.

She reviewed in her mind the facts of the case. The Australian man—or Mr. Black, as Nancy had nicknamed him—was her biggest question mark. But she still wanted to know more about Terry O'Leary. And Derek's appearance at the Selkirks' room this morning troubled her. What reason could he have for snooping in their room? *He's probably wondering the same thing about me,* Nancy told herself. That must be why he was sticking so close to her now, she realized with a flash of irritation.

As the ferry steamed across the harbor, the quaint medieval buildings of Galway City grew smaller and smaller, and the dark humps of land lying out in the ocean grew larger.

"If you thought County Clare was picturesque, wait till you see the Aran Isles," Bob said, joining them. "The smaller islands don't have car traffic, and some cottages still lack electricity or plumbing. The land is nearly as rocky as the Burren. Farmers have to make soil from sand and rotten seaweed."

Bess wrinkled her nose. "Ewww!"

Bob grinned. "I agree. If I lived here, I'd sure try to be a fisherman instead. But Aran Islanders are hardy, plain-living folks, used to fighting the elements."

"Most of them speak Gaelic, don't they?" Derek asked. "You know, the old Irish language."

Bob nodded. "Older folks do, and kids learn it in school. They're trying to keep it alive. But the same is true all over western Galway and Donegal. Look at the road signs; town names are usually in Gaelic as well as in English."

"How soon do we reach the island?" Bess asked.

"The ride over is three hours," Bob said. "Coming back, we can sail to Rossaveal, which only takes an hour. Too bad we only have time to see the big island, Inishmore. But the fort there, Dún Aengus, is spectacular. It's centuries old, and no one knows who built it, or why they needed to protect that lonesome bit of island. It's a mysterious ancient place, like Stonehenge."

Inishmore's port village, Kilronan, was a bit

touristy, with tour guides in minibuses buzzing around trying to pick up customers. Nancy was glad they had their bikes and could ride out of town on their own. The road to the ruined stone fort led straight out of Kilronan.

In only a few minutes the group was pedaling along a seaside line of cliffs. As usual, Rhonda and Rachel zipped off in front. But as Nancy and George began to follow, Derek pumped up behind them. "Can I ride with you two?"

"Sure," Nancy said, hiding her frustration.

From the looks of Derek's specialized cycling clothes and equipment, Nancy had assumed he was an expert cyclist. Now she learned differently. Derek had to look down at his gear levers every time he needed to shift. And despite his trim, athletic build, his legs weren't very muscular. As soon as he had to pedal hard, he lurched from side to side to give his legs an extra boost. George shot Nancy a meaningful glance behind Derek's back. She'd taught Nancy that extra motion like that dragged on the bike and slowed you down.

By the time the three of them reached the hill-top fort, the Selkirks' magenta bikes were already in the parking lot, along with Bob's silver racer. The McElheney van was parked there, too. Terry O'Leary sat in the driver's seat, eyes closed, snoring. "I guess he's seen this sight before," George remarked wryly as they parked their bikes.

Tourists swarmed over the broken stone ruins, perched at the edge of the cliff. Walking up a rocky rise to overlook the site, Nancy was impressed by how large the prehistoric fort was. It had been built in three concentric circles, the highest in the middle. Shallow depressions in the sparse grass showed where missing parts of the once-grand design had lain. The remaining stones, bleached pale by years of sea wind, reflected the sunshine with a hard glitter.

Nancy laid a hand on a nearby rock, awed by the thought of how long the rock had lain there. The stern gray stone was softened by patches of velvety moss and greenish gray lichens, flourishing in the wet sea air.

"Now there's a sight for you," Derek said, coming up behind her. With a sweep of his arm, he indicated the vast panorama of the flinty island and the mainland across the water. "That's a splendid view of Connemara over there."

Bess, cheeks still flushed from cycling, popped up behind Derek. "Connemara?" she said. "But we're looking east. Isn't that Galway?"

"The western part of Galway is also called Connemara," Derek said, pulling Bob's write-up out of the back pocket of his red spandex jersey.

With a glance Nancy signaled Bess to keep Derek occupied. Bess nodded. "But Carl was just telling me it was called the Gaeltacht," she said innocently, "because so many people there speak Gaelic. . . ." Nancy quietly backed away and left them.

She strode deeper into the fort, searching for the Selkirks. She soon spotted Rhonda, lounging on a large flat stone. Rhonda waved at Nancy. Nancy waved back, but a chill ran up her spine. It seemed disrespectful to her to climb onto these rocks that had endured so long, silent witnesses to the passing ages.

Still, since Rhonda was alone, it was an ideal time to question her. "We missed you at dinner last night," Nancy said, strolling over to her.

"I needed a night's rest," Rhonda said, propping herself on her elbows. "After my spill yesterday."

"Terry got your wheel fixed?"

"Oh, sure, good as new," Rhonda replied. No mention of the fact that it had been her sister's bike that had really needed the repair, Nancy noted.

"Any idea who hit you?"

Rhonda shrugged, her gaze sliding sideways. "Simple traffic thing, I reckon. Cyclists have them all the time."

"But after the trouble with the soda the first night . . . and your sister and the pub sign. . . ?"

Rhonda sat up and swung her legs over the side of the rock. She shot a piercing look at Nancy. "Look here, Nancy, what're you getting at?"

Nancy steeled herself. "I think someone's after you,"

she said. "The Australian man you were talking to yesterday morning—I saw him at Shannon, and I saw him again yesterday in Galway City. He's following us."

"I don't know any such bloke," Rhonda insisted. "Is this how you get all your cases, Nancy? By making things up? Well, excuse me, but I rode hard this morning. I'm ready to eat." She shouldered past Nancy and went toward Bob and Terry, who were laying out the picnic.

I blew it again, Nancy thought bitterly.

Reluctant to join the picnic just yet, Nancy looked around for Rachel. She spied her on the far side of the site, leaning dreamily on a shattered wall at the edge of the cliff.

Then Nancy saw Derek, hiding behind a nearby boulder, watching Rachel.

Quickly Nancy circled around the site, stumbling slightly in the overgrown ruts and declivities. Eyes on Rachel, she paused next to a taller fragment of wall. Her hand reached out to steady herself on its time-worn, pitted surface. She could see Rachel, about fifty yards away, but Derek had ducked behind the boulder and was out of sight. Where had he gone to?

Something above Nancy blocked out the watery Irish sunshine. There was a whistling sound in the air. She looked up.

A huge chunk of ancient stone was tumbling straight toward Nancy.

11

Over the Edge

Nancy twisted her body and sprang to the right to avoid the falling rock. It just missed grazing her left shoulder.

As her right foot landed, she came down at an angle on a broken bit of stone. Her ankle buckled, and she fell sideways. She tried to break her fall, but her shoe slid on a crumbling patch of dirt and shot out into open air, over the rim of the cliff.

Nancy clutched at the ground behind her. Her fingers closed on an upthrust rock and hung on tight.

The falling stone crashed on another rock, jolted and tumbled a few feet, then disappeared over the cliff. Holding on, Nancy cautiously peered over the edge.

Three hundred feet below, the ocean sparkled, cold and gray. There was a distant splash as the boulder plunged into the sea.

That could have been me, Nancy realized.

She twisted around to see where the stone had come from. The jagged fragment of wall sat there, impassive, grass sprouting from its cracks. A coating of mud showed where the fallen stone had been dislodged.

A stone cemented in place by soil doesn't just fall, Nancy thought. *Somebody pushed it.*

Nancy sprawled, shaking with relief, on the grass. Bob came rushing over. "Are you okay? Terry said he saw a falling rock nearly hit you."

"The rock missed me, thank goodness," Nancy said, rubbing her sore ankle. "But Bob, that stone has been there for centuries. Why would it fall today?" *And was it just coincidence that Terry was there to see it fall?* she added silently.

"Well, so long as you're all right," Bob said hurriedly. "Come over to the picnic and rest."

Nancy bit her lip. Why was Bob so blind to the fact that danger was dogging the tour?

George and Bess reached Nancy, with Rachel, Natalie, and Carl trotting up behind. Nancy looked around for Derek. He stood off to the side with Rhonda, muttering something in her ear.

Derek was near by just before that rock fell, too, Nancy reminded herself. She cast Derek a searching look. He simply turned away.

Fingers flying over the strings, a young fiddler sent a merry jig into the high-ceilinged community hall. Percussion was provided by the feet of a dozen dancers in black leather slippers and short black skirts, executing the skirling motions of a traditional Irish step dance.

"How young do you think that little girl is?" Bess wondered, pointing to the smallest dancer in the troupe. Barely four feet tall, she had the round face of a six- or seven-year-old. Her dark curls bobbed frantically as she hopped up and down to the music, eyes straight ahead. "She must have taken up stepping as soon as she could walk, to be this good already," Bess marveled.

Forehead furrowed, George studied the dancers' moves. "I can't believe how high they get their knees up. And see how they hold their upper bodies totally rigid, arms down at their sides? It must take perfect balance to move that way."

Rhonda, sitting on the wooden bench behind theirs, leaned forward. "It's even harder to do than it looks," she said. "With all the Irish folk in Australia, step dancing's popular, and I used to take lessons. I was a dismal failure, no joke."

Nancy answered with a thin smile. Rhonda had been clinging to her like a bur ever since they'd left the fort. With Rhonda around, Nancy could hardly investigate anyone's room at tonight's inn. Nancy recalled Derek confiding something to Rhonda that afternoon. Had he told her about finding Nancy in the hotel this morning? Was that why Rhonda suddenly wouldn't leave her alone?

The fiddler ended the song with a sharp downward stroke of his bow, and the dancers smartly stamped their feet together. The crowd burst into raucous clapping.

The leader of the troupe stepped forward, beaming. "Thank you very much," she called out as the clapping dwindled. "Now, it's not fair for us to have all the fun, is it? Who else would like to get their bones a-moving and their hearts a-pumping?" Hands flew up around the room. "Come on, gents as well as ladies," she coaxed the crowd.

Benches were pushed back to clear space on the linoleum floor, and the dancers fanned out to work with small groups of visitors. Nancy, George, Bess, and Rhonda, along with a couple of women from another tour group, teamed up with a raven-haired dancer named Moira. Lining up behind her, they copied her steps in slow motion. "Tap step, tap step, tap step, hop!" she called out. Pivoting around, she watched her pupils copy the steps. Nancy's mind was wiped clear of everything but the effort to dance. She found that as soon as she got her feet moving right, she forgot to keep her spine straight. When she got her back and feet together, she'd realize her arms were swinging outward for balance. She caught Bess's eye, and they both giggled.

George frowned at them and executed a tap-pivot-step move. "Arms straight down—but no fists," Moira advised George. She laid her hands flat against her thighs, fingers pointing down. "Like so. And don't hunch your shoulders."

Bess and Nancy traded glances and went into another giggle fit.

After an hour of tapping, stepping, and hopping, the visitors were glad to collapse back onto the benches and watch the trained dancers perform again. "Now I *really* appreciate how hard it is," George said to Nancy as the dance troupe launched into an intricate routine, pairing up, forming wheels, weaving lines together.

Nancy grinned and nodded, but as she turned her head she noticed Camilla leaving the hall by a side door. Nancy searched the crowd for Derek. She saw him leaning against a side wall, head close to Rachel's, murmuring in a low voice. Rachel smiled and blushed, and Derek bent closely toward her.

Nancy bit her lip. Which Selkirk was Derek interested in—Rhonda or Rachel? And how dare he hit on Rachel here, with Camilla looking on?

The night air felt cool against their flushed faces as they walked back through the village to their inn. George whistled a reel while Bess hopped and skipped along, but Nancy was quiet and distracted. She was keenly aware that Rhonda, Rachel, and Derek were walking arm-in-arm only a few steps behind them.

They soon reached the inn, a restored farmhouse overlooking one of Connemara's largest lakes, Lough Corrib. Nancy managed to smile as they said good night to the sisters and Derek, but she felt sour inside.

"So much for investigating," Nancy burst out, kicking off her shoes as they entered their bedroom. "And just when the case is heating up."

"My theory looks more likely all the time," George declared. "Someone's sabotaging the tour. One incident every day—and you're the latest victim, Nancy."

"Maybe so, George," Nancy said. "Rachel was nearby, but not that near. You know, both Derek and Terry know I was poking around the hotel this morning. What if one of them pushed that boulder at me as a warning not to snoop?"

Bess shivered. "I hate to think that."

"So do I," Nancy agreed. "But whoever the target

is, dangerous things are happening. And I don't think it'll stop unless we do something."

She picked up her daypack and took out the newspaper she'd found that morning in the Selkirks' room. She scanned the splashy front-page photo of a blond woman and an English football star, cringing from the prying cameras.

Bess peered over her shoulder. "Yuck, Nancy!" she exclaimed. "The *London Enquirer.* Did you really buy that sleazy paper? From what I see, those British rags are worse than supermarket scandal sheets in the States. Tacky celebrity gossip and hardly anything else."

Nancy shrugged. "I didn't buy it. I found it in Rhonda and Rachel's room this morning." She flipped the page. "Let's figure out why *they* were reading it. It may lead us to something."

She spread the paper on the bed, and the three girls lay side by side, poring over the columns of grubby print. Nancy's hopes faded as they turned one page after another.

Then George cried, "That's it!" She pointed to a small article at the bottom of a page.

Nancy frowned. "'Pop Star Breaks Down On Stage'? What's that got to do with the Selkirks?"

"It's not what it says, it's who it's by." George tapped her finger by the author's name.

Nancy and Bess gasped. "By Derek Thorogood,

London Enquirer Staff," the byline read.

"That sneak!" Nancy spluttered.

"So that's why he was snooping around Rhonda and Rachel's room," George said.

"If they've read this paper, they must know who he is now," Bess reasoned.

"Maybe not," Nancy said. "The article's buried so deep, they might not have seen it."

"It's true, they still seemed friendly with Derek tonight," George remarked.

Forehead creased in thought, Nancy considered this new twist. "But why? Why would a reporter be interested in the Selkirks? Who are they?"

"Spoiled rich girls from Australia," George suggested.

"That's not newsworthy enough," Nancy said. She drummed her fingers on the bed. "We need to do some research on them."

"But how?" Bess said. "We're in a tiny village in the middle of Connemara."

"Nothing's too far from anywhere else in Ireland," Nancy said. "We were in Galway City just this morning. It's got a university—there must be a library and cyber cafés there."

Bess looked doubtful. "We can't all three ditch the tour and go back to Galway City. Derek would notice, and so would Rhonda and Rachel."

"That's why we're not all going," Nancy said. "But

if one slips away . . ." She looked hopefully at Bess. "You're so good at research, Bess."

"Whoa, not me," Bess protested. "Go an extra day's ride out of the way?"

"It was a full day's ride along the coast," Nancy said, "but by the inland road it's not so far. Please, Bess?"

Rhonda and Rachel sat on one side of the breakfast room, dawdling over their streaky bacon and buttered toast the next morning. Rhonda kept glancing over at the table where Nancy and George sat. Bess had already slipped away to ride back to Galway City.

"I don't think they'll leave until we do," George murmured to Nancy. "They must know you're waiting to search their room."

Nancy grimaced and got to her feet. "Then we might as well go ride," she said. "But while they're so busy being suspicious of us, Derek could be upstairs pawing through their stuff."

"I can't believe they trust him more than they do you," George said as she and Nancy walked out into the front hall. "You're out to help them; he's out to dig up dirt on them."

Loud footsteps told them someone was coming down the stairs. They looked up to see Camilla, pouting, as she strapped on her helmet.

"Do you know where Derek is?" Nancy inquired in a casual voice.

"Derek? Ha!" Camilla replied. Her voice curled with scorn, and her eyes blazed. "Don't worry, Derek's gone—for good."

12

Vanished!

Nancy froze in surprise. "Derek's gone?"

With a huffy sigh, Camilla strode out into the paved courtyard. Nancy and George followed. "I found a note this morning," Camilla explained. "He checked out last night. By now he's at Shannon, waiting to fly to London to file his story."

"What story?" George asked.

Camilla checked over her shoulder whether anyone was listening. "I'll tell you as we ride."

The three girls quickly mounted their bikes and cruised away from the hotel. Once they were on the road, Camilla continued. "Derek came on this tour for one reason only: to do a smear job on the Selkirks."

"But why? Who are they?" George asked.

"Their father's Jacob Selkirk." George and Nancy looked blank. She added, "The media tycoon?"

"Never heard of him," Nancy admitted.

"Well, he started out in Australia," Camilla said, "but he's been buying newspapers in the U.K. over the past five years. He's as ruthless as they come. Last year he bought the *Clarion*—Derek's old paper, a top London daily. Right away Selkirk sacked a third of the staff, including Derek."

"So Derek hates him," Nancy guessed.

Camilla snorted. "I'll say. Derek was out of work for ages, till he finally got this post on that horrid rag the *London Enquirer*. Derek hates it. He'll never forgive Selkirk."

"So he decided to use the *London Enquirer* to get revenge?" George said.

"Spot on," Camilla said. "You see, Rhonda and Rachel were in London last winter. Every party they went to, every date they had, was covered in the tabloids. They certainly like to carry on—especially Rhonda. My friend's a McElheney agent in London and she tipped off Derek about the girls booking this tour. Derek decided to follow them and try to get an incriminating story. Or photo."

"So that's why he had that telephoto lens," Nancy murmured. "The ultimate snoop equipment."

"Too bad he's such an amateur photographer." Camilla sneered. "Not a single picture came out."

"But the Selkirks didn't carry on," George said. "Except to let Derek flirt with them."

Camilla rolled her eyes. "You noticed, eh? Derek said he was flirting to lead them into misbehaving. I played along. But then he started to enjoy it; he liked seeing the sisters compete for him. We had an awful row about it last night."

"And that's why he left?" George asked.

"Sort of. But really," Camilla admitted, "I just think he was tired of cycling, and tired of waiting for a story to materialize."

"So what will he write?" Nancy wondered.

Camilla sighed. "I suspect he'll just make something up, which could be even worse."

Nancy considered this new twist. Had Derek really left—or had he just told Camilla so? And if he was gone, would the danger stop?

Today's route lay along the wide lake called Lough Corrib. Terry had dropped off box lunches at a grassy picnic area on the lakeshore. Carl, Jim, Natalie, and Bob were already there eating when the girls rode up.

"I don't get the point of fly-fishing," Natalie was saying, motioning upshore toward the tiny figures of anglers standing thigh-deep in the lake. "They never move. How is that a sport?"

"It's a great way to get in touch with nature," Carl remarked.

"Plus, you end up with fresh grilled trout for lunch," Jim said, with a discouraged look at his thin ham sandwich. "Sounds good to me."

Nancy opened her box lunch, but she glanced back up the road, unspooling far across the level, brown-green moors. Rhonda and Rachel should have caught up with them by now. But she didn't want to say anything that would prod Bob into taking a head count. No point in making it obvious that Bess wasn't with the group today.

When Natalie announced that she and Jim were opting for the shorter route that afternoon, Camilla and Carl decided to join them. As the four cyclists were leaving, Bob got a call on his cell phone. "Right, run back and get her, then go up to Cashkellmara," Nancy heard him say. "Call back and let me know how it goes."

Bob flipped his phone shut. "That was Terry," he informed Nancy and George. "Rachel called for a pickup. I guess that means Rhonda's with them. We'll leave their lunches here in case they stop by later. So, shall we ride on together?"

"Fine," said Nancy, moving toward their bikes. "Hey, we heard that Derek went home."

Bob sighed. "I know. It's just as well. Now maybe the tour will be peaceful again."

Nancy responded quickly. "Why? Do you think he's behind all these accidents?"

Bob paused, perplexed. "Why, no. What makes you think that? I just meant he's such a ladies' man, I was afraid a fight would break out. What do you mean, all these 'accidents'?"

"Well, Rhonda passing out, Rachel getting hit by a sign, a car running them off the road," Nancy said. "The van hitting George . . ."

"Not to mention the rock falling at Nancy yesterday," George added.

Bob grimaced as he straddled his bike. "No one's been hurt."

"Luckily," Nancy replied, shivering at the memory of her close shave. As they pushed off, she added, "Frankly, Bob, I'm worried. We know who Rhonda and Rachel's dad is. What if somebody's out to hurt them? Shouldn't you bring in the police?"

Bob fell silent, gazing steadily between his handlebars. "Rhonda and Rachel insisted," he finally said. "That was their main condition when they signed up. No bodyguards, no publicity."

"It may be too late for that," George said. "Did you know Derek's from the *London Enquirer*?"

"A tabloid reporter?" Bob gaped. "Oh, this tour is a nightmare. I'll be lucky to keep my job." He looked at the darkening sky. "Here comes one of those famous Irish rain showers. Hurry up—let's get to the village over the hill."

Nancy, George, and Bob soon whizzed into a quiet

cluster of whitewashed buildings. They stashed their bikes and ran inside the nearest shop, just as the clouds broke open.

Rain drummed on the roof as Nancy and George admired piles of thick cable-knit sweaters in a soft off-white yarn. "Those are handmade by Aran Islanders," Bob said. "They're incredibly warm."

"And beautiful," George said, holding one up. "I'm definitely buying one."

"You'll need it tonight," Bob said. "We're staying on an island, in an old monastery. It's been restored, but it's still drafty."

"How do we get to the island?" Nancy asked.

"There's a road built out to it, on an old stone jetty," Bob said. "But when the tide comes in, the sea covers the road and you're cut off."

"How romantic!" George exclaimed. But Nancy, picking out a sweater for her dad, thought that romantic isolation might not be so good right now.

The old monastery's crumbling stone walls and tall, arched windows did look poetic, Nancy thought as she wheeled over the causeway to the tiny island. Inside, however, the place had been fitted up in complete modern style. Nancy and George were happy to find Bess snuggled by a fireplace in the lounge. "I'm glad you're back," she said, popping up. "I caught a bus from Galway City; they took my bike on the roof."

Nancy unzipped her windbreaker. "Any luck?"

Bess nodded excitedly and sat forward on the couch. "You'll never guess who Rhonda and Rachel's father is," she confided.

"Jacob Selkirk, Australian media magnate," George replied, plopping down beside her.

Bess looked hurt. "How did you know?"

"Camilla," Nancy said, perching on the arm of the sofa. "Derek was fired from a Selkirk paper, and he came on the tour to get a dirty scoop on the girls. But he gave up and left last night."

Bess shook her head. "Still, he wouldn't want to hurt them. But someone else does. Listen to this: Jacob Selkirk's newspaper, the *Sydney Examiner*, cracked a big Australian crime ring last fall. Ever since, the family's been receiving death threats."

George whistled. "So that's why Rhonda and Rachel lived in London last winter—for safety."

Just then, they heard Rhonda in the entry hall. "What do you mean, you don't know where she is?" she demanded. "What sort of security do you call that?"

"Look, Rhonda," they heard Bob's sharp reply, "you want total security? Hire a bodyguard."

"Have you ever *had* a bodyguard?" Rhonda shot back. "It's such a downer. No thanks!"

Nancy saw Bob in the doorway, wearily rubbing his temples. "Terry said Rachel called for a repair.

He was going to pick her up. He's not answering his cell phone, though. I called the bike shop in Cashkellmara to see if Terry and Rachel had arrived, but there's no answer there. I'll try Rachel's cell again." He unclipped his phone from his belt and dialed. The girls heard an answering ring outside. Bob perked up. "I hear her!"

Rhonda flushed. "Uh, no—that's on my bike. I kept the cell phone when I went on my own."

Bob's eyes began to bug out. "You rode away and left her without communication? Stranded with a broken bike at the side of the road?"

Nancy saw Rhonda's eyes fill with tears. "It wasn't broken then! Look, we had an argument. She got mad and rode away, and I happened to have the phone. Oh, where is she now?"

Nancy rose from the couch. After hearing Bess's news, she understood Rhonda's panic. Were Australian criminals stalking the Selkirks?

She broke into their conversation. "I remember seeing the bike shop when we rode through Cashkellmara. I'd be happy to ride back and check it out."

For once, Rhonda looked glad about Nancy's interference. "Thanks, Nancy, that'd be great."

"Better hurry, though," Bob told Nancy. "It's already three-thirty. The tide comes in soon. By five-ten, the causeway will be impassable. While you're gone, I'll call the local Garda and ask if any road accidents have been reported."

Nancy cycled back across the causeway, gazing uneasily at the encroaching waters on either side. She was well down the road on the mainland before she realized she hadn't taken a cell phone. In order to make it back across the causeway safely, though, she couldn't turn back.

Studying the map, Nancy spotted a small inland road that seemed the most direct route to Cashkellmara. She swung onto it and cycled steadily.

Then she saw a spot of red beside the road up ahead.

Nancy pedaled hard, feeling a lump in her throat. The closer she got, the more sure she was of what it could be.

It was the McElheney van, half overturned in a muddy ditch.

As Nancy approached, she spotted tire tracks on the banks of the ditch, half washed out by the recent rainfall. Terry must have crashed shortly after he had called Bob, Nancy realized; the rain had started soon after the call. But the tracks headed north. Rachel's breakdown had been south of here. Where had Terry been going?

Parking her bike, Nancy went to inspect the van. The passenger side door was jammed against a mound of dirt, but the driver's side door had been forced open a couple feet. She looked inside gingerly. No bodies—that was good—but there was a splatter of blood on the dashboard. She touched it. It was still sticky and fresh.

Beside the gearshift the mobile phone sat in its bracket. Nancy took it out and tried to turn it on, but the battery had gone dead.

She went around to the dented back door and opened it. The back of the van was empty; no magenta bike waiting for a repair.

Nancy began to search the immediate area. A set of large footprints led away from the van, clear in the mud. Only one pair, weaving from side to side. One person had walked this way, unsteadily . . . maybe dazed from the crash. *If these are Terry's footprints, he didn't have Rachel with him,* Nancy thought. As the prints reached the surrounding bracken they disappeared, leaving no impression on the tough sod.

Nancy frowned. If she had a cell phone, she could call Bob, or the police. Now she'd have to ride for help. She hadn't passed any houses along this road. That meant the monastery on the island was the nearest help. She jumped on her bike again and rode north a quarter mile or so.

Then she screeched to a halt. There was a second pair of tire tracks in the mud. But if a passerby had stopped to help Terry, why were these tracks so far from the wrecked van?

Nancy straddled her bike. These were smaller tires, probably a car's. Several muddy footsteps, all jumbled together, covered the pavement near the tracks, as if there had been a scuffle. Then the car tracks made a U-turn, heading south. These last tracks were sharply pressed in the mud, as if they'd been made later, after the rain.

There was no time to lose. Nancy sped back to the island, anxiously checking her watch. It was five minutes past five when she reached the causeway. The road looked like a paved strip of ocean, water rising to the top of its stone banks.

Nancy licked her lips. The causeway was only half a mile long—surely she could cover that distance in five minutes. But the seawater was considerably rougher than it had been earlier. Already the highest waves splashed onto the road.

And what if the rainstorm today made the water higher than usual? Nancy wondered tensely. Would the road stay clear long enough for her to reach the island?

13

Too Late?

Cursing herself for forgetting the cell phone, Nancy knew she had no choice but to ride on across the causeway to the island. She pushed off, hearing an ominous splatter beneath her wheels.

She swerved sideways to avoid a wave. Her wheels slid in a patch of brackish mud at the road's edge. Nancy's heart lurched as the bike tipped sideways toward the cold, roiling sea.

Nancy threw her body to the side and pulled hard on the handlebars. Somehow she managed to wrench her wheels back onto the slick pavement.

A few yards farther on, Nancy began to lose heart. She threw a glance over her shoulder to check out an escape route. But the road behind her was already submerged under a thin sheet of lapping tidewater.

Nancy stood up on the pedals, hearing a slushy whirr as her wheels spun. She was almost halfway across now. She plunged on, feeling her wheels grow increasingly unstable.

The water began to splash under her pedals, and she had to fight to make the wheels turn. Desperate, she jumped off the bike, sloshing through water up to her mid-calves. She covered the last several yards dragging her bike behind her in the water.

Stumbling up the final slope, Nancy turned to look behind her. The causeway was now completely underwater. She had made it, but just barely.

Wet and exhausted, Nancy staggered across the green lawn and into the monastery. She followed the cheery sound of familiar voices echoing off stone. Pushing open a stout oak door, she walked into the monks' ancient dining hall.

The rest of the tour group, gathered around a long plank table, stared at her as if she were a ghost. "Nancy, you got across!" Bess exclaimed.

"I thought you'd missed it for sure," Bob said. "We were waiting for you to call. I was afraid you'd have to find a place to stay on the mainland."

Nancy nodded and croaked, "I couldn't call. I forgot to take a phone. But I found the van—crashed by the side of the road."

Rhonda leaped up, her hand anxiously at her throat. "Rachel?"

Nancy shook her head. "No sign of her, or of Terry."

"A crash?" Bob spluttered angrily. "That Terry! He's had a couple of accidents before—little stuff, like that brush with George the other morning. But he was on a warning. Good thing he'd already delivered the luggage before he went to collect Rachel."

Rhonda wheeled to face Bob. "That's all you care about—the luggage? What about my sister?"

Bob cringed.

Nancy quickly interjected, "It looked like Terry might have been hurt. There was some blood on the dashboard, and one set of footprints leading away. Another car had stopped nearby, where there were more footprints. Someone else may have driven Rachel away."

Rhonda turned deadly pale.

Nancy crossed her arms. "Rhonda, is there something you're not telling us?"

Rhonda drew a deep breath. "Well, to start with . . . Rachel's bike didn't break down."

"But I saw her—" Jim began.

"That was me," Rhonda said. "I jammed my own bike's gears to make Rachel ride on without me. My plan was to wait for Derek Thorogood so I could ride with him."

Camilla narrowed her eyes. "Derek left this morning."

"Well, I didn't know that then, did I?" Rhonda declared. "Anyway, Rachel rode off, calling me a drongo and a boofhead and all sorts of names." She swallowed hard. "And that—that was the last I saw of her."

Nancy faced Rhonda. "Do you have any idea what may have happened to her?"

Rhonda nodded slowly. "When I was sitting there—waiting for Derek—I saw that blue car drive past."

"The same one that tried to run you off the road?" George asked.

Rhonda hesitated. "It went so fast, I couldn't be sure. But"—she dropped her eyes—"if it was who I think it was . . ."

"Rhonda, you've got to come clean with us now," Nancy said. "You know who was driving that car, don't you?"

"Yes," Rhonda said in a choked voice. "It was Stewart Smithson."

"Who's that?"

"He works for our father—at least, he used to, back in Sydney," Rhonda said. "He was our driver for a few months. When he showed up here in Ireland, he contacted me and told me Daddy had sent him to watch us."

"But I thought you didn't want a bodyguard," Bob said.

"That was mostly Rachel," Rhonda said. "She had

a huge argument with Daddy about it. She wants to live a normal life without guards. I can see her point, but I could see Dad's, too. Rachel whinged and grizzled about the bodyguards all last winter in London, until Dad got bloody tired of it. It made sense to me that he'd send Smithson on the sly."

She hung her head. "I guess I should have phoned Dad to check on Smithson's story. But we did know the man. And Smithson said he'd be discreet about it so Rache wouldn't know."

Nancy arched an eyebrow. "So that was who I saw you talking to in the alley that morning—the same man I saw at Shannon, and again in Galway? The one with the missing finger?"

Rhonda winced. "Yes. The one you asked me about, who I said I didn't know. I didn't want you to tell Rachel he was about!"

"But he clearly wasn't guarding you very well," Nancy argued. "That very first night here, you drank that bad soda—"

"That was a fake," Rhonda admitted, lifting her chin almost defiantly. "Smithson suggested we should frighten Rachel so she'd agree to have a bodyguard. So I pretended to pass out after sipping Rachel's soda."

"There was nothing in the soda?" Carl asked.

"Nothing at all," Rhonda said.

So it didn't matter that Terry had spilled the soda,

Nancy reflected. That was an innocent accident after all.

"What about the falling sign the next night?" Jim wondered.

Rhonda gritted her teeth. "That was a setup, too. I slipped Rachel a note to lure her outside the pub so Smithson could rig up an accident." She grimaced. "I didn't expect her to get hurt. When I talked to Smithson in the alley the next morning, he said the sign fell wrong. It was supposed to go in the other direction and miss her . . . or so he said."

"So later that day, when Smithson ran you off the road . . . ?" Nancy asked.

Rhonda nodded. "I knew he was going to do that, too. But he drove at us so hard, it finally scared me. That's why I switched bikes with Rachel, so I could go on to Galway City. I paged Smithson and arranged to meet him. That's when I told him to clear off for good."

"And did he?" Nancy asked.

"I thought he did," Rhonda replied. "He seemed to be gone. But I felt embarrassed that I'd helped him. That's why I kept close watch on you, Nancy, so you wouldn't learn about it. I knew you were suspicious. But I figured it was over."

Rhonda swallowed hard, and her eyes filled with tears. "Now Rachel's disappeared. What if Smithson caught up with her?"

Bob cleared his throat. "Rhonda, I think you'd better go call your father."

"Yes, you've got to find out if Smithson was really working for him," Nancy pointed out.

Rhonda nodded and walked out, footsteps dragging. Nancy sank into the nearest chair. The members of the group traded shocked glances in silence.

George broke the silence. "So it was Smithson who pushed that rock at you yesterday, Nancy."

Nancy saw a panicked look cross Camilla's face. "Uh . . . no, that was Derek," Camilla said.

Everyone swiveled to look at Camilla in surprise. "I saw him do it from a distance," she admitted. "I confronted him about it last night—that was what started our row. He told me he thought you were on to him, Nancy, and he wanted to stop you. But the rock came so close, it frightened him. It really did—you've got to believe that. He's not a bad bloke; he didn't mean to hurt anybody. That's a big part of why he left."

Just then they heard a stricken cry from the hallway outside. Nancy jumped up and ran out.

She saw Rhonda standing by the front desk, cradling the telephone receiver against her chest.

"What is it?" Nancy asked.

Rhonda turned numbly to face her. "Daddy says . . . he says he's received a ransom note from Smithson."

Nancy gasped.

Rhonda's face crumpled as she clattered the phone back on the hook. "He says he's got Rachel hidden somewhere in the Irish countryside," she forced out through her sobs. "And he wants three million dollars for her!"

14

Whereabouts Unknown

Nancy felt herself trembling at the awful news. So Rachel had been kidnapped!

She threw her arms around Rhonda and helped her walk back to the dining hall. One look at everyone's face told her that they had all heard Rhonda's announcement.

"Oh, Nancy!" Rhonda burst out. "You're a detective—you've got to help!"

Nancy sensed another wave of surprise run through Bob, Carl, Jim, Natalie, and Camilla. "A detective?" Camilla gasped.

Nancy lowered Rhonda into her chair. "Yes, a detective," she admitted. She traded glances with Bess and George, signaling to them that it was okay to reveal her secret. "I'm here on vacation, not on a case.

But yes, that's what I do. I'm strictly an amateur, of course."

"So that's why you were asking me so many questions," Bob said.

Nancy nodded. "Trouble kept breaking out, and I wanted to get to the bottom of it," she said, "to ensure our safety. And I wanted to protect Rachel and Rhonda—only they wouldn't let me."

Rhonda laid her head on her arms. "I thought things were under control. I thought Smithson was helping us!"

Nancy drew a breath. "I don't hold grudges, Rhonda," she said. "I want to do whatever I can to help. There's only one problem: I can't get off the island to begin investigating."

"I suppose we could call to the mainland for someone to pick you up in a boat," Bob suggested. "But it'll be dark soon. Maybe you should wait until tomorrow morning."

Nancy bit her lip. "Smithson's trail will be cold by then," she said. "He's a clever man—he's gotten away from me before. Bob, at least we should call the Garda."

"I already did, to ask if there were any roadside crashes," Bob reminded her. "But I'll call again."

"Listen!" Nancy hushed him, holding up one finger. "What's that?"

From outside came the grinding sound of a boat

cutting through the water. Nancy jumped to her feet and headed for the hotel's front door. The rest of the group followed close behind.

In the gathering dusk they could see a speedboat churning through the water between the island and the mainland. On its steel sides were painted the symbol of the Irish Garda.

A plainclothes officer standing in the stern of the boat was the first to hop off as it reached shore. "I'm looking for Bob Prendergast," he said.

Bob stepped forward. "That's me."

"Keith Mulryan," the officer introduced himself. "Special investigations." He flipped open a wallet to show his Garda identification.

"Boy, are we glad to see you," Bob said. "One of the members of our tour group is missing."

"Yes, Miss Rachel Selkirk," Mulryan said.

Bob gaped. "How did you know?"

Mulryan allowed himself a tiny smile. "We already knew you were missing your van and driver—Terry O'Leary, was it? Then Jacob Selkirk called to report he'd received a ransom note for Rachel."

Rhonda blew out a sigh of relief. "When Daddy makes a call, the law springs into action fast."

Mulryan looked over at her. "Are you the other Miss Selkirk?" Rhonda nodded. "I'd like a word with you and Mr. Prendergast."

Rhonda grabbed Nancy by the shoulders and

pushed her forward. "You should talk to Nancy first. She's a detective from the States, and she's been watching Rachel all along. She knew something was up."

Mulryan raised his eyebrows. "A detective? Well, that's a bit of luck for us."

"I hope I can help," Nancy said modestly.

"Your man O'Leary," Mulryan said, turning to Bob, "we think we're closing in on him. The van was found abandoned in the vicinity of—"

"Cashkellmara," Nancy finished his sentence. "I saw the site of the accident. His footprints went off into the bracken—he must be wandering about in a daze. He'll need medical attention, but don't arrest him."

Mulryan looked surprised. "But I thought he was our suspected kidnapper."

"Footprints show he was in the van alone when it crashed," Nancy explained. "Besides, we have a stronger suspect: a man named Stewart Smithson. He knew Rachel Selkirk and had already made a couple of attempts to hurt her."

Mulryan gave a low whistle and pulled out a notebook. "Can you give me a description of him?"

"About six feet tall, weight around two hundred pounds," Nancy estimated. "I'd say he's around thirty-five or forty years old. Short brown hair, dark eyes, ruddy complexion, Australian accent. He wears a black wool overcoat. Oh, and here's your identifying clincher: He's missing the little finger on his left hand."

"I'll radio out the description immediately," said Mulryan eagerly. "This is great."

"He may be driving a late-model blue sedan," Nancy said. "And—wait a minute." She ran over to her bike and dug out of her daypack pocket the paper on which George had written Smithson's license number. She ran back to the officer and handed it to him. "That'll help," she said.

Mulryan broke out into a grin. "It certainly will. This is the break we've been waiting for!"

"Officer, Nancy knows a lot about the case," Rhonda said. "I think you should take her with you to the mainland. She could identify Smithson if he's found."

"His car, too," Nancy added.

"And she'd be a friendly face for Rachel to see if she's found," Bob said.

"*When* she's found," Mulryan said with a confident smile. "I'd be happy to let you join us, Nancy. You've got a trained eye; that's always a help in any investigation."

Mulryan introduced a junior officer, Liam Murphy, who would stay on the island and conduct interviews while Mulryan rejoined the manhunt. Meanwhile, the speedboat driver radioed to the mainland the information Nancy had given them.

George disappeared for a moment and came back with the Aran Isle sweater Nancy had bought earlier that day. "You'll need this; it'll be cold out on the water, now that night is falling," George reminded Nancy. "I'm sure your dad won't mind if you wear it before he does."

Nancy grinned. "Thanks, George."

Soon the speedboat was cutting back across the channel, heading for Cashkellmara. A fine, cold sea spray spritzed Nancy as they flew along. She shivered, grateful for the warm sweater.

Even before they landed, Nancy could see a squad car waiting, its lights flashing. "We've got O'Leary," called out another plainclothes officer, standing by the car's open door. "You want to go talk to him?"

Mulryan nodded and ushered Nancy into the car. With a warning burp of their siren, they tore up the road. "He wandered into a café up in Cashkellmara," the second officer, Danny McGrath, reported. "Five or six miles from the crash site. He's not making a whole lot of sense, but maybe he can tell us something."

The front window of the simple roadside café was brightly lit as they drove up. Nancy followed the officers inside.

Terry O'Leary sat at a Formica-topped table, hands

cupped around a steaming mug of milky tea. His shaggy hair was damp, the curls plastered against his neck. Mud and grime streaked his face and hands. His gray pullover sweater was ripped and spattered with mud; small burs and brambles clung to the legs of his corduroy trousers.

A police officer was putting salve on the wound on Terry's forehead. "Augh, man, you're killing me!" Terry cried out, flinching in pain.

The officer clucked. "That's a nasty gash you've got, and no mistake," he warned Terry. "Be sure to keep a clean dressing on it, d'ya hear?"

Terry moaned softly in reply. He opened his eyes again. Seeing Nancy, he stiffened. "No, don't tell me . . . is Bob here?"

Nancy shook her head, sitting down across the table from Terry. "He's with the group at the hotel. Are you okay?"

"Don't tell him I wrecked the van," Terry said, clearly agitated. "He said he'd sack me if I crashed another one."

Nancy laid a gentle hand on his wrist. "Bob already knows about the accident," she told him. "But he'll be glad to hear you're not badly hurt. The important thing right now is to find Rachel."

Terry gave a groggy blink. "Rachel?"

"Yes. Didn't she call you to come get her for a repair?"

Terry stared vaguely at Nancy, as if trying to focus his mind. "Rachel . . . Rachel. No, she never called me. Somebody else did . . . a man."

"Jim de Fusco?" Nancy suggested. "He told me he'd called you about Rhonda. But she didn't need any help; she, er, fixed her gears herself. I thought you also told Bob that Rachel had called. I was there when he took the call."

Terry hung his head. "That's what I told Bob. But that was a bit of a cover story. You see, I . . . I stopped in a pub for a wee bit. Not for a drink, mind you, just to watch the football on television. Soccer, you call it." He looked away from Nancy to the surrounding officers, as if asking for support. "It's a very important match."

"Aye," one of the officers verified.

"I didn't take my mobile inside," Terry admitted. "The battery was dead—it only worked when it was powered by the car's engine. So when Jim called, I thought maybe Rachel had tried to phone while I was in the pub."

"You mean Rhonda," Nancy corrected him.

Terry blinked, "Rhonda, Rachel—I always get them mixed up. It must have been Rhonda I was after. But I didn't want Bob to know I'd stopped at the pub," he said sheepishly, "so I told him Rachel had called me herself."

Nancy squeezed her eyes shut in frustration. So

Terry's whereabouts had been a red herring; a clue that went nowhere. All along it had been Rhonda he'd gone to pick up, not Rachel. And meanwhile, what had Stewart Smithson been up to?

Terry was still rambling on. "I drove to where Jim told me she was, but she was gone. I turned around and drove back north—a long ways, it seemed like. It had just started to rain when I spotted her riding way ahead. I reckoned she'd fixed the bike herself."

"Think carefully. Was it Rhonda or Rachel?" Nancy asked.

Terry tried to concentrate for a moment, then winced with pain. "Don't know for sure. All I know is, a car came up behind me, real fast. With the rain and all, I didn't hear it at first. The next thing I knew, he was running me off the road."

Nancy sat up straight. "A blue sedan?"

Terry struggled to remember. "I think so. Like I said, it was raining, and I couldn't see so well. I looked in my mirrors . . ." His body sagged. "From then on, everything's a blank."

Nancy leaned back in her chair, frustrated. Was it Rhonda or Rachel that Terry had seen on the road? And if the driver of the blue car was Smithson . . .

Just then, a squawk rose from the radio clipped to Officer Mulryan's belt. He whipped it to his ear. "Mulryan," he said.

The dispatcher's voice came through, crackly with

static. "Keith, we've found the blue car. The license number matches and all. It's parked at the edge of the peat bog."

"Is Smithson in it?" Mulryan radioed back, throwing an excited look at Nancy.

"Negative, Keith," the radio voice replied. "But there *is* a magenta bicycle in the trunk."

15

The Bog Demon Awaits

"You're sure it's Smithson's car?" Mulryan asked.

The staticky voice answered, "Yeah. Same license and all."

"We'll be right there. Over." He clipped the radio back to his belt and gestured to Nancy and Danny. "Let's go to the bog and check it out."

As the Garda car hurtled through the velvety night, Mulryan thought aloud. "They must have left the car and gone on by foot."

Nancy considered this. "Maybe not. What if he got a second car? He must have known we'd be able to identify the blue one."

"In that case, he'd need an accomplice," Mulryan said, "to drive the other car here to pick him up. Well, I'll radio headquarters and have them phone round to nearby car hire agencies. We'll see if Smithson hired another car today."

"I doubt he'd use his real name to rent the car," Nancy reminded him. "Make sure they give the agencies his full description."

Mulryan nodded and radioed the message. After he was finished, he stared out through the window at the flat, featureless landscape approaching the bogland. "If they did go by foot, we'd have our work cut out. Tracing them through that bog would be a nightmare."

"What is a bog? Is it like a swamp?" Nancy asked, leaning forward from the rear seat.

Mulryan considered the question. "A bog is—well, it's a bog. The ground is soft and mucky for miles. The surface is what we call peat: a sort of gluey, dense soil. People cut it into chunks, cart it away, and let it dry into hard bricks to use for fuel. Most folk hereabouts heat their homes with peat fire."

"Of course, when people take away the peat, the bog just gets boggier," Danny McGrath added. "It's a fearsome place, all right. Some folks around here won't even drive on this bog road at night. They think evil spirits would jump out and attack their car." He grinned.

"But people can walk in it?" Nancy asked.

Mulryan shrugged. "There's no path, really—just a hundred little lanes, the boreens. They're like ridges of solid ground weaving around between the swampy bits. Even a local lad would have a devil of a time navigating it in the dark."

Swinging around the narrow roads, Nancy peered at road signs. It was hard in the dark to decipher the English names at the top, let alone the Gaelic ones below. But she could tell this wasn't the road she'd cycled over earlier.

As the next sign flashed past, Nancy called out, "What was that name?"

Danny McGrath said, "Clostermeade?"

Nancy straightened up. "I've heard that name before. . . ."

Danny shrugged. "It's nothing famous—just a wee village and a manor house."

"And the manor house is deserted," Keith Mulryan added. "The bog kept expanding and overtook the grounds. The house is practically cut off by now—no one goes near it."

Nancy snapped her fingers. "I remember! I heard Smithson talking about Clostermeade Manor. We were in a pottery shop in Galway City. He asked the sales clerk about the residence; he said his aunt used to work there as a maid."

McGrath looked over his shoulder. "Funny coincidence."

"My guess is he was lying," Nancy said. "He probably just said that to get more information from the woman. I suppose he'd cased out the area already and spotted this empty manor house. He'd want to learn more about it."

Keith Mulryan smacked a fist into the other palm. "That's it! It'd be a perfect place to hide out. Let's go."

They sped through the tiny village of Clostermeade. Mulryan pointed through to a hulking shadow on a low rise beyond the village. "That's the manor house. Pull over by the gates, Danny—just ahead, there."

Danny swung the car into a weed-choked paved area that looked like it had once been the foot of a driveway. A pair of rusted iron gates barred the old drive. Getting out of the car, Nancy examined the dilapidated wrought iron, its dented curlicues the evidence of a long-vanished grandeur.

"The blue car is about half a mile down this road," Danny said. "Should we go there first?"

Keith shook his head. "Smithson wasn't asking about Clostermeade Manor for nothing. I bet Nancy's right; Smithson's using this place as a hide-out. Why don't you drive on and check out the car, Danny? Then run back here and meet us."

"Okay. But you'd better take the torch," Danny said, handing over a monster-sized flashlight. "It's not safe for us to go splitting up. This man may be armed and dangerous."

Keith gave a lopsided grin. "Then radio for some backup. We might as well make use of all the chaps from Dublin they're flying in for this." He snickered. "I guess they don't think we westerners can handle a high-stakes operation."

Danny snorted. "Well, we'll show them."

Nancy and Keith Mulryan got out of the car, and Danny drove away. Keith switched on his huge flashlight and played its beam over the old gates. "Shouldn't take much to get through here," he said. He reached out and touched the rusty lock on the gates. The lock plate fell to the side, and one gate tipped open, shifting on its hinges with a loud creak.

"Better turn off your flashlight," Nancy warned him. Privately, she wondered how many stakeouts Keith had been on in this rural area. Not many, she guessed. "If Smithson is up at the house, we don't want him to know we're coming."

"Aye," said Keith, "but we'll need light to get through the bog. The drive ends up ahead; the bog devoured it." He aimed the flashlight at the broken pavement ahead.

Keith strode forward, sweeping the beam from side to side but keeping it low. He halted at the end of the pavement. "There're ridges of packed soil. You've just got to find them," he whispered. He began to feel his way forward.

The darkness soon closed in around them, despite

Keith's flashlight. Nancy kept her eyes trained on the ground before her, setting one foot directly in front of the other. A quick glance to either side showed gleaming dark muck, with very little grass and absolutely no trees.

The deeper in they went, the bleaker it seemed. No sounds of birds or small animals, the usual signs of life in a normal landscape. Her senses keenly attuned, Nancy imagined she could almost hear the bog breathe.

Then Keith Mulryan disappeared from in front of her.

Nancy gasped and halted her steps. Her hands flew out, searching for Keith.

She heard a squelching, sucking sound a few feet to her left. "Keith?" She crouched, groping in that direction.

A sudden sharp breath broke out by her ankles. "I've gone down!" Mulryan panted.

Nancy reached out and felt mucky hands grasp her forearm. She braced her bent legs and started to pull backward. Mulryan was clawing desperately for a solid ridge.

Nancy's muscles ached with the tension of pulling the man upward. But she dared not step in the other direction for more leverage. The open bog gaped there, too, like quicksand.

With one final great heave, Mulryan hauled himself

onto the footpath. He sprawled gratefully on the packed dirt. "Just an encounter with the bog demon," he joked weakly.

Nancy helped him to his feet. "I'll go first for a while," she offered. "Until you've recovered." Mulryan nodded.

They moved more slowly now, Mulryan staying only a few inches behind Nancy. She felt her shoulders hunch with anxiety. If she made a false step, she might sink like Keith had.

"Well, if we're having trouble, that means Smithson and Rachel are, too," she said to herself grimly. Then, with a sinking heart, she reflected that they must have come through here in daylight. That would have been nothing compared to this.

At last, Nancy sensed a line of shrubbery a few yards ahead, breaking up the bleak flatness of the bog. She pushed toward it, still setting one foot carefully in front of the other.

As she got closer, she could see a light faintly wink between the tangled strands of foliage. Her pulse quickened. Surely that was the manor house getting near. Was someone in there? Was it—Smithson?

Behind her, Nancy heard Keith stumble to the side of the path. His boots squelched, and he swore under his breath. Nancy halted, but she heard him haul himself back onto the path. She pressed on.

Reaching the bushes, Nancy discovered that it was

a ragged, overgrown boxwood hedge. She fought to pry open a gap in it. Sharp twigs whipped her face and hands. Keith joined her and threw his body weight beside hers. They finally flattened a section enough to struggle over it.

Ahead of them stretched an expanse of grass. Nancy stepped slowly forward, testing the uneven ground of the old garden for soft patches.

In the darkness, Nancy resorted to an old trick she'd learned from wilderness survival training. Shutting her eyes, she cut off her dependence on the sense of sight. Her other senses now came more sharply into play. Every sound around her, every variation in the terrain, even the airflow created by neighboring objects, all were magnified as she moved silently forward.

Several yards behind her she could hear Keith's footsteps pause. There was a soft creak of leather as he fumbled for something on his belt. What was he doing? Now was not the time to—

Keith's muffled voice said, "Mulryan here. Any word on that backup?"

Then a loud hiss of static escaped from his radio. The dispatcher's voice squawked forth, "About six miles off yet, Keith."

Nancy whirled around, her heart in her mouth. This close to the house, silence was absolutely necessary. What was Keith thinking?

The low beam of the flashlight revealed the officer's startled face. Even he hadn't expected the volume on his radio to be set so high.

Behind her, Nancy heard a wooden shutter clatter open. A harsh square of light broke into the darkness for a moment, then was switched off.

Nancy dropped to her knees behind a broken stone bench. Keith crouched behind a weathered wooden arbor nearby. Nancy heard him draw his gun from its holster and click off the safety latch.

And at almost the same time, Nancy heard from the house the answering click of a gun.

A harsh Australian bray rose from the house. "Whoever it is, I know you're out there. I've got the girl here. Come any closer, and I'll shoot her."

16

The Luck of the Irish

Crouching behind the bench, Nancy raised her head just enough to see Smithson's face framed in a broken-out window of the manor house. He held Rachel in front of him, in a headlock. Her pale face looked twisted in sheer panic. Nancy's heart ached for her.

Smithson shifted his position, and a slash of moonlight fell across his face. Beads of sweat glittered on his forehead, but the hand that held the gun was steady.

Over in the arbor, Keith Mulryan leveled his gun at the kidnapper. "You might as well come out, Smithson," he called out. "We've got you covered. Don't hurt the girl and everything will be all right."

Smithson swiveled to face the arbor. Nancy spied her chance. In the darkness, she might be able to slip across the shadowy garden and get into the house. She stretched out one leg to the right and shifted her weight, making as little noise as possible.

"And who would you be, then?" Smithson fired a sarcastic question at Mulryan.

"Keith Mulryan, Galway Garda," the officer replied in a confident voice. "I've got men stationed all around the property. You'll never escape. You might as well surrender."

Bending low, Nancy took a few lunges and found cover behind a knee-high terrace wall. From there she crept on all fours toward the house. There was a door in the side wall. Not too far . . .

"Oh, yeah?" Smithson countered. "Don't play me for a mug. Where are these men of yours? Stuck in that blasted bog? I could barely get through in daylight, and it's pitch-black now. Sorry, but I'm not scared of you and your gutless bog-slogging colleagues." He snickered cruelly. "I've come a long way to get my hands on one of the Selkirks, and I'm not giving her up. Do you know how much money she's worth to me?"

Nancy stepped carefully onto the slate step and laid her hand on the doorknob.

"Do you know how many years in prison she's worth to you?" Keith countered. "And you're in a foreign country; you'll never get her out of Ireland." Nancy had to admire Keith's coolness in a hostage situation.

"Maybe not alive," Smithson sneered. "But I don't care about that. My employers will pay me, anyway. They aren't in this for the ransom money."

"What are they in it for, then?" Keith asked.

"To hurt Jacob Selkirk," Smithson snorted. "The way he shut down their business, with his stickybeak reporters prying into everything."

So it was the Australian crime ring who'd hired Smithson! Rachel was just a pawn in some pretty desperate dealings.

Nancy clutched the doorknob and gave the door a gentle shove. It wouldn't budge. She suspected she could break the rusty lock open, but not without making a lot of noise.

As if on cue, noise arrived—a thin whine in the distance, growing rapidly louder. A police helicopter, its searchlights raking the vast stretch of bog behind the house, was approaching. Keith's backup!

"We're closing in, Smithson," Keith shouted over the chopper's roar. "Hand her over peaceably, and it'll make things easier for you."

The noise was loud enough now to hide the sound of Nancy's movements. She shoved the door again with both hands and one strong foot. It wrenched open. She squeezed through into a small paneled entryway, and pushed through a dark passageway to her left, toward where Smithson and Rachel must be.

She couldn't hear Keith's next words, but Smithson's gruff answer was audible enough. Nancy used the sound to guide her along this narrow, windowless servants' passage. "It's great that the money's on its way," Smithson was saying. "But after I get it, I might do her in, anyway. My bosses have given me what they call 'discretion to do as I please.' Maybe I'll cut off her finger, like someone did to me. Would you like that, eh, miss?"

Getting closer now, Nancy heard a muffled, frightened yelp from Rachel, followed by Smithson's ugly laugh.

"Your daddo didn't treat me too well when I was working for him," the kidnapper snarled. "I don't owe him no favors."

His voice was directly behind the door next to Nancy.

Now she could hear Mulryan's voice outside, shouting, "Hurt the girl, and it won't look good at your trial." There was an edge of fear to his voice now. "Did you think of that, Smithson?"

Nancy drew a deep breath and thrust open the door.

Smithson, taken by surprise, wheeled around. He swung his gun toward Nancy.

Somehow in the sudden motion Rachel was able to wrestle out of Smithson's grasp. He lurched after her, lowering his gun for a moment. Nancy leaped toward him. With a karate chop, she knocked the weapon out of his right hand.

With an enraged roar, Smithson threw himself at Nancy. His left hand, with the stump where his little finger should be, flailed in front of her face. He tackled her, knocking her to the floor.

Rachel launched herself at Smithson from behind, her face contorted with fury. "How dare you do this to my father!" she screamed, raining blows on his back with her fists.

Garda officers came swarming in through the window and the passageway door. It took three of them to pull Smithson up off of Nancy. She shook her head to clear her senses. A hand reached down to help her to her feet.

Rachel grinned down at her. "Nancy—I've never been so happy to see anybody in my life!"

Lying in a four-poster bed at the old monastery, Nancy thought she was dreaming, hearing the chop of a speedboat outside her window. Was she reliving last night's adventure?

But now there was sunlight streaming through the arched stone window. When Nancy got up and looked out, there was the Garda speedboat again, with Keith Mulryan standing at the stern. But next to him was an unfamiliar figure: a stout man of about sixty, in an overcoat that looked like expensive cashmere. Though his hair was gray, something about his rugged features told her he was Rachel and Rhonda's father.

Nancy quickly threw on some jeans and a sweater and hurried downstairs. Hotel staff seemed to be rushing about everywhere, bringing trays of coffee and breakfast food into the lounge. Nancy strolled in to find the entire tour group settled on sofas and chairs, gazing wide-eyed at the famous tycoon. He sat ensconced in a throne-like leather wingback chair.

"Nancy!" Bob called out, seeing her. "We didn't want to wake you; you had such a hard night last night. As you can see, we've abandoned cycling for today. Too much other excitement."

The man in the wingback chair looked up. "Is this the same Nancy who is the hero of last night's crime scene?"

Rachel, perched beside him, jumped up. "Nancy, this is my dad."

"So I guessed." Nancy smiled and shook Jacob Selkirk's hand.

"I flew in from London as soon as I could after I received Smithson's ransom note," Selkirk said.

Rhonda, sitting on a footstool by his feet, looked concerned. "But, Dad—your busy schedule!"

Selkirk waved a hand. "How important are all those meetings, really? I had a daughter to rescue." He circled an arm around Rachel's waist and gave her a squeeze. "But I see she's already safe and sound."

Officer Mulryan smiled. "And Stewart Smithson is safely behind bars," he reported. "They're keeping him in the Galway jail to await trial. By the way, we'll have to take statements from all of you later today, to use as evidence."

"The hospital in Galway called a little while ago," Bob added. "The word is that Terry is resting comfortably. X rays showed he had a pretty bad concussion, but nothing more."

Mrs. Keenan, the innkeeper, sidled into the room, carrying a tall stack of newspapers. "Mr. Selkirk, sir," she said with a little bow, "here are all the papers your assistant sent over."

Carl Thompson whistled. "You read that many newspapers every morning?"

Jacob Selkirk chuckled. "I am in the business, you know. But I requested these papers today because they all have one thing in common: Rachel's kidnapping is on the front page."

Nancy was impressed. Stewart Smithson had been arrested last night at nearly ten P.M. How could so many reporters dig up enough information to produce a story for this morning's edition?

Jacob Selkirk fanned out the newspapers on the coffee table and let everyone in the group choose one. Bess was quick to snatch up the *London Enquirer*. "I found Derek's story," she called out. "Page nineteen.

Here's the headline: 'Irish Tourism Booms with Step-dancing Craze.'"

Camilla clapped for joy. "A fluffy travel piece—not what his editor expected. Derek will probably get sacked. But I knew he didn't have it in him to be too sleazy."

"Derek left the tour a day too soon," Bess declared. "He might have had a cover story after all."

Selkirk looked up. "Derek? Who's that?"

Rhonda slapped her dad's shoulder. "A reporter you fired once."

Selkirk shrugged. "There're lots of those around, dear."

Rachel smiled. "I'll tell you the whole story later, Dad. But Derek's really not cut out for the tabloids. Maybe you can find a spot for him on the *Clarion* again."

The phone out in the lobby jangled, and Mrs. Keenan trotted out. A moment later, she returned. "That was the Cashkellmara bike shop, Bob," she said. "Miss Selkirk's bike is fixed."

"Her bike?" Rhonda looked at her sister.

Mulryan nodded. "We took it in. It was terribly banged up when we found it. Smithson rammed it pretty hard into his trunk."

Rachel shuddered. "That must have been after he knocked me out. I put up a real fight when he ran me off my bike."

Jacob Selkirk smiled proudly. "That's my girl."

"I guess he knew he couldn't just leave the bike by the roadside," Mulryan said. "We'd be sure to spot it and know she'd been abducted."

Nancy nodded. "His whole plan depended on buying time. That's why he disabled Terry's van; Terry had just seen Rachel riding up ahead and was sure to report it."

"Time was of the essence," Mulryan agreed. "If we had waited until this morning to hunt for him, he'd have been long gone."

Rhonda closed her eyes. "What a horrible man. To think he used to drive us to school."

Selkirk reached over and patted her knee. "If I'd known, sweetie, I'd never have hired him. He's full of smooth talk when you first meet him, sure enough. By the time I'd realized what a crook he was, I'd fired him—but unfortunately, that just gave him a grudge. Made him fair game for my enemies to use."

Rachel, snuggled next to her father, made a face. "Well, I'm in no hurry to retrieve that bike. I don't intend to go cycling anytime soon."

Rhonda sat up, surprised. "What?"

Rachel paused and waggled one mischievous red eyebrow. "Not unless I've got a bodyguard riding right beside me. Any chance you'd be interested in the job, Nancy Drew?"

The Riding Club Crime

Contents

1

Green Spring Farm

"Whoa, Tristram!" Nancy Drew said as the horse she was riding leaped into the air. A small gray shape with a furry tail scurried across the path in front of them. "Chill out, boy," she added, "it's only a squirrel."

"I don't know what's gotten into Tristram—he's usually pretty calm," Elsa Gable said. She stopped her horse, Barchester, next to Nancy and scanned the woods. Shafts of sunlight broke through the canopy of leaves above them. "He's been in these woods a million times. Why's he suddenly so scared?"

"Sneak attacks by mutant squirrels," George Fayne said from behind them. "Pretty terrifying, huh, Derby?" She reached down to pat her horse's sleek, golden neck.

Nancy and Elsa laughed. "Let's get going," Elsa said, "before any mutants get us."

Elsa was an old friend of Nancy, George, and George's cousin, Bess Marvin. She kept Barchester at Green Spring Farm, a riding stable in the country outside River Heights. She was also a counselor at Green Spring's summer camp, but she had a break while the campers were swimming. George and Nancy had eagerly agreed to ride with her when she'd called to invite them earlier that day.

Nancy led the way down the trail. It quickly brought them to the edge of a meadow. Purple clover and white Queen Anne's lace threaded the long green grass.

"The trail picks up again in the woods across the field," Elsa said. "Want to race?"

Before Nancy had a chance to respond, Barchester sprang into the meadow with Elsa hunched forward in her saddle. His jet-black coat gleamed in the sudden burst of sun. Tristram and Derby bolted after him, tossing their heads and whinnying. Nancy loosened Tristram's reins and nudged him into a gallop.

The breeze slapped against Nancy's face as she and Tristram zoomed through the field, his hooves pounding underneath her. She could hear Barchester and Derby galloping behind. *Are they catching up with me?* she wondered.

Seconds later, she came to the edge of the woods.

"Finish line!" she called, reining Tristram in.

"That was great!" George said, her brown eyes sparkling. She stopped Derby next to Nancy.

"I claim a tie for second!" Elsa said, pulling up by George. She flicked back her long chestnut hair, which had tumbled out from under her helmet.

"No way, Elsa. You're third by a nose," George countered.

Elsa grinned. "Whatever. Anyway, too bad Bess wasn't up for riding with us this afternoon. That would have made for an even better race!"

"Bess was in a race of her own. Her favorite shoe store is having a sale, and she wanted to get to the mall ASAP," George said.

"Maybe she can ride another time," Nancy suggested. "Bess likes horses. It's just that for her, shopping comes first."

Elsa's green eyes looked thoughtful. "Well, since Bess likes both fashion and horses, I might know the perfect job for her: an internship at *The Horse's Mouth.*"

Nancy frowned. "*The Horse's Mouth.* That sounds familiar. Is it a magazine?"

"It's a newsletter in River Heights that covers equestrian stuff," Elsa explained. "Anything to do with horses. The editor is a friend of Mrs. Rogers, the owner of Green Spring Farm. She told the counselors to spread the word that the newsletter needs an intern to cover equestrian fashion."

"Bess would love it," Nancy agreed.

"Remind me to call her when we get back to the barn," Elsa said. "In the meantime, we've got a jump at the end of that trail to get over. Nancy, you lead."

Nancy urged Tristram into the woods at a brisk trot. She could hear the other horses following them. When a fork appeared ahead, she tugged on the reins to slow her horse. "Which way, Elsa?"

"We have a choice," Elsa said. "The wimpy log fence to the left, or the giant post-and-rail to the right."

"You call that a choice?" George said, and grinned. "Who wants to be a wimp?"

"Would you be up for jumping it first, George?" Elsa said. "That fence is so big that Barchester always refuses it. But he'll do whatever Derby does. Don't ask me why, but Derby is his role model."

"People have role models, so why shouldn't horses?" Nancy quipped as she guided Tristram to the right. As they walked along single file, she asked Elsa how things were going at the camp. "Are you having fun?" Twisting in her saddle, she studied Elsa's face. Nancy thought she saw Elsa's eyes flicker down before they met her gaze.

"Basically, yeah," Elsa said.

Is Elsa worried about something? Nancy wondered.

"Working at a riding camp sounds great," George broke in. "How old are the kids?"

"Fourteen to seventeen," Elsa said. "It's a two-week program, and all the campers are members of the Green Spring Pony Club, which is part of the United States Pony Club. But even though the age limit for Mrs. Rogers's camp is seventeen, you can be in pony club until you're twenty-one. And don't be fooled by the name 'pony club.' Most of the kids actually ride horses."

Nancy thought about the official difference between a pony and a horse. A horse was larger than fourteen and a half hands, while a pony was under that size. Nancy also knew that a hand was the official horse measurement of four inches. But she was curious to know more about the riding club. "How do you get to be a member?" she asked. "Do you have to pass some test?"

Elsa shrugged. "You just apply and pay dues. The camp helps the kids polish their riding skills and get ready for pony club competitions."

"Competitions? Like horse shows and stuff?" George asked.

"Not regular horse shows," Elsa replied. "These are events for pony clubs to compete against one another. For instance, we're getting ready for the pony club rally that starts this Friday. Tomorrow, Mrs. Rogers and all of the counselors will choose five of the most qualified kids to be on Green Spring's rally team."

"What's a pony club rally?" Nancy asked.

"It's a three-day competition between different teams," Elsa explained. "There are regional rallies and national ones. If your team wins the rally in your region, it goes on to compete at the national level. The rally on Friday is a regional one; it's at the Chatham Fairgrounds, about half an hour from River Heights. Six clubs from around the area will be competing."

"What happens during the three days?" George asked.

"Well, this one is a Combined Training Rally, which means it has several events. The first evening we're there, the teams take a written test to quiz their knowledge of horses and riding," Elsa explained. "The next day is dressage. That takes place in a ring bounded by a picket fence about a foot high. Each rider takes his or her horse through a series of circles and figure eights and stuff. The horses have to go at different paces—walking, trotting, and cantering. And the rider has to wear special clothes."

"What kind of clothes?" Nancy asked.

"Basic black. Coat, boots, and derby hat. Oh, and white breeches," Elsa added. "The clothes sound kind of dorky, but the riders actually look pretty cool, especially when their horses have been cleaned and brushed. They're like something out of an old-fashioned movie."

"So the first full day of the rally is just dressage?" Nancy asked.

"Yes, and the second day is cross-country. That's a two-mile course across woods and fields, with about fourteen jumps scattered around. It's awesome. Most of the kids like cross-country best because they're not performing in front of an audience—just the judges who are posted at the jumps."

"What happens on the third day?" George asked.

"Stadium jumping," Elsa told her. "That takes place in a ring in front of the grandstand. The jumps are big, and the officials try to make them look scary and weird, with brightly painted poles and barrels. Sometimes the horses get skittish at the sight of them. If a horse refuses a jump, major penalties are added because the judges think a good rider should be able to make the horse do anything."

"That's unfair," George said. "I mean, horses aren't sheep. A horse has a mind of its own."

"Sure does," Elsa said. "But the rally is judged on the performance of each horse. Whichever team has the best horses and riders will go to the national rally. This year it's in Virginia."

Tristram's reddish brown coat and black mane glistened in the sunlight. Nancy gave him an encouraging pat on his soft neck. "Why only five kids for the team?" Nancy asked, twisting around again to see Elsa. "I bet all the campers are pretty tense about who will make it."

Elsa rolled her eyes. "The competition between them is ridiculous. I wish they'd relax." She sighed. "There are going to be hurt feelings tomorrow, but what can we do? We can't take more than five kids. The teams are the same all over the country: four riders and one stable manager to care for the horses and help the riders."

"Are the rallies fun?" George asked.

Elsa's face lit up. "The rallies are awesome. I guess I can't blame the kids for wanting to go. I just wish they'd appreciate what they're learning at Mrs. Rogers's camp for its own sake and stop worrying about making the team. Her program is really special. I don't know of any other pony club camp like it."

"How's it so special?" Nancy asked as she ducked under a low-hanging branch.

"Mrs. Rogers is a wealthy widow, and she's totally committed to helping kids who can't afford riding camp or keeping horses," Elsa said. "She offers a full scholarship and the use of her own horses to eight girls and boys. They have to be good riders and interested in the sport. The scholarship kids are some of her most serious riders. They make up about a third of the camp, I think."

"So the other kids bring their own horses?" George asked.

"Uh-huh. Mrs. Rogers owns about ten horses, including Tristram and Derby here—not nearly enough horses for all of the campers."

"What a great thing for her to do—use her money to help kids who can't afford her camp," Nancy said.

"Her scholarship is just the beginning of her good deeds," Elsa declared. "She also insists that at least two of the rally team members must be scholarship campers. She's devoted to them, and that's mainly why Green Spring is special. The other reason is Mrs. Rogers's personality."

"What's she like?" George asked.

"Maybe you guys can meet her when we get back to the barn," Elsa said. "She was busy giving lessons earlier. Anyway, she's really friendly and always in a good mood. She has a knack for making kids excited about riding. She also has tons of cool animals in her house—dogs, cats, ferrets, and even a monkey! She lives in this huge Victorian mansion with lots of rooms. Campers stay there instead of in cabins or tents."

"Sounds like camp heaven," George said. "I wish I could go—don't you, Nancy?"

"Too bad we're past the cutoff age!" Nancy said.

The trail widened, and the trees thinned. The girls were silent for a moment as they took in the sounds of nature. Nancy could hear birds singing and creatures rustling in the underbrush. She hoped a squirrel wouldn't hop out and surprise Tristram again.

A bend in the trail brought them face-to-face with a post-and-rail fence about four feet high. Beyond it was a cornfield filled with green stalks waving in the wind.

"That *is* a big jump," George admitted. "But I promised I'd go first, and I will."

Elsa's eyes sparkled mischievously. "You asked for it. Just don't jump on the corn, or the farmer will get mad."

Nancy held her breath as George positioned Derby about thirty feet back from the jump. Then she guided him toward the center of the fence.

Seconds later, Derby sailed over it, his golden coat and yellow mane bright against the green corn. George steered Derby to the border of the field, then turned to face her friends. "Just like flying," she declared, grinning triumphantly. "Who's next?"

"I'll go," Elsa said. "Barchester won't rest till he follows Derby." Moments later, Barchester's jet-black form leaped over the fence with inches to spare. "Your turn, Nancy," she added, joining George.

Nancy gritted her teeth. She was an experienced rider, but the fence was huge. Still, she was confident that Tristram wouldn't let her down.

Squeezing her legs against the saddle, she urged Tristram into the jump. He shot toward it, his body like an arrow. Nancy hunched forward as the huge animal launched himself into flight. *This is so cool,* she thought as the cornfield streaked up at her.

Tristram's hooves met the ground, and Nancy's eyes widened. A huge hole appeared under his left foot. Tristram lurched to his knees, with Nancy clinging to his neck. She couldn't let herself fall—or else she'd be trampled!

2

Stumbling into Danger

Nancy catapulted out of the saddle. Her face banged against Tristram's mane, but she held on to keep from falling under his legs. Tristram whinnied in fear as he struggled to stand up. Nancy held her breath as the mighty bay horse wobbled upward and hoisted his foot out of the hole.

Nancy exhaled against Tristram's neck as the horse steadied himself. She shimmied back into the saddle and grabbed the loose reins. A second later, the panicky Tristram crashed into the cornfield ahead.

"It's okay, Tristram," Nancy said in a soothing voice. She stopped him, then turned to look at her friends.

"Are you okay, Nancy?" Elsa asked.

"I'm fine. I just hope Tristram wasn't hurt." Nancy

guided him out of the cornfield, then jumped off to examine him for injuries. As she ran her fingers over his legs, she said, "He's lucky he didn't break a bone falling in that hole. But he seems fine. I don't see a scratch on him."

"I didn't notice that hole when I jumped the fence," George said.

"Me neither," Elsa said.

"Let me check it out." Nancy handed Tristram's reins to George. She walked over and inspected the hole. It was about a foot deep and wide, and it looked freshly dug. It also looked like the hole had been covered by a grid of sticks, which was now smashed. On top of the sticks were bits of grass. Someone had dug this hole on purpose!

Nancy beckoned to her friends. "This is so weird. Someone made this hole and then disguised it as smooth ground." She pointed to the grid. "See? They sprinkled grass on these sticks for camouflage. No one could see the hole until it was too late."

Elsa paled. "But who would want to hurt a horse . . . or a rider?"

"Has anyone ridden on this trail recently?" George asked. She looked at Elsa. "You and I were lucky. Our horses must have just missed it."

"I don't think any Green Spring kids came here today," Elsa answered. "We were busy practicing stadium jumping in the morning. But a bunch of us rode these trails yesterday, so this hole couldn't have been here then. People from all over the area ride through here, but I guess we were the first ones to land in the hole."

"Lucky us," George said dryly.

"So the hole was probably dug last night or this morning," Nancy reasoned, scanning the ground around it. "Do you guys have a minute? I want to see something."

George grinned. "Of course we'll wait. This is becoming a case, isn't it?"

Elsa brightened. "I'd forgotten you're a detective, Nancy. If anyone can figure out who did this, you can. I just hope this doesn't mean more danger for the campers and the camp."

Even though Nancy was only eighteen, she was already an accomplished detective. Bess and George, also eighteen, had helped her out many times. Nancy wasn't sure whether this hole more than just some isolated prank, but she wanted to check out the area for clues.

Nancy met Elsa's worried gaze. "Has anything weird been happening around Green Spring?" she asked.

"Well . . . ," Elsa began. "I haven't known of any other traps like that hole, but some strange things *have* been happening at camp. For instance . . ." She paused for a moment, and began speaking in a whisper. "Promise you guys won't tell anyone outside the camp? I just don't want to hurt Green Spring's reputation by blabbing about what happened."

"Of course I won't tell," Nancy assured her.

"Me neither," George said.

"Well, just this morning, the girth to a girl's saddle snapped while she was stadium jumping," Elsa explained. "The saddle slid off with Juliana on it. She fell right under the horse! It was a miracle she wasn't hurt."

"Was the leather worn? Could it have broken on its own?" Nancy wondered.

Elsa sighed. "No way. It was a brand-new saddle, and the cut in the girth was straight. Only a razor or a knife could have done that. The person who did it must have left a small part of the leather attached so Juliana would put on the saddle without noticing the cut."

"Juliana must have freaked," George said.

"You bet. And that's not the only thing that's happened." Elsa blew out her breath, then continued. "Two days ago, we found poison ivy mixed in with some horses' feed."

"Did the horses eat it?" Nancy asked her.

"A few of them did," Elsa said, "and they were fine. Fortunately, horses aren't allergic to poison ivy. They eat it in fields all the time and never get sick. But the counselor who handled it broke out in a rash.

She was so upset, she quit this morning."

All these things sound serious, Nancy thought. *Whoever is doing them has to be stopped before people—or horses—get hurt.* "Is that it?" Nancy asked.

Elsa frowned. "Isn't that enough? I mean, just before lunch today, three campers left because they were so creeped out by all the stuff that's happened."

"I don't blame them," George said. "I'm sure the kids are wondering whose saddle girth is going to go next."

"Mrs. Rogers gave everyone strict orders to check horses, tack, stalls—everything—for safety before we ride," Elsa explained. "The most frustrating thing is that camp used to be so much fun. Now it's a downer. These accidents have affected everyone's mood."

"One thing's for sure," Nancy said firmly, "they're not accidents."

"Let's fill in this hole so no one else gets hurt, and then I've got to get back to the stable," Elsa said. "Dressage practice starts in half an hour, and I'm coaching."

Once they'd returned to Green Spring, the girls unsaddled their horses, rubbed them down, then let them loose in a field to graze. Nancy took her helmet off and shook out her shoulder-length reddish blond hair.

"Let's go find Mrs. Rogers," Elsa suggested,

putting the helmets in a tack room box. "I want to tell her about that trap."

The girls found Mrs. Rogers working in her office in a corner of the barn. A small, plump woman of about sixty-five, with apple red cheeks and gray hair wrapped in a bun, Mrs. Rogers threw a dazzling smile at the girls as they stepped in the door. "Welcome!" she said in a hearty voice, standing up to greet them. "How nice, Elsa, to bring friends."

After the introductions were made, Mrs. Rogers studied Nancy. "Are you by any chance Carson Drew's daughter?" she asked her.

"I am," Nancy said, smiling.

"I met your father at a party at Josh Bryant's house," Mrs. Rogers said brightly. "Josh's farm is across the valley from mine. The party was a fundraiser for his own riding program, and Josh invited all the people he thought might contribute to it. Since your dad is a busy lawyer, he was high on Josh's guest list. Your father's a charming man, Nancy. You look quite a lot like him. I've no doubt you're a chip off the old block."

"Thank you," Nancy said.

"Did you girls have a nice ride?" Mrs. Rogers asked.

Elsa told Mrs. Rogers about the booby trap.

"Why, Tristram could have broken his leg!" Mrs. Rogers said, horrified. "Are you sure he's okay?"

"He's fine," Nancy assured her. "He didn't limp at all on the way home."

"Mrs. Rogers," Elsa said, "whoever set that trap might also be the one who cut Juliana's girth and mixed the poison ivy into the feed. He, or she, is really getting dangerous."

Mrs. Rogers drew herself up, her blue eyes resolute. "*Getting* dangerous? This person was dangerous from day one! Juliana could have been killed when her saddle broke. We've got to find out who's doing these things—and fast." Her gaze turned to Nancy. "Correct me if I'm wrong, Nancy, but I'm now remembering your father telling me that you're an amateur detective. He seemed very proud of your sleuthing abilities."

Nancy laughed. "Well, you know how dads can be." She met Mrs. Rogers's gaze. She knew what the camp director was about to ask: whether she would help solve the mystery. Nancy was eager to say yes, but how could she investigate without all the campers realizing her role? If she was going to do a good job, she'd have to go undercover.

Mrs. Roger seemed to read Nancy's mind. "I hate to intrude on your busy life, Nancy, but is there a chance you could help me out? You could go undercover as a counselor here so no one would know you're investigating."

"Brilliant idea!" Elsa exclaimed. Her skin flushed

with excitement. "But what about George? She'd be a help, too. Could she be a counselor too?"

"What do you say, George?" Mrs. Rogers asked.

"Count me in—if Nancy agrees," George said.

Nancy gave George a quick thumbs-up sign before Mrs. Rogers continued. "A counselor quit this morning, so our little ruse will make sense. I'll say I'm hiring George as an extra counselor because we need all the help we can get to prepare for the upcoming rally. I assume you girls have adequate experience with horses?"

"Enough not to blow our cover," George said, pausing for a minute. "Well, as long as we don't teach dressage," she confessed.

Before Mrs. Rogers could comment, loud voices cut through their conversation. A boy and girl were arguing in the tack room next door about their riding skills.

Mrs. Rogers and the three girls froze as they listened to the heated conversation. "Face it, Rafael, your family's broke! You can't afford to match me. I'll always be a better rider than you—and you know it."

3

One Weird Warning

Mrs. Rogers's kind face suddenly hardened with anger. With her fists at her sides, she marched into the tack room. Nancy, George, and Elsa followed. A dark-haired boy of about sixteen stormed by them, his black eyes blazing. A girl about his age stood by the window, her mouth set in a triumphant smirk. As she saw Mrs. Rogers, she blanched, and her mouth twisted into an unattractive scowl.

Mrs. Rogers didn't bother to get the girl's side of the story. "Clare, I heard what you said to Rafael. Your attitude is inexcusable! It's worse than arrogant. It's unkind. What makes you think you're any better than he is?"

The girl shook back her long dark hair. "I'm sorry, Mrs. Rogers," she said. Her gold eyes defiantly met Mrs. Rogers's gaze.

She sure doesn't seem sorry, Nancy thought.

"Your rudeness to that boy and to the other scholarship campers has to stop," Mrs. Rogers told her. "One more mean remark and you're Green Spring history! I don't care how talented a rider you are."

Clare's voice was sullen. "I understand, Mrs. Rogers. I apologize."

"Apologize to Rafael, not to me," Mrs. Rogers snapped. "Now hurry to dressage. You're late for practice."

"Yes, Mrs. Rogers," Clare said calmly. She headed out.

Nancy, George, and Elsa followed Mrs. Rogers back to her office. Once there, Elsa telephoned Bess to tell her about the job at *The Horse's Mouth.* When Elsa hung up, she was smiling. "Just as I suspected, Bess is thrilled," Elsa told them. "I gave her the editor's name and number. She's going to call him right away." She headed over to the door. "Now, I'd better get over to dressage."

Elsa hurried out, and Mrs. Rogers began to explain the camp schedule to Nancy and George. When she'd finished, Nancy asked her about Clare.

"Clare Wu is a classic snob," Mrs. Rogers said in a tone of disgust. "She's arrogant, controlling, and drop-dead beautiful. I think she has a secret crush on Rafael, but he doesn't return it. She's not used to rejection, so I can see how it could make her mad."

"And that's why she's so mean to him?" George asked.

"The situation is complicated," Mrs. Rogers admitted. "Rafael Estevez is a very talented rider. My scholarship kids are every bit as qualified as the other campers. But he doesn't rate with Clare, because his family isn't wealthy. I don't publicize who the scholarship kids are—it's kept confidential—but somehow the kids all know who's who. It bothers Clare that she's attracted to someone she thinks isn't high class."

"I don't blame Rafael for not liking Clare when she's so horrible to him," Nancy said.

"Clare can be nice when it suits her," Mrs. Rogers said, "and she was nice to Rafael at first. But he's a quiet kid. He keeps to himself. Clare probably thought she was being tolerant and good-hearted by courting a boy from a different background, but when he didn't pay attention to her, she got mad. She thought Rafael should feel grateful she liked him. This is a lot of inference on my part, true, but most of it seems pretty obvious."

"Man, what a viper!" George exclaimed.

"I've been trying to manage her for the past three years at this camp, and she just gets worse each year. That girl is one big headache. But a lot of kids seem drawn to her. I wish I knew why."

"Charisma," Nancy said. "I bet it lets her get away with stuff."

"I just hope that 'stuff' doesn't include digging holes and cutting saddle girths," Mrs. Rogers said grimly.

"One thing's for sure," George said. "Clare's charisma won't blind Nancy. If Clare's guilty, Nancy'll find out."

In a short time, Nancy and George learned everything they needed to know about their counselor jobs from Mrs. Rogers. By now it was late afternoon; time to drive home to pack for camp.

As the two girls headed toward River Heights in Nancy's blue Mustang, the summer sun glittered in the western sky. They'd promised Mrs. Rogers to be back at Green Spring after dinner so they could meet the kids before bed. As she dropped George off, Nancy asked, "Can you have dinner at my house, George? At around six o'clock? Hannah said she'd make fried chicken. I'll see if Bess is free too."

"Awesome! I'm addicted to Hannah's chicken."

Hannah Gruen was the Drews' housekeeper. She had been part of the family since the death of Nancy's mother, when Nancy was three. Hannah's talent in the kitchen was not lost on Nancy and her two best friends.

"Should I pick you up in my car?" Nancy asked.

"Nah. I'll just walk over to your house after I pack," George said. "But could we pick up my duffel bag at my house on our way back to camp? That way, I won't have to haul it with me."

"Sure thing," Nancy said. George jumped out of the car and jogged down the path to her door.

George and Bess showed up on Nancy's doorstep promptly at six. "Come in!" Nancy said happily. "Hannah's chicken smells great. Dad had to work late, unfortunately."

"We'll leave some for him," George said.

"Excuse me? Hannah's chicken? Leftovers?" Bess said skeptically. "No way, José." Nancy smiled and went to get sodas for her friends.

"So did you interview for that job at *The Horse's Mouth?*" Nancy asked when she returned. "The one Elsa called you about?"

Bess's blue eyes danced. "Sure did. And I got the job!"

"Awesome," Nancy said, and grinned.

"Congratulations, Bess," George said. "That was fast. When do you start?"

"I already have. Mr. Blackstone, the editor, put me to work on the spot. He's pretty much snowed under, so he was happy I could spend an hour today helping him open mail."

"What are your other duties?" Nancy asked.

Bess grinned. It was clear that her new job thrilled

her. "I'm the editor of a column on equestrian fashion. It's called 'Looking Hot to Trot.' It has the cutest heading—an illustration of two horses, boy and girl, dressed up in Victorian clothing. Mr. Blackstone is going to write it, but if I get good at doing the research, he'll let me take over."

"Will you get your own byline?" Nancy asked.

"You bet," Bess said.

"My cousin the reporter," George said approvingly. "You'll be famous in River Heights."

Bess giggled. "In the horse world, at least—if I'm lucky."

"Did you have to dress up in a black hat and boots to prove you know about riding fashion?" George teased.

"My new pink miniskirt and purple tank top showed Mr. Blackstone that I'm a fashion expert." Bess glanced down at her outfit fondly.

"Hey, girls," Hannah called from the kitchen. "Soup's on."

Nancy, George, and Bess set the kitchen table while Hannah brought out fried chicken, freshly baked bread, and a green salad. Nancy quickly sat down with her friends. "Thanks, Hannah," she said, passing the chicken. "This looks great."

"It's my secret recipe," Hannah said proudly, returning to the kitchen.

"Speaking of secret," Bess said, leaning toward

Nancy and George, "I opened the strangest letter for Mr. Blackstone today. It was an anonymous note criticizing Green Spring Farm and Mrs. Rogers's camp."

"What did it say?" Nancy asked.

"First, that the riding lessons at Green Spring are bogus," Bess said, counting off on her fingers. "Second, that Mrs. Rogers doesn't know a horse from a cow, and third, that the stable isn't up to fire safety codes. But Elsa's taught at the camp for a couple summers, and she's totally loved it." Bess buttered a piece of bread and shrugged. "Mr. Blackstone thought the note was completely lame, but he's investigating the charges just in case."

Nancy and George exchanged glances. "That note is obviously just one more effort to trash Green Spring," Nancy said. She and George briefed Bess on Green Spring's problems and their decision to go undercover to investigate them.

The girls heard Hannah clear her throat from the kitchen. "Nancy, I want you and George to be careful," she warned. "This person sounds dangerous."

"I promise we'll be careful, Hannah," Nancy assured her. "But only if you'll give us some of your chocolate cake." She caught a glimpse of Hannah frosting a brown cake.

"That's a small price to pay," Hannah said, icing the last bit of cake with a flourish.

After finishing dessert the girls helped Hannah

clean up and thanked her for dinner. Then Nancy picked up her packed duffel bag from the luggage rack in her room, and she and her friends headed outside. Nancy and George waved good-bye to Bess as she drove away, then they headed for Nancy's Mustang in her driveway.

Suddenly, Nancy stopped and pulled on George's arm. "Look!" she said, pointing at her car. White swirls of soapy writing covered the back windshield. "Get away from Green Spring, Nancy Drew!" it warned. At the end of the message, a picture of a horse's head crossed with a gigantic X glared at the girls.

4

Fire!

"How could anyone know I'm investigating?" Nancy asked.

"Someone must have overheard our conversation with Mrs. Rogers and followed us here," George said.

"Clare was in the tack room next door when Mrs. Rogers hired us," Nancy said. "Clare looks around sixteen; I bet she has her driver's license. She could have driven here, soaped the windows, and then driven back to camp."

"We'll have to ask some campers if they saw her," George said. "She would have been gone at least an hour."

Nancy sighed, feeling frustrated. "So our cover's blown already. Still, we might as well stay on as counselors. Even if the person knows what we're up to, we'll be in a better position to catch him or her if we're working at Green Spring."

"We might make him nervous just by being there," George said hopefully. "Maybe he won't try anything dangerous again."

Nancy thought George was being overly optimistic. Whoever was playing these tricks didn't seem the least bit nervous. Quite the opposite, in fact. The person seemed highly dangerous, and the only way to change that would be to catch him or her.

After cleaning off the windshield Nancy and George slid into the front seat of the car. They picked up George's duffel bag at her house before driving out to Green Spring Farm. It was nestled in a beautiful valley, among rolling hills and woods.

Once there, Nancy and George took a moment to scan the grounds. The only building at Green Spring aside from the bighouse was the stable. It was huge, with an indoor riding ring in the center surrounded by stalls, the tack room, a feed room, and Mrs. Rogers's office. A wide corridor with a soft earth floor separated the stalls from the ring. Outside the barn were several green pastures, where horses grazed during the day; two outdoor riding rings with white wooden fences; and a dressage ring. Now the pastures were empty, but Nancy and George could see horses gazing over their stall doors.

"We'd better get up to the house," Nancy said. "It must be almost time for lights-out."

The girls carried their duffels up the gravel path to the gigantic stone house with its four turrets, bay windows, wraparound porch, and overgrown gardens. "What a great place," George commented. "It looks like at one point it was really in pristine condition, but now its owner cares more about horses than being featured in some glossy home decorating magazine."

As Mrs. Rogers opened the door, a pack of dogs and cats rushed out of the house to greet them. "Scruffy, down!" she commanded. "You too, Inky and Nutmeg. And Marmalade, I'm watching you. You're *way* too friendly for a cat."

Sure enough, an orange cat with white stripes leaped up at the girls along with the dogs. "Marmalade thinks he's canine," Mrs. Rogers told them. She unwrapped a skinny brown creature from her shoulder and added, "Unlike Kula here, who knows he's a ferret. Anyway, come on in and meet the others!"

"Human, or animal?" George joked, as she patted the wiggly ferret.

"Both," Mrs. Rogers said. She led them into the wide front hall. At the bottom of the mahogany stairway, the banister post was carved to look like a fox. Gothic archways in the hall opened onto parlors and a dining room, where campers were busy snacking, playing board games, watching videos on two TVs, and playing hide-and-go-seek. The furniture, a mix of antiques and tag sale finds, lay scattered in a comfortable jumble around the rooms. It was clear to Nancy that kids and animals ruled in this house!

"Bedtime, kids," Mrs. Rogers proclaimed. A collective groan rose from the campers. "Don't forget—I'm announcing the rally team tomorrow. I'm not going to accept anyone who isn't well rested." With that, the campers began to stop their activities. Within a few minutes, they had assembled at the base of the stairs.

Mrs. Rogers raised her hand for attention. "Before you go up, I have some introductions to make. This is Nancy Drew and George Fayne. As you all know, we lost a counselor this morning, and these ladies are taking her place. I want you kids to behave for them." A sea of curious teenage faces gazed at Nancy and George. Mrs. Rogers finished by asking, "Have any of you seen Tarzan?"

A thin girl with platinum-blond hair said, "He and Inky got into a scuffle, so I put Tarzan in your room. Hope you don't mind."

"Not in the least," Mrs. Rogers said. Turning to Nancy and George, she explained, "Tarzan is my pet monkey, and Inky is my black Lab. They don't get along at all." She shot Inky, curled on a hallway chair, a withering look before leading everyone upstairs. She then retired to her room.

Elsa popped out of a bedroom door to greet Nancy and George. "I thought I heard your voices. I'm so glad you're here! Let me introduce you to the other counselor, James Fenwick—behind you."

Nancy and George turned to see a cute guy with chestnut hair and gray eyes standing in the upstairs hall. "Elsa told me you were coming," he said. "Let me know if you need any help or anything. But please excuse me now; I'm supervising the boys' room, and they seem especially wired tonight." He slipped through a nearby door.

"Everybody's off-the-wall tonight," Elsa said, craning to check out a pillow fight in her room. "They're excited about the team announcement tomorrow. Anyway, Mrs. Rogers asked me to show you to your rooms. You'll be sharing them with some campers."

Once they were farther down the hall, Elsa explained, "Mrs. Rogers has her own bedroom and bathroom on this floor." She pointed to a closed door at the front of the house. "Besides hers, there are four rooms on this floor and four upstairs. And of course, there are bathrooms on every floor." She stopped all of a sudden. "Here are your rooms."

Elsa gestured to two doors across the hall from each other. "George, you're on the left, Nancy, on the right. I'll see you guys in the morning."

Nancy said good night to George and Elsa and went into her room. Three girls, each about sixteen years old, stared at her from their canopied beds. "Hi," Nancy said. "I'm Nancy Drew. I've been assigned to your room."

"We know," said a stocky girl with curly blond hair. "I'm Cordelia Zukerman, by the way."

"Your bed's over there," a tall girl with long braids said, pointing to the corner. "Make yourself comfortable. Oh, and I'm Akiyah Hopkins."

"Nice to meet both of you," Nancy said. Turning to the third girl, who was dark-haired with high cheekbones and a shy smile, Nancy said, "What is your name?"

"Juliana Suarez," she answered softly. The girl with the broken girth, Nancy remembered.

"How many campers are there in all?" Nancy asked, tossing her duffel bag on her bed.

"There are supposed to be twenty-four campers, three counselors, and Mrs. Rogers," Akiyah explained. "But today we lost three kids and a counselor and added one kid and you two counselors. I've lost count!"

"How does Mrs. Rogers take care of so many kids?" Nancy asked.

"The three C's: cooks, cleaners, and counselors," Cordelia said flatly. "They keep the camp running so Mrs. Rogers doesn't have a heart attack from too much work. Still, this place can get pretty wild, especially in the evenings, when we kids and all the animals are thrown together. Did you see Flower, Mrs. Rogers's raccoon? Every night she escapes from her cage to sleep in the living room fireplace. That's pretty weird, if you ask me."

Nancy arched a brow. "Things do seem kind of eccentric around here—in a fun way," she added.

"Camp is tons of fun," Juliana said. Her face clouded over. "At least, until yesterday . . ."

"I heard about your saddle," Nancy said. "I'm glad you're okay. By the way, do you guys know Clare Wu well?"

Nancy's roommates exchanged glances. "You mean Clare 'Snotty' Wu who thinks she's so pretty and cool?" Cordelia said. "Why are you curious about her?"

"She was yelling at this boy earlier," Nancy explained. "I think his name is Rafael. I just wondered if she was always so chilly."

Akiyah snorted. "She was always a tough girl. None of us like her at all."

"She has this clique of friends," Cordelia said. "Some of them are George's roommates. Clare is sharing a room upstairs with a couple more 'Clare worshipers.' I don't know why anyone likes her—but they do. Of course, none of her friends talk to us, so I can't find out why they think she rules." She threw up her hands. "It's a mystery."

Nancy pulled a nightgown and toothbrush from her duffel bag and tossed them on her bed. "Not really. Some people probably like her because she's rich and pretty. They think she has power, and that some of it will rub off on them." Nancy was tempted to ask whether any of the girls had seen Clare snooping around Juliana's saddle or messing with the horses' feed, but she didn't want to plant the idea that Clare might be guilty. Instead, she asked, "Did you guys notice whether Clare was here around dinnertime?"

"Clare's been away since the late afternoon," Akiyah said. "I don't think she's even back yet. She got special permission to spend the evening in town with her brother. He's leaving for college tomorrow."

"Does she drive?" Nancy asked.

"Yup—her own little convertible Porsche her daddy gave her," Cordelia said in a mocking tone.

Nancy bit her lip. So Clare could have followed her back home and soaped her windshield. But what did Clare have against Green Spring?

"Hey, what's that smell?" Juliana asked, sitting up in bed.

Nancy sniffed. "Smoke!" she cried. She rushed to the open window where the breeze was blowing in the hideous smell. As she looked outside and down the hill, she saw orange and yellow flames billowing from a corner of the barn. "The barn's on fire. The horses!" Nancy shouted, springing out the door.

5

Tack Attack

Nancy ran out of the room and pounded on Mrs. Rogers's door. "Mrs. Rogers, wake up! The barn's on fire!"

The door flung open, and a bleary-eyed Mrs. Rogers came running out, still shuffling on her loafers. "I just called the fire department. We've got to save the horses!"

Kids were streaming out of their rooms and throwing on robes and shoes. "Campers!" Mrs. Rogers barked. "You stay here, for your own safety. Counselors, come with me."

James hurried out of his room wearing jeans and an inside-out T-shirt. Elsa, George, and Nancy joined him on the stairs, still in their regular clothes.

In less than two minutes they were evacuating the horses from the barn.

"Just open the stall doors that lead into the field," Mrs. Rogers commanded, throwing open Derby's door. The flames sizzled and crackled nearby. "If the horses refuse to come out, blindfold them with these and force them to follow you." She handed a bunch of rags to each counselor.

Nancy was relieved to see that the fire was confined to the corner feed room, but with the breeze blowing and hay and straw everywhere, the flames would surely spread fast.

Tristram bolted by Nancy into the field as the welcome sound of sirens blared through the night. Seconds later, two fire trucks were hosing down the barn.

Smoke filled the air as the firefighters worked. When the last ember had finally fizzled out, the fire chief turned off his hose and strode over to Mrs. Rogers. "Lucky you called us so quick, Mrs. R.," he said. "We got here just in time. Most of the damage is confined to that corner." He pointed to the feed room.

Mrs. Rogers sighed. "I can't thank you enough. It's your prompt work that saved the barn." She shuddered. "Thank goodness it's the feed room that burned, and not a horse's stall." She led everyone over to the charred room to inspect it. The sharp smell of burnt grain filled Nancy's nose.

"Obviously the feed is destroyed," Mrs. Rogers said, looking around. "We'll need to get more before the horses' breakfast tomorrow. But I was lucky. Nothing aside from the wall next to the feed was destroyed."

The fire chief walked over to a pile of ashes and flakes of burlap. "Looks like the fire started here," he said.

"We piled empty feed sacks in that corner," Mrs. Rogers explained. "Also, Green Spring's flag was there." A shred of green and gold fabric on a bent metal pole poked out of the ashes. "Can you tell how it started?"

The fire chief knelt down and studied the area. Then he asked Mrs. Rogers whether lamps and other electrical devices had been in the room.

"Just an overhead lightbulb," she declared.

"Unfortunately, I can't tell how the fire started," the chief said. "If someone set it with a match, there'd be no evidence left."

Mrs. Rogers blanched. "'Set it?' You mean on purpose?"

As they spoke, Nancy scanned the room for clues. If someone had set the fire on purpose, it was possible a clue had been dropped. If it was metal, it could have survived the fire. But she only saw charred wood, ashes, and bent metal feed cans. Nancy moved by the sooty windowsill to study the contents of the cans, but a flicker behind the broken window made her stop. Someone's shadow?

Before she could blink, it was gone. Nancy ran outside. The full moon lit up the field in which a group of frightened horses huddled. Beyond the field, dark woods rose against the sky. Whoever had slipped by the window had disappeared into the night.

Maybe it was one of the firefighters checking for sparks, Nancy thought. She hurried to the other side of the barn, where a group of firefighters was busy making sure no embers had spread. "Were any of you guys just around on the other side?" Nancy asked them.

One man glanced around at the crew and said, "Nope. We're all accounted for here, except the chief—he's with Mrs. Rogers."

Just then, Nancy remembered the note that Bess had opened at *The Horse's Mouth.* It had charged Green Spring's barn with not being up to fire safety standards. "Does this barn get inspected every year for fire safety?" Nancy asked the same man.

"Sure does," he answered. "In fact, we inspected this barn about four months ago. It was up to code, no doubt about it. Mrs. Rogers keeps this place ship-shape. The fire damage tonight might have been a lot worse otherwise."

Nancy thanked the man for the information, then walked back to the feed room. She ran into George on the way.

"The fire chief's wrapping things up with Mrs. Rogers," George told Nancy. "She told the counselors to go back to the house. The horses will stay in the field for the night, just to be on the safe side. At least it's nice out."

Nancy and George strolled back to the house side by side, with Elsa and Jimmy straggling behind. "That fire was pretty suspicious," Nancy said. "I saw a shadow at the feed room window. I think someone was spying—maybe to find out how bad the damage was."

George shook her head. "Those horses could have been killed. I mean, who would set a fire like that on purpose?"

"We know this person doesn't care about horses or people. Whoever's doing all this is out to wreck Green Spring no matter what's in the way." Nancy then recalled a possible clue. "Clare Wu was away from camp tonight, supposedly seeing her brother. She could have soaped my windshield—and also set the fire."

"You think she would have put her own horse in danger?" George wondered. "That's as low as you can go."

"We'll have to find out where her horse's stall is.

Maybe she was planning to free him if the fire got too close." Nancy opened the front door of the house to the sight of petrified campers grouped in the hall.

"Are the horses okay?" Akiyah asked in a whisper.

Nancy reassured the kids about the horses and the barn. Despite her soothing words, she could tell the campers' nerves were rattled. As Nancy tried to calm one girl, she abruptly turned away. "I don't care what anyone says—I'm *so* out of here. Mom and Dad can just come and get me tonight." She stalked to a telephone at the back of the hall.

As the other campers trudged back up the stairs, a pair of gold almond-shaped eyes caught Nancy's attention. Clare was back from her brother's.

Light streamed in through the window and woke Nancy at seven. Juliana and Akiyah were already putting on blue jeans and ankle-length riding boots. Juliana zipped a pair of brown suede chaps over her worn jeans.

"Nancy, will you please wake Cordelia?" Akiyah asked. "She'll get mad at us if we do it. You're an authority figure, so she won't mess with you."

Nancy smiled and straggled out of bed to wake Cordelia. Then she put on blue jeans, boots, and a sky-blue T-shirt that matched her eyes. A delicious smell wafted into their room. "Pancakes," Cordelia announced, hurrying into the hall in unlaced boots.

"We'd better get down there quick."

Sure enough, a pile of steaming blueberry pancakes awaited everyone. Sounds of giggling and jokes rose through the dining room as campers and counselors ate. After taking a bite of a pancake and swallowing it down, Nancy leaned over to George. "The mood here seems much better today," she whispered.

"The rally team is being announced at lunch," George said. "Everyone's really excited about that."

Still using a low voice, Nancy said, "I want to search Clare's car after breakfast. I'm curious to see if there's evidence of soap or matches."

Once she was finished, Nancy cleared her plate and headed to the kitchen to find Mrs. Rogers. She wanted to ask her permission to search Clare's car. As Nancy passed through the pantry she was startled by a high-pitched chattering noise coming from the far corner.

"Nancy, meet Tarzan," Mrs. Rogers said, bustling out of the kitchen. "Most people think he's kind of obnoxious, but who knows? Maybe you two will be friends."

A gray monkey was attached to a playpen post by a collar and leash. He shook his fist at Nancy and screamed. "Somehow I don't think we click," Nancy said wryly.

Mrs. Rogers picked him up, and he wrapped his arms affectionately around her. "Don't worry, Nancy, you're not alone. For some reason, he tolerates me."

With Mrs. Rogers's permission—and she got it very easily—Nancy searched Clare's car. Unfortunately, she found no clues. She reported back to the director in her office. "If Clare *is* guilty, what could be her motive for harming your camp?" Nancy asked.

Mrs. Rogers puckered her brow. "Maybe she resents the scholarship program because my quota kept her from making last year's rally team. I have a rule that at least two spots go to scholarship campers."

After their conversation Nancy joined up with George, who was helping a boy measure grain in a temporary feed room set up in an empty stall. Once the boy left to feed his horse, George started speaking. "Elsa told me the camp schedule today. After the kids feed their horses and clean out stalls, they divide into two groups, Green and Gold—Green Spring's colors. This morning, I'm helping Elsa coach stadium jumping to the Green Group in the outdoor ring, while you, James, and Mrs. Rogers supervise the Gold Group cleaning tack and grooming horses. We switch activities in the afternoon."

"Thanks for the drill, Sergeant Fayne," Nancy joked.

George laughed, and the two friends parted ways. Nancy headed for the tack room and began to set out cans of saddle soap, sponges, and buckets of water for the Gold Group. After a few minutes, Rafael Estevez appeared in the doorway. "Hi, Nancy," he said. "I just finished feeding Clown and cleaning out his stall. The schedule says the Gold Group does tack now."

"The schedule never lies," Nancy declared. "Come on in, Rafael. I got the supplies ready."

But Rafael didn't reply. He was gaping at something behind her. Nancy whirled around. She saw only racks of saddles attached to the wall—nothing the least bit strange.

Rafael pushed past her and grabbed a saddle off a rack labeled CLOWN. His hands shook as he lowered it, and in a flash Nancy saw exactly what was wrong: The saddle had been ruined—gouged by a sharp object. Ugly scratches covered the once smooth caramel color of the leather seat.

Rafael threw his saddle on the floor and collapsed on a nearby stool. He buried his face in his hands. Nancy wanted to try to comfort him, but she knew she had to tell Mrs. Rogers what happened immediately. "I'll be right back, Rafael," she said, patting his shoulder. Then she hurried into the office next door.

"This is outrageous!" Mrs. Rogers said after Nancy had delivered the bad news. "Rafael worked an extra summer job to buy that saddle." Like a tiny gray tornado, Mrs. Rogers whirled into the tack room with

Nancy following. As Mrs. Rogers studied the saddle and questioned Rafael, Nancy searched the room for clues. A glint on the floor under the saddle rack caught her eye.

Nancy picked up the object. It was long, sharp, and thin, and it gleamed wickedly in the morning sun that poured through the window. But it wasn't a knife. It was a sterling silver letter opener, with the initials JB monogrammed on the handle.

6

A Mixed-up Message

"Look what I found," Nancy said.

Mrs. Rogers and Rafael looked carefully at the letter opener in Nancy's palm. Gingerly, the camp director took it, and Rafael rose from his stool to get a better look.

"Can you think of anyone who has the initials JB?" Nancy asked.

Mrs. Rogers pursed her lips. After a moment, she said, "There are three people at camp who have the first initial J—James Fenwick, Juliana Suarez, and Jessie Greenstein. And there's one camper with a last initial of B—Todd Brown. But no one with that combination." She studied the letter opener, holding it up to the light. Her eyes widened. "JB," she murmured, “I wonder if this could belong to Josh Bryant.”

“Josh Bryant?” Nancy asked. “Isn’t he the neighbor you mentioned yesterday? The one who had the party where you met my dad?”

“Sure is,” Mrs. Rogers said. “Although ‘neighbor’ may be the wrong word. His farm is next to mine, but it takes a good half hour to ride there on horseback. The Kinderhook Creek separates our properties.”

“Has he been over here recently?” Nancy asked.

“He came to the barn yesterday morning.” She sighed. “It’s a complicated story. See, Josh runs his own pony club and summer camp. But it’s not a well-run program, and frankly, the campers don’t seem very happy there. Josh is often losing kids to my program. My camp seems more popular.” She smiled at Rafael. “You can be the judge of my words, Rafael. Am I bragging, or being unfair?”

“No way, Mrs. Rogers!” Rafael retorted. “Even if Mr. Bryant had a scholarship program and I could go there, I wouldn’t. That place is a joke.”

Some kids showed up at the tack room door. “The Gold Group has tack cleaning, right?” a girl asked.

“Yes,” Mrs. Rogers said, sweeping Rafael’s saddle behind her back before anyone could see the damage. “Why don’t you kids get started here while I finish my conversation with Nancy and Rafael in my office. Nancy has set everything up for you." The campers left to get started.

In Mrs. Rogers's office, Nancy asked, "So why was Mr. Bryant at Green Spring yesterday?"

"To take back a horse he'd lent me," Mrs. Rogers replied. "He had a fit because Katie O'Donovan ditched his camp for mine, so he came to retrieve Goldbug to get back at me. Those were his very words. I would have been short a horse if Katie hadn't brought her own."

"Katie O'Donovan?" Nancy said. The name sounded familiar.

"She's a new camper. Arrived yesterday," Mrs. Rogers explained. "You might have met her up at the house. I believe she's in Elsa's room." Nancy had heard a lot of names mentioned during breakfast conversation, but she couldn't put a face to all of them yet.

"Why did Katie leave the other camp?" Nancy asked.

Mrs. Rogers shook her head. "It's a shame, really. Katie was Josh's favorite camper. She's a terrific rider, and she owns a star horse called Black Comet. But she left because his riding instruction disappointed her. Josh just couldn't get his act together to provide a challenge for a rider like her. I never recruited Katie, but Josh is the grudge-bearing type. He blames me for her leaving." She smiled slightly.

"Anyway, I doubt I'll be invited to another party of his anytime soon."

Nancy glanced from Mrs. Rogers's face to the letter opener in her palm. "So Mr. Bryant was here to take back his horse. But why would he have brought his letter opener with him?"

Mrs. Rogers shrugged. "Beats me. Unless he brought it here to vandalize a saddle in revenge for losing Katie." Her eyes darted toward the saddle rack. "I have a thought, Nancy. Black Comet's saddle is next to Clown's. Could Josh have meant to harm Katie's saddle, but got Rafael's by mistake?"

Nancy shot a look at the saddle racks, each one specifically labeled with the horse's name. "It would be hard to mix them up," Nancy said. "Maybe he meant to hurt Katie's saddle, but then heard someone coming and settled for Rafael's. It's a little closer to the door."

Mrs. Rogers nodded. "That makes sense." She turned to Rafael. "I feel responsible for your saddle, so please don't worry about replacing it—I'll handle that. Maybe Nancy could drive you to Equestrian Outfitters, the riding shop in River Heights, either today or tomorrow." She checked the wall clock. "Meanwhile, it's time to switch activities with the Green Group. Stadium jumping is next."

Ten minutes later, Nancy and Mrs. Rogers had joined James at one of the outdoor rings. Several

Gold Group riders had already congregated at the gate on their horses. Nancy studied the jumps in the ring. They included multicolored poles and barrels, imitation hedges and chicken coops, and a large white board painted with a blue and red bull's-eye. The first horse to make the round was Clown, with Rafael riding on a borrowed saddle.

Nancy and James cheered him on, but when Clown approached the bull's-eye, he skidded to the side and refused to jump it. James ducked through the ring fence to give Rafael some pointers. On the next try, Clown sailed over the bull's-eye beautifully.

One by one, the rest of the Gold Group campers took the jumps. Many of the horses were fine on the course, but some were skittish like Clown. "Horses really have their own personalities, just like us," James told Nancy. "Some freak out at these jumps. Others just want to get back to the barn and eat hay. Like Victoria here."

Nancy watched Victoria, Clare Wu's red roan mare, execute a perfect round. The moment Clare finished, Mrs. Rogers clapped Nancy and James on the back. "Time for lunch," she declared. "It's served at the house. I'm announcing the rally team, so the atmosphere's going to be tense."

"Was it a hard decision—picking the team?" Nancy asked.

"It was especially difficult this year," Mrs. Rogers

admitted. "We had some very good riders with miserable horses, and some not-so-great riders with wonderful horses. I did my best to choose a strong team. I only hope the kids who didn't make the team won't be too upset."

A half hour later, all the campers and counselors were eating lunch served buffet-style under a tent next to Mrs. Rogers's house. As Nancy and George sat down at a table with their plates full of pasta salad and hot dogs, Nancy felt the tension mounting over who made the team. A timid girl with wavy brown hair and glasses sat next to Nancy. She pushed the food around on her plate without eating it.

Nancy and George introduced themselves. "I'm Katie O'Donovan," the girl said without making eye contact. She stopped speaking as Mrs. Rogers walked up to the front of the tent and raised a hand to signal quiet.

The teens leaned toward her, their faces full of eagerness and dread. Mrs. Rogers began. "I'd like to congratulate all you campers on the fabulous improvement in your riding skills. From the beginning of camp until now, your progress has been amazing. You should all be proud, proud, proud! The rally team was very hard to choose this year because we had so many strong contenders. Anyway, I won't keep you in suspense any longer." She took a dramatic pause. "I'll start by announcing the team captain: Akiyah Hopkins!"

A burst of applause and cheers rang through the tent as Akiyah joined Mrs. Rogers. Mrs. Rogers gave her a warm hug. "Akiyah is a superb rider," she went on, "and I'm sure she'll make a great team captain. I'm stepping aside now so she can announce her teammates." Mrs. Rogers handed Akiyah an envelope and told her to read from the paper inside.

"Just like the Oscars," George murmured to Nancy.

With trembling fingers, Akiyah ripped open the envelope. Everyone hushed. She drew out the paper and scanned it. Her face tensed.

"No way can I announce this," she breathed. She dropped the note as if it were poison. It flew up in the gentle breeze, then landed facedown on the grass outside the tent.

7

Swept Away

Mrs. Rogers bent down and snatched up the note. Then she fished for her spectacles in her skirt pocket and jammed them onto her face. She squinted at the paper in her hand.

Suddenly her eyes hardened. She crumpled the paper angrily and thrust it into her pocket. "Girls and boys," she began, holding up her hand for silence. But the campers had erupted in a flurry of questions and speculations, and it took a moment to gather their attention.

"I wonder what that note said," George whispered to Nancy.

"You and me both," Nancy said. "We'll ask Mrs. Rogers when we're alone with her and can talk about the case."

"Excuse me!'" Mrs. Rogers shouted. She took a whistle out of her pocket and blew it. Everyone instantly hushed. "That's more like it! Anyway, I'm sorry to tell you kids that someone substituted a very inappropriate message for the names of the team. I'd like to postpone the announcement of the team until dinner tonight, when we're in a better mood to celebrate. We'll break up now into our regular afternoon activities. I believe the Gold Group has dressage, while the Green Group swims. Later there's cross-country for both groups."

A groan of disappointment filled the tent. Nancy watched Mrs. Rogers trudge into the house carrying an empty salad bowl and a platter of cookie crumbs. The campers began clearing their plates in silence. Everyone seemed too stunned to speak. Nancy and George followed Mrs. Rogers inside with empty pitchers and plates of leftover watermelon slices.

Nancy and George set the dishes on the kitchen counter where Mrs. Rogers had cleared a space. "Thank you so much for your help, girls," she said. She glanced sideways at the cook, who was putting food away. "Let's go into the dining room," she murmured. "I want some privacy while we discuss the note."

The girls sat down beside Mrs. Rogers at the dining room table. "Let me know what you make of this, Nancy," she said, pulling the crumpled paper from her pocket.

Nancy scanned the message, with George looking on. "Close down your camp—or tragedy will strike!" it read.

Nancy handed the paper back to Mrs. Rogers. "This message is threatening more danger. I think we should call the police. But I'll continue with my investigation."

"I'll call them right away," Mrs. Rogers said. Just then, two girls who were fourteen years old entered the room. One girl looked defiant, and the other was rubbing tears from her eyes.

"Mrs. Rogers, Rebecca and I want to go home," the first girl said. "It's getting too creepy around here. Camp ends tomorrow, anyway."

"I'm really scared here," Rebecca whimpered.

Mrs. Rogers looked crushed, but she forced a smile. "I'm sorry you girls want to leave. But by all means, call your parents to bring you home if you feel in danger. I think you're safe here, though. And I'm about to call the police, to ensure our safety."

Rebecca shuddered. "The police? Things must be even worse than I'd thought. I'd like to call Mom and Dad right now, if you don't mind."

As Mrs. Rogers led them into the kitchen, Nancy and George exchanged glances. "If I don't solve this case soon, Mrs. Rogers won't have a camp," Nancy said gravely.

"We need more clues," George said, "and more suspects. Clare's our only one."

"She and JB," Nancy said. She briefed George on Rafael's saddle, and finding the letter opener with the JB monogram. Just as she finished her story, Mrs. Rogers returned to the room.

"Chief McGinnis is on his way here with an associate, Officer Rivken," Mrs. Rogers explained. "Unfortunately, Rebecca and Natalie have gone upstairs to pack." She threw up her hands in a weary gesture. "I guess the only thing for us to do now is get on with our afternoon activities."

Chief McGinnis soon showed up with Officer Rivken, a slim, dark-haired young man with alert brown eyes. Nancy, who was helping the Gold Group prepare for dressage, waved to the officers as they approached the ring. "I can give you all the information I have so far," she offered.

"Don't blow your cover by talking to us for too long," Chief McGinnis warned. "Mrs. Rogers has already given us the lowdown."

"My cover's blown already," Nancy said. She told the officers about the soaped message on her windshield. "But you're right, Chief McGinnis. It's better if most of the kids don't realize I'm a detective."

Officer Rivken nodded in agreement. "If they feel like you're a regular person, you'll catch more gossip from them. And the more information you can get, the better."

Nancy told them her suspicions about Clare, and also about finding the letter opener. Then the policemen set off to search the house and barn for clues.

The Gold Group finished its dressage session with Rafael taking Clown through his paces. Nancy watched the horse execute tight circles and loops in various gaits, from a walk, to a trot, to a slow canter. Letters posted around the ring marked places where the horse should change its gait.

Rafael shifted in his saddle, giving his horse subtle commands. Every movement of horse and rider was pitch perfect. "It's like a dance, like an old-fashioned minuet done by a horse," Nancy whispered to James, who was coaching.

"I prefer stadium jumping and cross-country," James said. "They're more exciting. But dressage is just as important to the overall rally score."

Suddenly they heard a voice behind them. Nancy recognized Clare's nasal tone. Turning, she saw Clare talking to a blond girl as they sat on their horses waiting for dressage to finish. "Will Rafael ever get Clown to go from a walk directly into a canter? He always lets him trot in between," Clare complained.

"Give him a break, Clare," the blond girl said. "Clown is Mrs. Rogers's horse, anyway. Rafael isn't used to him the way you're used to Victoria."

Clare rolled her eyes. "I don't care, Emmy. He thinks he's this great rider and he's not. I'm glad his saddle got trashed. Serves him right for being such a jerk."

"Wow, Clare, stop right there. That's harsh," the blond girl said. "Anyway, Rafael's finishing up, and he was the last of our group to go. It's our turn to swim." The girls took off for the barn at a brisk trot. Nancy and James exchanged glances.

"That Clare is something, huh?" he said.

"At least her friend told her off," Nancy remarked.

"Are you kidding?" James said wryly. "Emily's comment meant nothing to Clare. Clare never clues in when she's being dissed. I guess she thinks she's too cool for criticism. It goes right over her head. Though I don't now how, because it's so big."

Nancy laughed. "Anyway, it's a hot day. I'm looking forward to that swim." With that, she followed Rafael out of the ring.

Swimming and cross-country practice went smoothly that afternoon. At the end of the day Nancy returned to the house to shower. Dinner was informal, but Nancy put on a short, peach-colored skirt, white tank top, and sandals. It was just so hot. She swept her reddish-blond hair off her neck and secured it with a black elastic band.

Downstairs, she found George in white jeans and a black tank top serving herself tomato salad and a cheeseburger. "Get in line quick, Nan, before the hordes arrive," George advised.

Nancy slipped behind George just before a group of campers streamed into the tent. The two girls took seats at one of the picnic tables and began to eat. Nancy could tell that everyone was eagerly waiting for Mrs. Rogers to attempt once again to announce the team.

The camp director arrived in the midst of a dog pack. They all made their way to the front of the tent. "They want dinner, too," she explained as the dogs panted and wiggled around her. "But I don't want to keep you kids in suspense any longer. This time, we don't have a list to read. I've *told* Akiyah who her teammates are. She'll make the announcement now."

As Mrs. Rogers sat down from the small podium, Akiyah stepped up. "I'm proud to announce the Green Spring Pony Club's thirtieth annual rally team. Besides myself, we have"—she cleared her throat, then finished—"Katie O'Donovan, Rafael Estevez, and Clare Wu—with Cordelia Zukerman as stable manager."

Cheers and claps erupted through the tent as the rest of the team moved up to the front and joined Akiyah. There were only a few muffled moans of disappointment. As the team thanked Mrs. Rogers, Nancy leaned toward George. "I'm pretty full—and right now I'd really like to search Clare's room while I've got the chance."

"I'll save you a Popsicle," George promised. "Grape or orange?"

"Orange," Nancy said, smiling. "Thanks, George. And I'll let you know what I find." After clearing her plate, Nancy went upstairs. She remembered that Clare's room was on the third floor.

Nancy reached the third-floor hall without being seen by anyone. She peered into the room nearest the stairs. Her heart beat faster. Taped onto one of the dresser mirrors were several snapshots of Clare riding Victoria. *This is it!* Nancy thought, excited.

A sudden gust of wind whipped through an open window and swirled the pages of a comic book lying on a nearby table. Nancy glanced outside. Black clouds covered the sky, and a streak of lightning zipped to the ground. The world lit up like an X ray, then instantly darkened. Nancy had to turn on a light to search Clare's dresser—and she knew she had to work fast. Once it started raining, the campers would come inside.

The top two drawers of the dresser held clothes, but the third drawer was a jumble of papers, letters, more snapshots, and a notebook with Clare's name on the front. Nancy picked it up. On the first page, the words MY DIARY were written in capital letters.

But the rest of the page was in code! Not exactly pig latin, Nancy decided, but close.

Lightning streaked through the sky again, and the lights flickered. Gasps came from downstairs as the electricity died. Nancy bit her lip in frustration. Now it was too dark to read, much less decipher Clare's code. She put the notebook back and shut the drawer. Why would Clare bother to write in code if she wasn't guilty of *something*?

A refreshing breeze woke Nancy the next morning. Storms from the night before had wiped out all the heat. At breakfast, Mrs. Rogers announced that the team would separate from the rest of the campers for intensive practice. They'd leave for the rally tomorrow.

As she helped clear the breakfast dishes, Nancy told Mrs. Rogers about Clare's diary. "I'm getting nowhere with Clare, Mrs. Rogers," she added. "I'd like to widen my investigation. Maybe George and I could ride over to Josh Bryant's house and hunt around for clues. I'll bring the letter opener and ask him if it's his."

"Oh Nancy, be careful!" Mrs. Rogers cried. "Josh Bryant can be a spirited, mean man if ever there was one. Also, if you go on horseback, you'll have to cross the Kinderhook Creek that separates our farms. After last night's storm, the water will be turbulent." She pursed her lips. "Come into the kitchen with me—I'll draw you a map. I know a shallow spot where you should be able to cross the creek safely."

An hour later, Nancy and George were on their way to Josh Bryant's farm on Tristram and Derby. George had offered to carry a small backpack filled with bottled water, halters, lead ropes, and the silver letter opener. The girls rode through fields and down forest trails, always following Mrs. Rogers's map that Nancy had tucked in the waistband of her chaps. About twenty minutes into the ride, the woodland trail forked. "Which way?" Nancy whispered. She stopped Tristram and consulted her map. "We're in a patch of woods called Thunder Forest," she told George behind her, "but I don't see a fork on the map."

"I guess Mrs. Rogers forgot to put it on," George said.

Nancy shrugged. "The trail on her map seems to veer right, so let's go that way and see what happens."

A few minutes later, she and George heard rushing water. "We must be close to the creek," George called. Sure enough, the trail soon came to a steep bank leading down to a river about forty feet wide. *Mrs. Rogers was right,* Nancy thought. The creek was totally raging. Muddy water swirled over rocks, and the noise made it difficult for the two girls to talk.

Nancy had to shout over the rushing water. "Look to the right, George. There's a waterfall." About fifty yards away, spray shot up toward the sky where the creek crashed over a rocky cliff.

"If this is the shallow place Mrs. Rogers described, I'd hate to see what she calls deep," George said.

"It might be shallow. We just can't see the bottom because of the mud," Nancy said. "But just to be safe, let's go one at a time." Tristram hesitated at the water's edge, but Nancy urged him on. If the water was shallow like Mrs. Rogers had said, Nancy knew the horse would be strong enough to cross.

Tristram plunged in. The water splashed around his knees, and Tristram stepped carefully. "We're halfway there, boy," she told him soon, eyeing the trail on the other side.

Tristram tentatively took another step, but he slipped. Nancy grabbed his mane as Tristram's legs thrashed against the swift current. He struggled to swim forward, but it was no use. A wave of brown water crashed over a rock and swept Tristram and Nancy downstream. The spray from the falls fell on Nancy's face in a fine mist as they shot toward the precipice.

[illegible]

[illegible]

[illegible]

[illegible]

8

Hanging by a Thread

Nancy yanked the reins, hoping to head Tristram away from the falls. But no matter how hard she tried to guide him, the deep churning water pushed them forward. The roar of the falls grew louder and louder. Tristram panicked and flailed his legs as he spun in a whirlpool.

Nancy shot a look at George, who was galloping alongside her friend on the bank. George was shouting something, but her words were lost in the thunder of water crashing on rocks.

Suddenly George pointed to something ahead in the water between the riverbank and Nancy.

Nancy squinted. The spray was blurring her vision, but she forced herself to calm down and look. And then she understood. George had been trying to tell her about a rock—a flat, smooth rock that was barely higher than the water. It rose like a staircase about ten feet ahead. She tightened the reins. If she could calm Tristram she might be able to get him to climb onto it.

As she tried to guide Tristram, he resistantly pulled on his bit. The current sped around both sides of the rock, and Tristram was going with it. In seconds, they would sweep past the rock and over the falls.

Nancy stared at the rock, her eyes like lasers. She concentrated every ounce of her energy on forcing Tristram toward it. The rock was their last resort.

With his legs thrashing, Tristram stumbled onto a ledge below the water. "Good boy," Nancy breathed. "Get your footing." The ledge below the water was like a stepping-stone onto the larger rock. Nancy soothed Tristram so he could calm down and find solid ground. The horse swayed, his foothold precarious. But in moments he'd scrambled onto the ledge with all four legs.

"Steady, boy," Nancy said. She could feel his huge body shudder, and then balance itself on the underwater ledge. "Okay, now!" She slackened the reins, and Tristram surged forward. In one great leap, he bounded onto the rock.

Tristram shivered with fear as the river swirled below him. Nancy wondered if the panicky animal might bolt, plunging them both back into the water. Before Tristram had a chance to react, Nancy tightened the reins and faced him toward the creek bank where George and Derby waited tensely.

"Jump, Tristram!" Nancy commanded, slackening the reins. Tristram sprang toward the bank, barely making it as the water roiled beneath them.

"Whew!" George said, smiling with relief. "I'm so glad that rock was there."

"You and me both," Nancy said, after she'd caught her breath. "If you hadn't spotted it, Tristram and I would be over those falls by now. The rock was really hard to see since it was the same muddy brown as the water."

George shot her a wry grin. "We should have taken the left hand fork, huh?"

Nancy smiled as she turned toward the trail. "Well, George, let's go find it. The sooner we get to Mr. Bryant's fields, the better. I need to get in some sunlight, quick. I'm soaked!"

A few minutes later, they'd swung left onto the other path. It soon spilled them onto the creek bank again, but here the incline was very gradual and the river was narrower and much less turbulent. Nancy eased a quivering Tristram into the water, and the two horses had no problem fording it.

The trail continued through thick pine trees, and the girls pressed their horses into a canter. They were happy to finally reach a sunny meadow filled with butterflies. The girls lingered in the heat, and when Nancy felt drier, they galloped to the other side of the field. A farmhouse rose into view, its stone walls half hidden by ivy. Nancy and George passed through a gate into a gravel driveway overgrown with weeds. "Perfect," Nancy said. "There's no car in the driveway. Maybe Josh Bryant isn't here."

George held up crossed fingers as she gazed at the house and the nearby barn. "This place is weird," she said. "The house is a major mansion, but a bunch of its windows are broken, and the fence in the field is rotting. And look at all those birds' nests in the ivy over the front door." She pointed to the front of the house.

"Gross! I can see why Josh held a fund-raising party," Nancy said. "He could use cash to fix up this joint."

After a bit of light searching of the area surrounding the house, the girls found a section of the fence that seemed sturdy. They slid off their horses, replaced the bridles with the halters they'd brought in George's backpack, and tied Tristram and Derby to the fence with lead ropes. George also handed Nancy the silver letter opener, which Nancy placed in the back pocket of her jeans in case Mr. Bryant returned.

A small, mousy-looking girl of about fourteen

approached them from the barn. A yellow Labrador trotted next to her, wagging his tail in greeting. "Down, Duster!" the girl commanded as the dog began to jump on Nancy and George. "Where are your manners, boy?" she scolded as she gently grabbed his collar. Her gaze fell on the two girls. "Can I help you?"

"Is Mr. Bryant in?" Nancy asked.

"He's out on some errand," the girl said. "But I'm a camper here, so maybe I can help you."

"We just need to talk to Mr. Bryant," Nancy said, smiling. "How do you like camp?"

"Tomorrow is the last day, and it won't be a moment too soon," the girl said bluntly, making a face.

"What do you mean?" Nancy asked.

"This camp is the pits," the girl said. "Instead of teaching us anything useful, Mr. Bryant makes us slave away taking care of his horses. He calls the camp Happy Campers. What a joke! It's more like Labor-on-the-Cheap."

"Have you thought of coming to Green Spring next year?" George asked.

The girl's gray eyes flickered. "I heard that a bunch of weird things were happening there. Otherwise, I'd go there in a minute. See, because no one likes the camp, there are only three kids here this year—not enough to form a rally team. It's such a drag," she moaned.

"I'm sorry," Nancy said. "How did you hear about the stuff going on at Green Spring?"

The girl shrugged. "People talk. You just hear things." She checked her watch. "I'd better go muck out more stalls before Mr. Bryant comes back. He has a vicious temper." She tromped back toward the barn, and Nancy and George exchanged glances.

"This place sounds like not so much fun," George said. "We'd better check out the house before Mr. Bryant gets back. If his temper's as bad as that girl made it out to be, I don't want him to catch us trespassing."

Once inside the enormous house, Nancy and George split up to search for clues. Duster, the dog, followed Nancy. "You've found a new friend," George told Nancy on her way up the creaky stairs.

"Maybe he'll sniff up some clues," Nancy said. She followed Duster through the dining room and into the kitchen. He sat by his food bowl and pricked up his ears. "You're no help," she said, patting his head.

Turning from Duster, Nancy scanned the kitchen counters. Just as her eyes rested on an appointment book, she heard tires crunch on the gravel driveway. She hurried to the kitchen window and peered outside. A large blond man with a sour expression was climbing out of a Jeep. Mr. Bryant, Nancy guessed. She had to find a place to hide fast!

The front door slammed open, and Duster

bounded out of the room. Nancy scanned the kitchen. No closet in sight—just cabinets. *And most of the cabinets are too small to fit me,* Nancy thought. Suddenly she noticed a large cupboard with a sliding door.

Nancy climbed onto the counter and opened the cupboard door. Inside was a platform attached to a rusty cable. *A dumbwaiter,* Nancy thought—*perfect!* Hearing footsteps in the dining room, Nancy didn't waste a second. She scrambled into the dumbwaiter. Its cables creaked with her weight. Just as the steps reached the kitchen, she closed the door.

Nancy crouched in the tiny, dark space. As her eyes adjusted, she saw a thread of light coming through the crack in the door. *I hope George found a place to hide too,* Nancy thought, shifting her weight to keep her foot from falling asleep.

The dumbwaiter wobbled. The cable creaked again. Nancy held her breath. *This thing's about to go,* she realized.

Mr. Bryant hummed to himself as he puttered about the kitchen, opening cabinets, drawers, and what sounded like the refrigerator door.

A sharp crack filled Nancy's ears as a piece of the platform she sat on broke. The wood hurtled down, smacking against the basement floor. Nancy scurried back from the gaping hole.

Light flooded her eyes as the door slid open.

9

Horseplay

Mr. Bryant's face turned red with fury the moment he saw Nancy. He shot an arm into the dumbwaiter and grabbed her by the shoulders. His tiny eyes bored into her as he hauled her out.

Nancy stared at him. He was a stocky man with powerful shoulders, and greasy blond hair combed over a bald spot. She tried to think of an excuse for being in his house, but his glaring eyes made her mind go temporarily blank.

"Are ya spying on me?" he demanded.

"Uh, no, not exactly," Nancy said. She quickly fabricated a story. "See, I'm a counselor at Green Spring Farm, and Mrs. Rogers wanted me and my friend George to do her a favor—"

"I don't need any favors from Madeline Rogers," Mr. Bryant cut in.

"I said a favor *for* her," Nancy said. She felt annoyed. This guy thought the world was all about him! She dug into her back pocket and pulled out the letter opener. "We're returning this for Mrs. Rogers. She thought it might be yours. It's got your initials on it."

Mr. Bryant frowned as he took the opener and inspected it. "This is my letter opener," he admitted. "It's been missing for the past few months—ever since I held that fund-raising party."

"I found it on the floor of the tack room yesterday," Nancy explained. "Mrs. Rogers thought you might have dropped it when you came to Green Spring to pick up your horse."

"I didn't bring it to Green Spring yesterday," Mr. Bryant said. "Why would I bring it with me to pick up a horse?" He scowled at Nancy. "Is Madeline Rogers trying to play me for a fool? I'll bet she stole this letter opener from my desk at the party. After all, she was a guest there. And now her guilt is getting the better of her. She's finally returning it, but she's saying that I left it at her barn."

"It was definitely on the tack room floor," Nancy said.

Mr. Bryant reddened. "Are you contradicting me, girl? Let me remind you that you're trespassing." He turned his head suddenly and scanned the room. "You said you came over with a friend named George. Where is he? Stealing more silver?"

"George is a girl; her real name is Georgia," Nancy explained. "And she, um . . . went to find the rest room."

Mr. Bryant stared at Nancy, judging her words. He tapped the letter opener against his palm. "There's one thing I don't get about your story. If you were really here to return this opener, then why did you need to hide from me?"

Nancy glanced down, searching her brain for a good excuse. Her gaze landed on Duster. "I was hiding . . . because . . . I'm scared of your dog."

Duster wiggled up to Nancy and licked her hand.

"I want you out of my house. And your friend, too. She's been in that rest room long enough." Mr. Bryant pointed the letter opener toward the dining room. Nancy had no choice but to leave.

In the front hall, Nancy called upstairs for George. "I'm all set, George. Let's go!" she said.

"Coming!" said a muffled voice.

While waiting, Mr. Bryant prodded Nancy about how the camp season at Green Spring was going. It was clear from his tone of voice that he really didn't care.

"It's okay," Nancy lied. "And how is your camp season going?"

"Fantastically! It's a much better camp than Green

Spring, of course. Can't you tell from its name? Happy Campers. Who could resist it?" He threw up a hand, implying that anyone who chose Green Spring was an idiot.

"So your camp got its name because everyone here is happy?" Nancy asked.

"Yes indeed," he said. "And I think you're lying about Green Spring. I hear it's especially awful this summer, that it's having some, uh, problems."

"Mrs. Rogers's barn caught on fire the night before last," Nancy told him. "And someone complained to the editor of *The Horse's Mouth* that the barn wasn't up to code. Do you have any idea who would do this stuff?"

"Of course not," he barked. "Why would I? All I know is that Green Spring is way too regimented. Mrs. Rogers keeps her kids on too strict a schedule. They don't have fun because they're too busy. I think my camp is a much happier place."

George jogged down the stairs, just in time to stop Mr. Bryant from insulting Green Spring anymore. Nancy wanted to retort that the kids here didn't seem happy. How could they when he makes them do all the work? But then he'd know they'd been complaining to her, and she didn't want to get them in trouble. She shot George a look. "Let's go, George. Mr. Bryant wants us out of here."

"And don't let me see you snooping around my

farm again," he snarled, remembering his anger. He slammed the front door behind them.

Once outside, the girls untied Derby and Tristram, and replaced their halters with bridles. As they rode back to Green Spring Nancy told George about her conversation with Mr. Bryant, and how mad he was when he discovered her hiding.

When they were back at the farm, the two girls unsaddled their horses, rubbed them down, and then set them loose in a pasture. There was no sign of the campers anywhere. Nancy checked her watch. It was ten minutes to one. Lunch was probably just wrapping up.

Nancy and George hurried up to the house. Sure enough, the kids were clearing their plates and chatting about the upcoming afternoon activities. After Nancy and George had helped themselves to leftovers, Mrs. Rogers pulled them aside. "I'm so glad to see you girls," she said, "but I have some bad news. Akiyah slipped on the side of the pool when the Green Group had swimming. She bruised her left arm."

"That's awful," Nancy said. "She'll still go to the rally, though, right?"

"Yes, thank goodness," Mrs. Rogers said. "She's taking the afternoon off to rest. She'll miss cross-country practice."

"Was it an accident?" George asked. "I mean, you don't suspect sabotage or anything?"

"It definitely *wasn't* an accident," Mrs. Rogers said solemnly. "The side of the pool where she slipped was slick with oil, but no one admits to having spilled any. Someone must have spread it there on purpose."

"Let me check out the pool for clues," Nancy offered. "George, why don't you stay here and eat? You can tell Mrs. Rogers about what we did this morning."

"No problem, Nan," George said. She thrust half her turkey sandwich into Nancy's fingers. "Just do me a favor: don't let this case make you starve."

Nancy took a bite of the sandwich and grinned. "Thanks, George. I'll need every ounce of energy to figure this thing out." She walked through the tent and around the house to the pool. Whoever had mopped up the olive oil up had done an excellent job. Nancy scanned the pool for signs of it but found no traces of oil.

After thoroughly searching the pool area and finding nothing, Nancy cast her mind back to her morning at Happy Campers. *Mr. Bryant had been away from his house,* she remembered. *Had he been sneaking olive oil around Mrs. Rogers's pool?*

Nancy wandered back to the house, munching her sandwich and musing over the case so far. She felt she was stuck in a rut with her suspects and clues. Maybe a change of scene would give her a fresh perspective. She remembered that Rafael was owed a new saddle, and went back to the tent to look for Mrs. Rogers.

Nancy found the camp director talking with Elsa about Akiyah's arm. Once they'd wrapped up their conversation, Nancy said, "Why don't I take Rafael into River Heights so he can buy a new saddle? He'll need a new one for the rally, won't he?"

Mrs. Rogers beamed. "Brilliant idea, Nancy. I feel terrible about forgetting all about it. I've had way too many things on my mind lately. Please take Elsa with you. She knows exactly where Equestrian Outfitters is. And George and James can help me coach cross-country."

"A field trip!" Elsa said. "Let me round up Rafael, and we're out of here."

Forty minutes later, Nancy was parking her Mustang in front of a small shop on a side street in downtown River Heights. EQUESTRIAN OUTFITTERS appeared in black calligraphy on a sign over the door.

Nancy, Elsa, and Rafael climbed out of the car and walked into the store. Elsa and Nancy did a double take. "Bess Marvin!" Elsa said to the girl by the front counter. "I hear you got the job at *The Horse's Mouth.* Do I get a headhunter's fee?"

Bess grinned. "You'll have to take that up with Mr. Blackstone. But I warn you, he's a tough negotiator."

"What brings you here, Bess?" Nancy asked, smiling. "Business or pleasure?"

"Strictly business," Bess replied. "I'm interviewing Charlotte Neroni about the latest riding fashions. She is the owner of Equestrian Outfitters, so naturally she's an expert." Bess introduced everyone to Charlotte. She was an attractive woman in her early thirties with highlighted blond hair and a deep tan.

"So you kids are from Green Spring? Are you having fun there this summer?" she asked.

Nancy, Elsa, and Rafael nodded, not wanting to dwell on Green Spring's troubles.

"My late mother and Madeline Rogers had been best friends," Charlotte went on. "Madeline's a truly lovely woman."

"I'm just curious—do you know a man named Josh Bryant?" Nancy asked. She wanted to get as much information on Mr. Bryant as she could. If Charlotte's mother and Mrs. Rogers had been friends, Charlotte might know some of Mrs. Rogers's neighbors.

Charlotte looked confused. "That's a bit off the topic, isn't it? But I do know him. I went to a fundraiser for his camp at his house a few months ago. But I try to steer clear of him; I hear he's got a wicked temper. Why do you ask?"

"I met him at Green Spring yesterday," Nancy fudged. "And he seemed like such a grouch. So I just wondered how Mrs. Rogers puts up with him as her neighbor."

Charlotte shrugged. "At least he lives on the other side of the valley."

Within a few minutes Rafael had chosen a new saddle. After Elsa had paid the bill with Mrs. Rogers's check, the three said good-bye to Bess and Charlotte and drove back to Green Spring.

Mrs. Rogers greeted them at the barn with a compliment about Rafael's taste in saddles. "I'm happy to report that this afternoon's cross-country practice was uneventful," she told them, "except, of course, that Akiyah couldn't join us. Now, it's almost time for dinner. The theme is Italian, to celebrate our last night of camp!"

The campers ate a hearty dinner of lasagna, spaghetti, and eggplant Parmesan. When they were finished, they headed out to the barn to bed down their horses. As Nancy entered the building to help out, she bumped into Katie O'Donovan. Katie's gray eyes darted wildly, and her wavy brown hair stuck out in a messy halo around her head.

"Nancy, help me!" she begged, gripping Nancy's arm. "Someone has stolen Black Comet!"

10

A Slippery Clue

Nancy gaped at Katie. "Are you sure?" she asked.

"Yes!" Katie moaned. Her wire-rimmed glasses clouded with tears. "Nancy, I never would have quit Happy Campers if I'd known this was going to happen."

Nancy spotted George helping Cordelia lug water into her horse's stall. She motioned her over to them. "George, Black Comet is missing," she said.

George paled. "I'll get Mrs. Rogers right away. She's up at the house." George raced out the door, and Nancy turned back to Katie.

"Tell me what happened," she said.

"Well, when I got here, Black Comet wasn't in his stall, and his door to the field was wide open," Katie explained. "At first I assumed I'd spaced out and forgotten to latch it. Black Comet is smart. Without the latch, he could have pushed it open with his nose. But he wasn't outside."

"Let's go check out the field," Nancy suggested. She gave Katie a reassuring pat on the back. "Don't worry, Katie, I'm sure we'll find him."

Katie took off her glasses and wiped her eyes. Then she managed a shaky smile. "Thanks, Nancy," she said, sticking her glasses back on. "I'll try to keep calm and help you search."

Nancy led Katie into the pasture adjoining the stalls. The late summer dusk had given way to a moonlit night, and the four-acre field was twinkling with fireflies. Two horses—a dappled gray who was easy to see, and a chestnut with a white blaze on his face—were being corralled by their owners. There was no sign of any other horse. Nancy pointed to a huge oak tree down the hill. Despite the bright full moon, Nancy could see past the tree's spreading leaves.

"Black Comet's coat is so dark. Maybe he's hiding out there, and we just can't see him," Nancy said.

But a quick search proved her theory wrong. "Could he have jumped the fence?" Nancy asked. The four-and-a-half-foot fence was made of four horizontal boards painted white.

"He's capable of it," Katie replied. "But he never would."

Nancy looked around the field in every direction. "Look," she said finally, pointing to a gate at the bottom of the hill near the woods. "It's hard to see from here, but I think that gate's ajar."

Katie gasped. "Nancy, I think you're right. Now why didn't I notice?"

Nancy and Katie jogged down the hill to the open gate. On the other side, a trail opened into the woods; the same woods that separated Green Spring Farm from Happy Campers, Nancy observed.

"Whoever took Black Comet is probably riding him down that trail right now," Katie said grimly. Nancy agreed, but she didn't say anything. She didn't want to upset Katie even more.

"Nancy! Katie!" a voice called from the top of the field. The girls turned and saw Mrs. Rogers running toward them, with George and James in tow. "George told me about Black Comet, but I want to know more," Mrs. Rogers said. "Are you sure he's missing, Katie dear?"

Katie and Nancy briefed the others on what had happened. Mrs. Rogers took command of the situation. "Let's organize a search party," she said. "We'll round up some horses for the four of you to ride through the woods. Elsa and I will stay here with the kids. Oh, what a mess! I'm just grateful for the light of the full moon."

It wasn't long before Katie, Nancy, James, and

George were riding down the trail. They carried flashlights, but the bright silvery moonlight that penetrated the forest canopy was enough for them to see by.

After a few minutes, Katie spoke. "Even though we can see the trail, we can't see far through the trees. Black Comet is going to be hard to spot."

Nancy sighed. They'd be lucky if Black Comet was wandering in the woods. It was more likely that a horse thief was riding him down the trail ahead. *In that case,* she thought, *they might end up back at Happy Campers, with Josh Bryant and his famous temper greeting them.*

"Don't get discouraged yet, Katie, we've barely started our search," James said. But his voice carried a note of forced cheer.

Katie turned on her flashlight and pointed it toward the thick woods. "Black Comet!" she called. "Here, boy."

Sticks crackled deep in the woods. An owl hooted.

"Freaky," Katie whispered.

The moon passed behind a cloud, and the woods immediately darkened. Nancy turned on her flashlight to see the trail. "Hey, everyone, let's stop for a moment and listen."

As soon as the four had stopped, Nancy told Katie to call Black Comet again. But Katie's call was answered with total silence.

Once more, Katie called her horse. There was a sudden shuffle of twigs.

"Again!" George urged. This time, a faint whinny rumbled from the depths of the woods.

"Black Comet!" Katie squealed. She turned the horse she was riding toward the trees.

"Don't go in there, Katie," James warned. "You'll get lost. Let him come to you."

The whinny came again—this time, closer. "I'll go with her," Nancy said. "Black Comet's not that far away. We've got flashlights; we'll be fine."

Despite James and George's protests, Nancy led Katie off the path. In just a few moments the trees seemed to close over the trail behind them. There was nothing but unmarked woods in every direction. The trees weren't thick like evergreens, but low-hanging branches made them treacherous for horse-back riders. Nancy and Katie ducked several times to avoid getting knocked off their horses. Nancy suddenly stopped Tristram. "We shouldn't go any farther, or we'll get lost. Do you hear anything now, Katie?"

Once more, Katie called Black Comet. The girls held their breath, listening, but the woods were totally still.

Branches crackled behind them. Nancy jumped in her saddle. She turned just in time to see a large dark shape rushing toward them.

"Black Comet!" Katie cried. The white star on his face reflected in the moonlight, and announced him through the shadows. Katie quickly untied a lead rope from her waist and snapped it onto his halter. "Come on, boy. I'm not going to let you get away again." She bent over his neck and wrapped her arms around him, her face buried happily in his thick black mane.

"Okay, so we found Black Comet," Nancy said. "Now how do we get back to the trail?" The woods on all sides looked the same, dark and threatening. "George!" she called. "James! Where are you guys?"

"Here!" James and George said in unison. Nancy could tell they weren't far. She and Katie set off through the trees, stumbling toward their friends' voices. The two girls quickly reached the trail.

Katie led Black Comet beside her on the ride home. But instead of seeming cheerful, Nancy thought she seemed sad. "Is anything the matter, Katie?" Nancy asked her.

Katie said, twisted in her saddle to look at Nancy. "All these things that are happening at Green Spring are totally creeping me out. I mean, I'll finish my obligations to the rally team, but no way am I coming back next year. What happened to Black Comet is the last straw. I can't believe someone just turned him loose in the woods."

They passed through the lower gate into the

moonlit pasture. Nancy said, "You know, Katie, his disappearance may have nothing to do with all the weird stuff going on at Green Spring. He could have escaped on his own. You even said you weren't sure you'd latched his door. And someone could have left this gate open by mistake. There's no evidence that someone intentionally let him loose."

Katie rolled her eyes. "I just don't buy that, Nancy."

After putting away their horses, the four returned to the house. Mrs. Rogers was thrilled to learn their trip was a success. Nancy went straight to the kitchen for a snack of soda and cookies. On her way, Nancy passed Clare playing Monopoly with her friends in the main parlor.

Was Clare here all along? Nancy wondered, watching the four girls gossiping and giggling. Maybe. But Clare could have slipped down to the barn before dinner to set Black Comet loose. No one would have noticed.

Nancy caught Clare's gaze. Clare's gold eyes narrowed. They reminded Nancy of a tiger's, mean and proud. "Stop staring at me," Clare said coldly.

"Sorry," Nancy said. She continued toward the kitchen, but as she passed through the pantry, her eyes fell on the back stairway.

Clare's busy with her friends. Why don't I search her room again quickly? she thought.

Nancy hurried up the stairs to the third floor. Before peeking into Clare's room, she shot a glance behind her. The coast was clear.

Nancy yanked open the bottom drawer of Clare's bureau. She crossed her fingers that not all of the diary was in code. The diary was in the middle of the drawer, just where it had been yesterday. Nancy picked it up. And then she froze. Underneath the diary was a bottle of olive oil, half full.

11

Rallying toward Disaster

Nancy took the bottle out of the drawer. *Time to ask Clare a few questions,* she thought. But first, she wanted to tell Mrs. Rogers about her discovery.

She found the camp director tending to Tarzan in his pen. The monkey chattered at Nancy as he swung from a pole with his tail. "Stand back, Nancy," Mrs. Rogers warned as she took a cookie from her pocket. "Tarzan hasn't had his bedtime snack, so he's in a foul mood. When he gets like this, he's pure trouble. Though of course he knows better than to bite the hand that feeds him." She handed him the cookie.

Tarzan's manner immediately grew gentler. He was almost smiling as he gazed at it. Mrs. Rogers patted his head, then shut him in his pen as he nibbled away.

She turned to Nancy. "Something tells me you've got news."

Nancy showed her the olive oil. "I found this in Clare's drawer. I think we need to talk to her."

"Definitely," Mrs. Rogers said. "I'll get her. Let's meet in the kitchen where we can be alone."

A minute later, Mrs. Rogers and Nancy were quizzing Clare about the olive oil as they sat at the kitchen table. Several dogs lay at their feet, one in the throes of a dog dream.

Clare's face was closed and sullen. "I'm telling you, that olive oil is for my skin and hair. I take a tablespoon a day. It makes my hair much shinier." She shook back her long dark hair.

Nancy threw her a skeptical look. "Why wasn't it in the drawer when I checked yesterday?"

"Don't ask me. I didn't put it there," Clare said. "I keep it on my shelf in the bathroom. Why would I risk olive oil leaking on my stuff?"

"How much was in the bottle when you last used it?" Nancy asked.

"It was almost full," Clare said. "I bought it when I went to visit my brother the other day."

Nancy and Mrs. Rogers exchanged glances. Either Clare was lying, or someone had borrowed the oil from her bathroom shelf, poured it on the side of the pool, and then returned it to her bureau drawer. Perhaps Claire had been framed.

Nancy thought she'd try another tack. "Why was your journal written in code?" she asked.

Clare eyes flashed with anger. "Why were you snooping in my drawer, Nancy? First you find my olive oil, and now my journal? Excuse me, but my drawer is private!"

"Let me interrupt for a moment, Clare," Mrs. Rogers said. "Nancy is here to find out who is responsible for all these pranks. She's trying to keep Green Spring safe for everyone. You're a suspect because you told me that you resented my camp for its scholarship program. The quota, you said, kept you from making last year's team."

"Sure, I resented the quota, but that doesn't make me a criminal!" Clare retorted. "Anyway, I'm on this year's team, so why would I want to cause trouble for the camp?"

"Just answer Nancy's question please, Clare," Mrs. Rogers said. "Why was your journal in code?"

"So nosy people won't find out my true thoughts," Clare sputtered. She stood up. "Mrs. Rogers, I don't have to stand for this. I'm out of here."

"Sit down, Clare. You're in my house," Mrs. Rogers said, "and if I want to ask you some questions, I will. I could still remove you from the team if you don't cooperate. And if you breathe a word to anyone about Nancy's role here, your career at Green Spring is over."

"I won't tell anyone about Nancy being a snoop," Clare said. "But I'm not sitting down. I'm really tired, and I'm going to bed, whether you like it or not!" She stormed into the pantry and up the back stairs.

Mrs. Rogers sighed. "She has a point, Nancy. Why would she do all these terrible things if she's on the team this year? The more I think about it, the more convinced I am that Josh Bryant is our culprit. He was away from his house when you and George arrived this morning. He could have sneaked over here to pour that oil."

Nancy knew that Mrs. Rogers was probably right about Clare. She just wished she'd had better luck digging up clues at Mr. Bryant's. She'd have to check out his place again, threats or no threats.

The next morning there was a scramble of activity as kids and counselors prepared to leave camp. Parents showed up at ten with horse trailers in tow. After Nancy said good-bye to Juliana, her mother took Nancy aside. "Juliana has told me about all the dangerous things that have been happening here. I'm not letting her come back next year."

After Juliana had left, Nancy overheard Clare's friend Emily talking to her older sister. "It was weird at Green Spring this summer," Emily said. "All this creepy stuff kept happening, and I'm kind of relieved camp is over. I think I'm going to look for a new camp next year."

A sullen Mrs. Rogers appeared at Nancy's side. "Everywhere I turn, I hear kids saying they're not coming back," she said. "At the end of past summers, they've been upset about leaving, and can't wait until the next summer. The person who wants to shut down my camp is winning."

"Mrs. Rogers," Nancy said warmly, "I promise I'll find this person. I'm going to check Mr. Bryant's place again when I get a chance. And I'm hoping the rally will turn up more leads."

"Let's keep our fingers crossed, Nancy," Mrs. Rogers said. "We need some lucky breaks. Now, it's time to help the team get their horses ready to travel. I'm commuting back and forth from Green Spring to the fairgrounds, but the counselors and teams will stay there overnight. Elsa, James, and I will arrive at the fairgrounds early this afternoon to sign in and settle the horses. Do you think you and George could be there by dinner?"

"No problem, Mrs. Rogers. We'll see you then."

Nancy and George helped the team load their horses and equipment into trailers. They waved good-bye to Elsa and James, who were heading off to the rally in James's car. Nancy fished two sugar cubes out of her pocket. "I saved these from breakfast," she explained to George. "I think Tristram and Derby deserve a good-bye treat."

The girls fed the horses sugar and gave them big hugs. Then they climbed into Nancy's car and returned to their homes to drop off their clothes from camp and pick up fresh clothes for the rally.

The doorbell rang just after Nancy had carried her duffel bag into her front hall. In walked Bess.

"You'll never guess where I'm going," Bess announced. "To the rally!"

"That's great, Bess," Nancy said, smiling. "How'd you swing that?" She went to her room to get some clothes together, and Bess followed.

"Mr. Blackstone's sending me there to cover fashion. Stuff like what riding coat colors are hot this year."

"Awesome," Nancy said.

"And speaking of hot," Bess went on, "there's this adorable guy I met at Equestrian Outfitters. He came in to buy boots after you left. His name is Reed Fenwick, and he's on the rally team for his pony club. It's called Pine Ridge. He told me it's Green Spring's rival."

"Reed Fenwick," Nancy said slowly. "I wonder if he's related to James Fenwick. He's a counselor at Green Spring."

"James is Reed's older brother," Bess explained. "Reed doesn't seem bothered that his brother works for a rival team. Anyway, I'm excited that Reed will be at the rally too."

"I'm glad you'll be there, Bess," Nancy said. She collected her things. As the two walked out the front door, she took a moment to fill her friend in on the details of the case so far.

Nancy picked up George, and they drove to the Chatham Fairgrounds. Bess followed in her car. Once there, the three girls went immediately to dinner. Long metal tables covered with paper cloths held enough food for all six rally teams, the pony club directors, and the counselors. After pizza, salad, and ice cream, the team members left to face their first big challenge: the written test. It was held in a large room under the grandstand. Meanwhile, the counselors settled into the dorms, which they shared with all the kids. Two converted barns—one for girls, one for boys—were filled with rows of cots.

Bess sat on her cot and sorted clothes. "So is that little number hot in the horse world?" George teased, pointing to a lime green tank top that Bess was unfolding.

"It's hot anywhere," Elsa remarked, "*except* in the horse world. That color would make the calmest horse freak."

Bess shot Elsa a withering look. "James Fenwick invited me to go for a walk later, and I'm wearing this. Something tells me *he* won't freak."

"James?" Nancy echoed. "I thought the Fenwick you liked was Reed."

"It is," Bess said, "but his brother will have to do while Reed takes his test. Anyway, James is nice too. We met at dinner."

Bess quickly changed shirts and replaced her denim shorts with a white gauzy skirt and thong sandals. As she went out the door, a soft breeze blew inside, filling the dorm with the smell of horses and honeysuckle. "It's a beautiful night," Nancy told Elsa and George. "I'm going for a walk too, to explore the fairgrounds."

Ten minutes later, Nancy was wandering through a group of barns where the horses were kept. She headed toward the grandstand, which overlooked the racetrack. A light shone through some windows looking into the room in which the riders were taking their test. The night was clear, and from the bleachers she could see the amusement park at the far left of the track. The lights on the Ferris wheel glittered and danced. To the right of the track were a few farms, some dense woods, and fields where the cross-country event would be held.

Nancy climbed down from the grandstand and began to walk toward the amusement park. It looked like it was about half a mile away. A few feet away from the grandstand, a couple leaned over the racetrack fence. Nancy instantly recognized the figures as Bess and James. She moved away, not wanting to disturb them—but before she left, she overheard a fragment of their conversation.

"Do you feel competitive with Reed because you guys are on different teams?" Bess was asking.

"Not really. It's okay if Green Spring loses. I'll just root for Pine Ridge, since that's Reed's team," James replied.

Nancy slipped away, turning James's words over in her mind. He seemed perfectly cool about the prospect of Green Spring losing. She wondered if he could have anything to do with the sabotage. What if James was hurting Green Spring to give Reed a better chance of winning?

Nancy chewed her lip. She felt frustrated by the lack of clues and suspects. James was a long shot, she knew. Closing down Green Spring was an extreme way to give your brother an edge. Still, it couldn't hurt to check him out for clues. The boys' dorm was way too crowded at this time of night to search, but what about James's car?

Nancy headed toward the small parking lot in front of barn 5, where the Green Spring horses were stabled. She spotted James's silver Honda two cars down from her Mustang.

Please be unlocked, Nancy thought as she tried the

driver's door. To her relief, it clicked open. She climbed into the car and began to search. Tattered maps and wrappers from fast-food restaurants littered the floor and seats. Suddenly Nancy felt something lumpy under a paper bag. She tossed the bag aside, and caught her breath. A bar of white soap gleamed in the lamplight from the window.

Nancy picked up the soap and inspected it. Its edges were dull and scratched.

12

Terror at Dressage

Nancy replaced the soap and covered it with the bag. Nothing else in the car looked suspicious, so she climbed out and shut the door. As she headed back to the girls' dorm, Bess appeared from the opposite direction.

"How was your walk with James?" Nancy asked.

"Fun," Bess said. "And when we ran into Reed coming out of the test, the night got even better."

Nancy laughed. "Are you paying attention to what the Fenwicks are wearing? Your column covers boys' clothes, too, right?"

"Uh-huh, but the jeans they wore tonight won't make an interesting story. I'll have to pay extra attention to Reed's riding outfits." She shot Nancy a coy smile. "Just doing my job."

"Where are the Fenwicks now?" Nancy asked, looking around.

"In the boys' dorm," Bess replied. "The teams have to get up early tomorrow for dressage."

Nancy lowered her voice and told Bess about finding the bar of soap in James's car. "I don't know . . . soap is just a weird thing to have on the floor of your car," she finished. "And the corners were scraped, like . . . well, someone might have written with it."

"Do you really suspect James?" Bess asked, wide-eyed.

"Let's just say I've added him to my list of suspects," Nancy said. "He's been at Green Spring all along, and he has a motive: getting Reed's team to win."

"I can't believe James would go to that much trouble just to improve Reed's chances of winning," Bess said. "Plus, Clare's been at Green Spring all along too. And don't forget Mr. Bryant. Even though he wasn't staying at the camp like Clare and James, his letter opener was near Rafael's saddle. That's pretty incriminating."

"But why would Clare want to harm Green Spring when she's on the team?" Nancy asked.

Bess shrugged. "I don't know. Still, the soap proves nothing about James. It's like Clare and her olive oil—no proof. Josh Bryant is much more likely."

"Bess, I'll make a deal with you," Nancy said. "If nothing bad happens at the rally, I'll stop suspecting

James, and focus on Josh. After all, James is here, and Josh isn't."

"Makes sense," Bess agreed. "Now let's get our beauty sleep, Nan. I have to wake up early to cover the latest fashions in dressage!"

At breakfast the next morning, Mrs. Rogers gave her team a brief pep talk, then everyone headed for the Green Spring stables to prepare the horses for the morning event.

As stable manager, Cordelia Zukerman gave the other four team members advice on bathing and grooming the horses, and cleaning their tack. She made sure the stalls were always clean, and that feeding went according to schedule. From time to time, judges would roam the stables, evaluating each team's stable management skills.

"Cordelia, you're great at organizing us," Katie pronounced as Cordelia helped her polish stirrups.

"Could you help me brush Dido's tail please, Cordelia?" Akiyah asked, looking frustrated as her mare swished her tail at flies.

"How do I tie my stock?" Rafael asked. He was already dressed in formal dressage wear: a black riding coat, ivory-colored breeches, black boots, and a black derby hat. In front of a makeshift mirror in the tack room, he struggled with his stock, which resembled a large white tie.

"Dressage clothes look totally Victorian," Nancy told George in a low voice. "I mean, what news is there for Bess to cover if the style never changes?"

George shrugged. "Maybe the sock colors change each decade?"

"Well, even if the fashion hasn't changed since the eighteen hundreds, the clothes are kind of cool to look at," Nancy said, watching Rafael secure his tie with a large gold pin.

Mrs. Rogers bustled into the tack room. "Hey kids, why are you dressing so soon? Green Spring's round isn't scheduled until eleven. You'll get horse hairs all over your beautiful clothes!"

"No, we won't," Clare protested. "Our horses are squeaky clean. General Cordelia has made sure of that. Still, I think you guys are stupid to get dressed now. It's only ten."

Akiyah rolled her eyes. Leaning toward Nancy and George, she whispered, "Clare's being especially bad these days because none of her friends are here to distract her."

James called the other counselors over. "Why don't we go over to the dressage ring now and watch the other teams? I don't want to get in Cordelia's way."

The counselors told their team they'd see them later, then set off through the cluster of barns for the ring. As they walked, Nancy observed various rally teams tending to their horses. The morning light bounced off a variety of sizes and colors of horses. Newly brushed coats gleamed like satin. A beautiful chestnut mare, her coat a coppery brown, waited patiently while her owner combed her mane. A bright yellow palomino gelding stood next to her, swishing flies with his long white tail.

The counselors arrived at the dressage ring, which was in a grassy meadow near the amusement park. Bess was at the side of the ring, jotting down notes. Parents, counselors, and pony clubbers made up the rest of the audience.

A judge sat in a folding chair at the end of the ring by the letter C. He was studying a rider on a frisky bay.

Nancy did a double take. The judge looked familiar. She moved closer. There was no doubt about it—she'd know Josh Bryant anywhere. His pudgy frame overhung the flimsy chair, and his blond hair looked even greasier than it did.

"Do you see what I see?" George asked Nancy, appearing at her side.

"I wonder if Mrs. Rogers knows he's here," Nancy said. "I'm amazed he's qualified to be a judge."

The Green Spring team trotted up to the ring. "Hey, you guys look sharp," Elsa told them as the other counselors and Mrs. Rogers clustered around. The four riders looked terrific, Nancy thought, in their black habits and derbies. And their horses looked striking, too, all clean and brushed.

"Good luck, guys," James said, smiling. "We're all rooting for you."

Nancy took Mrs. Rogers aside and asked if she realized that Mr. Bryant was judging. With her hand shading her eyes, Mrs. Rogers looked toward the end of the ring. "I was hoping he wouldn't be here," she said. "But I'm not surprised. Josh has been judging events for years. Since he doesn't have a team entered, he's considered impartial. Of course, you and I know he's not."

The team scheduled before Green Spring finished, and everyone clapped. "Whoops, I'd better go wish Rafael luck," Mrs. Rogers said. "He's up first."

A couple minutes later, an announcer said, "The Green Spring Pony Club! Rafael Estevez, on Clown." Rafael walked Clown into the ring and saluted to Mr. Bryant. He expertly took the dappled gray horse through the intricate dressage paces. After a perfect round he left the ring, to the sound of polite applause. Katie followed on Black Comet. Mr. Bryant scowled as he watched his former pupil, but Nancy could tell the audience was impressed.

Clare went next, with Akiyah standing by. After saluting Mr. Bryant, Clare guided Victoria in tight circles of walks and trots. Victoria chomped at the bit, tossing her head nervously. "Settle down, girl,"

Clare whispered as she trotted by Nancy and George. But Victoria wasn't listening. Her mouth was foaming, and her eyes rolled.

"That mare is so skittish," Mrs. Rogers murmured. "She's the reason Clare didn't make last year's team. I thought she seemed calmer this year. Boy, did I misjudge that."

Clare urged Victoria into a perfectly controlled canter down the side of the ring. "Clare's a good rider, though," Elsa declared. "I'll think she'll pull this off."

A loud explosion suddenly shook the air. Smoke spewed from a clump of bushes next to Mr. Bryant's chair. Everyone jumped.

Victoria neighed in terror. Rearing up, she sprang forward and bolted through the ring. The audience screamed as the mare crashed through the short picket fence.

Clare yanked the reins, desperately trying to keep Victoria in the unpopulated field away from the fair rides. But it was no use. Victoria was uncontrollable. She raced into the amusement park area, and narrowly skirted the roller coaster. A cry rose from the crowd as she galloped straight for the merry-go-round.

"Turn her, Clare," Mrs. Rogers shouted, "or she'll trample all those kids!"

13

Cross-Country Craziness

Nancy froze, staring in horror at the runaway horse. Clare had to stop Victoria fast, or crowds of people would be injured. Kids and parents scattered in panic as the horse raced toward them. Clare leaned back in the saddle, jabbing the reins, straining to control Victoria. Screams overwhelmed the jolly music of the carousel.

Clare yanked the reins hard to the right in a last-ditch effort to avoid the carousel. Nancy held her breath. Finally, Victoria was turning—just four feet from the ride.

Shortening the reins, Clare forced control of the terrified animal. While kids cried in their parents' arms, still afraid of being trampled, Clare guided Victoria to an empty patch of grass.

Mrs. Rogers ran off to help Clare. George, Elsa, and James followed, but Nancy stayed behind. She wanted to see what had caused the explosion. Nancy hurried to the bushes and began poking around. Pieces of burned paper littered the ground. Nearby, the charred remains of a small firecracker told her what had happened. *One thing's for sure,* Nancy thought as she picked up the firecracker, *Clare couldn't have lit this—and she wouldn't have scared her own horse.*

Nancy shot a look at the judge's chair, which was now empty. Mr. Bryant was already returning to the dressage ring, though. Nancy studied him ambling across the lawn. His chair had been next to the bushes. *Could he have lit the firecracker and then tossed it in? Maybe,* she thought. The bushes were so close that he could have gotten away with it. James had also been around here, but Nancy couldn't remember exactly where he'd stood before the explosion.

Mr. Bryant scowled at Nancy. "Whatcha looking at, young lady?" he snapped.

"Did you see anyone hanging around these bushes?" Nancy asked.

"How could I have? I was watching the contestants' every move. You should tell that girl to control her horse better. She could have caused a mess out there."

He dropped back down on his chair, breathing

hard from his trip across the lawn. Nancy showed him the firecracker, and he summoned a rally official on his walkie-talkie. A few minutes later, everyone else returned to the ring. After the official made sure the ring was safe, Clare was allowed to try again.

While Clare was taking Victoria through her paces, Nancy spoke to Mrs. Rogers. "I'm hoping that firecracker was random, but I'm afraid the troublemaker has followed us here from Green Spring."

"I'm worried too, Nancy," Mrs. Rogers said. "We could pretend that the firecracker was a random occurrence, but my gut tells me it's part of the pattern."

This time, Clare's round was almost perfect. Akiyah and Dido were next, and they were very pleased with their results. When Green Spring had finished, Mr. Bryant stood up for lunch.

Back at the stable, the Green Spring team rubbed down their horses and returned them to their stalls. After Cordelia made sure that everything looked shipshape, the team members hurried to lunch. While munching on her grilled cheese sandwich, Nancy kept an eye on James—but nothing about him suggested anything the least bit suspicious. He chatted with everyone: the counselors, the team, and Mrs. Rogers. And he seemed completely at ease.

"Hey guys, we've got the afternoon off," Elsa announced. "Other teams are scheduled for dressage this afternoon. Let's have some fun!"

"Not so fast," Cordelia said. "Maybe you counselors can hang out, but the team has work to do. Tomorrow is the cross-country event. The route's being posted this afternoon, and we've got to study it."

The team members groaned. "You're such a drag, Cordelia," Clare said, pouting. "Always making us work."

"That's why we're going to win this rally," Akiyah said firmly.

After lunch, the team congregated at rally headquarters off the dining hall to study the cross-country map. James offered to stay with the kids to help plan their rides, while Elsa and George went to play tennis at some nearby courts. Nancy headed back to the dressage ring; she wanted to make sure Mr. Bryant was still there, judging the event as he should be.

Sure enough, he was sitting in the same chair, jotting down notes on the rider in the ring. Nancy watched the dressage with Bess for a while, then returned to her dorm to read and think about the case. She was sure the firecracker had been lit by whoever had played the other pranks. She just wished she had more leads.

The rest of the afternoon was uneventful. That evening, a buzz of excitement filled the air as the teams looked forward to competing cross-country the next day. Hands down, it was everyone's favorite event. The order of the teams was posted at dinner. Green Spring was scheduled to go first, at nine A.M. sharp.

The day dawned beautifully. After a breakfast of waffles and fruit, the Green Spring team gathered in their section of the stables to brush and feed their horses. Bess showed up, too, pad and pencil in hand, angling for an interview. "I know the attire for cross-country is less formal than dressage or stadium jumping," she said to the team. "Are there any new looks for this year?"

"Are you kidding?" Akiyah exclaimed. "Cross-country is the only cool event when it comes to clothes. We wear Polo shirts in lots of bright colors, and our horses get to wear colorful saddle pads. We also wear back protectors for safety."

"Bor-ing!" Clare complained. "I'd like to make bikini tops the dress code. They'd make a lot more sense in this heat."

Katie grinned. "And win us points with the judges."

"If you want to know the hip color this year, Bess," Akiyah said, "it's magenta. That's what *I'm* wearing."

Cordelia rushed over with Katie's saddle, and a lime green pad. "No time to gab, girls. Let's move. It's already eight thirty, and the horses aren't even tacked up."

The Green Spring counselors gathered early by

the entrance to the cross-country course. They'd offered to stand at different places along the so they could jump in if there was an emergency at any time. Elsa explained to Nancy and George that the course ran over two miles of countryside, and each rider had five and a half minutes to complete it. Judges stood by each of fourteen jumps that had been positioned around woods, valleys, fields, and streams. Red flags on poles were placed at certain points to guide the riders in the right direction. The jumps were identified with white flags and numbers.

A rally official drove the volunteers to their places in a Jeep, and handed them walkie-talkies. Nancy was asked to stand near a log jump—jump number 7—set directly in front of a clear, babbling stream in a little valley. A judge sat in a canvas chair by the jump, in the shade of an oak tree.

Nancy felt sorry for the riders since they had to wear long-sleeved Polo shirts and back protectors. She already felt hot in her pink T-shirt and khaki shorts. *At least the day was sunny,* she thought. She could just make out the next jump in the valley below the stream. It was an imitation chicken coop. Josh Bryant was the judge. A white flag with a black number 8 flapped in the breeze on one side.

Mr. Bryant glared at Nancy, but she was too far away to hear whatever obnoxious comments he might make.

At least I can keep an eye on him today, she thought.

Nancy checked her watch. It was nine fifteen. The first Green Spring rider should be coming soon.

A faint sound of galloping hooves grew louder and louder until Akiyah and Dido appeared on the crest of the hill. Akiyah's eyes were totally focused on the next jump as she urged Dido toward the log fence. *Go!* Nancy thought. With Akiyah hunched low over the mare's mane, Dido sailed over the jump effortlessly. She splashed through the stream, then climbed up a small incline that opened into a huge field.

Nancy took her eyes off Akiyah for a moment to glance at the judge. A thrill went through her as she watched the judge mark Akiyah's score. It was a perfect zero—meaning no penalties!

Dido raced through the field, with Akiyah guiding her around the flag that pointed toward Mr. Bryant's chicken coop. But as Dido turned, she suddenly lost her footing.

Nancy stared in astonishment as Dido slipped and stumbled. The mare could barely lift her legs. Akiyah urged her on, but she came to a standstill in front of the fence as if she were stuck in putty.

What's going on? Nancy wondered. She crossed the stream and ran down the hill. "Akiyah!" Nancy shouted. "What's wrong?"

Akiyah twisted in her saddle. "Dido's in a marsh.

She can't get enough traction to make the jump. Be careful, Nancy. You don't want to get stuck too."

"I won't," Nancy said, but already her sneakers were squelching in the wet grass. "Here, throw me the reins and I'll lead you to firmer ground."

Akiyah tossed Nancy the reins, and Nancy tugged. Stretching her neck toward Nancy, Dido lifted one hoof, then another, out of the swampy ground. Strange suction noises came with every step.

"Go, girl," Akiyah urged, squeezing her knees against the saddle. With Nancy and Akiyah's encouragement, Dido slogged her way out of the marsh and on to dry ground.

"Excellent!" Akiyah said, taking back the reins. "Now, what kind of person would put a jump in a marsh?"

"Do you have your map?" Nancy asked her.

Akiyah pulled her route map out of her pocket and held it so Nancy could see it too. The girls exchanged puzzled looks. "The flags must be wrong, Nancy. This jump isn't on the course," Akiyah said.

Nancy looked at the map again. Instead of veering right toward the chicken coop, the route headed left to the top of the hill. The next jump, number 8, was a post-and-rail on the other side.

Nancy called to Mr. Bryant, who was sitting by the jump about twenty feet away. It was very suspicious, she thought, that the messed-up jump was his.

"Come over here!" he shouted back unpleasantly.

"How lazy can that guy be?" Akiyah whispered. "He can't even be bothered to get out of his chair to help us!"

The girls went over to him. After studying Akiyah's map, Mr. Bryant said, "I admit this is odd, girls. I have no idea how or why those flags were rerouted."

"Did you notice anything weird when you got here this morning—like a person hanging around?" Nancy asked.

"Nope. You know, anyone could have switched the flags before the day began," he said. "Either last night or first thing this morning."

"How do you think the person got out here?" Nancy asked. "It's far from the fairgrounds."

He shrugged. "Don't ask me. A rally official drove all the judges to their fences. We just followed the flags. Whoever switched them must have done it before eight thirty this morning when we arrived."

Nancy studied him, measuring his sincerity. He stared back as if daring her to contradict him. *Sure, anyone could have switched the flags,* she thought, *and "anyone" includes* you.

Nancy scanned the area around the flags for clues. On the ground by the white jump flag, something caught her eye: something gold, glinting in the sun. She reached down and loosened it from the mud. A woman's bangle bracelet. But whose?

[illegible]

[illegible]

[illegible]

[illegible]

[illegible]

[illegible]

[illegible]

On the ground [illegible]

[illegible]

14

Monkey Business

A bracelet? Nancy thought. *Maybe Clare's . . .*

Nancy stood up and looked over at Akiyah and Mr. Bryant, who were studying the map again. She showed them the bracelet. "Do either of you recognize this?" she asked.

They shook their heads, then focused back on the map.

Nancy slipped the bracelet into her pocket, happy to have a clue. There was a chance the bracelet didn't belong to the person who had switched the flag, but it probably did. After all, Akiyah was the first person to ride the course, and the bracelet wasn't hers.

Nancy called rally headquarters on her walkie-talkie and explained the switched flag. After a brief investigation by a rally official, the flag was placed at its proper jump, Mr. Bryant was relocated, and Akiyah was allowed to start again.

The rest of Green Spring's run went smoothly. Each rider cleared the log fence perfectly. Not all the teams were so skilled, and Pine Ridge suffered a setback when Reed Fenwick's horse tapped the fence with his hind foot.

Even with her team's success, Nancy felt frustrated. Her duties required her to be on the course all day. She'd have to wait until later to investigate the case.

Every now and then she felt the bracelet in her pocket through the fabric of her shorts. Whose could it be? Clare wore several bangle bracelets, both gold and silver, but Nancy couldn't remember if she owned one like this. The shadows began to lengthen over the hills as the final team completed its round. Nancy knew where Josh Bryant had been all day, but what about Clare and James? They'd had the whole afternoon to plan more tricks.

After the event finished, judges and volunteers returned to the stables. Nancy found Clare giving Victoria a bath. She showed her the bracelet and asked if it was hers.

"No way," Clare said, sounding insulted. "I wouldn't buy a bracelet like that. It's too plain—like something my mom might wear."

Nancy turned to James, who was holding Victoria.

"Have you noticed anyone wearing this?" she asked.

James shrugged. "Can't help you, Nancy. But I'm not really tuned in to jewelry. If someone wore this in front of me all day, I still might not recognize it."

At dinner, Nancy kept a close watch on Clare and James, as well as on Mr. Bryant, who ate at a table reserved for judges. No matter how hard she studied them, though, she couldn't detect any suspicious behavior.

In the middle of dinner, Rafael said, "It all makes me nervous—that firecracker yesterday, and today, the misplaced flag. I wonder what's going to get us tomorrow."

"Don't say that, Rafael," Katie exclaimed. "You're scaring me."

"Me too," Cordelia said. "I'm not even sure it's worth being at the rally, knowing someone is trying to hurt us."

"Cordelia the 'iron lady' is feeling down?" Akiyah teased. "Things must be *really* bad!"

Nancy wanted to lift the team's mood. She decided to give them a pep talk. "Guys, you're doing great at the rally," she said, forcing a smile. "Your scores are awesome; you and Pine Ridge have the lowest so far! If you ace the stadium jumping tomorrow, then you're the winners. So don't let the firecracker or flag get you down. Just make it through one more day."

"But what if we win?" Katie asked, slumping her shoulders. "Our reward will be that we'll go to the national rally, and the person will probably show up there. This torture might go on for days!"

Nancy sighed. What Katie said was true. If they won the rally tomorrow, they'd go on to the nationals. And who knew whether these problems would just continue there?

While the rally teams went to bed down their horses, Nancy, Bess, and George took a walk so they could talk about the case. The three headed over to the amusement park to get some cotton candy.

"I have to solve the case by tomorrow," Nancy declared as she picked a piece of the pink fluff off the white paper holder. It melted in her mouth. "Unless, of course, we win. Then I'll have until the end of Nationals to solve it."

"Why can't you keep working on it after the rally ends?" Bess asked.

"Because without the camp or rally going on, the person will go into hiding," Nancy explained. "There won't be anything or anyone for him or her to hurt. Green Spring's reputation will be greatly affected by what happened this summer. We need to show that Green Spring's safe, so people will want to come back."

"It's true," George said gravely. "You should have heard the kids talk as they were leaving camp, Bess. They were totally weirded out. No one wanted to set foot at Green Spring Farm again. And all the strange things that happened here at the rally are just making things worse."

"So the only way to fix Green Spring's reputation is to catch this person and show everyone there's no more danger," Bess said. "Poor Mrs. Rogers. Her pony club is such a source of happiness for her. What would she do if she had to close it down?"

"I can't imagine her retiring," George said. "She's the type who has to keep busy with a project she loves. Without Green Spring, she'd be miserable."

"The thing that gets me about this case is the lack of leads," Nancy said. "Just when I rule out Clare, I find a bracelet. And just when I suspect Josh the most, he's stuck in a chair all day doing nothing wrong. And James's motive is weak."

"Now you're talking," Bess said. "James is definitely not guilty."

"Is that what he told you on one of your walks?" George joked.

"I just know it," Bess proclaimed, "thanks to my trusty sixth sense!"

"Those jumps look terrifying!" Bess said the following afternoon. Twelve brightly colored jumps formed a tight course inside the stadium jumping ring, which had been set up on the racetrack. Bess, Nancy, and George sat in the front bleacher of the grandstand with parents, counselors, and pony clubbers who'd completed their rounds that morning.

Green Spring was the first to go after lunch. Elsa, James, Mrs. Rogers, and Cordelia were prepping the riders at the front gate of the ring.

"The jumps are supposed to be scary," George told Bess. "Only the bravest horses and best riders do well in this event. It's a huge challenge."

"I've heard it's the hardest of the three events," Nancy said. "The horses have to make perfect rounds in just a couple of minutes without so much as nicking a fence. Refusals earn big penalties."

"Speaking of challenges," Bess said, "have you had any breaks in the case since last night?"

"Nope," Nancy said. "Things were quiet this morning, but Green Spring wasn't competing. It's our turn now, and I'm worried. I told Cordelia to pay extra attention to the saddle and bridle straps, and I just finished checking the grandstand and track for stuff like firecrackers and booby traps."

With the blow of a whistle, Rafael and Clown appeared in the ring. Bess flipped open her notebook and began taking notes, while Nancy and George fixed their eyes on Rafael.

After saluting Mr. Bryant in the judge's chair, Rafael made Clown trot in a tight circle at the top of the ring to warm up for his run. Once he was ready, he urged him into a canter, and headed into the first jump: A large board painted with multicolored butterflies. Clown sailed over it. The next jump was an imitation hedge painted electric green, and once again Clown cleared it. On and on Clown went, gracefully springing over the fences, each one brighter and more outlandish than the one before.

As Clown jumped the next to last fence with no problem, Nancy's heart beat faster. He was almost done—and nothing had happened! The last jump loomed ahead.

The fence was made up of two huge barrels lying on their sides, each one painted red, yellow, and green. They were topped by red, yellow, and green striped poles. It stood right across the ring from Nancy, George, and Bess.

Clown hesitated at the bizarre-looking fence, but Rafael confidently pressed him forward. Just as Clown reared up to jump, there was a commotion—from inside one of the barrels!

A brown furry creature swung out of the barrel and onto the pole. Nancy gaped. It was Tarzan, Mrs. Rogers's monkey. He screamed in surprise when he saw the airborne horse.

But Clown was even more surprised. The instant he saw Tarzan, he swerved toward the side of the ring, hooves flailing and nostrils flaring. Nancy froze as the huge animal loomed over her.

"Run," Bess shouted, "or we'll get crushed!"

15

Mirror, Mirror

Bess's notebook flew into the air as everyone scattered. Spectators screamed as Clown knocked through the barrel fence, then crashed against the side of the ring. A sickening crack filled the air. Clown was about to thunder into the grandstand.

Nancy scrambled onto the higher bleachers with Bess and George. She held her breath, watching the frantic horse sideswipe the fence.

Clown reared again, but this time away from the fence. Nancy exhaled with relief. The fence had bent from his weight, but the boards hadn't totally broken.

Clown bolted for the middle of the ring, and Rafael tightened the reins. Even though Nancy could hardly hear him, she could tell by his facial expression that he was soothing Clown.

Finally, Clown stopped by the butterfly jump. Rafael leaped off, and began inspecting his horse for injuries. The terrified animal tossed his head, sending flecks of foam into the air.

Mrs. Rogers and a man with a black bag ran into the ring to check Clown. Nancy guessed the man was a vet.

A sudden cry went up in the grandstand. "Catch him!" came a child's high-pitched voice. Nancy turned to see Tarzan leaping gleefully around the bleachers, trailing a leash. A group of kids was following him. Every time someone almost caught him, though, he skipped out of the way, chattering and teasing.

"That creature is like Curious George," Bess commented. "He's really mischievous."

"You're telling me," Nancy said. "He belongs to Mrs. Rogers. I wonder how he got from her house to that barrel."

"Got him!" a girl cried, holding up his leash. "Whoops!" she added as the monkey sprang at her. She dropped the leash the moment he bared his teeth.

"Allow me," George said. She dashed up the stairs three at a time and grabbed the leash. "Chill out!" she told Tarzan sternly. "No more monkeying around for you."

Tarzan obeyed, though his expression was sly. Elsa met George on her way down and took the leash from her. "Mrs. Rogers wants me to lock him in the stable until she drives home," Elsa said. "She can't figure out how Tarzan got here. Someone must have stolen him out of her house this morning. That's the last time she saw him."

"This is too weird," Nancy said, joining her. She glanced at the ring, where officials were checking for booby traps. One official pulled a banana peel and a dish of water from the barrel. "Someone must have put food and water inside that barrel for Tarzan so he'd stay put," Nancy added, "and then the sound of Clown's hooves scared him out."

"But who would do something like that?" Bess wondered. "It's mean to the animals, as well as to Rafael."

"It's terrible," Elsa agreed. "I think this is the last straw for a lot of Green Spring kids. I hope Mrs. Rogers will have enough takers for her camp next summer—but I wouldn't count on it."

"Think of all that scholarship money going to waste," Nancy said. "I wish I knew why this person is so desperate to shut Green Spring down. The program is great."

While Elsa hurried off with Tarzan, Nancy shot a look at Mr. Bryant. He was sitting in an umpire's chair at the far end of the ring. The judge had been there every moment of the day, except lunch. She turned toward the Green Spring team, huddled on their horses by the gate. James and Cordelia were standing by the riders. They were watching the officials who were inspecting the ring.

All her suspects—James, Clare, and Josh Bryant—were in plain sight, looking innocent and unconcerned. But Nancy knew that any one of them could have brought Tarzan into the ring while it was empty during lunch. Of course, Mr. Bryant would have been on a very tight schedule if he had to drive to Mrs. Rogers's house and back to fetch Tarzan. Clare and James, on the other hand, had the whole morning off.

Mr. Bryant announced that Rafael could take his turn again. This time, Clown had a perfect round. Akiyah, Katie, and Clare followed him, and they also scored perfectly. Nancy, Bess, and George hurried over to the gate.

"Congratulations, guys!" Nancy said, smiling. "You didn't make one mistake."

"I bet you won," Bess declared.

Mrs. Rogers grinned. "I bet you're right. But we won't know for sure until the last three teams perform this afternoon. Green Spring's scores on cross-country, stadium jumping, and the written test are perfect. But a couple of our dressage scores show penalties. So we'll just have to bite our fingernails until we learn the final results."

"And if you win, it's on to Virginia!" Bess said.

"I sure hope so," Mrs. Rogers said fervently. "I

also hope that whoever is plaguing us with these dangerous pranks gets caught by then. The last thing we need is for him to show up in Virginia."

After a solemn pause, Cordelia said, "Okay, everyone, let's get the horses sponged off and walked. They deserve a nice long rest after their awesome performances here."

The counselors offered to come back to the stables and help. Bess turned back toward the seats. "I'm staying here, guys," she said. "Pine Ridge is up next, and they're supposed to have cool stadium-jumping coats." She flashed a smile at James. "Or so Reed told me the other night."

James looked puzzled. "His coat is gray. How cool is that?"

"Hmm," Bess said playfully, "I'll give him a break and call it 'soft silver' in my article."

After waving good-bye to Bess, the counselors followed the team. On the way to the stable, they passed some food concession stands, and the smell of burgers, hot dogs, and french fries filled the air. James stopped for a second and took in the smell. "I'm hungry, and that smell is totally tempting. I'm stopping here for a cheeseburger. Don't wait for me, guys. I'll be back soon."

He veered toward a stand on the right and paused in front of it. Nancy eyed him. *Hungry?* she thought. *But we just had lunch less than an hour ago. Maybe*

James has a big appetite. Or maybe he has something he needs to do without the rest of us hovering over his shoulder. . . .

"I'm checking out his story," Nancy whispered to George. She slipped away from the rest of the group.

From behind a ticket kiosk, Nancy watched James linger by the burger stand until the team was out of sight. He then glanced furtively from side to side and hurried away without any food. Nancy followed him.

Picking up his pace, James headed toward the far side of the racetrack. Nancy was careful to keep at least thirty feet between them. Now and then, James would stop and look over his shoulder—but Nancy was quick. Each time he stopped, she'd slip into a crowd or behind a fence post before he could see her.

A racehorse starting gate stood at the edge of the track. James was jogging straight for it, putting too much distance between them. Nancy had to catch up, or she might lose him!

Nancy followed him onto the track. Once there, she broke into a quiet run. Her sneakers had no traction in the soft turf, though, so she could move only so fast. It was like having your legs paralyzed in a nightmare, she thought. She only hoped James didn't turn around. Besides a few scattered fence posts, there were no places to hide on the open track.

James was almost at the gate. A woman popped up from one of the stalls and waved to him.

Nancy scurried behind a fence post. *Did she see me?* Nancy wondered. Even from her distance of a hundred feet, the woman looked familiar. She was slender and attractive, with chin-length highlighted blond hair.

Nancy suddenly recalled the face. The woman was Charlotte Neroni, owner of Equestrian Outfitters—the store she and Rafael had gone to to buy his new saddle. Nancy remembered that she was the daughter of Mrs. Rogers's best friend, Eleanor Neroni, who had died a few years ago. But how were Charlotte and James connected?

Nancy scurried from post to post, trying to get close enough to hear their conversation. But before she could get to a good place, James suddenly hurried away. He was carrying a white legal-size envelope.

Nancy hunched down behind a post, hoping he wouldn't see her as he passed by. Nancy's gaze followed James as he jogged back the way he'd come. Nancy wondered what was in the envelope.

Nancy's curiosity shifted from James to Charlotte. Was Charlotte paying James to sabotage Green Spring? The envelope looked like it might contain money. Or maybe it held some sort of document. If she *was* paying him to hurt Green Spring, the big question, of course, was why.

Nancy followed James with her eyes before he blended into the crowd. *I can always catch up with him later,* she thought. Nancy quickly looked back at Charlotte. Her heart skipped a beat. The woman was already hurrying away from the starting gate, in the direction of the amusement park. In a minute, Nancy would lose sight of her.

Nancy slipped out from behind her post and jogged after Charlotte, but Charlotte had picked up her pace. As Charlotte approached the rides, the crowds thickened. Nancy could hardly see her.

I've got to run faster, Nancy thought. She broke into a sprint, dodging clusters of people, ticket kiosks, and hot dog stands. Nancy's spirits lifted as she caught sight of Charlotte's blond head bobbing in the crowd just ahead.

Charlotte stopped and looked around, as if deciding which way to go. She glanced over her shoulder, and her eyes flickered. *She knows I'm following her,* Nancy realized.

Charlotte froze, like a deer about to run. "Wait!" Nancy yelled. "I just want to ask you a few questions."

But Charlotte didn't waste another second. She sprang forward, frantically making for the carnival rides. Nancy increased her pace, barely keeping Charlotte in sight as she zigzagged through the crowds.

As Nancy ran through the carnival, she passed tiny kids holding huge clouds of cotton candy; green-haired teenagers throwing darts at balloons; and lines for rides snaking across the open spaces. Nancy almost collided with a child carrying a slice of pizza and a huge glass of soda. But in spite of all the obstacles, she kept track of Charlotte.

Suddenly a kid carrying a stuffed bear blocked Nancy's way. Nancy hopped to the side, trying to avoid him, but the kid spun around in front of her again. Tears trickled down his face as he stared up at her. "I'm sorry," she said. "Did I hurt you?"

"Where's Mommy?" he wailed.

"I don't know," Nancy said, her heart sinking as Charlotte's frosted head slipped out of sight. "Weren't you with her?"

A woman grabbed the boy's hand and yanked him toward her. "I told you not to wander off, Eric," she scolded. "Mommy got worried."

Nancy took off. Where was Charlotte? She pivoted in every direction, searching the crowds, but there was no sign of her. *Don't tell me I've lost her—I was so close!* Nancy thought.

Frustrated, Nancy scanned the area again. More and more people poured into the park. Lines to the most popular rides—the scrambler, the roller coaster, and the whirligig—lengthened by the second.

Nancy froze. Something familiar had just passed by her. But where did it go, and what was it? She looked around, her eyes searching for what she'd just seen. And then, as her gaze passed over the mirror maze, she found it.

Out of the jumble of mirrors, a zillion reflections of Charlotte's face glared at her.

Nancy bought a ticket, and stepped inside the maze. Charlotte's reflection had disappeared, but Nancy hadn't seen her leave. She had to still be inside.

Nancy quickly hit a dead end. With her own reflection staring at her from all sides, she tried a passage to the right. Once more, her own blue eyes gazed back at her from the mirror blocking her way. She turned around, ready to try another path.

Suddenly Charlotte's face filled every mirror in sight. Nancy whipped around. Charlotte's reflections laughed, teasing Nancy, delighted by her confusion. *Which was the real person?* Nancy wondered, frustrated.

Nancy turned down a passage to her left and caught a glimpse of Charlotte's back in the mirrors ahead. *Just let me out of here!* Nancy thought. *What if Charlotte escapes while I'm stuck in this crazy maze?* But in every passage she took, Nancy was a prisoner of her own reflection. Until she turned another corner. . . .

Just three feet away from Nancy, the real Charlotte froze. She was trapped. Thanks to the mirrors around them, Nancy anticipated Charlotte's next move. As Charlotte reached into her pocket, Nancy threw up her hands to shield her face.

Charlotte whipped out a Discman. She swung it against the walls, shattering their reflections. Shards of glass rained over Nancy's hands and arms.

16

The Mystery Team

Once all the glass had fallen, Charlotte shoved Nancy aside and ran down the passage. Gingerly, Nancy straightened and shook herself off. Glass clinked to the floor. Peering into an unbroken mirror, Nancy checked to see if she was okay. Other than a few minor cuts on her hands and arms from shielding her head, she was unharmed. With one more shake of her T-shirt just in case, Nancy took off after Charlotte, glass crunching underfoot.

There were more dead ends at every turn. By the time Nancy found her way out of the maze, she'd already lost a few minutes.

After warning the attendant about the broken glass, Nancy scanned the area for Charlotte, *Don't tell me I've lost her after all this,* she thought.

Nancy then noticed a slim blond figure moving quickly through the crowd. Charlotte! Nancy raced after her. The moment Charlotte noticed Nancy gaining on her, she broke into a run. But a huge ride was in her way: the bumper cars.

Instead of avoiding it, Charlotte headed right for the attraction. She leaped over the rail, into the middle of the crashing cars.

Nancy didn't flinch. She hurtled over the rail after Charlotte and caught up to her just as a car bore down on them.

"Hey!" the operator yelled. "What are you two doing? Get out of there!" He flipped a switch, and the cars whined to a halt.

Charlotte ran toward the far side of the platform, her loafers slipping on the smooth metal surface. She skidded for a moment, then fell. Desperately, she scrambled up, clutching a bumper car for support.

Wearing sneakers, Nancy kept her grip on the platform. Without slipping once, she caught up to Charlotte, and tackled her to the floor.

"Get off me!" Charlotte yelled. "I'll have you arrested for assault!"

"Okay, just as long as you also tell the police you attacked me with that glass?" Nancy retorted, pinning Charlotte in a judo hold.

"That was just . . . an unfortunate accident," Charlotte growled. Her body tensed, as if a huge fury was raging inside her. But suddenly, her shoulders sagged. Nancy could tell that she had given up.

Charlotte took a deep breath before speaking. "Lighten up on my shoulders, Nancy—and I'll tell you the whole truth."

The ride operator approached them. A hostile look flashed in his eyes. "Didn't you two hear me? Get out of here, now. I'm calling the police."

"Please call them right away," Nancy said as she loosened her grip on Charlotte's shoulders. "Ask for Chief McGinnis or Officer Rivken. Tell them Nancy Drew caught the person we've been looking for—the one who's been bothering Green Spring."

The man instantly calmed down. "Yeah—sure thing." After announcing to the bumper car passengers that the ride was temporarily closed, he hurried off.

"Okay, Charlotte," Nancy said. "You promised to tell me the truth. What was in that envelope you handed to James Fenwick?"

"Cash," Charlotte said bluntly.

"For what?"

"I gave him money to sabotage Green Spring," Charlotte said. She turned her face abruptly as a tear slid down her cheek. "His loyalty to it was easy to sway. His brother was at a rival camp; I think he'd been turned down by Mrs. Rogers last year because she didn't have room." More tears ran down her cheeks, and she angrily wiped them away. "He was a good worker for a while. He did most of the pranks at the camp, but he got cold feet at the rally. He wanted Reed to compete legitimately. So I had to do the work here myself," she complained.

"You set off that firecracker, and stole Tarzan?" Nancy asked.

"And misdirected the flag," Charlotte said. "The monkey was a pain in the neck. He bit me on the arm when I took him from his pen. I had to coax him into the barrel with a banana. I'm amazed *that* part of my plan worked—but it did," she added smugly.

"You said James did the stuff at Green Spring? Did he think of it all himself?" Nancy asked.

"Everything was my idea," she replied, shaking her head. "He just did what I asked."

"Do you know how Josh Bryant's letter opener ended up on the tack room floor at the camp?" Nancy asked.

"I wondered where I'd left that," Charlotte said. "Wrecking the saddle was the only thing I actually did at Green Spring. James was feeling bad about all the problems he'd been causing, so he went on strike for a day. I sneaked in with Josh's opener and slashed up the saddle."

"Where'd you get the opener?" Nancy asked.

"I lifted it from Josh's party a few months ago," Charlotte replied. "My plan to close Green Spring was already swimming around in my head. The opener was a way to throw suspicion onto Josh. But I have to admit, Nancy, you were too smart for me." Charlotte paused, her lip trembling.

Nancy continued with her line of questioning. "Are you upset because your plan didn't work?"

"I'm upset because I caused so much trouble," Charlotte replied.

Nancy wasn't sure whether Charlotte was sincere. "Well, why did you want to hurt Green Spring?" Nancy asked. "What did you have to gain? Your mother and Mrs. Rogers were best friends—so why shut it down?"

Charlotte's eyes snapped with anger. "That's just it," she declared. "Their friendship hurt me!"

"How?"

"My late mother left half her money in trust to Green Spring," Charlotte said bitterly, "because she and Madeline Rogers were best friends. Madeline wanted to start a scholarship program that would give aid to kids who needed it, and my mother thought that was a fine idea."

"You're angry at Mrs. Rogers because she got half your mom's money," Nancy said, trying to make sense of Charlotte's words, "so you've been attacking Green Spring for revenge?"

"Revenge is stupid," Charlotte replied. "What's the point of crying over spilled milk? I did this for money."

"Money? How would you get money by closing down Green Spring?" Nancy asked.

"Because my mother's will says that if Green Spring shuts down, the money reverts to me so I can set up a similar camp—one with a scholarship program," Charlotte explained.

Nancy was surprised. Charlotte was interested in needy children who want to ride?

"You did all these things so you could get enough money to set up a similar camp?" Nancy asked.

"No way!" Charlotte retorted. "I'm not interested in hanging out with bratty kids and their horses. In my mother's will, there's no provision for what would happen to the money if my camp program shut down. So I planned to create a second-rate program that would close after a year. Then I could do whatever I wanted with the money. I could quit my job at the store and take off for Hawaii."

"If you're unhappy with your job, there are plenty of legal ways to earn money," Nancy said reasonably. "You don't have to endanger teenagers and animals in some elaborate plot to shut down a riding camp. And why did you buy Equestrian Outfitters if you don't like working there?"

"My mother owned that store," Charlotte explained, "so I got stuck with it, instead of with the other half of her cash. That money should have been mine." Charlotte's sniffling became a sudden flood of tears. "I'm sorry, Nancy," she murmured. "I really am sorry. Yes, the money should have been mine, but I didn't mean to hurt anyone. I didn't actually *hurt* anyone—did I?"

"People were really scared," Nancy said. "A girl's arm was bruised when she slipped by the pool, a counselor got poison ivy, and property was ruined. It's lucky that you *didn't* hurt anyone very badly."

Charlotte looked at her with mournful eyes. "I missed my mother so much after she died." She paused for a moment. "I thought I deserved all her money."

Nancy was tempted to tell Charlotte that her mother had died, too, but that didn't make her feel entitled to things that weren't hers. She realized, though, Charlotte's mind had broken a little with grief. *There's no way this woman is thinking logically,* Nancy mused. *Maybe with time—and medical help—Charlotte one day will be cured.*

At that moment, Officer Rivken appeared and took charge of Charlotte. Nancy explained that James was also involved. They could probably find him back at the stables.

When the squad car dropped Nancy off outside Green Spring's tack room, James was in the doorway, chatting with Elsa, George, Cordelia, and Mrs. Rogers. His face paled when he saw Charlotte inside the squad car, and Nancy and Officer Rivken climbing out. The rest of the astonished pony club team gathered around as Nancy took James aside and started to question him.

She quickly told him Charlotte's story. His gaze flickered to Charlotte sobbing away in the backseat. "She told you the truth, Nancy," James said tentatively. "She paid me generously to do all that stuff at camp. I even swiped Clare's olive oil to pour by the pool. When I overheard Mrs. Rogers hiring you, I got worried. I followed you home and soaped your window, hoping to scare you off. But I guess it didn't work."

Mrs. Rogers stared at him. "You should be ashamed of yourself, James Fenwick. You could have killed someone! All those pranks were really dangerous. Did you only think of how much you were getting paid?"

James hung his head in shame. "I'm sorry. What I did was greedy, and stupid, and very wrong. But I wised up by the time the rally came, and I refused to work for Charlotte anymore. She paid me today for the things I did at Green Spring," he added, removing the envelope from his jeans pocket. "Here, Mrs. Rogers. Take this money and use it for your scholarships."

"I can't believe you would do those awful things, James," Elsa said. "I mean, what kind of example are you setting for Reed—and for our pony club?"

James's face reddened. "I never meant to set a bad example. I thought at the time that I needed the money, but it really wasn't worth it. I'm sorry, everyone," he added, scanning the stunned faces of the Green Spring riders, "and please, Mrs. Rogers, tell Reed I'm sorry too." James got into the backseat of Officer Rivken's car with Charlotte, and the car drove off.

Everyone on the team looked at one another in silent shock. Then Katie took a deep breath and said, "It's strange to think that James did all that stuff—but at least Green Spring is safe again."

The mood around the stable remained somber, but relieved. The competition was just ending. As soon as the stadium jumping finished, tension mounted. The final results would be announced at any moment!

Suddenly, the loudspeaker blared, "All teams please assemble on horseback outside the grandstand for the parade of winners!"

Fifteen minutes later, the six teams were grouped on the track in front of the grandstand. Elsa, George, Nancy, Bess, and Mrs. Rogers waited tensely on the sidelines. A rally official came forward with a large silver trophy and blue ribbons. He cleared his throat and announced, "And the winner is: Green Spring!"

Gasps of joy erupted as the teammates gave one

another the thumbs-up sign. Cordelia accepted the trophy on behalf of the team. Everyone cheered as the official pinned ribbons on each horse's bridle, and Cordelia called the counselors and Mrs. Rogers out to join them.

"Nancy, I want to thank you on behalf of the team for your great detective work," Cordelia said, smiling. "And I want to thank Mrs. Rogers for her wonderful pony club, Green Spring, which is just so awesome. Now that the mystery is solved, the camp and its scholarships can keep going strong." She held up the trophy. "Everyone, look out! Green Spring rules!"

Mrs. Rogers beamed. "Hooray! Thanks for your great work, kids, and yes—many, many thanks to Nancy for all her help."

"I want to thank my own winning rally team of mystery-busters," Nancy said, glancing at her two best friends. "Bess and George!"

"Oooh . . . does that mean we go to the *mystery* nationals?" George joked.

"Well, if there's a mystery, we always rally around," Bess said, with her trademark smile.

Werewolf in a Winter Wonderland

Contents

1

A Wild Night at WildWolf

"It looks like the Holiday Winter Carnival is finally going to get a break from the weather," Nancy Drew said. Light snow dusted the hood of her car as she pulled into Bess Marvin's driveway.

"I know," George Fayne said, reaching to put a new CD into the car's CD player. "At last. We've had nothing but snow, ice, and crispy-cold weather."

Nancy watched Bess pick her way carefully along the icy drive toward the car. Bess was George's cousin, but they looked completely different. George was tall, with short smooth dark hair. Bess was the same age—eighteen—but shorter, and she didn't have nearly as athletic a body as her cousin. Her wavy blond hair was lighter than Nancy's. Bess and

George were not only Nancy's classmates—they were also her best friends.

"Isn't this weather great!" Bess said as she plunked into the backseat. "The Carnival should be spectacular. I can't wait to find out what our work assignments will be!"

"You know, this might be the last Carnival for a while," Nancy said as she turned onto Clayton Avenue. It was the quickest route to Riverside Park, which sat near the Muskoka River. "The last two lost a lot of money."

"Well, the weather was so bad last year, for one thing," Bess pointed out. "Hardly any snow at all. Remember? It was so warm the ice wouldn't hold. And I don't just mean all the sculptures and cool stuff. There was barely enough ice on the Muskoka for skating the full seven days, let alone any real skating competitions."

"The weather wasn't good for a winter carnival, that's true," Nancy said. "But that wasn't the only problem," she reminded them. "Two years ago a lot of money was wasted, and last year half the money disappeared—along with the Carnival chairman. So they've brought in this new guy from Chicago to run things."

"Did you hear his name?" George asked. "It's Poodles McNulty. What kind of a name is Poodles?"

"Especially for a man," Bess said. "It must be some sort of a nickname."

"We might find out this morning," Nancy said, pulling into Riverside Park. Cars already nearly filled the lot. Nancy pulled her Mustang in to join them. The park was sparkling with fresh bright white snow and clear ice.

The three friends gathered up their sports bags and backpacks and got out of the car. Their boots crunched the packed snow as they headed toward the huge blue-and-green tent on the bank of the river. Branches of enormous sycamore trees leaned out across the frozen river near the tent. Maple and oak trees stood straight and tall against the watery-pale sky.

Nancy's new white ski suit showed off her slim body, and she was happy to find out that it also kept her warm and comfortable as they walked through the ice sculpture garden. "Wow, look at these—they're awesome," Nancy said. All around the girls were eight-foot statues of trees, animals, and people carved from ice. Sunshine broke through the sky and glittered through the sculptures.

The girls entered the tent to register for their work assignments. As they stood in line, Nancy recognized many faces—neighbors, friends of her family, shopkeepers around town, and colleagues of her father, attorney Carson Drew.

"There you are." Nancy's boyfriend, Ned Nickerson, strolled toward them. He was taller than Nancy and also had wavy blond hair. He leaned down to give her a kiss, and then gave her friends a warm smile. "Do you have your assignments yet?"

"We just got here," Nancy said, leading the others to a registration line. "What about you?"

"I'm on the team that'll organize the torchlight parades," he answered. "And I'm also going to help with some of the sporting events—the golf tournament and the Polar Bear Plunge."

"Like the Polar Bear Plunge is a *real* sporting event," Bess said. "Give me a break! It's just a group of people in bathing suits jumping through the ice into the river in below-freezing weather."

"I don't know," George said. Her mouth twisted into a crooked smile, as if she still weren't sure about what she was going to say. "I'm thinking about doing it this year."

"Yikes," Bess said. "You would."

"Oh, and get this," Ned added. "I'm one of the judges for the Snow Princess competition."

"That should be right up your alley," Nancy said with a grin.

"Nancy!" a familiar voice called from behind. "It *is* you!"

Nancy turned. "Brianda!" she said. "I haven't seen you since you graduated. Do you all remember each other?" she asked. "This is Brianda Bunch. She was a couple of years ahead of us in school—I knew her when we worked together on the paper. You're in college now, right?" she asked Brianda.

"Yes, finally. My family moved to the West Coast right after I graduated. I worked a year there, and finally started college this past fall—studying journalism at Columbia."

"You must be on school break too," Bess said.

"I am," Brianda answered. "And I came here to hook up with some old friends and get in one more Carnival. It looks like I'm going to be one of the on-call hosts, hanging out to give visitors a quick tour of the Carnival if they want. I'm staying at WildWolf while I'm here."

"WildWolf," Nancy repeated. "That's the animal preserve a few miles out of town, right? We've all been there. It's really cool. Come to think of it, you and I did a feature article on it once. Wait a minute—I remember. Your family's connected to the place . . ."

"That's right," Brianda said. "My cousin is Markie Michaels, the executive director of the preserve. She's an ethologist—a scientist who studies animal behavior. Her specialty is wolves. Hey, would you like to come out tonight? It's Tuesday, so they're having a Howl-o-rama."

"That's when the wolves and the humans howl back and forth?" Bess asked.

"Right," Brianda said. "If you come early I can

give you a behind-the-scenes tour. We have some new pups. They're not out for public viewing yet, but I can show them to you. They're incredible."

"I'd love it," Nancy said, "as long as we aren't scheduled to work here tonight."

Bess and George agreed it would be fun. Only Ned begged off. "I can't make it tonight, but I'll take a rain check," he said. "I have to go meet with the torchlighters now, so I'll talk to you later." With that, he bounded off toward a corner of the tent.

Before Brianda left, the others made plans to meet that night at WildWolf. Then Nancy, Bess, and George got their Carnival assignments.

"I'm working at the Heat Hut," Bess said, looking through her orientation kit. "And the cool thing is that I work different shifts every day, so I'll have a good chance of seeing everything before the Carnival is over."

"We'll be able to stay in touch there, too," George pointed out. "The Heat Hut is definitely the place to hang out and get warm—a perfect place for breaks."

"And lattes and hot chocolate and cookies and nachos and all sorts of goodies," Bess added. "What about you, Nancy? Where are you working?"

"I've got several jobs," Nancy said. "You know how they have hosts who stand by to welcome everyone and direct visitors to all the activities and venues?"

"You did that last year, didn't you?" George asked.

"Exactly," Nancy said. "This year I'll be in charge of that team. I make rounds to be sure that all the hosts are on call and helping out, and to see if they have any questions. Oh, and they asked me to be one of the Snow Princess judges, too."

"So you and Ned will be working together for that one," Bess said. "That'll be fun. What are you going to be doing, George?" she asked.

"I'm coordinating the softball-in-the-snow games, and also working with the lighting crew for some of the evening activities," George told them. "I hope I get to work the Crystal Palace for the opening tomorrow."

"That's one of my favorite parts of the Carnival," Nancy said. "That huge ice castle with all the colored lights shining through."

The three split up to meet with their various coordinators and teams for a few hours. As prearranged, they met back at the car at three o'clock. After a late lunch of tacos and burritos at Smoky's Hothouse they headed out to WildWolf.

It was four o'clock and still light when they arrived at the preserve. Nancy pulled off the country road onto a mile-long drive to the gate that opened into WildWolf. They drove another couple of blocks until they came to the visitors' parking lot and a compound of wood-frame buildings. Brianda was waiting for them at the office door. She introduced them to her cousin, Markie Michaels, and Markie's assistant, Christopher Warfield.

"We're so glad you could come," Markie said. She was tall and pretty, with reddish-brown hair.

"Welcome," Christopher added, extending his hand. He had deep green eyes and a British accent. He was stocky, but he looked very muscular.

Brianda immediately took Nancy and her friends to see the wolf pups. The preserve was huge—it was comprised of six four-acre enclosures that were bordered with double security fences. Four to ten wolves lived in each enclosure. WildWolf had an international reputation and was visited by students, scientists, and people from around the world who were interested in animal welfare, nature, education, and research.

Brianda took them into a small building where the wolf babies were being examined by a vet.

"They're so fluffy," Bess exclaimed as she took one in her arms. It looked like a cross between a puppy and a bear cub.

Nancy picked up another wiggly pup with thick brownish fur. It was warm and incredibly soft, and it wriggled up her chest to her shoulder. It nibbled on her hair and murmured baby mumbles in her ear.

"Aren't they amazing?" Brianda said.

"I'm in love," Nancy said, cuddling the pup.

They played with the babies until it was time for

the Howl-o-rama. Then they went back to the first wolf enclosure. It was dark, but a large moon flooded the landscape with a vanilla glow. People started to fill two small bleachers which sat a few yards from the fence—even though a hanging thermometer registered twenty-two degrees.

Markie came out and introduced herself, and said a few words about the preserve and its inhabitants. Then she began the howl. She threw her head back, and a long mournful sound poured from her throat: "*Ah-oooooooooooooooooooooooooo.*"

From the distance, an echoing call filled the air. Then another wolf from another pen responded, beginning on a different note, so that the two animals howled in harmony.

Markie answered back and motioned for the people in the bleachers to join in. Nancy, Bess, George, and Brianda sent out loud howls and were rewarded with responses from all the packs.

Soon the air filled with an eerie counterpoint of animal and human howling. Nancy's skin sparked with tiny explosions as she sang with the wolves.

During a particularly loud chorus, Nancy noticed a modern sound muted beneath the primitive sound of the howling. She seemed to be the only one who heard the steady rolling crunch of the snow. Suddenly everyone stopped howling and looked toward the new sound. An old pickup truck was shooting toward them along the road that divided two large enclosures.

Christopher Warfield pulled the truck to a grinding halt near the bleachers and hopped out of the truck's cab, leaving the door swinging open. He raced over to the fence where Markie stood. Nancy watched the two of them closely. They were too far away for Nancy to pick up any words from scanning their lips, but there was no question about the news that Christopher had brought. It wasn't good.

"I'm going to see what's going on," Brianda said. She marched down the bleachers, her boots clomping along the wood slats. Brianda joined her cousin and Christopher at the fence, and the three of them huddled for a few minutes. Then Markie and Christopher ran to the truck, and Brianda returned.

"We've had a little problem," Brianda announced to the crowd with a thin smile. "Nothing too bad—but Markie needs to help Christopher clear it up. We're going to cut the Howl-o-rama short this evening. We hope to see everyone back next month. The drive is lit all the way back to the road, so you shouldn't have any trouble finding your way. But be careful—there's ice under all that snow. We don't want any of you sliding into a drift."

Nancy could tell that Brianda was trying to look confident and reassuring—but it was obvious that she was very upset.

"What's happened?" Nancy asked her friend privately as people shuffled off the bleachers. "Is there anything I can do?"

"Just stick around until everyone else has left, okay?" Brianda asked in a very low voice. Then she continued to help people down from the bleachers and point them to the parking lot.

Nancy, Bess, and George waited for Brianda to rejoin them after every car had pulled away. Brianda's porcelain skin was flushed a pale pink, and her large blue-gray eyes sparkled with tears in the harsh glow of the security lamp. "It's horrible," she cried. "Khayyam and Liz are not with their pack. Two of our prize alpha wolves—they're *gone.*"

2

A Wolf in Sheep's Clothing?

"Gone?" Nancy repeated. "But how? When?"

"I'm not sure," Brianda said. "There's no break in the fence. Somehow, though, they got out."

"You mean . . . *escaped?*" Bess said softly.

"Or were they stolen?" Nancy suggested.

"Without a break in the fence, they couldn't have escaped," Brianda said.

"So if they were taken, it would have to have been by someone who knew this place," Nancy concluded. "And also knew how to handle the animals."

"Khayyam and Liz are alpha wolves—leaders of their pack," Brianda said. "It would not have been easy to capture them."

In the distance Nancy saw snow flying along the

gravel road. The pickup truck and a couple of SUVs raced up. "Looks like they've got everyone in on the search," Brianda said. "They're going to kick you out, too, so I have to make this fast. This isn't—"

"Girls, we're closing up for the evening," Markie called out, interrupting her cousin. "So I'm going to have to ask you to leave. Bree, can you join us in the office, please? Right away."

Nancy waved and smiled. "Bye. The howling was great." She knew it would be better if Markie didn't know that Brianda had told them what happened.

The WildWolf crew went inside the office, and Nancy and her friends started for the parking lot.

In spite of what Markie had said, Brianda escorted them to their car.

"This isn't the first time something bad has happened here," Brianda whispered to the girls. "Markie told me there have been several scary incidents. Personally, I sense that someone is trying to destroy this place and ruin all of Markie's hard work." Nancy could hear the distress in her friend's voice.

"Nancy, I know your reputation," Brianda said. "Help me figure out what's happening here before my cousin loses everything?"

"Of course, Brianda," Nancy said without a moment's hesitation. "I'll look into it and do whatever I can. WildWolf is as of this minute in a sort of lockdown, it seems—outsiders aren't welcome. So listen carefully to everything—take notes if you can. It'll help to have you on the inside. And let's talk tomorrow at the Carnival."

"Thanks, Nancy," Brianda said. "Thanks a lot." She quickly turned and ran back to the office building.

Nancy drove her friends back to town. After dropping Bess and George at their houses, she pulled into her own garage. Nancy sat for a moment in her car, going back over every minute at WildWolf. When she shivered, she told herself it was because it was so cold. But deep down she wondered if it was because there might be two wild wolves on the loose somewhere around River Heights.

At eight o'clock Wednesday morning Nancy's alarm and her bedroom phone both rang at the same time. With one hand she hit the alarm button, and with the other she picked up the receiver.

"Turn on your TV," Brianda said on the other end of the line. Nancy used the remote to turn on her small television set on the bookshelf. The screen showed a local reporter, Susie Oliver, speaking earnestly into a microphone. Nancy caught the point of the broadcast in the middle of the reporter's sentence.

"—standing here in the pasture of local sheep farmer Philip LeRoy, who is understandably concerned about the breaking news we've been bringing to you this morning." The reporter turned to a man who was standing next to her. He looked like he was between fifty and sixty years old—it was hard to tell exactly.

"So, Mr. LeRoy, what was your reaction when you heard that there are two wolves missing from the WildWolf animal preserve, which is not far from here?"

"The same reaction I had the last time it happened," LeRoy said. "I'm mad. Wolves have escaped from that place before, and they attacked my sheep one night about this time of year. I tried to get that place shut down the first time it happened, but nobody'd listen. They'll listen now, I promise you that. WildWolf should be shut down, and all the animals should be destroyed."

"That's outrageous!" someone said out of the camera's range. Nancy recognized the voice, and the camera panned over to Markie's face. "The wolves aren't running loose," she said. "They could not have 'escaped,' as you put it. WildWolf is a supersecure animal preserve, and it meets the strictest federal guidelines for such a facility."

Markie managed a fake smile. "Have you ever visited our preserve, Mr. LeRoy?" she asked. I think your opinion might change if you saw our establishment."

"No, but I don't need to," LeRoy sputtered.

"You *do* admit that two wolves disappeared from WildWolf last night," the reporter said to Markie.

"Yes, but they couldn't have gotten out by themselves," Markie responded.

"Are you saying they're not out there somewhere?" LeRoy demanded. The camera moved so that all three were in view.

"Of course not," Markie said. "But if they are, it's because someone maliciously stole them and *then* turned them loose. Perhaps to cause trouble for WildWolf—to scare everyone who lives around here and to try to shut the preserve down." She gave LeRoy a harsh look.

"Are you accusing *me?*" he yelled. "Are you saying I'd do such a thing? I'll sue you! I want a tape of this program for my lawyer."

The camera zoomed in on the reporter. "As you can see, not only do we have a couple of opinions as to what happened—we also have controversy about *why* it happened. Animal experts from around the state are currently searching for the wolves. Let's hope they find them soon. More news to come on the noon wrap-up. This is Susie Oliver, live from a farm outside River Heights."

"Nancy, I talked to Markie," Brianda said. She was still on the phone. "She'd like to get together with you. She's totally okay with your helping us out. So you can come take a look around any time you want."

Nancy didn't have to report to the Carnival until that afternoon, so she told Brianda she'd be there within the hour. As she pulled on a heavy sweater, Bess called to see whether Nancy had seen the news. Nancy told her about Brianda's call, and Bess agreed to go with Nancy to WildWolf.

They arrived at the preserve five minutes before nine. Markie, Brianda, and Christopher were waiting in the main office building, which was filled with the aromas of warm banana-nut muffins and hot chocolate. They all followed their noses into the conference room and sat around the large table. Brianda and Christopher passed out muffins while Markie spoke.

"People have been trying to shut us down since we opened five years ago," Markie said. "Some people have a basic fear of wolves."

"And that's also one of the reasons WildWolf exists," Christopher pointed out. "So that people can learn more about wolves, see how beautiful they are, and respect them. They're not mean—they're just wild animals."

"Markie has this great reputation all over the world," Brianda chimed in. "She's the one called in to testify in cases involving wolves. She's appeared before a congressional hearing in Washington, D.C. And she was asked to make a speech in London just last month at a big international conference."

"Brianda, thanks for the buildup, but I don't think that's the point here," Markie said.

"Well, I do," Brianda insisted. "I think someone's trying to ruin your reputation by causing trouble at WildWolf."

"That's possible," Christopher added.

"It's not going to work," Markie said. "I'm determined to stand my ground. We're not going down without a fight—and I mean a *fight!*"

"What about the Carnival?" Bess said. "If the wolves are out there running around, do you think they'll head for the Carnival? It would be total chaos if someone saw them there."

"Actually, if they're out there somewhere, they won't go near Riverside Park," Christopher answered. "They're scared of people. There's never been a case in North America of a wild wolf deliberately attacking a person."

"I'd like to take a look at their enclosure," Nancy said.

Christopher, Brianda, and Bess stayed in the office while Markie took Nancy out to the area where the missing wolves lived. The rest of the pack was still there, so Nancy wasn't able to go inside, but she and Markie walked around the double fences. Nancy didn't see any breaks in the wire.

At the part of the enclosure that was the furthest away from the buildings, Nancy saw something on the ground. "What's this?" she wondered aloud. She crouched down to examine a small pile of a grainy, cereal-like mixture. Nearby were two more small piles. She estimated there was maybe a quarter-cup of the mixture in each pile.

"Is this some kind of wolf feed?" she asked.

Markie shook her head. "No," she said. "We don't give the animals anything like that."

"And you don't grow any grains?" Nancy asked.

"We don't grow any crops here at all, except herbs for the kitchen," Markie answered.

Nancy took three pieces of paper from her notebook and fashioned small envelope-type pouches. Then she pinched a sample of the mixture from each pile and dropped them in each of the three envelopes. She placed the packets carefully in the small zipper compartment of her backpack.

Nancy talked to Markie all the way back to the office but didn't learn anything new. As she finally drove back out of the preserve she told Bess about the grainy mixture.

"That's all you found? You don't have a lot to go on so far, do you?" Bess asked, frowning.

"Next to nothing," Nancy said. She stopped at a crossroads and looked at the signs. "That's Norwaldo Road," she read. "They said on the news this morning that that's the road to Philip LeRoy's farm. Let's go pay him a little visit."

"Why?" Bess said. "He was mad this morning. He didn't look like someone who welcomes strangers."

"No, but he *did* look like someone who enjoyed telling his story. Maybe he'd like to tell it to a couple of newspaper reporters," she said, smiling.

After a mile of driving Nancy spotted LeRoy's mailbox leaning over the road. She turned into his driveway, which was bordered by pastures. She parked in front of a two-story white house with dark green shutters and took her notebook and pen from her backpack. Then she and Bess trudged toward the house along a rough path dug out of the waist-high snow. Nancy knocked on the door. Within a few moments, it opened.

"Who are you?" Philip LeRoy asked. His face was a rosy red color and his dark eyes pierced into Nancy's.

"I'm Nancy Drew, and this is Bess Marvin. We're reporters for the *River Heights Gazette,* and we're here to get an in-depth story on your feud with Wild-Wolf."

"It's no feud," LeRoy said. "It's a just cause—and it's justice I'm after!"

"Could we have a few minutes?" Nancy asked. "I'm scared of the idea of wolves running loose. I'd like to tell your story. Maybe we can fix this problem so wild animals don't threaten River Heights any-more."

Philip LeRoy blinked, and his expression softened a little. "Come in," he said. "I don't have much time, so please make it quick."

Nancy asked a few questions, repeating several of those that Susie Oliver had asked earlier. LeRoy answered them with the same responses. Then she grilled him about the sheep attacks.

"Exactly when did a wolf attack your flock?" she asked, her pencil ready.

LeRoy stood up and walked behind his chair. "I'm not going into that. My attorney says not to."

"Well, did you see the attacks?" Nancy asked. "How many wolves were there? Are you sure it was wolves and not wild dogs or coyotes?"

"I'm not answering that either," he said, squinting at her. "Say, are you really reporters? You look kinda young to me."

"We're with the student edition," she answered. "I would really like to get an exclusive about the wolves who attacked your sheep."

"I don't think so," he said, walking to the door. "This interview is over."

"Mr. LeRoy—," Nancy began.

"I said it's over! No more questions."

Nancy and Bess hurried out the door and down the path to Nancy's car. In her rearview mirror Nancy could see Philip LeRoy watching her drive away.

"He's scary," Bess said. "I'm glad we left."

As Nancy pulled onto Norwaldo Road, she noticed a service road leading to two large barns far behind LeRoy's house. Trees shielded both sides of the road. "We haven't *quite* left yet," she said.

She drove down the service road and parked the car behind three huge spruce trees so that it couldn't be seen from LeRoy's house. Then she led Bess through the snow to one of the large barns.

"What are we looking for?" Bess whispered, even though there was no one nearby to hear.

"I just want to see the setup," Nancy said. "See where the sheep are kept, see how the wolves might have gotten in. He said on the news this morning that the attack was at night, at this time of year—so the sheep would probably have been in a barn."

Nancy lifted the heavy crossbar and pulled open the barn door. As they went in the door slowly creaked shut behind them. Nancy propped it open with a large rock so that they could have some light.

Even though it was day, the huge room was dark, dingy, and mostly empty. Thin rods of pale sunshine slid through the cracks in the wall and crisscrossed from one side to the other. Gritty dust filled the stripes of light.

"There aren't any sheep in here," Bess said. "There aren't even any animal stalls."

"It's just a storage room," Nancy said. There were

a dozen or so large sealed barrels in one corner. "I think there's a door over there," Nancy said, pointing to the opposite corner.

She walked to a large steel door, pulled it open, and was immediately engulfed in a cloud of frigid cold. "It's a walk-in freezer," she told Bess. "There are more barrels in there."

As she closed the freezer door she heard an ominous scraping noise at the barn door. She turned in time to see a booted foot roll the rock doorstop into the large room. The barn door slammed shut. Nancy raced to the door, but it was too late.

As the crossbar thudded down into its iron cleat, she felt a similar thud in the pit of her stomach.

3

An Unfortunate Meeting

"Nancy, we're locked in!" Bess said.

"He couldn't have seen us drive back here from the house because the trees shielded the road," Nancy said. "He must have followed us."

She looked around the big room. It was even darker now that the door was shut. There were no windows, and even though the room was at least two stories high, there was no loft.

She walked around the room, pushing at wallboards, hoping to find one or two that were loose and could be pushed out enough for the girls to squeeze through. But after a half hour they were no closer to freedom than when the door had slammed shut.

"What are we going to do, Nancy?" Bess asked.

"There's got to be a way out of here," Nancy said.

She paced, her boots shuffling across the dusty wooden floor. "Wait a minute. Remember when we worked at Uncle Bud's pizza place that summer?"

"Yeah," Bess said. "I wish I were there right now instead of trapped in this stinky barn."

"Remember the walk-in freezer?" Nancy asked, walking back to the door in the corner. "Bring that rock that we used for a doorstop over here."

Bess rolled the heavy rock over to Nancy, who was standing in front of LeRoy's walk-in freezer. Nancy continued, "Uncle Bud's walk-in had a back door so they could get deliveries straight from the alley outside."

"I remember that," Bess said.

"Keep your fingers crossed that this walk-in has a back door too." Nancy opened the front freezer door and propped it open with the rock, just in case. Then she walked to the back of the long room. "I've got it," she called back. She tried the door and it opened. "Kick away the rock and come on through."

Nancy heard the other door close with a pneumatic *whoosh*. Bess appeared through the frosty haze, and the two darted out the back door.

They raced to Nancy's car. She didn't admit it to Bess, but she was really relieved to see that the car was still there. Within minutes she was charging down the service road and back out onto Norwaldo Road.

"Look at me, I'm just a mess," Bess said, brushing at her jacket. "I think I have cobwebs in my hair. I need to freshen up before we report for work at the Carnival."

"I need to change clothes too," Nancy agreed, "and I want to make a stop at the chemistry lab at Riverside College. I'm going to drop off the samples of that grainy stuff I found at WildWolf so they can analyze them."

"It's noon now," Bess said, looking at her watch. "Why don't you drop me off at home. I'll drive to the park after I get cleaned up."

"Good idea," Nancy said. "Let's meet up with Poodles McNulty at three."

"Maybe we can find out where he got that name," Bess said with a smile.

Nancy drove Bess home, dropped off the samples at the college, then went to her house. A familiar smell greeted her as soon as she got out of the car.

She followed the delicious aroma into the kitchen. "Hannah," she said, "I could smell your homemade chicken noodle soup clear out in the driveway. The whole neighborhood is going to be lining up for a taste."

"Don't tell your father I made his favorite soup while he was out of town," Hannah Gruen said.

Nancy felt a warm comforting feeling tumble through her—not only from the soup's scent, but also from the familiar sight of Hannah stirring the pot on the stove.

Nancy's mother had died when Nancy was only three years old. Shortly after that, her father had hired Hannah to come live with them. Housekeeper, cook, and loving nurturer for Nancy, Hannah had virtually become part of the Drew family over the years.

"Look at you!" Hannah said, bustling over to pull twigs from Nancy's hood. "Where on Earth have you been? You haven't been out looking for those wolves, have you?" she added with a frown.

"Well, sort of," Nancy admitted, sitting down to a large bowl of soup and some of Hannah's delicious biscuits. While she ate Nancy told Hannah about her activities the previous night and that morning.

"Well, you're old enough—and experienced enough—to know what you're doing," Hannah said. "But you *know* I'll worry about you anyway."

"I'll be careful," Nancy said.

By one twenty Nancy was walking around the Carnival grounds. She was dressed in multiple layers: a thermal unitard, a silk turtleneck, black ski pants, and a long, purple wool sweater. She had slathered plenty of sunscreen on her face and pulled a black-and-white knit hat down over her ears. She was toasty warm even without a coat, although her parka was in the car just in case.

She spent most of the next hour talking to her

team of high-school-student hosts. "Remember, although you're working," she concluded, "we are all encouraged to participate in any of the activities that we choose. For example, I've signed up for the cross-country ski race Thursday night. If you want to participate in any of the sports, feel free to do so."

"That's *any* activity, right?" Brianda asked, walking up to the group. She wore a hot-pink snowsuit that looked really great with her pale skin and dark hair.

"Sure," Nancy said. "It doesn't have to be a sport. If you want to enter the ice-carving competition, grab your chisel or saw and sign up. We have plenty of backup, so we can all enjoy the Carnival. Go look around and I'll see you all at the meeting with Mr. McNulty in half an hour."

Nancy and Brianda went to check on Bess at the Heat Hut. Over choco-lattes Nancy told Brianda about how she'd dropped off the samples at the chem lab.

"And we also paid a visit to Philip LeRoy," Bess added.

"Yes, we pretended we were reporters and asked him a few questions," Nancy said casually, "but he didn't tell us anything he hadn't already said on TV." Then she changed the subject. "Have there been any wolf sightings by the people searching?" she asked.

"Nothing," Brianda said. "No word from anywhere in the state."

At three o'clock Nancy, Bess, and Brianda joined the other workers for a pep rally with the new chairman of the Carnival, Poodles McNulty. The meeting was held next to the Crystal Palace in an outdoor amphitheater, where the Snow Princess would be crowned. The two-story ice castle was draped in black canvas, waiting for the big unveiling later.

The stage was bare when Nancy and her friends took their places on folding chairs. Sun streamed toward them through a pale gray sky streaked with stripes of light blue and peach.

A low rumble of conversation rippled through the air until familiar singsong-y music hushed the crowd. To the accompaniment of "Who's Afraid of the Big, Bad Wolf," a tall, stocky man with a thick cover of spiky red hair loped onto the stage.

He swung his arms as if to conduct the music, and a few people in the crowd sang along.

"Hello, you hardy souls," he bellowed when the song stopped. "Welcome!" He spoke with a lilting accent that Nancy recognized as an Irish brogue.

"Hello!" the crowd boomed back.

"I'm Poodles McNulty, and I'm one hundred percent ready to get this Carnival rockin'. Are you?"

"Yes!" the crowd answered, adding applause and whistles.

"I've heard that some people think wild wolves on the loose is a reason to stop these festivities. Well, they're wrong! We're not going to let a little thing like wolves hanging out in the woods shut us down, are we?"

"No!" There were more cheers and hollers.

"Now, we're not fools," he said, his voice taking on a more serious tone. "We've doubled our security efforts to ensure the safety of our guests—and all of you, of course." His face wound into a huge smile full of sparkling white teeth.

"So relax, and enjoy the extra publicity we're getting because of the two escapees. I've been contacted by national news organizations who are sending journalists here to cover our Carnival. We have those two four-legged rascals to thank for that. So be sure to toast them with some cocoa at the Heat Hut, and have a wonderful time!"

He closed with a reminder about the crowning of the Snow Princess and the Crystal Palace lighting later. Then he asked if there were any questions.

"Where'd you get that name?" boomed a voice from the back of the crowd.

"An excellent question, my friend," McNulty boomed back. "As you can probably tell, I'm Irish," he said, brushing his gloved hand over the top of his auburn spikes. "Before I moved to this country, I was a professional boxer there. The nickname 'Poodles' is a traditional one in Irish sporting circles, and it's stuck with me since my days in the ring. And I want you all to call me 'Poodles,' too. None of that 'Mr. McNulty' stuff, okay?"

Poodles finished by leading a rousing cheer, and then he vaulted off the stage to continued applause. As the crowd began moving out, Ned came up to join Nancy and her friends.

"Well, he's sure getting this party off with a bang," Ned said. He was dressed in a green down ski suit that matched his eyes.

"He sure is. Have you seen George?" Nancy asked.

"I saw her a little while ago," Ned said. "She's working with the crew that will be lighting the Crystal Palace later. If I can get away, let's meet at Smoky's in about a half hour. I'll let George know, too." He waved and hurried off.

Thanks to her orientation training, Nancy was able to give Bess and Brianda a short tour of all the activities and highlights of the Carnival.

"Oh look, a fortune-teller," Bess said, pointing ahead. About a block away a small wooden cabin was painted with brightly colored designs. A neon sign in the shape of a crystal ball glowed above the entrance. "Let's go in."

"Oooh, good idea," Brianda said.

"Okay, let's go," Nancy agreed.

When they got inside the cabin, they found that it was empty. The walls were lined with masks, feathers, hats, and bright, exotic clothing. A small heater fanned them with periodic blasts of warm air. "Doesn't look like anyone's here," Bess said. "Hello?"

"I hear something in the back," Nancy said. She started toward the curtains that ran across the back of the small room. Suddenly the curtains parted, and a medium-sized figure stepped through. The person was completely encased in a swirling velvet cape of midnight blue. A full face mask with pale blue lips, a wig, a satin headdress, and gloves completed the outfit. Nancy couldn't tell if the fortune-teller was a man or a woman.

The person motioned for Bess to take a seat on the front side of a small table. The fortune-teller seemed to study Bess's face and palms, and then wrote a note on a piece of paper and folded it into fourths. Handing it over to Bess, the person motioned for her not to open it yet. This routine was repeated with Brianda.

Finally, Nancy took the seat. She stared at the fortune-teller. Nancy had an odd feeling when the person's piercing stare drilled right into her through the tiny eyeholes in the mask. She felt immediately as if she should be on her guard, but she was having a hard time focusing her thoughts. Nancy felt locked into the fortune-teller's gaze. It was almost as if she *couldn't* look away.

A tiny tingling fluttered across the back of her neck as the gloved hand pushed her note across the table. With a wave of its hand, the fortune-teller motioned them out.

Nancy led her friends outside. The sudden shock of cold air seemed to clear her thoughts. She turned to Bess and Brianda. "Okay, let's see what we've got."

"Well, this sure strikes home," Brianda said. "'BEWARE of wolves in sheep's clothing.'" She read the note again and frowned at Nancy.

"Mine is sort of the same idea," Bess said. She smiled faintly, and Nancy could tell she was a little rattled. "'Beware of the bite,'" Bess read. "'It IS worse than the bark.'"

Bess crumpled her note and stuffed it in her pocket. "Well, it looks like the fortune-teller got the cue from Poodles," she said. "Use the missing wolves as a way to punch up the Carnival with extra excitement."

Bess jutted out her chin. Nancy knew that meant her friend was trying to be defiantly brave, even though she was probably a little frightened. "What does yours say, Nancy?" Bess asked.

Nancy unfolded the paper. The tingling at the back of her neck returned as she read. There, in large black letters, was her fortune: BEWARE . . . DANGER.

4

The Message Is Crystal Clear

For a moment she felt like she was back inside the cabin, staring at those eyes behind the mask again. She looked at the fortune again, but her thoughts were interrupted by George's voice.

"*There* you are," George said. "Ned said I should meet you all at Smoky's. So I go, and no one's there. I've been walking all over . . ." She stopped and waved a hand in front of Nancy's shocked face. "Hey, what's the matter with you? Earth to Nancy, Earth to Nancy, come in."

The image of the fortune-teller vanished in a wisp of midnight blue as Nancy shook her head and refocused her thoughts. "Hey, George, I'm glad you could make it. Let's go to Smoky's. I'll tell you all about what happened when we get there."

Ned had already found a table by the time Nancy and her friends arrived. Smoky's had set up a tent in the Park for the Carnival. All the familiar tables, bright tablecloths, and candles were there, along with plenty of tall heaters to keep the customers comfortable. A truck behind the tent, complete with oven and refrigerator, supplied Smoky's famous treats.

Within minutes of taking their seats, Bess and Brianda had shown Ned and George their fortunes and had told them all about the experience.

"Show them what you got, Nancy," Bess urged. "Hers was the scariest one," she told the others.

Nancy unfolded her fortune and pushed it over to George. "This *does* seem a little different," George said. "It doesn't have any cutesy references to wolves in it. It looks like it's really serious—not a joke."

"I agree," Brianda said, rereading the words. "Nancy, yours is sort of . . . more personal."

"I'm feeling kind of weird," Bess said in a hushed voice. "If it *is* personal . . . what if that fortune-teller can really see into the future? What if it's true?"

Nancy agreed that her fortune seemed different than the others. It had given her an odd feeling, too. But she could tell that Bess and Brianda were beginning to get worried, so she decided to play it cool until she was completely sure.

"Don't forget," she pointed out, "the fortune-teller is a paid entertainer. Everyone's talking about the missing wolves right now."

"Poodles is encouraging it," Ned reminded them. "He thinks it's good for business."

"Exactly," Nancy said. "The fortune-teller surely picked up on that. Everyone's probably going to get scary fortunes, and ones that have a wolf-like theme. It's all a gimmick to flood the Carnival with mystery and excitement."

"Yeah, but yours was different," Brianda said. "The message—"

"Food's here," Nancy interrupted, relieved to see the platters heading toward their table. She had decided a change of subject was just what the party needed.

"Guess what," George said, dipping her burrito in salsa. "I'm going to be helping with the lights for the unveiling of the Crystal Palace."

"So we heard," Nancy said. "I know you really wanted to be in on that."

"It's *so* cool," George explained. Her dark eyes glinted with reflections from the heater near their table. "It's going to be the most spectacular setup ever. We rehearsed for hours this afternoon."

"Have you seen the palace and everything?" Bess asked.

"It's really something," George said with a nod.

"Huge—two stories high. And parts of it have been hollowed out, so we can get in there and set up lights. There are lots of towers and windows and decorations cut out around the top."

"And all carved from ice," Brianda said. "I'm always stunned by what they can do."

"With a lot of hard work and a dozen chainsaws," Ned added.

"When the name of the Snow Princess is announced," George told them, "they're going to turn out all the other lights in the area—that's new this year. Then the drapes will fall away and we'll flip the switches. Thousands of lights will go on inside the Palace, and all these different colors are going to shoot out through the ice walls. It'll be amazing."

"I think this will be the best Carnival ever," Bess said. Nancy was relieved that her friend seemed to be over her jitters from the fortunes they'd gotten earlier.

After lunch Nancy and her friends took off to perform their various duties. Bess headed to the Heat Hut, and George went to the Crystal Palace. Ned left to meet with the torchlight parade committee, saying he would see Nancy at the Snow Princess judges' table.

The Carnival opened at dusk to a huge crowd. Nancy and Brianda walked to the park's entrance where the other members of Nancy's team of hosts were gathered. Nancy watched while her team passed out maps and offered to direct visitors or to escort them to different activities and events.

Finally Nancy reported to the outdoor stage. Huge heaters perched atop poles radiated warmth onto the stage and into the audience. In front of the first row of seats was a long table. Nancy took her seat at the table with the other Snow Princess judges. Ned was already there, and he introduced Nancy to Susie Oliver, the local television reporter she had watched that morning. Susie was going to be the emcee for the competition.

"I saw your interview with Philip LeRoy and Markie Michaels," Nancy said to Susie. "So what did you think? Was Mr. LeRoy telling the truth? Or is he just trying to get WildWolf shut down?"

"You know, I can't decide," Susie said. "They both seemed to make sense to me. Frankly, I don't care who's right as long as those wolves get back where they belong. I really don't like the idea of those beasts running around the woods."

"I don't think you really have to worry," one of the other judges said. Ned introduced him as Jax Dashell, detective with the River Heights police force. "I'm on special assignment, heading up the Carnival security detail," he explained.

"And you don't think we have to worry about the missing wolves?" Susie asked. She was even prettier in person than she was on television. About thirty years old and shorter than Nancy, she had short, spiky, nearly white hair.

"No," Detective Dashell said. "Wolves are frightened of people. They like to keep what the animal handlers call a long flight distance between themselves and human beings."

"Has it occurred to any of you that we've got more than a wolf problem on our hands?" said the last judge at the table.

"Willy, I already know what you're going to say," Detective Dashell said.

"Nancy, this is Willy Dean," Ned said. "He owns a mailing service. Willy has an interesting twist on the wolf story."

"Okay, okay, don't believe me," Willy said. "But I tell you I've seen it, and it's no joke." Willy was average looking—brown hair, brown eyes. But he had muscular arms and shoulders, as if he did serious weight training.

The music started, announcing the beginning of the Snow Princess parade.

"Seen what?" Nancy asked, leaning closer so she could hear Willy over the music.

"The werewolf," Willy answered, opening his judging book to the first page. "You know, one of those creatures that's a regular person in the daytime, but turns into a wolf when the moon is full. I've seen one running around here lately."

The lively music cut off Nancy's startling conversation with Willy and heralded the parade of finalists for the honor of being crowned Snow Princess. Each finalist had already performed in a talent competition and had been interviewed by the Carnival committee. Tonight they were appearing in ballgowns on the heated stage. The judges were to evaluate them on poise and appearance. These points would be combined with totals from the other two competitions to determine this year's Snow Princess.

Susie introduced five women who walked across the stage in gorgeous white gowns. Some of the dresses were plain but very elegant. Others were glitzier, decorated with lace or beads.

Without talking, the judges recorded their votes. Susie collected them, and she, Poodles, and a couple of other people huddled around a computer, adding up the totals.

Susie then went back to the microphone with a note in her hand. "Ladies and gentlemen," she announced. A low drum roll stuttered from the back of the stage. "The Carnival committee and I are proud to introduce you to this year's River Heights Holiday Winter Carnival Snow Princess . . . Miss Julie Taylor!"

The women on the stage all gasped and clustered around the new Snow Princess. Susie placed a rhinestone tiara on her head, and the Snow Princess was led by Poodles to the canvas which had been draped around the Crystal Palace. She and Poodles grasped the cord that would bring down the curtain.

All the lights around the area dimmed and then blacked out, as George had predicted. Everyone waited a moment in the dark, staring at the drape. Nancy held her breath as the drum roll grew louder, more urgent.

Finally the Snow Princess pulled the cord and the canvas shroud dropped from the Crystal Palace. Lights burst on with an elegant fanfare.

But only one color—blood red—spiked through the ice. And it shone through large block letters carved into the wall, letters that warned: BEWARE . . . DANGER.

5

Who's Afraid of the Big Bad Wolf?

A weird sound—a sort of collective gasp—rustled through the crowd. Nancy felt her skin ripple in response. A few startled screams punctuated the last gasp.

As Nancy stared at the blood-red words glowing on the wall of the Crystal Palace, she reached into her pocket and wrapped her hand around the fortune.

"Nancy," Bess whispered next to her. "That's your fortune. It's the same message!"

Nancy clenched the paper until her fingers started to hurt. Then she shook off the anxious chill and stood up. Instantly, everyone moved into action. Some people scurried away. Others pointed with tentative, nervous-sounding laughs.

"Raise the drapes," Poodles McNulty yelled. "Get those drapes back up." A few members of the production crew began reattaching the black canvas drape to the metal ring. Then they hoisted it into place, masking the ice building from view again.

Nancy raced to the large lighting booth to find George, and Ned followed close behind. George was working frantically with the rest of the technicians.

"Tell me it was a joke," Nancy said, "or some crazy scheme cooked up by Poodles McNulty."

"I don't know," George said. "We're shocked too. We're trying to put the pieces together now."

"Okay," boomed Poodles, rushing in. "You had your fun and stirred up the crowd. Whoever did it gets a gold star for ingenuity and marketing. Which one was it?" He looked at each of the lighting technicians with a tight smile. He acted as if he was okay with what happened. But Nancy could tell he was simmering beneath that smile.

"Don't worry—I'm not firing anyone," Poodles said. "It was just a prank—I know that." He looked into each person's face. When he got to Nancy's, he seemed to study hers longer than the others.

"No one's taking the credit?" Poodles asked, pausing for a moment. "Okay—just get the original lighting plan back in place. No one leaves until it's done." Then he charged back out of the room.

"Boy, he really gave you a once-over," Ned said to Nancy.

"He was probably trying to figure out who she is and what she's doing here," George offered.

Nancy smiled and nodded at her friends. *Was that it?* she wondered. *Or was it something else?*

"I have to get to work," George said. "We have to reprogram everything." She lowered her voice. "I'll let you know what we find out," she promised Nancy.

"Let's go," Nancy said to Ned. "I want to see something." Nancy and Ned left the lighting booth and went behind the curved wall—the "shell"—that formed the back of the amphitheater. When they got to the edge of the shell they could see the draped Crystal Palace next door.

Nancy stopped Ned and they ducked into the curved shadow that the shell cast across the snow. The wind had picked up a little. The drapery surrounding the Palace rippled as the wind blew across it. Every few seconds a gust would hit the opening where the two ends of the drapery came together. The black canvas would lift up slightly and blow away, revealing the ice building inside.

"There's Jax Dashell," Nancy pointed out. The detective was standing nearby. "He must be guarding the Palace. I need to get past him. If you can get him away from his post for a few minutes, I can sneak through the opening in the drape."

"I'm on it," Ned said. He hurried out from behind the shell and up to Detective Dashell.

Some of their conversation traveled to Nancy's ear on the dry, cold air. First she heard words like "shock," "Willy," "werewolf," and "panic." Then Ned pointed toward the stage. "Come on," he said, loud enough for Nancy to hear. "You'd better talk to them. You can still see the Palace from there."

Ned led Detective Dashell away and toward the stage. As they passed by Nancy, hiding in the shadows, she held her breath. Then, while they climbed the steps to the stage, she darted inside the drapes to the Palace, pulling the ends of the cloth together behind her.

Even in the darkness the Crystal Palace glistened. Someone had set up a couple of portable worklights on poles. They weren't very bright, but the dim bulbs caused a dramatic effect. The lightbeams shot around and through the ice, forming sparkling patterns on top of patterns.

Nancy hurried right to the wall where the threatening words had appeared. She examined the carving. From the gouges and pointed holes she figured that the letters were hammered out with a chisel rather than cut with a chainsaw.

She turned on her penlight so she could pinpoint the area around the carving. Her eyes narrowed as she concentrated. She didn't want to miss anything.

And she knew she didn't have much time before Detective Dashell returned to his post.

She scanned the ground carefully. Suddenly her breath caught in her throat. An icy breeze wafted by. Something fluttered in the dark shadows near the floor. She crouched and pinned the area in her penlight beam. Several small, purple twists of silk stuck to the wall of ice.

As she stared at the fluttering fabric her mind flashed back to a colorful picture. She was in the fortune-teller's cabin at the moment its host swept in—and the fortune-teller had been wearing a cape bordered with purple fringe.

Her heart stepped up a few beats and she pocketed two of the purple fragments, leaving the other pieces for subsequent evidence-gatherers. Then she ducked out of the Palace without being seen. Circling around the amphitheater shell, she headed straight for the fortune-teller's cabin.

She stepped inside the painted building. "Welcome, Miss," a friendly elderly woman said. She had grayish hair and wore a filmy, bright-colored dress layered over a tunic. Chandelier earrings trailed down and rested on her shoulders.

"We've had strange things happening this evening," she continued. "Would you like to know what it means for you? Show me your palm and I'll tell you." She smiled warmly.

"Actually, I wanted to speak to the other fortune-teller," Nancy said.

"But there is no other one," the woman explained. "I am the only fortune-teller."

"There was someone here earlier," Nancy said. "With a mask and a cape." Nancy looked around.

"A white mask with pale blue lips?" the woman asked. She looked at the back corner of the room. Nancy followed her gaze to see a couple of bare nails poking out of the wall. "I wondered where it went. Was the cape dark blue, by any chance?"

"With purple fringe," Nancy added with a nod.

"Oh boy," the woman said. She dropped her dramatic, mystical air and talked like a real person. "I just got here. I was called away earlier on an emergency. Thank goodness it turned out to be a false alarm. I'm still feeling a little rattled."

"That must have been really scary," Nancy said. "Who called you about it—the police?"

"I don't know who it was," the woman admitted. "Some guy raced in the back door saying the Carnival office got a call that my house was on fire and I had to get right home. I just panicked and ran. I didn't stop to ask any questions."

"And you don't know who called?" Nancy asked.

"No," the woman said. "I just figured it was a neighbor. But when I got home, everything was fine."

"Can you describe the man who raced in with the message?"

The woman thought for a moment, then shrugged her shoulders. "No. I can't picture him at all. I was just so scared. Hey, do you think he's the one who stole my costume? Seems like a lot of trouble to go to for just an old cape and mask." She paused for a moment. "Why are you asking all these questions, anyway?"

"Just curious. I'm glad it was a false alarm."

"Me too. I don't like the idea of someone ripping me off like that, though. Thanks for helping me figure everything out. How about letting me read your palm? No charge, of course."

"I'll have to take a rain check on the fortune," Nancy said, smiling. "See you later."

Nancy ducked out of the cabin and went back to the amphitheater.

"I couldn't find you," Ned said. He sounded worried. "Did you hear me earlier? I made up a story about Willy revving up a group backstage with talk about a werewolf," he said proudly. "Then I asked Jax to calm the crowd down before anyone panicked."

"I heard parts of that," Nancy said. "Good job—it worked."

"For a little while, anyway," Ned said. "We looked around, and of course Willy and the group weren't there. Finally he decided they had all left. By the time we got back to the Palace, you were gone."

Nancy told him what she'd found stuck to the Palace. Then she described her meeting with the *real* fortune-teller.

"Nancy, I don't get this," Ned said. "You're saying that the person who gave you, Bess, and Brianda your fortunes was a fraud?" Ned stared at the snow for a minute. "Wait a minute," he continued. "That means the fake one was there *specifically* to give you those fortunes!"

"It could be," Nancy said. "So far, I can't figure out any other reason for the whole charade."

"So the fake fortune-teller was targeting you," Ned said again. "But how would the person even know you were going there? That doesn't make sense."

"How about this," Nancy suggested. "Someone is following us. Maybe it's the person who stole or released the WildWolf animals. He's not *planning* to do the fortune-telling bit. He's just keeping tabs on us. But then he hears us talk about getting our fortunes told, and he sees an opportunity to scare us. So he runs around to the back of the fortune-telling cabin."

"He tells the real fortune-teller that she's got an emergency at home, to get her out of the way," Ned added.

"Right," Nancy agreed. "She rushes away, and he looks around and sees the costumes. Maybe he's even been in the cabin before, so he knows there are disguises available. He pulls on the mask, gloves, and cape, and waits in the back of the room."

"Knowing you three are on your way," Ned finished.

"Exactly," Nancy said. "He hands us the fortunes and clears out as soon as we leave."

"So you think he's got something to do with the wolfnapping, and knows you're on the case?" Ned asked.

"What I know for sure is this: Someone who didn't belong in the cabin was in disguise, handing us fortunes. Why? And it also seems like more than a coincidence that my fortune was exactly the same as the message in the Crystal Palace wall."

"So the fake fortune-teller was the same person who carved the nasty message in the ice," Ned concluded.

"Maybe," Nancy said. "If so, he's smart—the kind of person who sees an opportunity and goes for it."

"Well, just the idea of someone following you in the first place bothers me," Ned said.

"I'm totally with you on that one," Nancy said. "So we need to find out if our assumptions are true, and if so, who this impostor is, and why he—or she—is doing all this."

Ned looked at his watch. "Okay, I'm in trouble," he said.

"I thought I heard the band tuning up," Nancy said. "It must be time for the torchlight parade."

"Yep—and I'm supposed to help get it started. Let's meet at the Heat Hut after, okay?"

"I'll be there," Nancy assured him.

"Be careful!" Ned called back.

Nancy quickly checked on her team, but it really wasn't necessary. Everyone was lining up for the torchlight parade.

At last she made it back to the Palace area, where Detective Dashell was still manning his post. She told him about the bogus fortunes she and her friends had gotten from the fake fortune-teller. She even confessed to sneaking into the Palace and finding the fringe in the ice. He nodded as she talked, but his smoky blue eyes narrowed when she told him about her conversation with the true fortune-teller.

"Okay, I've heard enough to tell you that I want you to back off, Nancy," Detective Dashell said. His face had a kindly expression, but his voice was stern, and she could tell he meant what he said.

"If you're being followed and threatened," he said, "it's time for us to step in. I've been on the police force for a few years, so I'm aware of your skill in solving cases. But we can't have you putting yourself in danger. I'll follow up with the fortune-teller and try to track down the fake one."

"Will you tell me if you find out anything?" Nancy asked.

"If it will keep you off the trail, yes."

"Deal," Nancy said. She left to pick up Bess for the parade.

It began with a few men wielding flaming torches as they walked to the river. Behind them, white horses pulled carriages which carried the Snow Princess and her court. Costumed figures were next—Jack Frost, winter elves, and the cast of the ballet company's production of *The Nutcracker*.

Poodles McNulty began a group sing of "Winter Wonderland," and the spectators chimed in. Laughing and singing, Nancy and Bess joined Ned at the end of the parade.

As they neared the river the music wound down. Before another song could begin, a new sound floated along the river and filled the ears of the paraders. It was the same eerie wail that had chilled the blood of humans for centuries. The howl of a lone wolf rose and fell through the thin air.

Nancy turned to find the source of the sound. Everyone around her followed her lead. There, on a bridge spanning the Muskoka, they saw the silhouette of a wolf sitting on its haunches. As they watched, it leaned its head back and pointed its long, tapered nose toward the sky. Another mournful cry left its throat and filled the air.

While a third howl poured out from its lungs, the beast rose up on its back legs, standing tall in the moonlight.

6

The Hair of the Wolf

This time the crowd's reaction was stunned silence. Everyone stood still and stared. There was no collective gasp—not even any screams. Some people seemed to be holding their breath.

Nancy was *not* holding her breath. In fact, it was coming pretty fast—faster than comfortable. She couldn't take her eyes off the figure on the bridge. It almost seemed as if none of this was real. People carrying torches, a werewolf howling in the moonlight . . . it was like watching an old horror movie, except she wasn't in her comfy house with a big bowl of popcorn in her lap. She was outdoors in the bitter cold, mixed signals rushing through her brain.

The beast on the bridge let out one more bone-chilling howl before loping off on two legs into the shadows on the opposite bank of the river. By the time the air was quiet again the wolf had disappeared into Ripple Woods.

The silence continued for a moment or two. It was suddenly broken by a smattering of applause. Everyone was wearing gloves, so the claps were muffled, but the sound grew and was soon accompanied by full-fledged cheers.

"It was an actor," Bess said, letting out a large sigh. "Of course—it *had* to be."

"I guess so," Ned concluded. "Just part of the whole opening night festivities. Poodles is really trying to spin this thing positively, that's for sure."

"I can see everyone thinks it's part of the show," Willy said out loud. "You all figure that was just entertainment for the Carnival. But I'm telling you, I've seen that creature before. He was slinking across a field. Now you tell *me* how that wolf's got anything to do with the Carnival!"

Willy walked off, mumbling to himself.

The torchlight parade ended at the riverbank. The *Nutcracker* cast performed a few highlights of the ballet on the hard ground, and the crowd dispersed pretty quickly after that.

Everyone was buzzing about the scary message in the Crystal Palace wall and the werewolf on the bridge. Most people seemed to think the performance was part of the fun, but Nancy picked up a nervous jitter underlying all the excitement. Carnivalgoers walked quickly to their cars and sped from the parking lots out into the wintry night.

Nancy's friends had chores to complete before leaving their jobs for the evening. She checked all her hosts out for the evening, answered a few questions about the next day's schedule, and finally headed for home.

"Wow, does this feel good," she said out loud, finally sinking down into her bed. Although the thermostat was set the same as it always was this time of year, she just couldn't seem to get warm. She pulled the covers close up around her face, but sleep didn't come easily. She thought back over the day—from being locked in Philip LeRoy's barn to the crazy evening at the Carnival.

She couldn't chase from her mind the figure covered in wolf hair standing on the bridge until a veil of sleep finally draped over her brain.

For the second morning in a row, a ringing phone jarred Nancy awake.

"Hi, it's me." This time it was Bess's familiar voice. "Has Brianda called you yet?"

"No," Nancy answered, sitting up and yawning. "What's up?"

"She and I talked last night before we went home. We both have late shifts today," Bess explained, "and we thought we'd see if there's anything that we can do to help on the case this morning. Maybe there's some lead you want us to follow up on?"

"Hey, thanks," Nancy said. "Actually, I'm not going in until this afternoon myself. I was going to call the chemist and see if he knows what that stuff was that I found near the wolf enclosure. Markie couldn't identify it, so it must be something brought in from outside."

"Do you want me to call?" Bess offered.

"I'll do it," Nancy answered. "But stand by. After I talk to him let's have breakfast, and we'll go from there. Want to call Brianda and ask her to come too?"

Bess hung up, and Nancy took a shower. She pulled on jeans and a heavy white cable-knit sweater. After chugging a glass of juice she called the college and talked to the chemist. Then she called Bess back. Brianda had just arrived at Bess's house. Nancy told them to meet her at Net 'n Nosh computer café. "Bring your laptop," she told Bess.

Within fifteen minutes they were all seated at a window table. It was perfect weather—not as cold as the day before, but way too cold for the ice to melt. The sunlight bathed everything in a bright glow.

"George is already working," Bess told Nancy and Brianda as they ordered their breakfasts. "They're still trying to get all the schematics restored for the lighting program. Someone really hacked away at it to get the red lights shining perfectly through that scary message."

"I haven't heard from Ned this morning," Nancy said. "He's probably already on the job too. I'd really like to talk to George, so I'm thinking about going over to the Carnival early."

"Did you talk to your chemist friend?" Brianda asked, sipping her foamy latte.

"I sure did—and guess what? That substance I found is a homemade animal feed. It's fifty percent standard grains, plus some other grasses and herbs that would appeal to *sheep*."

"Sheep!" Brianda said, her upper lip fluffy with frothy cream.

"Exactly," Nancy confirmed. "That's why I had you bring your computer, Bess. See what you can find on Philip LeRoy. I know he's been interviewed for the newspaper as well as television. Those interviews will be in the archives somewhere—you can start there. Get me anything you can find out about him."

The waitress brought breakfast. Brianda had ordered French toast, Bess a Belgian waffle, and Nancy a vegetable omelet.

"That might take a while," Bess said, pouring blueberry syrup over her waffle. "There are lots of sites I can check."

"Whatever you can find out will be great," Nancy said.

She told Bess and Brianda about her meeting with the real fortune-teller. Both girls were visibly distressed by that news. The three talked over the theory Nancy had about being followed and fooled by the fake fortune-teller.

"I don't like being followed," Bess said, looking out the window. "It's not the first time—but that doesn't make it any easier."

"I told Detective Dashell what happened, so I'm sure he's looking into it. But Brianda, while Bess is tracking down info on LeRoy, I'd like you to check back with the real fortune-teller. Find out whether she's remembered anything more about the man who got rid of her so he could take her place."

"Okay. So what did you two think of the werewolf?" Brianda asked.

"Everyone seems to think it's part of the fun," Bess offered. "I'm hoping they're right."

"That's what I've heard, too," Brianda said. "I mean, there are no real werewolves, right? I just hope it's not someone trying to scare people about our missing wolves. Markie's so afraid Khayyam and Liz will get hurt, or worse, if they're out there just running around and some nutcase sees them."

"Let's get to work and make sure that doesn't happen," Nancy said. "Let's find the wolves first."

They quickly finished breakfast and went to the Carnival. It was a few minutes past ten. Brianda left immediately for the fortune-teller's cabin. Bess took her computer to the Heat Hut, where she could work at a table in the back until her shift started.

The temperature had dropped ten degrees, so Nancy pulled on a pair of blue snow pants that she'd brought. With those and her hooded parka she knew she could handle the frigid air.

Her first stop was the lighting booth at the amphitheater. George welcomed the break. "We still don't know who did it," she said. "The lighting schematic was computer-driven, so the person probably knew theater lighting. Sabotaging the original program and substituting another is pretty standard tech stuff. Speaking of techies," George said, looking over Nancy's shoulder.

Nancy turned around and saw Bess scampering across the icy ground toward them. "I've got to go to work in a few," Bess said. "But I wanted you to have what I found so far. I went back to the computer café to print out a couple of articles that LeRoy wrote for livestock magazines."

"Look at this," Nancy said, scanning the sheets. "It seems that Mr. LeRoy customizes his winter feed for the flock."

"He includes a few recipes there," Bess added. "He even has his own web page, and he sells packages of his grain concoction to people all over the world."

"I'll bet that's what was in those barrels in his barn," Nancy said. "Bess, this is excellent."

"I'll search some more on my breaks," Bess said. "Come by later! See ya." With a broad grin she went back to the Heat Hut.

Nancy had an hour left before she reported for duty. She strolled over to the fortune-teller's cabin, but there was a line outside. She didn't see Brianda, so she walked on. She kept an eye out for Detective Dashell, but didn't see him either. Nancy ended up at the field next to the park where a rousing softball-in-the-snow game had started.

Nancy stopped for a while and watched the game. When the inning was over and the teams changed sides she saw Philip LeRoy stride toward second base.

"Well now," Nancy mumbled. She walked to the parking lot near the softball field. She recognized the truck parked at the end of the lot as the one she'd seen in LeRoy's drive.

Nancy looked around. The lot was empty. Everyone was on or near the softball field, playing or cheering. Nancy walked casually to LeRoy's truck and peered into the empty truck bed. It looked clean, but she knew that you don't always see everything in the first glance.

It took about five minutes to finally spot what she'd hoped to find: a few small piles of a grainy mixture like the one she'd found at WildWolf. She gathered some up, leaving the rest where it was. She put a couple of tablespoons of the mixture into an empty film canister she had in the small sports pack strapped around her waist.

She then crouched and checked all the tires. The first two were packed with snow and a few twigs and leaves in the tirewells. Then she saw something dark buried in the snow behind one of the wheels. She flashed her penlight into the tirewell. Her pulse skipped so rapidly that she felt a tingling on the sides of her neck. A sudden shiver made the penlight beam bobble up and down.

She stripped off the glove of her right hand and reached into the packed snow on LeRoy's truck. She hardly felt the cold on her fingers as she pulled away a clump of gray-white hair with dark brown tips.

Nancy folded the hair into a tissue and stuffed it into her bag. Then she stood up and went back over the truck bed, inch by inch. She found a couple more large hunks of the hair jammed under a flap in the corner of the truck bed. She put the smallest hunk in her bag and left the other, folding the rubber flap back down over it.

Her heart was still pounding. *Get a grip,* she told herself. *That could be cat hair or dog hair. There are lots of animals on his farm from which this hair might have come.*

She walked quickly back into the Carnival grounds. "But it could be wolf," she muttered. "Markie will know for sure. And if it is . . ."

Nancy stopped at the Heat Hut for a mocha latte. Bess was too busy to talk, but she gestured that she'd meet Nancy at three o'clock. Nancy checked in for work and began making her rounds, talking to her team of hosts.

She came across Brianda at the two-story snow slide near the south end of the park. For a week, carpenters and other Carnival workers had constructed the manmade hill. They had packed snow onto a carefully engineered scaffolding, building it up until it was a superslide. Every year this was one of the Carnival events that drew the biggest crowd—especially among River Heights teens.

This Thursday afternoon was no exception. Nancy and Brianda sat on a nearby bench and watched the fun. The slide was already superslick from all the people who had used it. The frozen snow was polished to a high shine.

Dozens of people patiently climbed the stairway, one slow step at a time, while those at the top prepared to skid to the bottom.

Nancy unzipped her sports pack. "I want to show you something," she told Brianda. "I found—"

Her words caught in her throat when she heard the first crunch. It wasn't the soft crunch of snow. It was another sound—brittle and snaplike. Nancy knew it was a sound that didn't belong with the snowslide.

Then she heard a loud *craaaaaaack*. The sun was so bright on the two-story pile of snow that when she saw the hill seem to shudder, she hoped it was a mirage. But it wasn't her imagination. As if it were experiencing a mini-earthquake, the two-story snow-slide shivered again, then convulsed into a small avalanche. Sliders and climbers tumbled down in a booming tidal wave of snow and ice.

7

A Fortune Comes True

Nancy's latte dropped in a splash of coffee and white chocolate, staining her blue snow pants and the snow at her feet. She raced to what had been the foot of the slide. It was now a jumble of snow, hats, boots, ice, and people.

She heard several people calling for help, so she dug right in, pawing with her hands to free people from the globs of snow and ice. Brianda followed her lead. Others joined them, and Ned and Willy soon showed up to help as well.

"I suppose you all think this was an accident," Willy muttered. "I'm telling you it's not. It's more of the curse of the werewolf, and that's the truth."

"Not now, Willy," Ned said. "Let's just work at getting these people out of here."

"Not now, Willy . . . not now, Willy. That's all anyone ever says to me. I can't get security to listen, I can't get the police to listen. *Somebody's* got to find that beast and stop him or this Carnival's going to fall apart just like this snowslide."

Jax Dashell and Poodles McNulty arrived within seconds of each other. A few doctors jumped in to set up a triage in the snow. They checked all the injured and ranked them as to how seriously they were hurt. When the emergency crews arrived with their ambulances—which happened quickly—the ones with the worst injuries went to the hospital first.

Detective Dashell and other security officers took charge of the rescue effort, pitching in to get everyone free. Poodles supervised the maintenance workers who arrived with hand shovels, snowblowers, and small trucks with digging equipment.

It took over two hours to rescue everyone. By the time the last person was pulled out of the avalanche, Nancy's arms and shoulders ached and she was emotionally drained. Many of the people caught in the avalanche were her friends or others she knew at school. Finally, she, Ned, and Brianda sank down onto a bench.

Nancy couldn't help remembering a few hours earlier when she had sat on the same bench to enjoy her latte and watch the fun.

Brianda checked her watch. "Nancy, my shift is

almost up. If it's okay with you, I'd like to get back to WildWolf. Markie's probably heard about this by now, and she'll be worried."

"No problem," Nancy said. She remembered the wolf hair in her pack that she had found on Philip LeRoy's truck. "I need to talk to her again," she told Brianda. "Have her give me a call."

As Brianda walked off, Jax Dashell dropped onto the bench next to Nancy and Ned. "Thanks for all your help," he said, looking around. "What a mess!"

Nancy followed his gaze. There was still a three-inch glaze of snow on the slide itself, and a pile left at the top. Here and there she could see part of the wood scaffolding—the base structure—peeking through the icy snow that was left.

But at the bottom of the slide there were piles everywhere, still littered with hats and boots and gloves. When it came down, the avalanche had rolled along the street at the bottom of the slide, picking up people, trash cans, a cart selling roasted chestnuts, and everything else in its path. Then it had tossed them several yards away. Police had roped off a wide area with yellow "Do Not Cross" tape.

"Did we really get all the people out of there?" Nancy asked. "Is everyone accounted for?"

"Thankfully, yes," Detective Dashell answered. "And there were no critical injuries—nothing life-threatening. Broken bones, and some pretty bad sprains. And there were a few that looked okay, but the medics still thought they needed some X rays. They've all been taken to medical centers. The rest—the ones with minor cuts and scrapes—are being treated in the extra ambulances. It's a miracle it wasn't worse."

"It was bad enough," Ned murmured, shaking his head.

"Well, I'm going to talk to some of the people being treated here," Detective Dashell said, "and see if they can tell me anything about what happened." He smiled at Nancy and Ned and then left.

"That's just what I was thinking of doing," Nancy told Ned. "I'm going to walk around this area and talk to some of the witnesses."

"You're not starting to think like Willy, I hope," Ned said. "Are you saying this might not have been an accident?"

"There's only one way to find out," Nancy said, "and that's to start asking questions."

When she stood up she saw George rushing down the street toward the scene. Nancy hurried over to the temporary border of yellow police tape. She introduced herself to the police guard posted there. "You probably saw me talking with Detective Dashell on that bench," she said in a very businesslike manner, pointing back at the area around the slide.

The guard nodded slightly. "Well, this is George

Fayne," she said quickly. "She's here to help us with the investigation."

Without waiting for a response Nancy turned to George, saying, "We've been waiting for you. Jax is in the ambulance." Then she pulled the tape up out of the way and ushered George into the confined area. They jogged away from the guard without looking back—and without being stopped.

"I heard there'd been an accident, but I can't believe this," George said when they rejoined Ned. "I had no idea it was so bad. It looks like the thing exploded."

"Ned can tell you about it," Nancy suggested. "I want to interview some of the people who witnessed the avalanche while it's still fresh in their minds."

Ned and George walked off. Ned pointed and talked, and George just shook her head.

Nancy talked to several witnesses—people who had been watching the sliders, vendors in nearby kiosks, and a few people who had been at the bottom of the staircase, waiting to climb up for a slide. But they weren't much help. No one had seen or heard anything that Nancy herself hadn't witnessed.

About thirty yards from the slide, she came upon the chestnut vendor. She helped him gather dozens of chestnuts from the snow. "My cart's a total loss," he told her. "But at least I'm okay—and the chestnuts. I can clean them up and salvage a little from this disaster, I guess."

"Did you see what happened?" Nancy asked.

"Nah, it hit me from behind," he said. "By the time I heard it coming, it rolled right over me. I've been selling chestnuts at the Carnival for thirty years. I've never seen one like this one so far. And this is only the second day. Warnings in the ice, howling werewolves, and now this. We never had a problem when one of the locals was in charge. Now we got this outsider—this Poodles guy."

"You don't think all those things are his fault," Nancy said. "Even the slide?"

"He's running the show, isn't he?" the vendor said. "Look, my wife is on the committee that hired this McNulty guy. Some on that committee didn't want him. He's got a reputation for 'pushing the envelope,' as they say—for going too far. Well, that seems to be just what's happening around here."

Nancy finished helping the chestnut vendor clean up and then returned to Ned and George. "I want to get closer to the slide," she told her friends. "Maybe we can piece together what happened."

She led George and Ned around to the back of what had been the slide. It was now just splintered, broken scaffolding, half buried in snow and ice. A small opening led into the wooden framework that formed the base for the slide. "Let's go in," she suggested. "But be careful. It probably isn't too stable at this point."

She pulled out her penlight, and Ned got a flashlight from his backpack. "Keep a light on the structure above us," she told him, pointing up. Scaffolding rose upward for two stories. "Watch for cracks in the wood. We don't want this framework to slam down on us."

It was grayish blue up at the top of the scaffolding. "No talking," Nancy whispered. "That's the top of the slide, and there's still a lot of snow packed up there. Loud noise can cause avalanches, and there's enough snow left to do more damage. If any of us hears anything strange, we grab the other two and all get out to safety, okay?"

George and Ned nodded, and Nancy stepped into the open framework. It was like walking into a two-story house that someone had just started to build. Hundreds of pieces of wood, some vertical and some horizontal, had been nailed together and crisscrossed to support the snow and ice above.

Nancy's penlight gave off just enough light to show them the way without glaring back too brightly against the snow that was packed on the ground. Ned kept his own flashlight beam up on the scaffolding, watching for cracks or places where a two-by-four had splintered and broken away.

Nancy cautiously tiptoed along, avoiding the footprints in the snow in front of her. *Someone has been in here before us,* she noted silently.

Eventually, the three of them came to the end of the path. They had reached the area underneath the long diagonal slide itself. It was really dark at this point. Wood beams slanted toward the ground, supporting the ice and snow that still remained after the avalanche. Nancy could hear the wind on the other side of the wall they had reached. Every time the wind whistled, what was left of the slide would creak.

When she heard the creaking, she felt as if an icy waterfall was trickling down her spine. "It's too dangerous to poke around in here," she whispered. "Let's get out."

She motioned for Ned to lead them back out through the framework. Ned and George hurried along, but Nancy moved more slowly. She paused often to examine the ground more closely and then the wooden poles around her. She was looking for something—anything—that could give her a clue to what had happened.

She realized that Ned and George were no longer in sight ahead of her. *They're probably already back outside,* she told herself. *Sounds like a good idea to me.* As she neared the opening, Nancy swung her penlight beam back and forth across the ground. Her cheek felt a sudden chill, and she put her gloved palm against it. When she took her glove away, the palm was damp.

She patted her cheek again as a small clump of snow plopped past her and onto the ground. Then another glob landed on her shoulder.

She looked up and another small puff of snow landed on her cheek. She knew she was under the top of what was left of the snowslide. It was dim up there—hard to see what was up above. She waved her penlight around, but its beam just didn't travel that far up. She heard an odd sound and thought she saw something moving on the wood crossbar above her.

Suddenly she heard a long, drawn-out creaking noise that grew louder and louder. She took a gigantic step toward the opening to the outside, but she didn't make it.

She looked up just in time to see a small wall of snow plunge down from the top of the rickety structure. In the split second before the snow reached her, she saw someone standing at the top of the framework. Then the smothering blue-gray cold buried her.

8

In the Light of the Full Moon

For a moment she felt paralyzed. She couldn't move her arms or legs. Only the top of her head peeked out from the mass of snow that engulfed her. Even though the lower part of her face was completely covered by the pile, Nancy instinctively tried to take a breath. She gulped in wads of snow that froze the inside of her nose and burned her mouth.

Her arms felt strapped down by the weight of the snow, but she knew not to panic. She forced her head to move from side to side and her shoulders up and down. She moved only tiny distances at first, and then inches. She kept pushing, each time moving a little more snow out of her way, until she freed her upper body enough to yell for help.

"Nancy! Nancy!" Ned's voice seemed to warm her

and give her a spurt of extra strength.

"Over here," she called out. "Hurry!"

George and Ned both rushed to help her. "I'm so glad we didn't wander off," Ned said. "We were right outside the door when the snow just rushed down." All the time he was talking he and George were pushing the snow away from Nancy.

"I haven't been here too long," Nancy told them. "But long enough."

While her friends worked to rescue her she told them about seeing the person up on the scaffolding just before the snow buried her. When her arms were finally released she was able to help with her legs. Finally the three emerged into the late afternoon sun.

"I'm going to find Jax," Ned announced, hurrying off to the area where the ambulances were parked.

"And I'll get you something hot to drink," George offered.

In just that short time she had been confined by the snow Nancy's physical strength had been sapped. Her legs felt shaky, so she stumbled over to a log and sat down. Ned rushed back, followed closely by Jax Dashell.

"Ned tells me you had your own private avalanche," Detective Dashell said. "And it sounds like it was no accident."

Nancy told him what she'd seen. "I saw someone

up there, but I couldn't identify him. He's probably long gone by now," she concluded. "What about the real avalanche?" she asked. "Was there anything suspicious about it? Have you come up with anything from your witness interviews?"

"Not really," Detective Dashell answered. "How about you?"

"Nothing," Nancy said. "But I'm sure that what happened just now wasn't an accident."

"Do you think you need to see a medic?" Ned asked. "There are still some over there." He tilted his chin toward the remaining ambulance. "They could check you out."

"There's nothing wrong with me," Nancy said. "I wasn't buried long enough to get hypothermia. I'm just cold." She took the mocha latte that George handed to her. "This will definitely help. I lost my last one."

"If you're sure you don't need me any more right now, I'm going over to talk to Poodles," Ned said. "I want to see if there's anything more I can do to help with the cleanup."

"That's cool," Nancy said. "I'll be fine." She took a sip of her latte and turned to Detective Dashell. "This is off the subject," she said, "but I saw Philip LeRoy on TV yesterday with the administrator of WildWolf. LeRoy said that wolves had escaped before and attacked his sheep. Did he ever file an official report about that?"

"I'm not sure," Detective Dashell said. "I'll check and let you know. Meanwhile, I'm going up to take a look at the top of the slide. I'll see you all later."

"I need to get home and change clothes," Nancy said. "These feel wet and sticky."

"I'll go with you," George said. "We finally got the Crystal Palace lighting program back up to speed, so I'm off for the rest of the day. I feel like I've been locked up in the lighting booth for days. It'll feel good to get away from this place for a while."

"Were you talking about the Crystal Palace lights?" Ned asked, rejoining them. "I just talked to Poodles. He's canceling most of the activities scheduled here for this evening. They need to get some major earthmovers in here to clean up this mess."

"What about the sporting events?" Nancy asked. "Most of those are at other venues—out on the lake or at one of the courses or fields. George and I are signed up for the cross-country race this evening."

"Most of those are still on—including the cross-country," Ned answered. "I've signed on to stay and help with the cleanup."

"Okay." Nancy nodded.

"Talk to you later tonight," Ned said as he left to meet the cleanup crew. "One of you better win that race."

Nancy finished her latte and dropped the cup in the trashcan. It almost seemed like a silly thing to do, since the ground was covered with litter and debris. She and George then stopped at the Heat Hut to talk to Bess for a few minutes. She had heard about the avalanche, of course, because a steady stream of distressed witnesses and shocked victims had descended on the Heat Hut. Bess had decided to stay on past her shift to pass out hot chocolate and coffee.

Nancy told Bess and George about her discoveries in Philip LeRoy's truck, and showed them the clumps of hair.

"Nancy, if that's wolf hair, LeRoy must have stolen the wolves," Bess said. She talked very fast as she began to put two and two together. "What do you suppose he did with them? I hope he didn't hurt them. Do you think he let them go? Or maybe they really did escape, and he caught them going after his sheep. That would be horrible for WildWolf. Wait a minute—if he found them with his sheep, he would have called the police. Or at least put together a press conference!"

"Whoa!" George cried, putting her hand up to stop her cousin. "Like you said at the beginning—*if* it's wolf hair. We don't even know that yet."

"Right," Nancy agreed. "I told Brianda to set up another meeting with Markie so I can show the hair to her. She'll probably be able to tell us right away what it is."

"You're right, you're right," Bess said. Her blue eyes squinted when she grinned. "If there's anything we've learned from working on cases with Nancy, it's to get the facts first."

"It's about five o'clock. George and I are leaving right now," Nancy told Bess, returning her smile. "We're going to stop at the college and drop off this new batch of grain mixture at the lab. I want them to cross-check the stuff from LeRoy's truck with the samples I found at WildWolf. Then we'll go change clothes and get ready for the cross-country race."

"I forgot that's tonight," Bess said. "Good luck." A small crowd of people walked in. Nancy recognized them as some of the rescue volunteers.

"Looks like we're going to be busy for a while," Bess said. "I'd better get back to work. Talk to you later."

Bess bustled back to the front of the room to take orders. Nancy and George stopped at the office tent to check Nancy out of her work shift. The coordinator there told them that Friday's schedule was still up in the air, so they should check by phone before coming in.

About half an hour later the girls left Riverside Park and the Carnival grounds. After a stop at the college chemistry lab, Nancy drove to George's house. While George cleaned up, Nancy called WildWolf and talked to Brianda.

"Some people phoned in leads," Brianda said

when Nancy asked about the missing wolves. "But no one's found a real trace. Markie is so upset."

"Well, I might have found *just* that—a trace," Nancy said. She told Brianda about the clumps of hair. "I'm in the cross-country race, so I probably won't make it out there tonight," Nancy continued.

"Markie and Christopher won't be here tonight anyway," Brianda said. "They got a lead out near Westfield, and they left a little while ago. They may be there all night, searching. But she should be back tomorrow. Come out any time—just call first to make sure she's here. What about work tomorrow? When should I come in?"

"Work shifts might be weird tomorrow because they don't know how long it will take to clean up the avalanche and get the scaffolding all torn down safely. They're going to be plowing and moving large dump trucks in and out. If you don't hear from me tonight, I'll call early tomorrow morning."

Nancy talked for a few more minutes, trying to reassure Brianda. She hung up just as George emerged, dressed in her red ski suit and carrying her skis and poles. "I am *so* ready for this," George said. "Let's go!"

Nancy drove them to her own house. Hannah was relieved to see her. She had heard about the snowslide avalanche, and was horrified about the additional attack on Nancy.

"Did I or did I not tell you to be careful?" Hannah said. This time her frown was not pretend, and she wasn't smiling.

Nancy put her arms around Hannah's shoulders in a sort of half-hug. "I'm just fine now, and I'll be extra careful from now on." It was a familiar and affectionate exchange between the two. "George and I are cross-country skiing in a little while. How about whipping up some of your famous pasta and shrimp while I shower? We could use some carbo-loading!"

By the time they finished eating it was seven thirty—almost time to report to the starting line. Nancy finished pulling on her white ski suit. She still felt a little chilled, so she threw a ski mask and scarf into her bag—and off they went.

There were a couple dozen people in the field. Nancy recognized some of them as being pretty good skiers, but she was sure that George could take them all. She looked over at George, who was giving her skis a final buffing. She was a real outdoors person, and Nancy was sure that being locked up for nearly two days in a cramped lighting booth had been really hard for her.

Nancy did a few warmup stretches and pulled on her green ski mask and scarf. Then, with a shudder, she shook off the final uneasiness lingering from her near-burial. As she snapped into her ski boots she realized that she was really looking forward to the race. She was eager to get away from the city for a quiet evening in the snowy countryside. *A great place to think,* she thought. *And I've got a lot to think about.*

Everyone lined up, and for a moment there was nothing but the soft sound of skis sliding back and forth on the snow. The starting gun broke the mood, though, and suddenly the race was on.

Nancy loved nighttime cross-country skiing. She'd only done it once before, but she remembered it vividly. It had been an eerie event, but breathtakingly beautiful. This night lived up to her memory. The racers slipped across fields covered with a few feet of snow. The pristine white surface sparkled with thousands of diamond crystals in the bright light of the full moon.

The only sound she heard was the *swoosh, swoosh* of the skis and the occasional crack of a branch nearby laboring under a coating of ice.

George seemed to sail ahead of everyone. It was almost as if she were on wheels. Nancy knew she was using all that pent-up energy she had stored while working inside for so long.

Nancy quickly lost sight of George and didn't see her for the next hour and a half. Although there were skiers around her, she felt alone with her thoughts. When she finally reached the finish line she had finished in the middle of the pack. She was thrilled to see George standing in the winner's box, holding a trophy high for the photographers.

"Congratulations!" Nancy said when George finally joined her. "I knew you'd do it."

"That was the best," George said. "It felt so wonderful to be out there, didn't it?"

"It did," Nancy said. "I loved it."

"Let's not quit yet," George said. Nancy could see the exhilarated expression in George's eyes even though she was also wearing a ski mask. "I know a short cut back to the car. Let's skip the shuttle ride back and stay on our skis. We can take our time."

"Sounds good to me," Nancy said. It was a little before eleven, and clouds had begun to skitter across the sky, yellowy white in the moonlight. The two pushed off along George's shortcut.

As her skis skimmed along the top of the snow, Nancy's shadow bounced ahead and then disappeared again as the moon was swallowed by a passing cloud. She felt a sudden chill, as if the temperature had plunged ten more degrees. For a few moments it was very dark. Then the moon was free of cloud cover again, and light flooded the snowy field.

For a long while there was no sound except from the movement of their skis. They didn't even try to talk. Nancy wanted nothing to break the almost mystical snow silence. But something did . . . something horrible.

A familiar wail chilled her blood. It was very close by. Even George stopped cold. They stood for a minute, waiting for a repeat of the howl. But it was deadly quiet again.

Then, without warning, a hairy gray figure rushed from behind a tree and charged into George, knocking her hard to the ground.

9

Wild Weather at WildWolf

Nancy snapped out of her skis and rushed to where George grappled with the hairy figure. Nancy swung her ski pole at it, scoring a hit on its side. With a human-sounding yelp the figure rolled away and jumped to its feet. Then it raced across the field and out of sight.

"George! Are you all right?" Nancy knelt next to her friend, who was still lying in the snow.

"There's something wrong with my arm," George said, cradling her left arm in her right. "It got sort of bent back when he . . . it . . . whatever it was jumped me."

Nancy darted back to snap her skis on. Then she helped George up and fashioned her scarf into a sling for George's arm. Slowly, they skied the rest of the way to the car, with George using only one pole.

Nancy drove quickly to the medical center emergency room. While George was being X-rayed, she called Detective Dashell and told him what had happened. He knew the area where they'd skied and told her he'd go right out. They both agreed that the snow should yield plenty of footprints for tracking.

George was finally released. "She has a badly sprained shoulder," the doctor told Nancy. "But I tell you, those were nasty scratches on her back. She said she thought it was some kind of wild animal, so we might have to have her start rabies shots, just in case. We took some cultures, and we'll be back in touch."

Nancy stopped at the pharmacy to fill George's prescription and then delivered her home.

When she finally got to her own house, Nancy found her answering machine full of news. She listened to the messages as she got ready for bed. Brief messages fired out from Ned, Brianda, and her Carnival coordinator about the next day's schedule. The next message was from Bess, and she had obviously been in touch with everyone else.

"YES!" Bess's voice yelled from the worn-out tape. "Go George! I called her first to tell her that you guys were on the late news. George holding up that major trophy, and you cheering. So cool."

"Wait'll you hear what *wasn't* on the news," Nancy mumbled to the answering machine.

"There's still a lot of cleanup to do," Bess chirped. "So they're only holding the events that are away from the park for the first part of the day. They're doing the polar-bear plunge—Ned's helping with that. And they've set up a temporary Heat Hut near the river, so I'll be working there. They're also holding the ice-fishing competition, and the golf match and softball tournaments. George is third-base coach for the game."

Nancy collapsed onto the bed. "Then in the evening," Bess's voice continued, "everything should be back to normal in the Park again. They're going to do the Crystal Palace lighting and the whole deal. I talked to Brianda and she said to tell you that Markie is home, so come out to WildWolf as soon as you can. I'll see you at the Hut whenever you get to the Carnival."

The last message was from Jax Dashell. "I found the spot where George was hurt," he said. "One path of weird footprints led into and out of that spot, but the snow was smeared around so that there were no really clear prints. There were some pine branches lying around. I figure whoever it was used the branches like brooms to sweep away the prints. I took some photos that we'll blow up. That might help, but I can't promise anything. Oh—and LeRoy never made a complaint about wolves attacking his sheep."

"What was a werewolf doing in the country?" Nancy mumbled. "Willy *couldn't* be right, could he?" She fell asleep before she answered herself.

On Friday morning Nancy woke up later than she'd wanted to—at about eight thirty. She checked her alarm clock and discovered she hadn't even set it. "Today I get some answers," she announced to the empty room.

Before she even got out of bed she called George. "I know Bess called you, so you should know everything that I know about today's plans. How do you feel? Do you need anything?"

"Nah, I'm okay," George said. "This isn't the first sprain I've gotten—and it won't be the last. I hope it will be the only one caused by a werewolf, though. Have you heard from Detective Dashell yet? What *did* happen last night?"

"We don't know yet." Nancy told her about Jax Dashell's call. "I'm going out to WildWolf this morning to have Markie take a look at that hair. I'll let you know what I find out. It's going to be hard to keep in touch by phone if you're out on a softball field though. Let's use Bess as our message center. Drop into the Heat Hut off and on and let her know what you're doing and where. I'll do the same, and we can keep tabs on each other that way."

Nancy called Brianda to tell her she was on the

way. Then she showered, dressed, drank a protein smoothie, and grabbed a protein bar, then headed out to the wolf preserve.

As she drove, heavy, wet, fat snowflakes began falling. Then the wind picked up and swirled the snow around until finally the air seemed completely white.

"Perfect weather for the Polar Bear Plunge," Nancy murmured. "But good luck at third base, George."

Brianda greeted her at the WildWolf office door. She immediately took Nancy into the conference room and closed the door. Nancy could hear loud voices arguing from the main office across the reception area—even through the closed doors.

"Is that Markie and Christopher?" Nancy asked.

"Yep, and they've been going at it like this almost all morning."

"Does this happen often?" Nancy asked.

"It has been lately," Brianda said.

Nancy walked to the door and opened it a crack. The office was across the large reception area, and the door was closed. Nancy could hear their heated voices, but couldn't pick out many words.

"What are they arguing about?" Nancy whispered.

"This morning it was about procedures at WildWolf again," Brianda said.

Nancy motioned to Brianda to stop talking. She

then slipped out of the conference room and tiptoed across the reception area. She stood outside the office door and listened to the argument.

"If *I* had gotten the position as director, we wouldn't be having these problems," Christopher said.

"But you didn't," Markie responded. "*I* did. And I deserved it. You work for me, so you'll do it my way."

"Someday you're going to be sorry you ever got this job," Christopher warned. Nancy heard his footsteps pounding toward the door, so she scurried back across the reception area and into the conference room.

She kept the door open a crack and watched Christopher storm out the front door.

"So he was considered for Markie's job too?" Nancy asked Brianda in a low voice.

"You got it," Brianda said. "In fact, I gather from Markie that the competition was pretty hot. I think Christopher has always resented Markie for beating him out."

Nancy heard the office door open. She opened the conference room and saw Markie standing at the window next to the front door.

"Hi, Markie," Nancy said. Brianda followed her out of the conference room.

"Oh, hi," Markie said. "I didn't realize you were here." Her large eyes blinked in a rim of tears. She looked back out the window. "It looks like a real storm is blowing in," she said. "I know we need to talk, Nancy, but Christopher is gathering up the other curators. If we're getting a storm, we have to go on rounds immediately and make sure everything's secure."

"Do you need any help?" Brianda asked.

"No, we've got a routine mapped out," Markie answered. "Nancy, I hate to ask since you came all the way out here, but could you hang out until we're finished? We could talk then."

"Absolutely," Nancy said.

"Good. Help yourself to coffee and anything else. I'll be back as soon as I can."

As soon as they saw the trucks and other vehicles take off, Nancy turned to Brianda. "I'm going to look around in the office," she said. "You don't have to join me if you'd rather not. You can just stand guard out here."

"Are you kidding?" Brianda said. "I'll do anything I can to help my cousin—even snoop into her business!"

The office was divided into two large rooms. The first had several desks and computer stations. The back room was Markie's personal office.

Nancy directed Brianda to go through Christopher's desk in the front office. "He probably wouldn't keep anything important out here, where it could be accessed by anyone," Nancy pointed out. "But we need to look through it just in case."

Nancy went into Markie's office. After a cursory look through desk drawers and file cabinets, she found what she was looking for: a cabinet with two locked file drawers. Using her lockpick, she opened it. First she found the employment contracts for both Markie and Christopher.

"I'm not finding anything important," Brianda said. "What have you got?"

"Christopher's contract," Nancy said. "It says that if Markie leaves her position for any reason, he will be immediately named interim director until a permanent person can be found."

"Hey, that means that if she gets fired, he gets the job," Brianda said.

"Exactly. And it goes on to say that if the board finds his work satisfactory, he will be installed as permanent director, and they're not obligated to search any further to fill the job."

"So maybe he meant it when he warned her," Brianda said, her voice hushed. "Oh, Nancy, maybe *he's* causing the problems around here to make her look bad. Then she gets fired, and he's the alpha."

"Could be," Nancy said. "Hmmm, this might be something." She pulled a folder from the open drawer. "It's full of reports and letters from Christopher to the board of directors. They're all complaints about how Markie runs things at WildWolf. It looks like he's waged a systematic campaign against her."

"But this file is in her office, so she knows about it," Brianda pointed out.

"She sure does." Nancy laid out some letters on the desk. "Look at this. Every letter or report from Christopher has been answered by Markie."

"That must be why she's still got the job," Nancy said. "Apparently, she's satisfied the board that she's in control out here."

"So far," Brianda said. "Why does he even stay, I wonder? His plan clearly isn't working."

"If he wants Markie's job, he might think his best recourse is to stay here and keep chipping away at Markie's credibility," Nancy said. "In fact, maybe he's decided to step up the heat a little and cause a few problems that are not so easily explained away by Markie—such as wolves 'escaping' from WildWolf."

"Nancy, do you suppose . . . ," Brianda started. "Christopher could have kidnapped the wolves to make the board—and everyone else—think that Markie isn't capable of running a safe, secure animal preserve."

"It would be very easy for him to pull off," Nancy noted. "He knows how to handle the animals." She packed everything back into the appropriate folders and drawers and relocked the file cabinet. "I don't want to wait. I want to talk to Markie now."

"We can use my SUV," Brianda said. "They're making the rounds of all the enclosures and outbuildings. We're bound to find them."

The snow wasn't actually falling anymore. Driven by the hard wind, it was blowing horizontally, parallel to the ground, and was so thick that visibility was nearly zero.

When they got to the huge enclosure where the missing wolves had lived, it looked empty. Brianda explained that although no one could find any breach in the fence, they had moved the rest of the pack to another area in the preserve—just in case.

"I want to go in," Nancy said. "I haven't been inside yet. This is my only chance to look for evidence here. If there was any that was missed by the others, it'll soon be blown away or buried."

By the time Nancy and Brianda got inside the second fence they were in a near whiteout. Nancy knew immediately that they needed to abandon their original plan and retreat to the warmth and safety of shelter. The snow was now so thick that she couldn't even see Brianda, even though she was standing just a few yards away.

"Brianda," Nancy called. "We've got to leave. Come on." She heard Brianda's answer through the howling wind and looked in the direction of her friend's voice.

Just then she had that spooky feeling that she was

being stared at from behind. Nancy turned and saw two yellow eyes glinting at her through the blowing whiteness. Her pulse pumped as fast as the snow pelting her cheek. She was looking into the yellow eyes of one of WildWolf's famous residents.

10

A Blizzard of Clues

The wolf stared at her, and Nancy immediately diverted her gaze to its nose. She racked her brain for all the wolf behavior knowledge she'd gained from Markie. She knew that the wolf wouldn't attack them if they followed the rules.

She felt Brianda breathing next to her. "Brianda," she said. "Remember the rules." Then Nancy listed them off in a quiet voice.

"Stay alert. Stand your ground. No eye-to-eye staring contests. Don't give the wolf orders the way you would a dog. Don't turn your back on the wolf."

Nancy took a deep breath. "Okay, let's just back slowly out of here." She felt Brianda moving with her backward toward the gate. After a few minutes the wolf turned and trotted away into the snow. Still cautious, Nancy and Brianda continued backing up until they felt the gate behind them.

When they got back to the office, the others were already there.

"Brianda! Nancy!" Markie cried out when they arrived. "We saw Nancy's car still here, but not yours. We thought you'd gone off on some errand. I was worried about you out in this storm."

"It wasn't an errand," Brianda said. "We were looking for you . . . and we got caught in the wolf enclosure, which we *thought* was empty . . . and . . ." Brianda crumpled into a chair, shivering. A staff member got her a blanket and started a pot of tea.

"I don't understand," Markie said. She looked from Brianda to Nancy.

Nancy related their experience with the wolf. Markie and the others were horrified by the story. "Are you all right?" Markie asked Nancy and Brianda. "Are you sure you're all right?"

"Yes, we're fine," Nancy said. "But I would like to talk to you privately."

"Of course," Markie said. "But I need to find out what happened with those wolves." She looked around at the other employees. "What's going on here, gang?"

All of them looked at each other, shrugged their shoulders, and denied knowing anything about it. All of them but one.

"Christopher?" Markie asked. "Do you know something about this?"

"All right, all right," he bellowed, standing up. "I admit it. I put the remaining members of the pack back in the enclosure. I thought they'd feel more secure during the storm if they were in familiar territory. They're already unsettled, with Khayyam and Liz gone. It seemed to me that—"

"*Seemed* to you," Markie repeated. "That's always the problem! You do what 'seems to you,' rather than what I ask you to do. You know better than to move the pack without consulting with me first."

"You know what? I'm tired of consulting with you on every blasted little thing!" Christopher stomped toward the door. "As you Americans say, *I'm outta here*. You'll have my letter of resignation in one hour."

No one moved as Christopher's words echoed around the room. Everyone watched the door. It was like they were all waiting for him to pop back in, saying, "Kidding."

But after a few minutes, it was clear he wasn't coming back anytime soon. "Okay, everyone, I'm sorry about that scene—and all the others you've witnessed over the last few months," Markie said. "Let's just move on, okay?"

She walked to the window. "The visibility is still practically nil," she said, "but any of you who would like the rest of the day off, please feel free. Those of you who don't want to risk the drive, you're welcome to stay until the weather clears, of course. Let's go fix some lunch. Nancy, if you can stay yet a little longer, you and I can eat privately and talk."

Several of the employees took off in SUVs or on cross-country skis, but a couple of them stayed. Nancy joined Markie, Brianda, and the others in the kitchen. Everyone pitched in to pull together a feast of leftovers—soup, sandwiches, and pie.

Nancy, Markie, and Brianda ate alone in the conference room.

"Brianda said you had something to show me," Markie said. "Something to do with my missing wolves?"

"First I'd like to talk to you about what's been happening out here," Nancy said. "I'm sorry that I overheard your argument with Christopher this morning. But I really couldn't help it."

"I know," Markie said, her mouth twisting into an expression of embarrassment. "Sorry about that."

"I'd like to know a little more about your working relationship with Christopher," Nancy said.

"Well, apparently it's over, for starters," Markie said. "It really hasn't been the best since we opened WildWolf."

"I told Nancy about Christopher competing with you for this job," Brianda admitted. Nancy felt sure that Brianda wouldn't tell her cousin that they had been going through her office files, though.

"Yes, it was pretty unpleasant at the time," Markie told them. "But I liked Christopher and admired his work. And I told him so. I really thought we had put the rivalry behind us and were both willing to work for the good of the preserve. Apparently, that was a stupid assumption."

"Do you think it's possible that Christopher stole the wolves?" Nancy asked. "Is he capable of releasing them into the wild?"

"But why would he do either of those things?"

"To sabotage you," Nancy said gently. "To get the board to fire you and perhaps put him in your place."

Markie was visibly distressed. "I never even thought of him," she answered. "I hate to think that would be possible. As much he might resent me, I truly believe he loves the wolves too much to endanger them."

"It's just an idea," Nancy said. "Think about it. Go back in your mind to the time around the disappearance. Right now, nearly everyone's a suspect."

Nancy reached into her pack and pulled out the tissues and placed them on the table. She opened them to reveal the hair that she had found in Philip LeRoy's truck.

"Where did you get this?" Markie asked, picking up a puff of hair and holding it gently in her palm.

"Do you recognize it?" Nancy asked, without telling her where it came from. "Is it wolf hair?"

"Not only is it wolf hair," Markie answered, "it's Olympia's."

"How can you be sure?" Brianda asked.

"Wolves lose their undercoat of hair in the spring," Markie explained. "It sticks to scratching posts, and it skips around the ground like tumbleweed. We gather it all up and store it in containers. Then we sell it to raise funds."

"Sell it?" Nancy repeated.

Markie stretched her arm across the table. "Feel my sleeve," she urged.

Nancy and Brianda patted the soft oatmeal-colored sweater. "It was knitted from the wolf 'wool' we gathered," Markie told them. "It's wonderful stuff. You can spin it like sheep's wool and then knit or crochet it. It's warm and snug, and really special to wear."

"And you're sure this is Olympia's hair?" Nancy insisted.

"Absolutely," Markie said. "Do you see these brown tips at the end of each gray strand? This is definitely Olympia's hair. We have a barrel of it."

"But Olympia isn't one of the missing wolves, right?" Nancy said.

"That's right. Olympia was born here, in fact," Markie answered. "She's never even been off the preserve. I just saw her when we made our rounds."

Nancy put down her mug of ginger tea and sat back in her chair. "What's the matter, Nancy?" Brianda asked. "You look surprised."

"Mmm, nothing," Nancy said. *How did Olympia's hair get on Philip LeRoy's truck?* she wondered.

A creaky noise like the winding of a spring interrupted Nancy's thoughts. She followed the sound to a large painted wood clock on the wall. It looked like a cuckoo clock. Instead of a bird coming out the little door, though, a wolf rode out on the little platform. And instead of twelve *cuck-oos,* they heard one long rolling howl with twelve beats: *Ahoo-oo-oo-oo-oo-oo-oo-oo-oo-oo-oo-oo.*

"Can you believe that clock?" Brianda said, shaking her head.

"It's pretty wacky," Markie agreed. "But one of our board members had it made for us in Germany. That's why it's in our conference room and not in my apartment."

"It got my attention," Nancy said. She went to the window and looked out. "The storm has thinned out a lot. I can even see a ray or two of sun trying to get out around the clouds. I really need to get back into town," she said.

"I'm not on until three o'clock, but I think I'll follow you in," Brianda said. "I'd like to see some of the games without being on call as a hostess."

"I'm coming in this evening myself," Markie said.

"I want to see the Crystal Palace. I hear they finally have it all ready to light tonight. If you ride in with Nancy, Bree, you can leave your car here and ride back with me tonight."

"Sounds good," Nancy said. She helped Markie take their lunch dishes back to the kitchen while Brianda changed clothes. Markie asked the other employees if they'd heard from Christopher, but no one had.

The storm had left its mark on the countryside. One of the WildWolf staff drove a plow just ahead of Nancy along the drive out of the preserve, making it easier for Nancy to drive on the road. She didn't have such a luxury when she got out to the country roads.

The snow had definitely stopped, and the sun was even peeking out. But the morning storm had made the road that led away from WildWolf nearly undrivable.

"I'm glad we left when we did," Nancy said. "It's going to be slow going." She dodged drifts higher than her car and used all her driving skills to stay on the road. It was so hard to tell where the road stopped and where the drifted ditches alongside it began.

The car swerved and slid, but Nancy maintained control. She stole a look at Brianda, whose face was white. "It's okay, Brianda," she said. "Don't be nervous."

Nancy wished she felt as calm as she tried to pretend she was. This was the slickest road she'd ever driven on—and she'd been on some really bad ones. She saw a small bridge ahead and knew it would be icy under the new snow. She did everything right as she approached the bridge, and she did everything right going over it.

But even her skill couldn't save them. Her heart seemed to sink into her stomach as she felt the tires skid across a snow-covered sheet of ice. "Hold on!" she said through clenched teeth as she felt the car leave the ice and sail through the air.

11

Frozen in Midair

Instinctively, Nancy turned the steering wheel—even though the car was still up in the air. The car came down on the other side of the bridge, on the left side of the road. She pumped the brake gently, so the car's momentum began to slow. The ice was too much of an obstacle, though. One last skid and the car finally stopped. Nancy's body slid into her door with a *thunk* as the left front wheel sank into a soft snowdrift.

Nancy and Brianda each took a deep breath. "You should patent that and make it a thrill ride at the Carnival," Brianda said with a giggle.

"Are you okay?" Nancy said, unfastening her seat-belt.

"I am," Brianda said. She sounded surprised.

"Good," Nancy said. "Now let's see if we can get out of this somehow." The left front corner of the car was buried so deep in the snow that Nancy couldn't open her door. Brianda got out first, and then Nancy climbed over the gearshift and went out the passenger door.

Nancy quickly got a shovel out of the trunk and began digging away at the snowdrift. After twenty minutes, Brianda took a turn. Nancy was about to call for help when she heard a welcoming sound in the distance. A vehicle was driving their way.

"It's Willy," Nancy said as the truck came closer. "He must have had a pickup or delivery out here."

Willy Dean's shipping service truck drove up behind them and stopped. Willy jumped out of the truck's cab and hurried over.

"Looks like you missed the runway a little, Nancy," he said, shaking his head. He got right to work hauling a large chain, a heavy cloth, and some rubber mats out of the back of his truck.

"I had a pickup near here," he told them. "Philip LeRoy's farm. Do you know he makes a private blend of sheep feed right there on that little farm? And he ships it all over the world. This batch is going to a ranch in Wyoming."

"Yes, I read that somewhere," Nancy said.

"Now you two ladies just stand out of the way," he told them. "I'll have this car out in no time. Hey, did you hear that the werewolf was sighted again last night?" he asked, walking to Nancy's car. His eyes widened as he talked, and his lip quivered a little. He seemed genuinely afraid.

"Philip said that a farmer friend of his saw the werewolf in one of his pastures," Willy continued. "Mind you, I don't mean one of those WildWolf animals, or just some big dog."

He padded the chain with the cloth so that it wouldn't scratch Nancy's car, then took the gridded rubber sheets and placed them tight behind Nancy's tires. "I told you, I've seen him myself. He looks like a wolf, sure . . . at first. But then, about the time you start realizing he's bigger than any wolf you ever saw . . . he stands up!"

He walked back from the snowdrift to where Nancy stood. "He stands up on both of those back legs and then he runs. He's sort of stooped over." Willy bent the top part of his body a little toward the front. "But he runs on those back legs. Just like a human being."

He walked toward his truck, then paused and looked back at Nancy and Brianda. "I've read a lot about those creatures," he said. "They look like animals, but they're not. They run like humans, but they're not. They're some sort of in-betweens—and they're dangerous." He climbed into the truck cab. "Well, let's get this puppy back on the road."

Willy backed his truck along the road and pulled Nancy's car out of the snowdrift and back onto level ground. She and Brianda gathered the rubber sheets from all over the snow and handed them to Willy. He disconnected the chain and the blanket and returned all the gear to the truck. Aside from a small dimple in the bumper, there was no damage to Nancy's car.

"Thank you so much," Nancy said as Willy climbed back up into his truck cab.

"My pleasure," Willy said. He gave her a big smile and cocked his head to one side. "I hope I didn't scare you with all that werewolf talk," he said. "I probably should just keep my mouth shut about it. No one believes me anyway."

"Well, I don't really think we have to worry about it," Nancy said.

"Okay," Willy said. "I'd better get this feed sent. I'll probably see you at the Carnival. I'm trying to get up the nerve for the Polar Bear Plunge."

He backed up and waited. As Nancy started to get into the car, Willy called out one last message from his open truck cab window.

"Just think about this," he yelled. "No one around here really knows Poodles McNulty. And no one ever saw a werewolf around here until he came to town. And no one has ever seen both Poodles and the werewolf at the same time."

“This has been one strange morning,” Nancy said as Brianda climbed into the car. Nancy carefully pulled away.

Brianda spoke for the first time since Willy had driven up. “Nancy, do you believe in werewolves at all?” she said quietly.

“No, I really don’t.”

“Well, I didn’t either—until this week,” Brianda said. “Now I’m not so sure. Do you think Willy really thinks Poodles McNulty is a werewolf?”

“Sounds like it,” Nancy said, chuckling. “I don’t know—I sure can’t picture that.”

Brianda joined in the laughter. It was a great way to release tension.

Nancy stopped at the college and talked with the chemist. Her suspicions were confirmed. All the samples of the grainy mixture from LeRoy’s truck matched all those from WildWolf.

When she got back to the car she told Brianda about the results. “I finally have some ammunition for Detective Dashell,” she concluded. Armed with the reports she drove to the Muskoka River, site of several Carnival events. It was three o’clock.

The rest of the afternoon passed quickly. Nancy and Brianda joined the crowd that was watching the Polar Bear Plunge. It was a crazy event. Several people, some in bathing suits, some in regular clothes, jumped into the freezing cold Muskoka.

Medics stood by in case any hearts actually stopped. None ever did, although a spectator might have expected it from all the screaming and yowling that went on. Willy Dean chickened out, but Ned jumped right into the frigid river for all of thirty seconds.

People who strolled over from the main Carnival venue brought good news. The snowslide mess was cleared. Everyone began buzzing about what a great evening it was going to be.

George showed up after the softball game to tell Nancy that the threats carved into the Crystal Palace had been filled and smoothed away. At six o'clock the lighting of the Crystal Palace would begin the Friday Night Extravaganza.

The Extravaganza promised something for everyone. There would be ice dancing on Wawasee Cove, complete with a live swing band. The individual ice carving competition would be held in front of the Crystal Palace. And a rock group would turn up the heat along the banks of the Muskoka.

Nancy told Ned and George about the chemist's reports. "I'm going to find Detective Dashell and tell him," she said. "And I have to see what time you and I need to report for work, Brianda. How about the rest of you? What are your schedules?"

"I'm off until the Palace lighting," Ned reported.

"I'm off until then too," George said. "Even with my arm in a sling, I'll be able to help with the show."

"Great," Nancy said. She motioned to the temporary Heat Hut on the riverbank. "Somebody should check with Bess and see if she's working tonight."

Nancy checked in with her coordinator, who told her that there were so many changes in the schedule that she hadn't been able to contact all the volunteers affected. She had posted a couple of people at the gate to pass out flyers about the changes.

"Just wing it from now on," the coordinator told Nancy. "Your team has done a great job so far. A huge crowd's predicted for this evening. Do the best you can to keep in touch with your team."

Nancy set out immediately to find Jax Dashell. It didn't take long. She told him about collecting the two sets of samples and the wolf hair, and then showed him the reports.

"This is pretty convincing," the officer said.

"None of this really proves he had anything to do with the missing wolves," Nancy pointed out. "But it does seem to indicate that he has at least been to WildWolf, which he denied in the television interview. It is circumstantial evidence, but the exact custom-mixed grain that was on his truck was also on the preserve. And hair from WildWolf was on his truck, too."

"Well, there's enough here to at least question Mr. LeRoy," Detective Dashell said, folding the reports and putting them inside his jacket.

"I've seen him at the Carnival," Nancy alerted the officer. "He might show up here again."

Detective Dashell handed her a card. "Here's my cell phone number," he said. "If you see him, call me. Don't try to talk to him yourself."

Nancy agreed and the officer walked away. Nancy took a minute to enter his phone number into her own cell phone and then put it on her automatic dialing list. That way she only had to press the number 9 to dial the rest of the number.

Next Nancy went on her rounds and looked for her team. She walked around one of the spectacular iced-up fountains, its gushing water temporarily frozen in midair. As she came around to the back she heard a familiar voice.

"What's going on, Miss Drew?" Philip LeRoy asked. His tone was belligerent, and he seemed ready for a fight. He stepped in her path, freezing her just like the fountain water.

"Excuse me, Mr. LeRoy," she said. "I'm working, and I don't have time for a break right now."

"Oh, you're working all right," he said, his face twisted into a sarcastic sneer. "Working to get me in trouble."

Nancy's eyes darted from side to side. They were standing in a sort of alley behind the fountain. To their left was the rest of the alley, which seemed to lead to a dead end against a wall. To their right was the fountain, which was so big that it hid them from view. She wasn't in a good spot.

Nancy took a breath and focused her thoughts. "I don't know what you're talking about, Mr. LeRoy. If you'll excuse me . . ." She started to turn and reverse her path, but he darted around and blocked her again.

"I thought I made my point the morning I locked you in my barn," he spat. "Now I find out that I wasn't completely clear. Someone saw you inspecting my truck at the softball game."

"Whoever told you that was mistaken."

"I might believe you," he said, "if I hadn't found out who you are. I've been checking you out." He put his hand in his pocket, and Nancy went on high alert. Every cell in her body was tuned to every move he made, every word he said.

"And what did I find?" He pulled his hand out of his pocket. Nancy flinched, but he held only a piece of paper. "You're a private detective."

"I'm telling you you're mistaken," she said firmly. "Now let me by."

Philip LeRoy stepped closer, completely blocking her from moving away. "This conversation is not over," he warned.

12

When Wolves Fly

Nancy's adrenaline zapped through her, and she felt herself switch to "flight or fight" mode. But she was trapped, so flight wasn't possible.

She casually dropped her hand—the one holding her cell phone—behind her back. While LeRoy rambled on, she flipped open her phone. With her thumb she counted along the buttons until she reached button 9, the number she had assigned to automatically dial Detective Dashell's cell phone.

She pushed the 9 button, then the CONNECT button. *Come on, Jax,* she thought to herself.

"So did you find anything interesting on my truck?" LeRoy demanded.

"I found wolf hair," she said. LeRoy teetered a

little and stepped back. "And I found samples of one of your grain recipes at WildWolf," she added. He seemed shocked and said nothing for a moment.

"Wolf hair!" he finally sputtered. "That's impossible."

"I'm afraid it isn't," Nancy replied.

"Maybe it was yanked from one of the wolves that attacked my sheep," he said defensively.

"The hair was gathered from natural shedding and had been cleaned to sell," Nancy said. "It was *not* pulled out. I think you lied about the wolf attacks—you never reported them. Did you steal the two wolves from the preserve?"

LeRoy's face flushed from its usual rosy red to a purplish hue. "What? You must be crazy!" he blustered. "Maybe I lied about the sheep attacks, and maybe I didn't. If I did it's because I know it's only a matter of time before it *does* happen. And I'm going to get that place closed—"

"What place, Mr. LeRoy?" Detective Dashell's welcome voice demanded from behind Nancy. She took a deep breath.

"I suggest we excuse Miss Drew and have a private conversation," Detective Dashell said. He nodded at Nancy who walked around LeRoy and a few yards past. She stopped when she was a safe distance away so she could hear the rest of the exchange between the two men.

"You have two choices, Mr. LeRoy," the officer continued. "You may accompany me voluntarily to the police station to make a statement and answer some questions, or you can be arrested for harassing Nancy."

Nancy couldn't see LeRoy's expression clearly, but she heard him gasp. After a few moments, he spoke. "I'll go with you," he said. "And I'll be happy to tell you a few things about that WildWolf and why it should be shut down. But you *won't* hear me confess to taking those animals."

Detective Dashell nodded at Nancy and escorted Philip LeRoy away from the frozen fountain.

Nancy finished her rounds, talking to the hosts she ran into. Then she stopped by the fortune-teller's cabin. She wanted to see whether the woman remembered any more about the man who had impersonated her. The door was locked, though, with a CLOSED sign on the front. By five thirty she was more than ready for refreshment at the Heat Hut.

When she walked in, Bess and George hurried to greet her. "I thought you'd never get here," Bess said. "George and Brianda told me everything that's happened. Here I am, stuck in this place, and you're out getting attacked by werewolves and real wolves and having all kinds of excitement!"

"Yes, well . . . some of it I could have done without—including the recent *human* attack." She told her friends about her impromptu meeting with Philip LeRoy.

"Oh, I hope he confesses," Bess said. "And tells them where the wolves are so they can be returned to WildWolf."

"Ever the optimist," George said with a disbelieving tone, but she gave her cousin an affectionate smile. Nancy and her two best friends walked back to George's table.

"And that would leave only the case of the werewolf," Bess said as Nancy and George took seats. "That needs to get solved really soon because it's starting to give me nightmares. I'll get you a latte," she said to Nancy.

"How is your arm holding up?" Nancy asked George as Bess walked to the counter.

"It's okay," George said, gingerly moving her injured shoulder. "I haven't had to take any of the pain medication the doctor gave me."

"Excellent. Did you have a chance to check with the others? How does everyone's schedule for this evening look?" Nancy asked.

"Bess is off at six for the rest of the evening," George told her. "Ned is going to be at the Crystal Palace at six o'clock for the ice-carving competition, but he's free after that. Brianda's schedule is pretty much up to you, I guess. We're all meeting at Uncle

Bud's at six o'clock. That's in about fifteen minutes. We might as well wait for Bess."

Bess brought Nancy's drink and hurried back to spend her last several minutes of the shift taking care of the people lined up at the counter.

At six o'clock Bess signed out, and she, Nancy, and George walked to Uncle Bud's Pizza—another famous River Heights restaurant that had opened a heated tent at the Carnival. Brianda was already there. Ned strolled in a few minutes later.

The five of them placed their orders, and then Nancy caught up Ned and Brianda on the latest news about Philip LeRoy.

"Hey, looks like the field has narrowed," Ned said. "For a while there were so many incidents and so many suspects, I didn't know who might be doing what."

"Wow," Brianda said. "I hope this is the end of it. At first I was sure LeRoy was the one who either stole or released the wolves. But then I switched to Christopher Warfield. Now I'm thinking it *was* LeRoy after all."

"Pretty weird story about Christopher Warfield," George said to Nancy. "Brianda told us about that scene. What do you think about it?"

"I'm not ready to rule him out yet, in spite of the evidence implicating Philip LeRoy," Nancy said. "Christopher has a motive, and the best opportunity of anyone. Plus he's the only suspect who we know is able to handle wolves."

"I still think that Poodles McNulty carved the message in the Crystal Palace wall," George said. "Remember how he acted? He was totally pumped about all the controversy. He even said he thought that wolves running loose would be good for Carnival business. That woman you told us about on the hiring committee predicted he might go too far to juice up the Carnival publicity. How do we know that he's not involved in all this somehow?"

"He *did* say he was going to put the River Heights Holiday Winter Carnival on the map," Ned added.

"Is no one but me worried about this whole werewolf deal?" Bess anxiously asked the group. She pulled a piece of pizza from the platter. The strands of cheese connecting it to the next piece stretched longer and longer as she pulled. "I want someone to tell me what that's all about."

"I'll bet Poodles hired an actor to play the werewolf just to capitalize on the missing wolf story," George pointed out.

"Willy Dean thinks it's more than that," Ned said. "He thinks there's a real werewolf."

"Brianda and I have an update on that story," Nancy said. "Willy thinks Poodles *IS* the werewolf."

"Well, I hope Poodles is just as much a showman as everyone thinks, and that the first story is the right one—it's an actor *playing* a werewolf," Bess said.

"Of course it is," George said. "What, do you think werewolves are *real* now?"

"Hey, you're the one who was attacked by one," Bess fired back. "You tell us!"

"Well, we have to admit one thing. We now know of four people—Willy, Nancy, George, and that farmer—who've seen this whatever-it-is when there was no crowd around to witness the sightings," Ned concluded. He gulped nearly half a glass of soda.

"There's one issue that no one's mentioned yet," Nancy said. She broke off a corner of a pizza wedge and popped it into her mouth.

Everyone looked at her expectantly. "Well?" Bess said. "What?"

"There seem to be *two* sets of crimes here—one set directed at WildWolf, and one set directed at the Carnival. Is this one case, or two? Are the two related? If so, how—and perhaps most importantly, why?"

After dinner Nancy and the others walked to the Crystal Palace to watch the ice-carving competition. The Palace was still in its canvas drape, awaiting the unveiling and light show after the competition.

Ice carving was one of the oldest Carnival traditions—a craft that was passed down through generations. Some used hammers and chisels and other sharp instruments; others used chainsaws. Willy

Dean used both. When the competition was over, Willy was the fourth person in his family to reign as champion for three years in a row. Ned led the others over to congratulate him while George went into the amphitheater's lighting booth.

"I see you recovered from your little accident this morning," Willy said to Nancy and Brianda.

"Thanks again," Nancy said. "This carving is really beautiful." They all admired the magnificent sculpture of an elephant carrying a sheaf of grass in its trunk. "It's so lifelike."

"Just a virtual version," he said. "I worked in the zoo for a couple of years before I saved enough money to open my shipping business. I used to—"

Willy was interrupted by a blare of trumpets. They all looked over to see Poodles McNulty ready to pull the cord and drop the drape that covered the Crystal Palace. The lighting was about to begin. The crowd gathered nearer.

With another fanfare Poodles pulled the cord, revealing the two-story, multitowered ice castle. George and her coworkers flipped a few switches, and thousands of lights turned on inside the Palace. Red, purple, blue, green, and gold lights flooded the elaborate structure and radiated through the ice, out into the frosty night.

A third fanfare sounded, but as the last note faded

away, a bloodcurdling howl rose up. Although Nancy had heard that sound twice before, it still was enough to make her jump. She felt as if all the blood had drained from her skin, leaving it as cold and clammy as the slush under her boots.

She looked up with the rest of the crowd to see the werewolf on the top of the Palace. More people gathered to watch.

"I told you he was real," Willy said, his face white with fear.

As with the previous appearance of this creature, half the crowd seemed frightened while the other half was delighted and cheering. Bess and Brianda huddled together, and Nancy felt Ned move a little closer to her.

George emerged from the lighting booth. She raced over to the ground spotlight that was trained on the roof of the palace. Wheeling it around with her good arm, she followed the beast with the light as it darted from tower to tower.

"Come on," Nancy said to Ned. She led him around to the back of the Palace. Leaning against the back wall of ice was a two-story ladder. "I thought so," Nancy said. "Looks like our werewolf came prepared for a getaway. Give me a hand." Ned helped her pull the ladder away just as the werewolf rushed to the edge of the roof.

The beast looked frantically down at them, his

glance darting from Nancy to Ned, and then back to Nancy again. He paced back and forth for a few seconds. Then, staring straight into Nancy's eyes, he leaped off the edge.

13

Let's Start Over

Nancy's heart vaulted into her throat when she saw the werewolf flying off the roof and sailing down toward her. She and Ned jumped back and skidded out of the way.

But they needn't have worried. The beast landed perfectly in a snowbank and then somersaulted out onto his feet. Ned dove toward the figure, but the werewolf hopped back and held his hands up in a defensive posture.

"Wait a minute," he said. "Wait! Don't be afraid. I'm not really a werewolf."

"I'm not afraid," Ned said. "I'm angry. I don't like anything flying at my girlfriend."

"Who are you?" Nancy asked. "And who hired you?"

"I'm Gabriel Winthrop," the man said, peeling off his wolf head. "I'm just a stuntman, doing a job. Poodles McNulty hired me to give the crowds a thrill."

"I knew it," George said, running up to join them.

"And you were hired only to perform here at the Carnival?" Nancy asked.

"Right," he said. "This Carnival is my only venue—I was hired to be on the bridge last night, and on the Palace tonight. That's all." His eyes shifted from Nancy to George. He was clearly nervous and uncomfortable.

"There have been rumors of a werewolf running around out in the country," Nancy said. "Several people have seen it. Was that you?"

A couple of security guards and a River Heights policewoman, along with Poodles, rushed up as Nancy asked the question.

"No way," said the stuntman. "I'd have to be crazy to be running around outside the city as a werewolf. Somebody'd probably shoot me." He looked at Poodles, and then back at Nancy.

"Are you okay?" Poodles asked Winthrop. "I almost lost it when you jumped off the building."

"Yeah, but—" Winthrop shrugged his shoulders. "I gotta tell them," he said to Poodles. He looked back at Nancy.

"Okay, it was me last night—out in the country," he confessed. "I was the one who crashed into you," he said to George. "I'm sorry. I never meant to hurt anyone. It was an accident, honest. I'll be glad to pay your medical bills."

"What were you doing out there?" Nancy asked.

"I had this gig," he said, "playing a werewolf at a party out at this hunting cabin. My car broke down on the way home. I knew I'd never get anyone to help me way out there late at night—especially dressed like this. I wasn't too far from home, so I decided to leave my car and just walk. I sure didn't think I'd run into you two out skiing."

"Wait a minute," Poodles said. His face was starting to flush, and he sounded angry. "You didn't tell me you ran into them."

"He sprained my shoulder!" George exclaimed.

"But I swear it was an accident," Winthrop said. "I heard you two, so I howled to scare you away. But you just kept coming, so I hid behind the tree. And then you came right toward me. I guess I panicked. I decided to make a run for it, and smashed right into you."

Poodles turned to Nancy, Ned, and the security people. "Look, he said he was sorry," Poodles said. "It sounds like it really *was* an accident. I'll make sure your medical bills are taken care of, George.

Gabriel really is a good guy. And you must admit, we sure added a touch of excitement to this event. That's what I was hired to do. I got the whole idea when I heard about the wolfnapping at that preserve."

"All right," George said, frowning and smiling at the same time. "At least I won't need rabies shots . . . I assume."

"Poodles, did you have anything to do with the missing wolves?" Nancy asked.

"Absolutely not!" Poodles said. "I had nothing to do with it whatsoever. And I'm sorry it happened. But as long as it did . . . it was a logical springboard for pumping some life into the River Heights Holiday Winter Carnival."

The security people and the policewoman talked briefly to Poodles and the stuntman. Since neither appeared to have done anything illegal, they all left.

"Let's go tell the others," Ned said.

"You go ahead," Nancy said. "I want to call Jax Dashell and see if he's made any progress with Philip LeRoy." She could hear Poodles speaking into a microphone at the front of the Palace. He was already introducing the stuntman to the crowd and whipping the onlookers into a frenzy of cheers and applause.

Ned walked around the Palace and Nancy hit the 9 on her cell phone. "I'm just calling to see what's happening with LeRoy," she told the officer when he answered.

"I questioned him pretty rigorously," Detective Dashell said. "He seemed shocked that anyone would suspect him of stealing the wolves. I kind of get the impression that he's afraid of the animals, so his having stolen them would probably be out of the question."

"I suppose," Nancy said. "What about the grain samples and the hair? How does he explain those?"

"He swears he's never even been to WildWolf, and he has a pretty good alibi for the night the wolves disappeared. He even offered to take a lie detector test on the spot."

"Do you suppose he's got an accomplice?" Nancy wondered. "Someone who does all the actual handling of the wolves?"

"I'm thinking that if LeRoy is involved, he definitely has to have someone else doing the dirty work," the detective answered.

"Okay," she said. "I suppose you've already heard what just happened out here."

"Yes, one of our officers called it in a few minutes ago. Let me guess—you're the 'young lady' who was at the foot of the Crystal Palace when the werewolf guy made his leap."

"You guessed it," Nancy confessed.

"I'm going to repeat my warning to be careful," Detective Dashell said before hanging up. His voice had a very serious tone. "This case isn't solved yet—not by a long shot."

Nancy went back around to the front of the Palace. A large crowd was milling around, admiring the gorgeous lighting effects and talking about Poodles's werewolf. Bess, George, Ned, and Brianda were waiting for her. Nancy repeated what the detective had told her about his interrogation of Philip LeRoy.

"I don't believe it," Brianda said. "All that trouble you went to, collecting the feed samples and the wolf hair . . ."

"The evidence still counts," Nancy pointed out. "If LeRoy is telling the truth and he didn't drop the grain or pick up the hair, someone else did. Either he has an accomplice or someone planted the evidence to implicate him."

The rest of the evening was nothing but fun for Nancy and her friends. They strapped on skates for an hour of spirited ice-dancing to swing music. Then they grabbed warm drinks and settled in for a couple of hours with the rock band on the riverbank.

They finally parted to head for their homes. George couldn't drive because of her arm, so she was riding with Bess. Nancy asked them to come by the next morning for breakfast. She wanted to take her car to the shop for a once-over after her accident. Bess could follow her and drive her from the body shop to the Carnival.

When Nancy finally got into bed she tossed and turned, working over all the clues in her mind. She was sure the answer was right in front of her if she could just get it into focus.

On Saturday morning Bess and George arrived for breakfast as planned. Nancy noticed that George seemed to be moving her injured arm more, although it was still in the sling. Over juice, scrambled eggs, and Hannah Gruen's melt-in-your-mouth cinnamon-apple scones, Nancy hardly talked. She was lost in the threads of thought she'd fallen asleep with. She knew that they could be untangled if she worked with just one thread at a time.

"Earth to Nancy, Earth to Nancy." Bess's words jolted Nancy out of her thoughts. The phone was ringing. She reached for the portable on the kitchen counter. It was Brianda, and she was in tears.

"Oh, Nancy, I'm so glad I got you. I have terrible news. Remember the four baby wolves you and the others played with last Tuesday when you came out for the Howl-o-rama?"

Nancy's stomach clenched with a pang. She could

still feel the warm, fluffy body of the wolf pup crawling up to her shoulder to nibble her hair and cry in her ear. "Yes," she answered, though she dreaded to hear what Brianda would say next.

"They're gone," Brianda said, her voice dropping to almost a whisper. "They've disappeared."

14

Howliday on Ice

"Oh, Brianda, I'm so sorry," Nancy said. "What happened, do you know?"

"They just vanished like Khayyam and Liz did," Brianda said. "And—"

"What happened?" Bess whispered. "Tell us."

Nancy motioned to Bess to wait, and focused on Brianda's voice.

"There are no clues that anyone can find," Brianda continued. "The babies are just gone. Apparently they were taken during the night."

"They wouldn't just wander off by themselves, would they?" Nancy asked

"Never," Brianda said. "Not at this age. Even if one was really precocious and adventurous, not all of them would be. We couldn't lose a whole litter at once unless something happened to them—something bad."

"Has anyone heard from Christopher?" Nancy asked.

"That was my next piece of news," Brianda said. "Christopher left River Heights the night he quit his job and returned to California—that's where he came from. He's called Markie a couple of times, and he was being very friendly. He even asked Markie for a job recommendation for someplace out there."

Brianda sighed, but it sounded a little like a sob. "Nancy," she said, "please help us find the babies—help us find *all* our missing wolves. Markie is trying to be very professional, organizing searches and working hard to figure out what happened. But she admitted to me last night that she doesn't have a clue. She's so depressed—it breaks my heart."

"I'll do everything I can," Nancy promised. As she put the phone back in its cradle on the counter, she felt more determined than ever to find the answers—*and* all of the missing wolves.

She told Bess and George why Brianda had called. "Not the babies," Bess said, her eyes wide. "Who would do such a thing? And *why*?"

Nancy was quiet for several minutes. Finally she spoke. "Let's start from the beginning of this case. Sometimes the best plan is to give up on the original idea and look at the problem from another perspective," she said. "Instead of trying to determine whether the motive behind the crimes is to close down WildWolf or to close down the Carnival, let's try something different."

"Like what?" George asked.

"Like, what if there's another motive altogether?" Nancy suggested. "For example, why would someone steal wolves from WildWolf?"

"For pets?" Bess asked. "Even though Markie says that's a bad idea? Hmm . . . maybe. Or maybe for their hides," she added with a shudder.

"Maybe to use as attack guard animals," George suggested in a hushed voice, "or even to hunt."

"Or maybe for *all* of those reasons," Nancy concluded. "Maybe someone wants to steal these prize animals to sell to anyone who can afford it. And they don't really care what they'll be used for."

Nancy bit into a scone. Her thoughts tumbled quickly as she added up the clues from the past five days. "Suppose the person wants to steal and sell the wolves, and caused all the incidents at the Carnival as distractions," she suggested. "It has to be someone who knows something about computer-driven theatrical lighting, and who knows about Philip LeRoy's homemade sheep feed *and* has access to it."

"But not LeRoy, right?" Bess asked.

"I'm not ruling him out completely," Nancy answered. "But it doesn't *have* to be him. And it helps if the person is a skilled ice carver. Most of all, it has to be someone who knows something about animals—not only how to steal them, but also how to *ship* them, perhaps even illegally, to different points around the world."

"And since you—and even your friends—seem to have been targeted a few times, it has to be someone who knows you're on the case," George pointed out.

"A couple of these requirements fit some of our suspects," Nancy said. "But I can think of only one person around here who fits most of them. Bess, would you boot up my computer and see if you can get into the zoo database?"

"Sure," Bess said, jumping up. "What are we looking for?"

"Willy Dean said he worked at the zoo. I want to know everything you can get about his experience there," Nancy said. "George, could you call around town and see if you can locate a werewolf costume? If the costume shops don't have them, try some of the theaters or college theater departments."

While Bess and George got to work, Nancy called Ned and then Brianda and asked them to meet her in an hour at the Heat Hut.

"I got it," George called out from the living room, where she had used her cell phone. She returned to the kitchen, where Nancy was just finishing up her calls. "I found one at the Patches Costume Shoppe," she reported. "It's the same werewolf costume that Gabriel Winthrop used. It was turned back in yesterday and it's all cleaned up, ready to go."

Bess joined them with a printout from Nancy's computer. "Willy Dean was in charge of shipping at the zoo, and his job included sending animals around the globe," she read. "I also pulled up his bio and job history, and guess what? He spent four years in Chicago as an actor and lighting technician at a small theater!"

Nancy, Bess, and George stopped at Patches and picked up the werewolf costume, then drove to the Heat Hut. Nancy quickly brought Ned and Brianda up to speed.

"Are you going to call Detective Dashell?" Brianda asked.

"Not yet," Nancy answered. "I want to make sure we have the right man."

"How do we find that out?" Bess asked.

"We set a trap," Nancy said. "Last night when we were at Wawasee Cove, I poked around that old, abandoned ice-fishing shed down on the far end. It looked like it hadn't been used for years. It'll be perfect."

"So what's the plan?" Brianda said.

Nancy looked at her watch. "It's high noon," she announced. "We're going fishing—and I hope we catch a big one!" Nancy gave her friends their roles in her plan and then set it in motion.

Ned called Willy Dean. Ned and Nancy had rehearsed what he'd say, and the conversation went like clockwork.

"Hey Willy, I need to talk to you," Ned said. "I consider you my friend, and something's going on that I think you should know about. I figure if you have a heads-up on this, you can be ready to prove your innocence."

Ned held the phone receiver out a little. Nancy huddled with Ned so she could also hear.

There was a long pause. Finally, Willy spoke. "My innocence?" he said. "Innocence about what?"

"Look, I don't want to go over it on the phone," Ned said. "You know Nancy—I'm crazy about her, but she can really get caught up in this detective thing. She's got this idea that you're the guy who stole the wolves from the preserve. She also thinks you're behind some of the bad stuff that's been happening around the Carnival."

"You're kidding," Willy said. "What makes her think that?"

"I don't know exactly. She mentioned something about a fake fortune-teller and wolf hair. Oh, and she says she saw you try to bury her with all that snow under the superslide."

"Mmmmmmm," Willy said. "That's going pretty far. Maybe I should talk to her."

"That might make things worse," Ned said. "You don't want her to think you're threatening her or anything like that. But I do know she's talking about going to the police with her theory. I don't want to sabotage her or anything, but I just think it's fair to let you know what she's planning."

"What are you suggesting?" Willy asked.

"I thought we could meet in an hour—maybe at the amphitheater. I know you and I know you'd never do anything like all this. I can tell you what she's thinking you've done, and that'll give you a chance to get your own evidence ready to prove she's wrong. But you have to promise you'll never tell her I talked to you."

"No problem," Willy said. "How soon is she planning on talking to the police?"

"Not until later today. She bought that abandoned ice-fishing shack on Wawasee Cove and wants to fix it up as a present for her Dad. He's out of town right now, and she wants to get it cleaned up before he gets back. So she's going to be out there from about one o'clock on. That's why I suggested you and I get together about then. She'll be so busy she won't notice I'm gone."

"Sounds good," Willy said. "I'll be there."

After Ned hung up the phone, Nancy went over the plan with her friends several more times. She knew that if she was right, Willy might get dangerous. She wanted to make sure all her backups were in place.

George, her arm still in a sling, went to the amphitheater to watch for Willy in case he *did* go there to meet Ned. But Nancy was sure he wouldn't.

Nancy, Bess, and Ned drove to Wawasee Cove. They went into the small shack on the ice and started setting it up. The shack consisted of four walls and a flat roof just sitting on ice a yard or two thick. There was no floor. What had once been a hole cut in the corner to fish into had long since filled in.

The only "furniture" in the small room was several wooden crates and one beat-up wooden chair. Nancy, Ned, and Bess stacked several crates and the chair in a corner and draped a painter's tarp over them. Ned, wearing the werewolf costume, crawled in under the tarp.

A hole in the roof had been cut to allow a stovepipe through. Fast-food wrappers and Styrofoam dishes littered the room. It was dark inside with the door closed, so Nancy lit the kerosene lantern she had brought. The smoke curled up through the hole in the roof.

She didn't have to wait long. She heard a car drive down the abandoned road leading to that end of the cove. Then she heard the car stop. Soon there was a short rap on the wooden door, and it opened without the visitor waiting for an answer.

"Well, it's you, Nancy," Willy Dean said. "I wondered who was in here. I thought this place was abandoned." He seemed very nervous.

"Well it was, but I bought it. It was really cheap and I'm going to give it to my father for a holiday gift. Do you know my friend Bess Marvin?" Nancy smiled at Bess.

"I've seen her around—hello. Aren't you a good daughter, Nancy," Willy said, sitting down on one of the crates. He was shaking. "I'm glad to find you here. I'd like to have a little talk."

"What about?"

"I understand you've been thinking I might have something to do with all the problems that have been going on around the Carnival," he said. "And even at WildWolf."

"Who told you that?" Nancy said.

"Never mind," Willy said. "I thought we'd have a little talk and get this all straightened out." He was breathing fast and seemed more nervous.

"We don't have to talk, Willy. I have proof, and I'm going to use it. And the police will be here shortly to receive it."

Willy jumped to his feet, knocking the crate into the old chair. "Well they're not going to find any of us here," he said. He reached out with his burly arm and grabbed Bess, yanking her over to the dark corner where he stood. Holding tightly to Bess, he pulled an ice pick from his back pocket and held the point against her side. "Now, let's go for a ride," he said to Nancy. "You drive. I've got some shipping crates that ought to fit you two perfectly."

"I've heard the werewolf uses this shack for his hideout," Nancy said without flinching. "Do you suppose that's true?"

Right on cue a horrifying howl pierced the cabin darkness, and the werewolf leaped out from under the tarp.

In the dim light from the kerosene lamp Nancy could see Willy turn as white as a ghost. He let go of Bess and fell backward, kicking the kerosene lamp into a pile of litter in the corner. A blaze surged up almost instantly, and the tiny room filled with acrid smoke and flames.

15

The Culprit Is Iced

Nancy grabbed the tarp and threw it on the fire. Bess helped stomp out the flames. Ned, dressed as the werewolf, opened the door to let out the smoke and stood guard, staring at Willy. Then he peeled off the full-head mask and signaled to Brianda, parked nearby, to call Jax Dashell.

"All right, all right," Willy said. "I see what's happening. You win. But get me out of here. I hurt my leg when I fell—I think I broke something."

Willy was still very white and shuddering. Nancy knew he shouldn't be lying on the ice, so she and Ned carefully eased him onto the tarp and dragged him off the ice and up onto shore. Once there, they wrapped him up in the cloth.

"The police and doctors are on their way," Nancy

assured him. Bess went to tell Brianda to call for an ambulance too.

"You stole the alpha wolves and the babies, didn't you?" Nancy asked Willy.

"I did," he admitted. "It took me years to set up an international black market network for those animals. And I was finally ready to make a little money on WildWolf."

"Your experience with the zoo helped," Nancy prompted.

"Yep. Not only to develop the contacts around the world. I also learned to tranquilize and capture animals without damaging the merchandise."

"But you didn't care what happened to them after they were sold," Bess charged. "How could you work with animals at a zoo and still not care about the abuse those wolves might get from your clients?"

Willy just shrugged. "I planned to pull off some pretty bold thefts during Carnival time," he said. It was like he was talking to himself now. "I figured they'd get less attention with all the hubbub this year."

He turned back to Nancy. "You know, you're not the only detective in this room. I did some major sleuthing of my own. For instance, I found from my snooping out there that Brianda was staying at WildWolf. And, of course, I already knew your reputation as a detective. So when I saw you and Brianda hanging out, I figured you were working on the kidnapped wolves case."

"That's when you started following me?" Nancy asked.

"Well, first I tried to just get to know you—sort of be your friend." He smiled broadly. "I already knew Ned a little, so I figured I could keep tabs on you if we all sort of hung out together."

"You were the fake fortune-teller who gave us our fortunes, right?" Nancy guessed.

"Yes, I was," Willy said with a sigh. He related a scenario that was like the one Nancy had already guessed: that he had been following them and overheard they were heading to the fortune-teller's. Then he just took advantage of the situation.

"It was perfect," he concluded. "I was able to slip you a fortune that matched the warning I had carved in the Crystal Palace wall."

"Why did you carve that message?" George asked.

"Again, I wanted all the talk around town to be about the Carnival," he answered. "I figured that would stir up the rumors and take the heat off the wolfnapping. I was especially proud of the lighting effect—blood red was a great idea."

Willy slumped into the tarp, then looked at Nancy. "I thought for sure that would discourage you—even scare you a little. I hadn't figured you out as well as I'd thought."

"What about the wolf hair in Philip LeRoy's truck?" Nancy asked. "And the bits of his custom sheep feed at WildWolf? Did you plant those to implicate LeRoy?"

"You *are* good," he answered, surprised. "Congratulations for pulling those clues together. Sure, I did that. LeRoy is paranoid about having the wolf preserve so close to his farm. He was an obvious suspect. It was easy to steal the samples from one of his shipments. I dropped the evidence at WildWolf when I kidnapped the first two wolves."

He wiped his sweating brow. Nancy could hear the sirens in the distance. "I spent quite a bit of time prowling around out there at night," Willy confessed. "I needed to get really familiar with the operation before I made my move. On one trip I noticed the barrel of wolf hair, and I pocketed some to plant around LeRoy's property."

"And the snow slide?" Nancy asked. "Was that an accident, or more of your handiwork?"

"I take full credit," he said proudly. "It was actually pretty easy. Just a few cuts with my chainsaw through strategic points in the scaffolding. Again—just a distraction from my *real* work."

"But how could you do that without getting caught?" Bess wondered.

"That was probably very easy," Nancy guessed. "In the weeks before the Carnival, chainsaws were the accessory of choice around the park. Dozens of workers were carving ice blocks, castle towers, and other sculptures around the area."

"You guessed it," Willy nodded. "No one looked twice at someone carrying a chainsaw around. When I saw you and your friends snooping under the slide after the avalanche, I decided it was time to remove you from the picture altogether. Too bad I wasn't successful," he muttered.

By this time Detective Dashell, his backup team, and the ambulance had arrived. The detective read Willy Dean his rights and arrested him while the emergency team treated him for shock and put his leg in a cast. Then they hoisted him onto a gurney.

"Before you leave, Willy, please tell us where the missing wolves are," Nancy urged. "It might even help your case with a jury."

For a minute he looked defiant. Then he seemed to lose the fighting spirit. "The babies are at my house," he said, "in the basement. The alphas are on their way to the Philippines, but they're probably still somewhere in the American West."

A relieved Brianda called Markie immediately and told her the news. After Willy was taken away, Detective Dashell escorted Nancy and Brianda to Willy's home to retrieve the wolf pups. Although they were evidence, Nancy and Brianda were allowed to take them immediately to WildWolf for holding until the trial. Detective Dashell also promised Brianda that he would do whatever it took to track down the alpha wolves.

When Nancy and Brianda got to WildWolf, Markie hugged Nancy and handed her a large gift-wrapped box.

"You didn't give her that crazy wolf-howl clock, I hope," Brianda said with a laugh.

"No," Markie said with a warm smile. "This is the only thing I could think of that would let you know how grateful we are, and how much this means to us," she told Nancy.

Nancy carefully unwrapped the package. When she lifted the lid, she gasped with delight. Inside lay a gorgeous wolf-hair sweater and matching cap.

That evening, under a midnight-blue sky with ice-crystal stars, Poodles McNulty held a special ceremony on the amphitheater stage next to the Crystal Palace. "We are all indebted to River Heights Holiday Winter Carnival employee Nancy Drew for cracking the wolf-napping case," Poodles told the huge crowd. "She has brought the wolf-napper to justice and closed the book on that scary period in River Heights history."

Poodles paused until the cheers died down, and then spoke again. "Nancy has told me that she had some help on this case, and I've asked her to introduce her team." He handed the microphone to Nancy.

"Thank you all very much," Nancy said. "Some of you might have been here when George Fayne turned the light on the werewolf on top of the Palace. Now it's her turn to be in the spotlight." George nodded her head briefly at the applauding crowd.

"And I'm sure you already know Bess Marvin," Nancy continued. "She's been one of those serving you warm treats in the Heat Hut. Well, she helped turn up the heat on the culprit, too." Bess smiled and waved.

"You've probably seen Ned Nickerson around the Carnival the last few days," Nancy said, taking Ned's hand. "He's had a lot of jobs, including helping with the snowslide cleanup. Yesterday he imitated a werewolf and helped catch a criminal." Ned bowed to the audience.

"Finally, you might have turned to Brianda Bunch for help finding your way around the Carnival," Nancy said, gesturing toward her friend. "She's been a hostess the last several days. I turned to her for help too—help on this case. And she stepped right in. Now that you all know the werewolf was a fake, consider a visit to see some real wolves at WildWolf, which is run by Brianda's cousin. It's a fascinating place." Brianda smiled and cocked her head shyly. The crowd cheered again as Nancy turned the mike back over to Poodles and returned to her friends.

"Did you ever notice the same thing I did?" Poodles crowed. "Every one of these young detectives is a Carnival employee." Poodles pumped his fist in the air. His face glowed with an expression of pride and enthusiasm as he worked the crowd into more cheers.

He looked at Nancy and motioned to an assistant to hand him some envelopes. "Nancy, the Carnival is especially thankful for your hard work. With the wolfnapping case solved, the people of River Heights and guests from around the world can really enjoy the rest of the Carnival. As a token of our appreciation, here are gift certificates for you, George, Bess, Ned, and Brianda. Take these to Albemarle's and redeem them for new skis and designer ski clothes with our thanks."

This time it was Nancy and her friends who cheered. "This is so cool," Bess whispered to Nancy as they all went up to collect their gifts. "I can't even think about what might have happened to the baby wolves if you hadn't solved this case, Nancy."

"Not only that," George added, "but she figured out what was going on here at the Carnival. And look at that crowd—this Carnival is going to have a record turnout."

"Hey, what did you expect?" Bess concluded. "With Nancy Drew on the case, the River Heights Holiday Winter Carnival was bound to be a *HOWLING* success!"

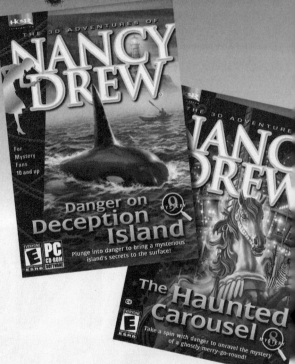

Have you read all of the Alice Books?

❑ THE AGONY OF ALICE
Atheneum Books for Young Readers
0-689-31143-5
Aladdin Paperbacks 0-689-81672-3

❑ ALICE IN RAPTURE, SORT OF
Atheneum Books for Young Readers
0-689-31466-3
Aladdin Paperbacks 0-689-81687-1

❑ RELUCTANTLY ALICE
Atheneum Books for Young Readers
0-689-31681-X

❑ ALL BUT ALICE
Atheneum Books for Young Readers
0-689-31773-5

❑ ALICE IN APRIL
Atheneum Books for Young Readers
0-689-31805-7

❑ ALICE IN-BETWEEN
Atheneum Books for Young Readers
0-689-31890-0

❑ OUTRAGEOUSLY ALICE
Atheneum Books for Young Readers
0-689-80354-0
Aladdin Paperbacks 0-689-80596-9

❑ ALICE IN LACE
Atheneum Books for Young Readers
0-689-80358-3
Aladdin Paperbacks 0-689-80597-7

❑ ALICE THE BRAVE
Atheneum Books for Young Readers
0-689-80095-9
Aladdin Paperbacks 0-689-80598-5

❑ ACHINGLY ALICE
Atheneum Books for Young Readers
0-698-80533-9
Aladdin Paperbacks 0-689-80595-0
Simon Pulse 0-689-86396-9

❑ ALICE ON THE OUTSIDE
Atheneum Books for Young Readers
0-689-80359-1

❑ GROOMING OF ALICE
Atheneum Books for Young Readers
0-689-82633-8
Simon Pulse 0-689-84618-5

❑ ALICE ALONE
Atheneum Books for Young Readers
0-689-82634-6
Simon Pulse 0-689-85189-8

❑ SIMPLY ALICE
Atheneum Books for Young Readers
0-689-84751-3
Simon Pulse 0-689-85965-1

❑ STARTING WITH ALICE
Atheneum Books for Young Readers
0-689-84395-X

❑ PATIENTLY ALICE
Atheneum Books for Young Readers
0-689-82636-2

❑ ALICE IN BLUNDERLAND
Atheneum Books for Young Readers
0-689-84397-6